THE AMERICAN

THE
AMERICAN

ANDREW BRITTON

KENSINGTON BOOKS
http://www.kensingtonbooks.com

KENSINGTON BOOKS are published by

Kensington Publishing Corp.
850 Third Avenue
New York, NY 10022

All Kensington titles, imprints and distributed lines are available at special quantity discounts for bulk purchases for sales promotion, premiums, fund-raising, educational or institutional use.

Special book excerpts or customized printings can also be created to fit specific needs. For details, write or phone the office of the Kensington Special Sales Manager: Kensington Publishing Corp., 850 Third Avenue, New York, NY 10022. Attn. Special Sales Department. Phone: 1-800-221-2647.

Kensington and the K logo Reg. U.S. Pat. & TM Off.

Library of Congress Card Catalogue Number: 2005928272

ISBN 0-7582-1333-6

First Printing: March 2006
10 9 8 7 6 5 4 3 2 1

Printed in the United States of America

For my mother, Anne

ACKNOWLEDGMENTS

I would like to start by gratefully acknowledging Linda Cashdan of *The Word Process*. Linda proved almost prescient in her advice; even the suggestions I didn't take were later recommended by my publisher and ultimately found their way into the book. I couldn't have done it without her.

Special thanks go to Mark A. Jones of the Wake County Sheriff's Office, who was extremely generous with his time and knowledge; to Officer Rodney Parks of the D.C. Metro Police Department, for all of his insight; and to Erika Lease, M.D., for her wisdom and, more importantly, her friendship.

My heartfelt appreciation goes out to the talented team of professionals at Kensington: Steven Zacharius, the president and CEO, Laurie Parkin, Michaela Hamilton, and Wendy Bernhardt. I am also eternally grateful to my editor, Audrey LaFehr, for her boundless support and enthusiasm.

I owe a debt of gratitude to my literary agent, Nancy Coffey, who believed in this novel from the start.

And to Jeralyn Valdillez, for supporting me when the only thing I was writing was research papers.

PROLOGUE

WASHINGTON, D.C.

They whispered amongst themselves. For an announcement of lesser magnitude, they said, it might have been a more suitable venue.

It was natural for them to complain. Nothing less was expected by those who had organized the event; indeed, the interns who had arranged for the seating and distributed the press passes would have been stunned by anything approaching a compliment. When the frequent interruptions led to a substantial delay in the proceedings, few were surprised. Nevertheless, every effort was made to accommodate them. Additional chairs were brought in for the latecomers, and the proffered urns of coffee and pitchers of chilled water were re-filled at a near constant rate. Ornate chandeliers hung high above their heads, providing the requisite amount of light. The cameramen complained anyway, but to no avail. That the room might have been graced by natural light was never a consideration. The six massive windows were wired shut for security purposes, and draped in flow-ing burgundy curtains that perfectly matched the color of the carpet. Above the sparkling crystal chandeliers, a forgotten pair of star-shaped balloons drifted absently across the gilded ceiling. Although the walls were missing the usual procession of paintings, they were replaced, and perhaps surpassed, by towering marble pillars in the Corinthian order.

For the most part, they agreed that the usual trappings of power were in evidence. What the room was clearly lacking, though, was space. They were wedged tightly against one another, and the shared discomfort was noticed by all. As the hearing progressed, however, the vocal complaints began to subside. Soon they were scribbling furiously and shooting pointed glares at those who continued to talk. Finally, the hushed whispers faded away completely, and they listened with rapt attention to the man who was currently holding court, standing before a backdrop of his seated peers.

"Today I believe we have reached a consensus among some of the most respected and influential people in Washington, including those whose input is vital to the president's decision-making process. I am fully confident that he will react favorably to many of the conclusions the committee has reached this afternoon. I'll take one more question . . . I see you fidgeting over there, Susan. Let's have it."

A small peel of laughter rippled through the assembled crowd of print and television reporters as the CNN correspondent blushed slightly and posed her question to the man behind the podium. "Senator Levy, what do you hope to achieve by delivering this ultimatum to the interim Iranian government, and do you see this administration going down the same path that led to a controversial outcome in Iraq?"

The senator frowned at that last addition, a fact not lost on anyone present. "First of all, our goal here is to make clear to those in power in Tehran that the United States will not sit idly by while preparations are being put in place to cause direct harm to the people of this nation. We have not—and I'd like to be very clear on this point—yet considered the possibility of armed conflict, or even the staging of troops in the region, for that matter."

Levy paused for a moment, ostensibly to give the impression that he was gathering his thoughts. In reality, it was just for effect. "At this point, we have concrete evidence that Iran has restarted the process of refining uranium for use in nuclear weapons, proof that was lacking when the decision was made to remove Saddam Hussein from power. As it stands, the president has refused to recognize the new leadership in Tehran, and I—we—support him fully in this decision. Additionally, we now have tentative commitments from President Chirac of France and Prime Minister Berlusconi of Italy. Both leaders have assured us that, if some agreement for partial compensation can be reached, all companies in their respective countries with oil interests in Iran are prepared to terminate their contracts and pull out of the region at the earliest available opportunity. Although these implementations are predicated on talks that are scheduled to take place in late November, this is a huge step toward reinforcing the sanctions that are already in place. Let me assure you that our efforts to form a united front against Iran's nuclear ambitions will not be deterred."

Levy paused again, the momentary lull inviting a wave of clamorous voices. Ignoring them, he focused his gaze on the attractive young correspondent in the third row. "In response to the second part of your question, Susan, I'd like to stress that we're looking for strong U.N. participation in this matter. The proof of weapons production that I referred to is currently in the hands of the Security Council, and once the examination of that evidence is finished early next month, we expect that there will be a strong resolution and condemnation of the actions that have been undertaken by the new regime. No, I'm sorry, that's all," he said as another storm of voices erupted in his direction. "Thank you for being here today."

Senator Daniel Levy stepped down from the dais amidst a flurry of questions that he had no intention of answering. A four and a half hour hearing was bad enough, but the raised voices of twenty-six fellow senators and the incessant blinding light of camera bulbs had left him with a throbbing head and a dull pain in his stomach. Levy was sure that his recently diagnosed ulcer was a direct result of the trouble brewing once more in the Middle East. The recent death of Ayatollah Khomeini, the supreme leader of Iran, had resulted in the appointment of an ultraconservative cleric on decidedly unfriendly terms with the United States. Despite his comments of a few moments ago, he was fully aware that the possibility of war in the region was once again looming on the horizon.

He left the Caucus Room and took a sharp right, moving at a brisk stride down two short flights of marble stairs. As he walked, he was joined by his chief advisor, Kevin Aidan.

"So, we're about to start this nonsense all over again," Levy said. He ran a hand through his thick silver hair and spoke under his breath, ever distrustful of his small but highly efficient Secret Service detail. Members of Congress were not usually entitled to this level of protection, but as the Senate Majority Leader and the Chairman of the Senate Armed Services Committee, special attention was paid to his security, especially in the wake of recent events. "We spent billions in Iraq so our citizens could be treated to images of their sons and daughters dying on network television. What the hell did we get in return, Kevin?"

Aidan glanced at the senator out of the corner of his eye. He had to look down slightly, as Levy was at least a full head shorter than he was. He idly wondered if the senator harbored any lingering insecurities over his stature. On the other hand, one of the most powerful men in Washington need not concern himself with such trivialities. *After all*, Aidan reminded himself, *That's what I'm here for*.

"Sir, the best bet right now is to stick to the party line. Maybe you can try to distance yourself from this later, but you're currently seen as Brenneman's biggest supporter. We're already running polls—if public support starts to swing the other way, we'll see about revising our stance."

Levy raised an eyebrow, somewhat amused at this statement. Although he highly valued his advisor's input, the senator always considered Aidan's youth and inexperience when weighing his opinion. Having just appeared on national television throwing the full weight of his office behind the president, he could hardly reverse himself at any point in the near future without looking like a traitor to his party. Besides, he strongly believed that he was doing the right thing, and while he didn't mind complaining in private, he knew that he would endure as much political fallout as was necessary to prevent Iran from taking its place on the nuclear stage.

These thoughts faded from his mind as they passed through the elaborate marble rotunda of the Russell Senate Office Building. Levy never ceased to be amazed by the beauty of the architecture and the exquisite craftsmanship that was obviously put into the structure; it continually reminded him of the importance of his job and how fortunate he was to be in his position. He was snapped from his reverie by the sound of a Secret Service agent speaking quietly into his sleeve. The man looked up at Levy.

"Sir, they're ready to go. We'll be moving in the second vehicle." The senator nodded slightly in response and moved through the entrance to the building. The weather outside was customary for Washington, D.C., in mid-October; blustery winds forced a light rain to fall at a sharp angle, threatening to tear away the umbrella that Aidan held over his employer's head. The agents escorted the senator quickly to the second of two white Suburbans.

Levy knew that the first vehicle contained four men armed with automatic weapons, and that the head of the detail would ride in the passenger seat of the second. He vaguely recalled that there would also be a chase car following at a discrete distance. When he glanced down the street to his left, however, he could see no evidence of any such vehicle.

When the detail was first assigned to him, the senator had thought that the highly visible presence of his guardians was both unnecessary and embarrassing. He had said as much to the president himself, but when the reason behind the changes was made clear to him, the senator agreed that the threat appeared to justify the additional security.

That didn't mean that he had to like it, though. Strict limits had been set on his Secret Service detail; the agents were not permitted to step foot inside his residence except in case of an emergency, and his daily commute was not to be affected in any way. The twenty-five-minute drive from his office to his home across the river was one of the few quiet, uninterrupted parts of his day, and he would not have the placidity of those moments spoiled by sirens and the blared horns of angry, displaced motorists. Although the lead agent had strenuously objected to these conditions, Senator Levy *was* one of the most influential politicians in Washington, and they weren't really conditions, anyway; they were demands. In the end, a five-minute telephone call had settled the dispute.

The watchful agents that comprised his detail were not paid to like the senator, which was a good thing, as they didn't. They *were* responsible for his safety, though, so they were relieved as always that the seven-second transfer from the Russell Building to the Suburban was uneventful; it was a maxim in their business that the principal was always most at risk when entering or leaving a vehicle. In their rush, the experienced agents failed to notice the young, well-dressed man who had followed them outside. He waited for the small convoy to pull away from the curb and for the chase car to follow fifteen seconds later before descending the marble steps of the Russell Building and moving slowly down Constitution Avenue. Along the way, he lifted his own umbrella against the rain and extracted a slim cellular phone from his coat pocket.

The man who answered the call chose to ignore the tinge of arrogance that accompanied the expected message. At the same time, he couldn't help but feel a sliver of contempt for the Congressional staffer whose name he had been given two months earlier, and on whose information he was now completely reliant.

He waited patiently in the driver's seat of a rented black Chevy Tahoe on Independence Avenue, just opposite the James Forrestal Federal Building. The vehicle was legally parked, with sixty minutes remaining on the meter, and the tint in the windows was not of such a degree to cause suspicion among any unusually attentive traffic officers. The man had extensive experience in such matters, and although he recognized the inherent danger of his occupation, he was not one to leave the elements he could control to chance.

Adhering to this principle, he had carefully selected the place in which to position his vehicle. From the intersection with L'Enfant Promenade, Independence Avenue ran west for almost 3 miles. From his location, he had a clear view of two traffic lights. The closest was approximately 65 meters away. The second light was at least another 200 meters down the road, which placed it well beyond the range of his weapon and his ability.

The traffic signals held his interest for only a moment, as his preparations were more reliant on the rush-hour traffic and the inclement weather than anything else. He couldn't depend on the lights to work in his favor, as his proficiency with computers was not so extensive as to allow him to break into the Department of Transportation's signal grid undetected. At the same time, the other two variables were natural occurrences that never failed to bring D.C. traffic to a near standstill.

His cell phone beeped and he looked down at the numbers. The target was less than two minutes out.

"So, what are you doing this weekend?"

Megan Lawrence lifted an eyebrow and turned in the seat to look at her partner, Frank Benecelli. They had been paired together for three months, and she had been getting the feeling that he was working up the courage to ask her out.

"Why? You have plans for us?" she asked with a grin. Benecelli blushed and muttered something under his breath. Megan thought it was amusing that an Italian American could be so introverted and awkward in conversation, but she couldn't deny that she found him reasonably attractive. It was a moot point anyway, as she *did* have plans for the weekend; Sarah was celebrating her sixth birthday on Saturday, and both mother and daughter were excitedly looking forward to spending the day together.

Sweeping her long red hair back from her face and into a haphazard ponytail, Megan focused her sparkling green eyes on the vehicles she could see ahead and in her peripheral vision. Silently, she rebuked herself for letting her thoughts wander. There was no room for that in this job. Besides, she had the next two days off and would soon have plenty of time to relax.

"God, look at this weather. It's days like this that remind me Washington used to be a malarial swamp," Aidan complained. Senator Levy was distracted, staring out at the wind-rippled surface of the Capitol Building's reflecting pool. His stomach pains had not receded since the hearing adjourned, and he wondered if he should move his doctor's visit up to next week. *Better yet*, he thought, *maybe I should just quit this job altogether.* Although he was aware that his retirement would devastate his ambitious chief advisor, the senator knew that nothing would please his wife more. Lately Elizabeth had been dropping hints about moving to the estate they had recently purchased in the rolling hills of Virginia, the state that had elected him to his lofty position, and her wishes seemed to be taking the form of demands with each passing day.

Still, Levy could not begrudge her this desire, as she had faithfully stood by him through a turbulent political career spanning nearly three decades. The house just outside of Charlottesville was in need of extensive remodeling, and a warm glow spread throughout his body at the thought of making a home there with his wife, and how much she would enjoy the process.

"Senator?" He broke from his thoughts and turned to peer at Kevin Aidan. "We need to talk about your meeting with the governor next week. He's going to ask you about school funding, so I think we ought to—"

"Later, Kevin. Let an old man rest for a moment," Levy joked as he leaned back in his seat and closed his eyes. The light drum of the rain on the roof of the vehicle dulled his senses as he drifted back into fantasies of retirement. He took no notice when the vehicle splashed through a miniature lake of rainwater as it made the sharp right turn onto Independence Avenue.

From the moment he received the second call, the man in the black Tahoe worked quickly but efficiently. His hands were steady as he peeled away the threadbare blanket covering the object on the seat next to him. Lifting the awkward rectangular weapon onto his lap, he flipped a latch to move the optical sight into place, then swung the firing-pin mechanism down into position.

What he held in his hands was known as the M202A1 66mm launcher, also designated as the Flash launcher by the U.S. military, for whom it was specially manufactured. This particular weapon had been conveniently lost during a live-fire training exercise at Fort Bragg the previous spring with a full complement of three M74 rockets. The semiautomatic launcher was actually capable of firing four rockets in four seconds, but it was only issued with three, and the army's investigation would have been far more extensive if ammunition not assigned to the missing weapon had also disappeared.

As the launcher was already loaded, he had twenty seconds to spare. He used this time to move himself and the bulk of the weapon simultaneously into the passenger seat. After extending the trigger into the firing position, he scanned his mirrors and peripheral visibility. Through the rain streaking down his rear windshield, he saw the first of the two Suburbans approach.

The man took a deep breath and exhaled slowly. Looping the strap into the crook of his right arm, he cracked the passenger side door and waited to see if fate would spare the life of Senator Daniel Levy.

As luck would have it, the first light was green. He breathed a soft curse as the convoy began to roll through the intersection, and so it was with a slight pang of relief that he watched as an errant motorcycle swerved directly in front of the lead Suburban. The driver braked hard to avoid clipping the bike, and the man holding the launcher in his lap heard a brief squeal of tires when the following vehicle stopped. In a quiet show of impiety, he thanked God with a fervent whisper and pushed out onto the sidewalk.

"*Weapon!* Move, move, move!" Heads snapped up as the shouted words came over the radio. The agents in the first vehicle swung frantically in their seats to search for the threat. Senator Levy was jolted awake from a light sleep, and he turned to his advisor with a confused expression. Reading panic in Aidan's face, he immediately turned to look out of the rear window. The world around him was blocked out by sheets of rain. It was only then that he felt the first wave of paralyzing fear.

Spurred on by a surge of adrenaline, the young driver of the second vehicle broke protocol and attempted to maneuver around the first, but the sudden stop had left the vehicles too close together. He clipped the rear bumper of the lead Suburban, forcing the heavy SUV to grind to a halt. It was all the time the man needed. The weight of the launcher kept it steady on his shoulder as his eyes found the primary target. He squeezed the trigger and the first rocket screamed toward the second vehicle, its deadly path marked by a thin contrail of white smoke.

The senator saw a brief flash through the driving rain and closed his eyes as the agents screamed into their radios.

The man immediately adjusted his aim after he saw the projectile slam into the back end of the second Suburban. The M74 rocket was filled with 0.61 kilograms of a thickened pyrophoric agent, known as TPA, with chemical properties similar to those of white phosphorus. The results were devastating to behold. Another rocket tore into the lead Suburban just seconds after the vehicle carrying the senator was reduced to a heap of smouldering metal. The particles expelled from the warhead's casing ripped into nearby vehicles and passersby. One agent managed to get the rear door open just before the impact and was thrown 20 meters from the vehicle, his scorched body writhing on the damp pavement until he expired a few moments later.

The chaos was unimaginable on Independence Avenue, as the street was filled with people returning to work from their lunch hour. The screams of terrified onlookers were lost on the man as he turned his attention to the chase vehicle that had initiated the first warnings over the radio. The fact that he had fired two rockets within five seconds had given the agents in the last car little time to react, and he could see there were only two of them, one behind the wheel. He lifted the launcher, but immediately pulled it back down when he realized that the agent exiting the passenger side already had an MP5 submachine gun up at his shoulder. Benecelli squeezed off a 3-round burst that missed the assassin by inches, the 9mm slugs tearing into the red-brick wall of the Arts and Industries Building. Then Benecelli's line of sight was blocked as his target moved behind the bulk of the Tahoe.

Meanwhile, the man with the launcher was beginning to feel the chance for escape rapidly slipping away. The angle at which he had parked the rented truck had given him a direct route to the National Mall through the Smithsonian's Haupt Garden. Still shielded by the

Tahoe, he took two steps back toward the wrought iron entrance, then turned to sprint through the gate and down the tree-lined path. He stopped and turned once more before reaching the sharp right curve that led out to the Mall. His breath was coming hard, but his hands were steady as he checked to make sure that the final round was properly seated in the weapon. Then he lifted the launcher to his shoulder for the third and final time.

The rain was driving harder now, heavy curtains of water sweeping over the buildings and the approaching sidewalk, obscuring much of their view and drowning out the cries of the wounded. On the other side of the Tahoe, Agent Megan Lawrence moved carefully to the left, her standard-issue Sig Sauer P229 up in a modified Weaver stance as she covered her advancing partner. Benecelli held the only automatic weapon in the vehicle, and she couldn't help but realize how completely outgunned she was. Megan commanded her mind to remain clear as she focused on the slowly widening gap between the front windshield of the truck and the narrow path next to the Arts and Industries Building. She did not think about her six-year-old daughter or the close friends she had just lost, although both thoughts were screaming for her attention. At that moment, all her awareness and considerable skill were focused on Benecelli as he began to edge around the front of the vehicle.

Her partner hesitated just before moving into position for the shot, and it was only then that Megan heard the terrible whine of the solid-fuel rocket as it sped down the path and into the passenger side door of the Tahoe. Standing frozen in place, she watched in horror as the triethylaluminum filler burned its way through the vehicle's frame like it was made of plastic. Jagged pieces of metal coated in smouldering particles of TPA embedded themselves deep into Benecelli's face and chest, and the last thing she heard were his screams of agony before her world faded to black.

CHAPTER 1

CAPE ELIZABETH, MAINE

It wasn't an easy climb to the top of the 170-foot slope, especially after an hour-long swim in the icy waters of the North Atlantic. Nevertheless, Ryan Kealey was pleased to feel only a slight sense of exertion when he finally reached the small clearing above the cliffs. He took a long moment to admire the view, then moved off at an easy pace down a gravel footpath. It wasn't long before he came across a ragged beach towel draped over a solitary fence post. Using it to dry his unruly black hair, Kealey continued along the path until the trees parted and the house he had purchased eleven months earlier came into view. The thoroughly remodeled home stood three stories tall, with elaborate French doors and windows tucked neatly into the cedar-shingled exterior. The expensive slate roof was a recent addition, as was the exterior fireplace centered on the inlaid stone patio. Ryan had done most of the stonework himself, but had contracted out for the roof. While he was proud of his abilities as a handyman, he recognized that there were limitations to his skill.

As he approached, the door leading to the kitchen was suddenly flung open, and a young woman rushed out to envelop him in a ferocious hug.

"Damn it, Ryan, I've been looking everywhere for you! I've got some news you definitely don't want to hear," she said with an infectious grin.

Kealey smiled back, charmed as always by her youthful exuberance. "Then I know you'll save us both the trouble and keep it to yourself," he said with a laugh.

She bounced alongside of him as he moved through the open door into the warm interior of the house.

"You'll never believe it," she said breathlessly. "I overheard the dean saying that your attendance record is even worse than that of your 'most consistently inebriated student,' were his exact words, I think, and *then* he said—"

"Katie." He interrupted her excited rambling with gentle good humor. "I need that job even less than he wants me there. I wouldn't worry about it." Kealey occasionally lectured at the University of Maine as an associate professor of International Relations, but lately just hadn't been inclined to make the trip. Although he was becoming increasingly bored with the teaching, he had to admit that something good had come of it as he surreptitiously glanced at Katie Donovan out of the corner of his eye.

She was pouting as though put off by his lack of interest in her story, but the theatrics didn't last long. "Honey, I've been running around since six this morning," she said. "I'm going to take a shower."

"Care for some company?" he asked with a mischievous grin.

"Oh, I see how it is," she retorted, wearing a knowing smile of her own. "You're more than happy to jump in the shower with me, but you couldn't care less when it comes to hearing about my day."

He shrugged. "I guess we'll just have to compromise. I'll scrub you down while you tell the story."

" 'Scrub me down,' huh? Is that what you call it now?" He opened his mouth to protest, but she had already peeled off her T-shirt and tossed it in his face. Then she was running up the stairs, screaming in mock fear as Ryan followed close on her heels.

Much later, he stood on the second-story balcony with a cup of coffee and stared out across the frigid gray expanse of the ocean. He watched as the towering thunderheads several miles offshore seemed to grow at an alarming rate, and could soon feel the strong gusts as they brought small sprinkles of rain inland. If he strained, he could hear the distant peel of thunder over the television tuned to MSNBC in the master bedroom. Every major news network had been providing continuous coverage of the preceding week's attack in Washington, as they were prone to do with any disaster—natural or otherwise. As he sipped the warm coffee, he heard the screen door slide open and Katie approached from behind, gently wrapping her wind-tanned forearms around his waist and resting her chin on his shoulder.

"You're expecting a call, aren't you?"

Ryan raised an eyebrow at that. They had been together for only six months, and though they had once had a short, awkward discussion about the work he used to do, the subject did not often come up. Once again, he was amazed by how perceptive she could be.

He turned to face her, instinctively reaching out to touch her cheek, smooth beneath waves of shimmering golden brown. As her troubled blue eyes searched his face, he found he could only answer truthfully.

"I guess I am. The call is a given. It's whether I go or not . . ." He turned to gaze at the approaching storm. "I just don't know."

She leaned in to kiss him gently on the lips.

"Yes, you do."

Later that evening, Katie left for Orono to attend a night course in physics. From the front door he watched as she tossed her books haphazardly into the rear seat and sped off in her battered Corolla, throwing him a cheerful wave along the way. Although she couldn't have known it, her prophecy was fulfilled when the telephone rang just before eight. Ryan hesitated and kept his fingertips on the receiver for several seconds before lifting it to his ear.

It was still dark the following morning as Ryan streaked north on I-95 in his dark blue BMW 645Ci. He had scribbled a short note punctuated with an apology and left it on the kitchen table, but guessed that Katie would still be furious when she finally got back from Orono. Although the concern skirted the edge of his mind for a while, it was soon replaced by the pleasure of the car's performance and the scenic beauty of the surrounding countryside.

As the first rays of the sun filtered through the passing forest, dense tree cover overhead rained dying leaves of brilliant red and yellow onto the roof of his vehicle and the approaching road. The trip seemed to pass faster than he had expected, and it wasn't long before he pulled into the daily parking lot at Bangor International Airport, the heavy sedan easily navigating the numerous speed bumps leading into the garage. It was just past 7:30 when he collected his electronic ticket from a pretty blond attendant at the United Airlines counter, who managed to flash him an alluring smile despite the early hour. By 8:45 he was on the next flight to Washington, D.C.

About the same time he landed at Dulles International, Katie Donovan was rocketing recklessly up the narrow driveway bordered with pines to the house on Cape Elizabeth. She was in a dangerous mood, having spent the morning arguing with her faculty-appointed advisor over the course her dissertation was taking. As a second-year PhD candidate in applied mathematics, she had already spent so many years in school that the thought of leaving it all behind to start her career was becoming an increasingly attractive idea. The argument had degenerated into a shouting match; she had definitely burned some bridges there, but took solace in the fact that she would be spending the rest of the afternoon with Ryan.

Opening the front door, Katie announced her arrival with a flourish, but there was no answer. The sound of her heels clicking against the polished hardwood floors echoed throughout the house as she walked through the empty rooms. In the kitchen, she looked around in puzzlement before noticing the sheet of paper on the table.

The note was apologetic, but Katie still found herself growing angrier each time she read it. How could he just take off without even saying good-bye? Over the past six months she had opened herself to him, shared so much, and in return he had revealed almost nothing of his past, except that he had briefly worked for the Central Intelligence Agency. It had taken a considerable degree of craftiness and charm to get that much out of him.

She picked up a framed photograph of the two of them standing on a pier at Kittery Point, Ryan's arm loose around her waist. She admired his dark Irish good looks, lean physique, and easy smile, then caught herself and slammed the picture down on the antique wooden cabinet, leaving a small mark in the lacquered surface. Tears welled in her eyes, and she wiped them away angrily as she stormed out of the house. Feeling suddenly childish, it occurred to her that he would probably be disappointed if he could see her now. She felt a rush of shame, which quickly turned to anger again as she drove away even faster than she had arrived, which was very fast indeed.

CHAPTER 2

WASHINGTON, D.C.

To avoid the challenge of getting into Langley while listed as a visitor, Ryan had agreed to meet the person he spoke with on the telephone "off campus," so to speak. He waited in a brightly lit café just off the George Washington Parkway, seated in a far corner of the room facing the door. The atmosphere was pleasant on a Friday afternoon, young professionals and college students busy making plans for the weekend, exchanging small talk and gossip, casting flirtatious glances across the crowded room. Many of these glances were aimed in Ryan's direction, but he didn't notice; sitting alone in the bustling atmosphere of the café, he could not help but feel old and out of place.

After almost twenty minutes had passed, a cold gust of air swept through the room as the door was pulled open. The man who entered was so unremarkable in dress, height, and build that he immediately blended into the background. That kind of practiced anonymity was to be expected, though, as Jonathan Harper had nearly twenty years of field experience to draw from. He had begun his career as a young analyst working the Soviet desk, but it wasn't long before the bland-featured, exceptionally intelligent young man had found his way into the Operations Directorate. By the mid-1980s he was running agents behind the Iron Curtain and making arrangements for those few defectors whose positions within the Committee for State Security made them valuable assets to the CIA. Now, at the pinnacle of his career, Harper had the number-three spot at Langley as the deputy director of operations. He lifted his hand slightly to acknowledge Ryan's presence as the younger man stood up, coffee cup in hand, to follow Harper back out into the cold.

"You look well, my friend. College life seems to agree with you," Harper remarked as the two men strolled slowly along in the direction of the Mall. The sky was a pale gray, and the bite of the air seemed to promise an early snowfall. Ryan glanced to his left and guessed that the words were meant sincerely. Sometimes it was difficult to tell as Harper's face never seemed to give anything away. With his hair carefully parted on the right, his conservative but expensive style of dress, and a solemn expression that seemed to be permanently etched into his features, Jonathan Harper, as Kealey had always thought, looked more like an aging minister or banker than an intelligence officer.

"I can't say I'm unhappy."

Harper took a moment to digest those words. It was the same way with Ryan every time.

"Got a lot of time on your hands, though, I'll bet."

Kealey hesitated. "I try to keep busy. I'm teaching now, and I met someone. It's not a bad life, John." He turned his penetrating gray eyes onto Harper's. "What I have now is worth having . . . it's good, secure."

They strolled along silently for a while. Jonathan didn't find the words convincing. He knew about the twenty-four-year-old student Ryan was seeing, and he knew about the tenuous teaching position at the university. Slinking by in some backwater, feigning interest in the mundane. Waiting for time to erode away the memories of what he had seen, and maybe what he had done . . . If asked, Harper would have said that Ryan was worth more than that. He did not imagine that the younger man wouldn't know he was being checked up on. Kealey *wanted* to be convinced; otherwise, he wouldn't even have bothered making the trip.

"You've seen it all over the news, I imagine. It's just fucking unbelievable. A hit on three cars in broad daylight, and we have nothing. Except, of course, for six dead civilians, one a pregnant woman, and seventeen injured. The media's all over this, and so the president is all over us. Evidently he was pretty close to the senator." Harper shivered as a brisk wind swept through the bright orange leaves of the trees overhead. "This guy took out Levy's entire detail, Ryan. I'm not talking about people who barely managed to squeak by on the Civil Service Exam. They weren't riding out desk duty for the pension, either. They were professional protection officers rotating off the presidential detail, for Christ's sake."

"I heard on the news that one survived. A woman."

"Yeah, her name is Megan Lawrence. Seven-year veteran. That's a sad story—she's got a six-year-old kid, and she's not expected to pull through. Fuck it." Harper whipped his empty Starbucks container toward an overflowing trash receptacle. It bounced off the top and hit the ground, where the wind promptly pushed it back onto the sidewalk. A female jogger dressed in colorful attire approached, her blond ponytail bouncing in accordance with her footfalls. She shot Harper a dirty look as she passed them by.

"Levy was on his way back to Alexandria; he and his wife had a place on Gentry Row. The route was checked out by the detail and given approval, but it was one of five possible choices, and selected at random less than a half hour before they left the Russell Building. So we have a list of people that had access to that information, and it's short. The Bureau is taking a hard look at each and every one of them. From what I gather, they already went to McLaughlin on the D.C. Circuit for the wiretaps. We should know more in a day or two, if they're willing to participate in the new spirit of cooperation."

"Why was a senator receiving Secret Service protection anyway? I thought that came down to the Capitol Hill Police."

Harper hesitated meaningfully before answering. "I can show you why. We have a tape—more than one. I think, actually, that you might know the person who did this."

With this revelation, it was as though time suddenly stopped for the younger man. Cold fingers inched their way up from the base of his spine, threatening to seize his throat in a terrible grip. He was lost for a moment, until just as quickly the feeling passed and he felt Harper's reassuring hand on his shoulder.

"Watch the tapes, Ryan. Watch the tapes and tell me what you think. That's all."

The two men walked slowly back in the direction of the café, Harper awarding himself silent accolades. Kealey was lost in another, more terrifying world altogether.

CHAPTER 3

WASHINGTON, D.C.

A lthough the nation's capital is home to many prestigious medical facilities, including University Hospital in Georgetown, the only adult burn unit in the metropolitan area is located in the Washington Hospital Center on Irving Street. Within forty-five minutes of the rocket attack all but three of the victims had been routed either directly or indirectly to this center, including Megan Lawrence, the only Secret Service agent to survive the initial devastation.

Naomi Kharmai wearily climbed the worn stone steps that were in constant contradiction to the modern building they adorned. She had spent the morning at Washington General speaking with bystanders who hadn't seen or heard anything that could be of real use to her, or more importantly, to her immediate supervisor. The clouds had made an appearance earlier in the day, and the sky was a white sheet overhead. The warmth of the pale sun on her back lifted her spirits slightly as she walked through the main entrance past the intense scrutiny of a security guard.

Her interest extended to what she could learn, but no further. She was not burdened by the sight or knowledge of the terrible injuries that so many of the witnesses had suffered; rather, it was the lack of progress finding information that was such a crushing disappointment to her.

Taking the elevator up to the fifth floor, Naomi asked to see Megan Lawrence. After bluffing or outright lying through a series of questions and filling out the appropriate paperwork, she was finally escorted to Lawrence's room by an exhausted young resident.

"Her injuries are very severe," he confided in a low voice, although there was no one within sight to overhear. "She sustained multiple fractures to the skull when her head hit the pavement, but somehow she was only slightly concussed. That's the least of it. She suffered extensive third-degree burns over thirty percent of her body, penetrating down to the hypodermis. Most of the burns are on her chest and arms, upper legs. There wasn't much pain at first . . . Her nerve endings were seared, but she started to feel it on Monday. We've had her on a morphine drip for two days."

"Will she live?"

The resident shook his head slowly and looked away. "The chemicals inside that rocket produce effects almost identical to those of white phosphorus," he said. Kharmai was familiar with the statistics relating to that particular substance, but did not volunteer this information. "She's demonstrating the initial symptoms of osteomyelitis of the jaw, a very rare condition associated primarily with exposure to highly toxic chemicals. The triethylaluminum that was released on the street oxidizes when exposed to air, and the particles continue to burn even after they are embedded in epithelial tissue, so you can imagine how painful these injuries are. The chemicals have also caused irreparable damage to her liver and kidneys, and frankly, she's just too far down on the donor list for it to make a difference."

Naomi thought that if she had truly been related to Lawrence as she had claimed on the forms, the resident's blunt analysis of the woman's condition would have sent her into hysterics. Her fears were confirmed when she pointedly flashed her credentials to the Secret Service agent seated in front of Megan's door, and the doctor did not seem surprised. *How did he know who I was?* she asked herself angrily. She fervently hoped that news of this visit would not be leaked to the press, but knew that it would probably be a matter of public record within the hour. The interview with Lawrence was the most important of the day, though, and she could not rush through it just to avoid reporters. Before she entered the room, the young resident pulled her back gently.

"Listen," he said, "I don't know if you've had experience with this kind of thing or not, but what you do when you walk in there means a lot. She'll look to your expression to gauge her own appearance, her own condition. She's aware of the prognosis—but she doesn't need to be reminded of it every time someone walks in."

Naomi gave a terse nod and pulled away from the doctor abruptly.

As the agent followed her through the door to keep an eye on the proceedings, she could not keep the sickened expression from her face. The woman on the bed was hardly recognizable as a human being, her body and face scorched by burns so deep that they appeared quite dry and dark red. The lingering smell of garlic pervaded the air, which Naomi knew was the result of the necrosis eating away at the subcutaneous layers of skin. Although the most heavily burned parts of the woman's body were covered by white sterile dressings drenched in saline, Naomi could see that this was easily the worst of all the injuries she had encountered so far.

"Agent Lawrence? My name is Naomi Kharmai. I'm with Central Intelligence, and I need to talk to you about the assassination of Senator Levy."

"I've already given my supervisors a full account, as well as the FBI. Capitol Hill PD sat in on that one. Aren't you supposed to be sharing information with them?" Megan asked resignedly.

Although the deterioration of her jaw had slurred her speech, Naomi could still detect the lyrical, lilting quality of Megan Lawrence's voice. She thought that a few days ago it would have been a pleasure to listen to this woman speak. "I'm sorry, Agent Lawrence, but you know how it goes. We're going to need a firsthand account, and I have some pictures I'd like you to take a look at." Naomi hoped that by addressing this woman as "Agent," she might foster a little professional courtesy. To Megan, it just sounded patronizing.

"Look," Megan tried one last time, "if we could maybe talk later, I just don't feel—"

"You know, I don't really have time later, so if you don't mind—"

"Time?" Megan interrupted, a look of disbelief spreading across her misshapen features. The man leaning by the door stood a little straighter at the tone in her voice. "You want to talk to me about *time?*" Lawrence was shouting now, the garbled sound of her speech gone, crystal-clear words echoing off the clean white walls. "*You* have all the time in the world! I'm never going to leave this room alive, and my daughter is about to lose her mother. She doesn't *have anyone else!*" She collapsed back onto her bed, the anger dissipating as quickly as it had appeared. Her own words brought it all rushing back, though, and the reality of her situation was suddenly sharp, stinging deeper than any physical pain as tears began to stream down her ravaged face.

In three quick strides the heavy agent in the corner reached Naomi's side, grabbed her arm roughly, and dragged her out of the room. As he pulled her down the hallway, the sound of Megan Lawrence's sobs followed them, blending with Naomi's furious protestations. The agent did not let go of her arm until he watched her leave the building.

Outside the hospital, a light snow had begun to fall, early winter in October. She stood motionless for a long moment, finally stepping off the curb to stalk angrily to her car. Behind her, the doors were pushed open and a voice called out in her direction. She turned to face the young resident from the fifth floor.

"I thought you should know." Naomi waited impatiently until the doctor continued. "She has less than a week left. Her husband passed away three years ago, and she won't see her daughter again because she doesn't want that image to be the girl's last memory of her mother."

The resident watched Kharmai's face long enough to realize that the words meant nothing to her. Then he turned and retreated from the cold, heading back to finish his shift.

CHAPTER 4

LANGLEY, VIRGINIA

Kealey was standing before a bank of monitors and audio equipment in a darkened room occupied by the Directorate of Science and Technology. He wore a visitor's pass around his neck that identified him by number, although the laminated surface also bore a photograph of himself taken three years earlier. The crowded space was filled with young analysts looking at data, monitoring rows of numbers, and occasionally speaking quietly to each other over Styrofoam cups of cold coffee. Ryan Kealey, standing next to the chief analyst, Roger Davidson, was lost in the sense of anonymity that seemed to blanket the room.

"Okay, this copy arrived in June of 2003 via the Saudis—God knows how they got it. Originally broadcast on Al-Jazeera, it's the usual fare, so it didn't get a lot of attention at first. Declaration of *fatwa*—a religious proclamation—issued on a standard feed, decent resolution. Remember, we're looking at the background . . . This isn't surveillance tape, so we didn't really need to run any compression. We got what we were looking for when we adjusted this spot here—you see?"

As the analyst manipulated strings of data on a laptop computer, the corner of the screen on the second monitor darkened, revealing a small group of people. Some were reading from what Kealey thought were handmade military field manuals, while others were stripping and cleaning weapons.

"Got it?" asked Davidson. "Okay, this tape was shot at midday, at least according to the time-and-date stamp. My tech officers swear up and down that it hasn't been altered, so we'll call that fact for now. Now, you can see the glare *was* initially blocking out this group of people, so we've . . ."

Ryan tuned the analyst out as he leaned in to stare at the tape. The group of men were seated on the sand beneath a worn canvas tarp lashed to wooden supporting poles. For the most part, they appeared to be of Arab descent, dressed in loose, dark clothing or flowing robes covered in dirt and dust. All were wearing the traditional kaffiyeh, including one man half-turned away from the camera, the sun giving light to blond hair that strayed from beneath the head covering. The angle did not reveal the man's face, only the clean, straight line of his jaw, obvious even beneath the heavy beard.

Ryan Kealey stared at the frame for a long time.

He turned and caught Davidson watching him with a satisfied smile on his face. "Harper said you would pick up on that right away." He tapped emphatically on the screen where the image was located. "I don't think it's an accident that this guy is facing away from the camera. He's far more disciplined than the others, probably because someone has a file on him somewhere. He's a player, but he wasn't always so careful. I'll show you what I mean."

The analyst kept the image on the screen and started a different segment of tape on another of the room's many flat-screen monitors. "This is a copy of a tape found in the Khyber Pass four months ago. The original was badly damaged by fire, probably in an attempt to destroy it. Mostly they were successful, but we recovered about two minutes of intermittent footage.

"In this one, we have what appears to be a high-level meeting of lesser Al-Qaeda operatives and members of the *majlis al shura*, the governing council. Although the time and date are not displayed, we believe that it was recorded well *after* 9/11, as our intelligence indicates that this man, Abu Musab al-Zarqawi, was still busy recruiting for Ansar al-Islam in northern Iraq until early 2002. In fact, the most recent sighting came in May of that same year, when a Pakistani army captain supposedly spotted him in Peshawar . . ."

Kealey might as well have been alone in the room, his attention completely focused on the monitor. At that moment, the man with whom al-Zarqawi was speaking briefly glanced up in the direction of the camera. The face was without expression, but the flashing green eyes seemed to stare right through the glass, as though catching sight of an old friend from across a crowded room.

"Son of a bitch," Kealey whispered under his breath. He turned to Davidson, abruptly interrupting the man's impassioned commentary. "I've seen enough. Take me to Harper."

Seated in the deputy director's seventh-floor office, Ryan could catch distant views of the Potomac River across treetops lightly dusted with snow. The sight of the water reminded him of his old house on Cape Elizabeth, and he suddenly felt the urge to call Katie. Would she even pick up the phone? She could definitely hold a grudge, as he had discovered much to his chagrin on several other occasions . . .

"Ryan, I take it you feel sure enough to move on this?" Harper asked.

Kealey snapped back from his thoughts, turning his full attention to the other man.

"It's March on that tape, John, I'm positive. If we can place him here during the attack, well, that's another question. It would help if we had some witnesses to talk to. If their stories match up, then we might have a foundation to build on."

Harper nodded his agreement and turned to the only other person in the room, a small young woman seated on the other side of the coffee table. "What did you turn up in the interviews, Naomi?"

"Nothing new from the civilians, sir, but the Secret Service has already consulted with their person on the scene. They've faxed me a copy of her account. She only got a brief look, but it's enough to confirm the other descriptions: Caucasian male, late twenties to early thirties, medium height, lean build. More importantly, she was the only witness confident enough to pick someone out of the photographs. Iran doesn't have an embassy here in Washington, of course, but they *do* have a special-interest group located in the Pakistani embassy. Our people were watching the building five minutes after the attack, and there was no real fluctuation in traffic in or out.

"That's the bad news. It's going to be tough to stick this to the regime in Tehran. However, it's possible, even likely, that this new government has direct ties to Al-Qaeda. If we can dig something up there, we would definitely have a silver bullet to hand to the U.N."

Harper was looking thoughtfully out the window as she spoke. When he swiveled back in her direction, he nodded briefly and gave her a polite smile. "Thanks, Naomi. Would you mind excusing us for a moment?"

She didn't move for a couple of seconds, then stood up without looking in Kealey's direction. "Of course, sir."

"I take it she's cleared for this." Ryan asked after she had left the room and closed the heavy door behind her, perhaps slightly harder than necessary. On the other side of the wall, a light flashed red next to the door frame, announcing that they were not to be disturbed.

Harper nodded wearily. "Naomi Kharmai. From what I'm told, she's a rising star in the CTC," he said, referring to the Agency's counterterrorism department. "She's finishing up her master's in computer science at GWU. From London, originally, but she speaks four languages, including Arabic and Farsi. That's why she's in on this. Otherwise, I'd probably get someone with a little more experience."

Ryan wasn't surprised to hear that Kharmai was British. The accent was a dead giveaway, but there were other factors to take into account. Although the CIA depended on foreign assets for much of its hard intel, many were also brought in as full-time employees at Langley, especially in recent years. Of course, they underwent a rigorous security screening before they were offered positions, and even then, they were periodically checked up on by the internal Office of Security. Most of the Agency's foreign-born recruits were never aware that they were lightly surveilled by their own employer from time to time, without regard for rank or seniority.

"Do I have to ask who Lawrence identified?"

Harper shook his head and pushed an 8 x 10 across the coffee table. When Ryan picked it up, he found himself staring at the same person in the videotapes. It was the man he knew as Jason March.

"Obviously, we've known about this for some time," the DDO was saying. "There's more, of course; one of ours was attached to the Special Forces team that cleared those caves. In addition to the videotape, he bagged some papers that had been partially burned. They were shipped directly over to our embassy in London. Technical Services didn't get much, but the senator's name came up as a possible target. That was enough to get him a protective detail, for all the good it did.

"If it *is* March we're dealing with, then we're in serious trouble, Ryan. Can you imagine what the reaction will be if word gets out that an American national is that high up in Al-Qaeda? There will be chaos, pure and simple. It'll be a field day for the media . . . This guy makes John Lindh look like a boy scout." Jonathan tapped his pen methodically against the sleek finish of his desk as he considered. "Kharmai's pretty quick, you know," he said thoughtfully. "That's quite a leap, from Iran to Al-Qaeda, and she doesn't know about March or his involvement, if in fact he was involved."

"I'd say it's a safe bet, John," Kealey said. "And it's definitely cause for concern. As you said, Senator Levy's name was known to Al-Qaeda, and Levy just happened to be the most outspoken critic of the Iranian hard-liners. If Al-Qaeda is being directly supported by the new regime, then they're going to have access to the money and equipment needed to pick up where they left off."

Harper finished the thought. "Which means we could be looking at a serious problem. I get the feeling that March would be able to tell us a lot right now." He turned to look directly at the other man. "Where is he?"

"Out of the country, no question." Ryan's response was quick and definitive. "He would have had prior arrangements in place; he knew that once we had a positive ID, he would have no chance at moving through any standard point of embarkation. On the other hand, he wouldn't take the obvious route out anyway.

"It sounds impossible, right? The assassination of a well-guarded politician in Washington, D.C., during daylight hours. There was definitely a huge amount of risk involved, but there are Metro stations all over the place, including one right behind the Smithsonian. Hell, there's at least eight different ways to leave the city from Union Station alone. He counted on the heavy tourist presence on the Mall despite the weather, and he set up just outside the security perimeter for the White House. He probably scouted out the locations of the countersniper teams, at least those with fixed posts. Maybe that information was provided to him . . . It's difficult to say. In short, he hasn't lost a step. You can't count on him to make any mistakes."

CHAPTER 5

IRAN

The young woman leaned back against a late-model Range Rover and shivered slightly in the cold night air as she watched the small plane approach through scattered clouds. She wore the long black chador that was customary dress for the female populace, although her head covering was pushed back to reveal lustrous black hair framing her oval face. The woman reasoned that this small violation of her country's stringent standards of dress could be easily forgiven in her lonely surroundings. The makeshift airfield was located almost 5 kilometers south of the Atrak River, a major perennial that cuts through the desolate coastal plains extending from the Caspian Sea. This portion of Iran was virtually deserted, and so made an ideal landing spot for the aging multiprop Cessna, which was making its final descent after having left Azerbaijan three hours earlier under a false flight plan.

Once the plane rolled to a stop on the compact dirt of the runway, the exterior door swung open and a sole passenger emerged, carrying only a duffel bag in his right hand. She watched with interest as he carefully climbed down from the elevated fuselage and moved toward her. From his youthful appearance, she guessed the man was in his late twenties, early thirties at most. He walked with a crisp, confident stride that propelled him effortlessly across the perilous surface of the desert sand.

"Hello," she said. Then, in rapid Farsi, "My name is Negin. I will take you the rest of the way. I have been instructed to ask if you are carrying any weapons—you will be searched on arrival."

"I'm unarmed. How far?" he asked in kind. Although she had been told the man understood the language, it was still a little unsettling to hear her native tongue spoken so fluently by a foreigner.

"Less than two hours. They are waiting for you," was her response. Fifteen minutes later, the Range Rover emerged from the dark expanse of the desert and turned onto the cracked asphalt of the main road to Mashhad, speeding east toward the holy city as the stars burned far overhead.

Mashhad is the capital of and the largest city in the Khorasan province of Iran, home to approximately two million souls. His hosts could hardly have selected a better location for this meeting, March thought, as the very name of the city means "place of martyrdom." One would have to search long and hard to find a community more virulently opposed to Western culture. Although he had few doubts about his own abilities or capacity for survival, he might have feared for his safety were it not for the presence of the other men seated around the simple wooden table before him.

An amusing thought suddenly occurred to him: despite his recent atrocities, the director of the Central Intelligence Agency would probably greet him at the airport with open arms and a suitcase full of cash were he to sacrifice the people in this room. The occasional looks of distrust that were cast in his direction were enough to convince him that he was not the only one to envision this scenario.

Most, however, were uncomfortable meeting his eyes and chose to stare down at the notepads on the table or to distant corners of the room.

His real name was not Jason March, nor did they know him as such. It was, however, the pseudonym he had been identified with most over the years. On a hilltop overlooking the Syrian coast seven years earlier, March had proven his loyalty to these men and their cause. None, however, was aware of this fact, and he did not volunteer the information. About the man seated before them they knew very little, except that he could accomplish anything. This was the only statement made about the American that was not disputed.

"You achieved a great deal in Washington, my friend. I trust the contact we provided was to your satisfaction." The speaker was an Egyptian national, Mustafa Hassan Hamza. Despite having been sentenced to death in absentia by an Egyptian court in 1981, he had remained active within the organization. After the invasion of Afghanistan by American forces in late 2001, he had narrowly escaped the country with his life. The subsequent decimation of Al-Qaeda's ranks had resulted in rapid promotion for the man who now held the rank of assistant commander within the Islamic terror network.

"I was impressed with your source's efficiency and dedication," March replied honestly. He did not give compliments freely. "It is a shame that he will most likely be discovered by the FBI; in fact, this may have already occurred. They can be quite efficient in their own right."

"Do you have any recommendations?" the Egyptian asked.

"Through our mutual friend in South Africa, I have already provided your source with the means to evade capture. As I said before, I do not think you will be disappointed by his commitment to this organization."

Hamza appraised the man seated before him with increasing admiration. Once again he was reminded of how fortunate he was to have such a powerful weapon at his disposal, not to mention the inherent propaganda value of an American working against his own country. Nevertheless, his lack of knowledge about the man's past was a constant source of worry for Hamza. How long could a man commit treason on such a grand scale before his conscience rallied against him?

Another thought ate at him occasionally, though he had all but dismissed it: how far would the Americans go to plant someone in his organization? He did not think they would kill one of their own greedy politicians, but deep down he was aware that this was not necessarily true, and the doubt was a heavy stone in his stomach. There were people within the Western intelligence services who were very much like him, in that they did not consider themselves bound by law or moral imperative. Hamza himself had often been heard to say that these few exceptional individuals posed a greater threat to the organization than the entire might of the American military combined.

The Egyptian did not betray any of these thoughts, his face an impassive mask. He turned to another man seated directly across from him, who had not spoken for the duration of the meeting. "Minister Mazaheri, thank you for being here this evening. I believe you have news to impart."

The newly appointed minister of intelligence and security nodded and went on to address the group, his eyes focusing intently on each face from behind simple steel-framed spectacles. "His Excellency is most pleased by what you have accomplished. He was angered by the American accusations, and wishes to thank you for the actions you have initiated against them. Tomorrow he will issue a statement declaring his intention to reopen the nuclear facility at Natanz." This revelation brought murmured approval from the small group of men around the table, the few who were trusted enough to be told of this development.

"Of course, production is already well under way. Recently installed gas centrifuges have dramatically increased the speed of the enrichment process, and our heavy-water reactor at Arak is currently producing weapons grade plutonium. We have, however, encountered several difficulties. The IAEA has its suspicions, as always, and is insisting on access to our facility in the south. This proposal is rapidly gaining support within the U.N. El-Baradei can be quite persistent. Additionally, we have been forced to import some of the components needed for the carbon casing and injection core. It will be difficult to bring these materials into the country without alerting the Americans."

The Iranian leaned forward, resting his hands on the rough surface of the table. His face was twisted in hatred when he spoke again. "This new resolution implemented by the West will set back the program by ten years or more if it is allowed to continue. For years we have survived only through the greed of European oil companies who regularly undermined the American sanctions. Now it appears that the French are starting to fall into line, as are the Italians . . . It is the opinion of my government that there is only one way to dissuade them from supporting these latest measures."

Hamza absorbed these comments silently, one hand carefully grooming his thick black mustache as he considered this statement. "A large-scale attack on U.S. soil. Many American deaths. Extensive news coverage and public backlash. These are the things that you need to cause a division, to break their will."

Ali Vahid Mazaheri nodded in agreement. "What do you suggest?"

"There are many options," Hamza said. "First, a suitable target must be found. Everything depends on the target. A decisive strike will shatter the coalition; however, we may need assistance from His Excellency in mounting such an operation. Your government has seen how effective Al-Qaeda can be, even in our current weakened state." He sent a respectful nod in the American's direction. "Our Western friend has taken many risks that have once again brought us to the attention of the world. Speed is critical at this juncture if we wish to cause immediate disarray in the American leadership."

The minister inclined his head slightly, a small smile etching its way across his face. "An interesting proposal. What do you require?"

"At first, nothing. Merely your support."

"You have it. My country is in your debt, and it shall be repaid many times over. I will convey your proposal to His Excellency."

"You have my gratitude. I am confident that we shall both prosper from this agreement."

Hamza smiled and stood, as did the Iranian minister. Both men shook hands and then embraced, causing the small group surrounding the table to break into spontaneous applause.

Jason March stood to the side, his face wiped clean of any emotion. Inside, though, he felt a wave of pleasure ripple through his body as a vision of Washington ablaze seeped its way into his mind. The image of fire erupting from the windows of the White House was so powerful that Hamza had to speak his name several times before he snapped back to reality.

"Yes, what is it?"

Hamza frowned slightly at the man's tone. He was still, after all, a traitor to his native country. A man who changed sides once could do so again. Hamza wanted to test this man's loyalty; to do so, he was about to take a serious risk.

"Follow me. There is someone I would like for you to meet."

The ancient Ford Cortina moved steadily through the darkened streets of Mashhad, stopping at various locations, sometimes for several minutes at a time, before moving off again unexpectedly with a sudden burst of speed. Although hundreds of volunteers would have jumped at the chance to drive Hassan Hamza about the city, he placed trust only in his own instincts, and rightfully so; he had seen many other experienced operatives die at the hands of the American Special Forces by exercising less caution than was necessary in their chosen profession. The American seated next to him had not spoken since leaving the heavily guarded two-story residence northeast of the city center. Hamza wondered what was running through the other man's mind.

After forty-five minutes had passed, Hamza decided they had not been followed. In any city in Afghanistan, he would not have attempted such a meeting, but he felt reasonably secure in this part of northeastern Iran. He turned abruptly into a dusty alleyway, the sedan clattering to a stop between buildings of pale stone.

"Follow me. You have nothing to worry about," he assured the other man. He handed the American a woolen watch cap. "Put this on."

March pulled the material down low over his blond hair, which, if left uncovered, would be immediately noticed and stored away for future use by the city's many inhabitants. Given the chance, the people in this area would eagerly criticize the decadent West; however, he was aware that they might easily change their tune when presented with a generous reward for information. Such was the fickle nature of humanity, March knew. Most people would gladly sacrifice their principles for money.

The two men moved quickly down the alley, and then past a row of dilapidated, low-slung brick buildings. March noticed that the street was unusually dark, the bulbs in the streetlights above having been either removed or destroyed. Despite the late hour, an old woman wandered down the uneven street in their direction, her gait unsteady. She averted her eyes as she passed the two men, another fact that was not lost on the American. He decided that the organization had taken substantial measures to ensure their security in this area, perhaps even to the point of bribing people house to house. Certainly, the local officials would have been well compensated for their cooperation.

They stopped at the fifth house on the left. March hesitated before pushing through the wrought iron gate, sensing that something was amiss. Hamza's easy smile did little to alleviate his sudden fear. As his acute senses suddenly focused, he picked up a silhouette in his peripheral vision. A sniper lay prone on the low roof of the building, the rigid bone of his eye socket just millimeters from the scope of a Russian Dragunov rifle.

March was impressed by the man's discipline, but thought the weapon far too large and difficult to maneuver in an urban environment. He personally would have opted for the Galil with its folding stock, but never would have suggested it to the man on the roof. He almost laughed out loud at the idea of an Arab militant using a weapon manufactured in Israel.

Approaching the door, two more guards suddenly entered his line of sight, AK-47 rifles held down by their sides. The men tensed momentarily as they approached, then quickly relaxed as Hamza spoke with one of the guards in hushed tones. A portable radio was lifted to lips cracked by the harsh sun, words were exchanged, orders issued. Moments later, the door swung open and the two arrivals were hustled inside.

Jason March waited, his back aching in the uncomfortable wooden chair. The past few days had been tedious: nonstop travel under assumed identities, the constant fear of discovery, the constant apprehension. Only now was it coming to a peak; he felt as though he was about to be tested, and his answers would determine not only his place within the organization, but whether he would leave this building alive or not. Through his supreme confidence, March retained a measure of caution. He had come too far to throw it all away now.

Low voices outside the door announced his visitors before they pushed into the room. Hamza entered, quickly followed by a surprisingly tall, gaunt individual whom March recognized immediately. The man had made few changes to his appearance despite the leaflets dropped by army helicopters that offered a reward in excess of 25 million dollars for his apprehension.

Saif al-Adel cursorily examined the person who had abruptly stood upon his entrance into the room. He was instantly suspicious, as the man's appearance seemed to embody Western decadence in its entirety. The eyes, on the other hand, told a different story altogether, the hatred visible deep within the vivid green irises. It was this hate he wanted to explore. Soon he would have the answers he needed to proceed.

CHAPTER 6

WASHINGTON, D.C. • CAPE ELIZABETH

It had taken all her powers of persuasion, but Naomi Kharmai was finally able to liberate the personnel file from Jonathan Harper's protective care. It lay closed before her now, although she had already examined it thoroughly. Naomi sipped at her tea in the deserted café as she recounted the information she had learned about Ryan Thomas Kealey. He was thirty-three years old, the last three of which had been spent in the Central Intelligence Agency as part of the Special Activities Division. Within those three years, the file confirmed that he had been awarded the Intelligence Star for courageous action in the field.

She considered this award for some time. Although the circumstances that had resulted in the conference of the medal were sealed, Naomi recognized immediately that Kealey must carry a fair degree of influence within the Agency as a result of his actions. She had noticed earlier, with some surprise, that he was on a first-name basis with Deputy Director Harper. Perhaps this also explained why Ryan was not attached to the CTC; certainly, they would have eagerly recruited him given the opportunity.

The file also recorded his activities before joining the Agency. Kealey had left the U.S. Army as a major in 2001 under pressure from Special Forces Command. Naomi took that to mean the Joint Chiefs of Staff, whose approval would have been needed in order to indict a soldier with Ryan Kealey's background. The 201 military record cited numerous awards: the Distinguished Service Cross, the Legion of Merit with one Oak Leaf Cluster, the Bronze Star with two Oak Leaf Clusters—the list went on and on. Kharmai knew little about military decorations, but was aware that this man would be held in high esteem by anyone wearing the uniform.

Naomi could see that he was educated as well, holding a bachelor's of science in business administration from the University of Chicago. His graduate degree had been awarded by Duke University in 1994. By that time, Kealey was already a first lieutenant fresh out of Special Forces Assessment and Selection, soon to be followed by successful completion of the Q course at Fort Bragg.

Unbelievable, she thought. He had achieved the rank of major in eight years, and that time included two years attached to another unit, the 1st SFOD-D, which she did not recognize. That was phenomenal advancement. The man was obviously being groomed for high command. She wondered what Ryan Kealey could have done to derail such a successful career.

She had a sudden insight and flipped open the file to the last page, looking for the signatory: MG Peter Hale, USASFC. With or without Harper's authority, Naomi Kharmai decided she would find a way to talk with Kealey's last commanding officer.

It was fast approaching dark when Ryan finally returned to Cape Elizabeth two days later. There was little reason to wait around in Washington while the analysts did their work, so Harper had given him a brief reprieve. Katie had not answered her phone for the duration of the trip, so he couldn't help but feel slightly apprehensive when he saw her little car parked outside the house.

The interior was almost as cold as the air outside. He went directly into the living room, where he proceeded to carefully stack wood in the immense stone fireplace. It wasn't long before the fire began to spread a pleasant warmth throughout the house. He turned to find Katie leaning against the doorjamb wearing tight jeans, a loose woolen sweater, and a look of consternation. She was watching him quietly. It seemed to Ryan that the temperature of the room had suddenly dropped again. Judging from the scowl on her face, he wasn't about to receive a warm welcome home.

"Hey," he said, after a brief, awkward silence. "I missed you."

"I can tell, the way you rushed in here to talk to me."

He lifted his hands in a gesture of exasperation. "I called you. It was a last-minute thing. Why didn't you answer?"

She was momentarily caught off guard. *That's a good question,* she thought. "You know why! I can't believe you just took off like that. It's . . . I don't know, it's like you forgot I was even here."

A look of pain came over his face. "Katie, you know that's not true. And it's not fair."

"Did you lie to me?"

"About what?"

The scowl became a skeptical glare. Clearly she wasn't buying it. "About leaving, Ryan. Did you really retire last year?"

"Of course I did." Her arms were crossed, her expression doubtful. "Katie, I would never mislead you like that."

She looked into his face for a long moment, gauging his sincerity. "If you left the Agency," she said slowly, "why were you in such a hurry to get back to Washington?"

It was a fair question to which he didn't have an answer. She had won a small victory, but it didn't register in her unhappy features. When she spoke again, it was clear from her tone of voice that she was already tired of arguing.

"You know, I'm scared to ask where I rank in all of this. Is it below the CIA? Below a bunch of crazy terrorists in some shitty third-world country?"

"It's not a question of rank, Katie."

She smiled sadly and lowered her glistening eyes. "That's a terrible answer, Ryan."

He dropped his own head and silently cursed himself for the stupid remark. God, he had never been good at this kind of thing. It had cost him more than one good relationship over the years. It had never bothered him much before, but Katie meant more to him than the rest of them combined, and his chest tightened when he suddenly realized that he might be losing her. When she finally filled the silence, he was surprised by the intensity of the relief that he felt.

"Look, I know what you do is important," she said in a small voice. "I would never say otherwise. I don't try to make you talk about it—that can be separate from us. I'm not sure if I can deal with that yet, but I'm willing to try."

She looked up at him hopefully. "That's the important thing, right? That we're both here and willing. I just want to know where I stand in this thing we have going. Where *we* stand."

"I'm sorry," he said. "You're right, I wasn't thinking." A slight hesitation, the following words no less meaningful for it. "I don't think you know how important you are to me, Katie . . . In fact, I'm sure of it."

She desperately tried to hold on to her anger, but it was already slipping away. A small smile spread over her face. "Do you mean that?"

He held out his hand. She walked over to him, and they hugged gently at first, Kealey finding her lips with his. Then he pulled her closer, and suddenly they were holding each other tighter than was necessary, for reasons neither could explain. Ryan speaking quietly into her ear, "You're all I need, Katie. You and me, in this place, is all I could ever ask for."

With her eyes squeezed tightly shut, arms wrapped around him, Katie wondered how she could have been so angry in the first place. She knew what he was trying to say, and for some reason it didn't matter that he couldn't get the words out.

"I love you, too," she whispered.

About 28 kilometers south of Jableh on the Syrian coast, a casual observer would have noticed many things about the scenic beauty of the surrounding landscape. He would have likely described the orange sun high in the dying light of day, the fiery red sky contrasting sharply with the sparkling water of the Mediterranean. The gently sloping hills leading down to the water's edge would have been mentioned, as would the unpaved road slicing its way through the heavily wooded contours of the land. A description might well have been provided of the only building visible for many kilometers, a low-slung villa with whitewashed walls and a roof of Spanish tile that seemed to burn in the sunset. The observer would not, however, have been able to detect any sign of human life in the picturesque scene.

Beneath a heavy canopy of towering pine trees interspersed with the occasional oak, a figure lay perfectly still in the shade and the dirt. Captain Ryan Kealey listened attentively to the environment around him, waiting patiently for communication from the other members of his ODA over an encrypted radio. Glancing to his rear, he was pleased to see no sign of the five other soldiers.

"Sapper Six, Gold One, over."

Kealey lifted his Motorola radio and spoke quietly, careful to avoid the staccato sounds of a whisper. "Sapper Six, give me your sit rep, Gold One."

"In position, no targets visible at this time. I've got eyes on Blue Two on my left, over."

"Keep me updated, Gold One. Six, out."

Without looking back, Ryan lifted his right hand in the air and circled with his index finger, signaling the others to rally at his location. Within thirty seconds, he was surrounded by his team members. "Okay, guys, how we doing?" he asked in a low voice.

"Good to go, sir." The speaker was the newest member of the team, Staff Sergeant Donald Bryant.

Kealey looked into the youthful, eager face and saw himself just four years earlier. He was grateful that this soldier's first combat experience would be a fairly straightforward operation. The other men nodded in the affirmative without saying a word. This was just an extension of training, as far as they were concerned.

"We're going to move up to the woodline. Remember, when our snipers give the word, we'll be moving down that hill pretty quick. There's almost no cover, so keep your distance. Thomas, Mitchell, check the car. Once you get a visual confirmation, move to your entrance point. In the house, don't pass any room without clearing it

first. I mean that." He fixed each man with a serious look, and then broke into a relaxed grin. "Piece of cake, fellas. You know why we're here. Let's take care of business and head on home."

A few little smiles at that. There was a sudden burst of static from the radio, followed by a clear, calm voice. "Sapper Six, Blue Two. I have a visual. One vehicle, looks like a black Mercedes. No tint, I have . . . one driver, two passengers. Permission to go green light, over."

Kealey responded immediately. "Gold One, do you have the target?"

"That's a Roger, Sapper Six."

"Snipers, you have a green light. We're waiting on you. Sapper Six, out."

Kealey gave a hand motion, and the soldiers around him moved from their improvised perimeter toward the edge of the treeline. The men picked their way quietly around the heaviest areas of vegetation; each had used electrician's tape to secure any loose pieces of metal that might give away their position. No one expected the enemy to send out patrols, but the elite soldiers comprising Operational Detachment Alpha 304 were not about to take the risk.

With the exposed section of the slope less than 50 meters away, the thunderous report of a long-range rifle could be heard through the trees, rapidly followed by two more shots.

"Six, Gold One! Vehicle is neutralized, I say again, vehicle is neutralized!"

"Let's go!" Kealey called out. The troops were already running, suddenly breaking through into open ground. A thought was calling for his attention, but he couldn't quite grab it . . . something about the direction of those shots . . .

Halfway down the hill, Ryan realized there was no one in the car, and that it had braked to a halt in the middle of the road, unscathed. The windshield was in-

tact. Automatically he called out, "Cover!" The members of his team immediately hit the ground in the prone position except for Bryant, who was slow in getting down. Kealey watched in disbelief as a ragged exit wound appeared in the young soldier's back, immediately followed by the echo of a rifle shot across the valley. The man did not make a sound, only taking two more faltering steps before crumpling to a heap on the ground.

The four surviving soldiers were pouring lead into the car on the road below. Ryan could make out two armed men crouching behind the vehicle and a third lying still by their side, streams of his blood mingling with the dust of the road. Peering through the telescopic sight mounted to his M4A1, Ryan fired a 3-round burst into the head of the primary target. Adjusting his aim, he could see that one of his men had already taken care of the other terrorist. Kealey was suddenly aware that Staff Sergeant Mitchell was not moving, and then saw the halo of blood around his head, the heavy M249 machine gun inches from his lifeless fingertips.

"Blue Two, what the hell is going on up there?" Kealey shouted into his radio. There was no response. "Blue Two, report!"

Silence.

"What the fuck is going on, sir?" yelled Sergeant Alvarez.

"Gold One, sit rep!" There was still no answer. Ryan had to struggle to keep his voice from shaking. The fear was thumping in his chest; he felt it and hated himself for it, but his men were completely exposed on the side of the slope, and he didn't have time to think about what had gone wrong. The decision came quickly.

"Thomas, Watson! When we open up, move back to the treeline as fast as you can! Alvarez, fire on March's location!" he screamed.

A look of shock and confusion crossed the sergeant's face. "Sir, we can't—"

"Do it!" was the vicious response. "Now!"

Intermittent streams of fire erupted from the barrel of Alvarez's M16A2. Kealey fired in the same direction, although he couldn't spot the sniper, whose ghillie suit allowed him to blend easily into the surrounding vegetation. He cursed the diminished range caused by the shorter barrel of his weapon, which would have been ideal for the close-quarter combat initially anticipated.

He called out to Alvarez: "Loading!"

Rapidly changing out his magazine, Kealey's eyes never left the ridge where his snipers were positioned. He guessed that the line of earth was 400 meters away, a difficult shot even under the best of circumstances, almost impossible with the standard iron sights. He saw a flash of light followed by the roar of the rifle, and out of the corner of his eye caught the awful sight of Alvarez's head breaking apart. That first fatal shot was followed by four more. It took all of Kealey's self-control not to flinch away as he pressed his cheek against the warm metal of his assault rifle. The heat shield encasing the barrel was perfectly balanced in his left hand as he eased back on the trigger, firing until the bolt locked back on an empty magazine.

A few minutes passed without any movement on the ridge.

"Thomas! Watson!" he called out.

There was no answer. A sick feeling clenched his gut as he realized that he was probably the only man alive on the hill. Easing his head slowly around, he could see the lifeless bodies of the other two sergeants in his detachment. His detachment. As the commander, he was responsible for the lives of these men. Was it right that he should be the only one to survive? Suddenly not caring, he got to his feet, a lone figure standing tall on the side of the hill, long shadows cast behind him by the fading sun. Feeling a sudden impact, Ryan looked down at the small hole in his chest, the sight almost blocking out the terrible sound of the rifle in his ears.

He fell to the ground, for some reason absorbed by the hissing of the radio inches from his outstretched hand. Presently he was aware of a man standing on top of the ridge, the image blurred by pain. Through the red haze creeping into the edge of his vision, Ryan thought he could make out the lightweight Parker-Hale M85 rifle held loosely in the crook of the man's right arm. The same weapon that, for the past eight months, had been lovingly attended to and cared for by one man, and one man only. The incredibly still figure of Sergeant First Class Jason March continued to blur as the pain intensified, and Kealey found he could no longer breathe.

He couldn't breathe . . .

Ryan Kealey awoke without a sound, pieces of information slowly entering into his mind, each a revelation more startling than the one before.

The thin sheets were clinging to his sweat-soaked torso. As the shaking slowly left his body, Ryan was suddenly aware that Katie was whispering quietly in his ear, her arms wrapped around him protectively from behind, silken fingers gliding over the raised scar on his chest.

"Baby, are you okay? God, you were shouting so loud . . ." There was a noticeable tremble to her voice. "Your dreams . . . They're getting worse."

He didn't respond, preferring to think of nothing for as long as possible. He just wanted to take comfort from the proximity of her body. Maybe she understood, as she fell silent while his ragged breathing slowly subsided.

Thoughts swirled around him in the dark, intruding when he could no longer hold them at bay. Jason March had murdered men that were like brothers to him. If the regular army fostered lifelong friendships, the relationships built within the Special Forces community were like family ties, carrying no more or less importance than actual blood relations. Now the man he had hoped was dead had returned from the other side of the world to commit even more vicious crimes.

Kealey thought that he was uniquely equipped to kill March. He felt that he owed it to the men who lost their lives on that hilltop far away from home. Where it would end, he wasn't sure. Ryan only knew that he would be there to make sure it did.

CHAPTER 7

WASHINGTON, D.C.

"I'm due at the White House in two hours, John. I can't go up there empty-handed. What do you think we're looking at here?"

Jonathan Harper glanced up at Robert Andrews, the recently appointed director of the Central Intelligence Agency. It was a difficult question to answer; the combined efforts of the CIA and the FBI had yielded very little new information in the past week. Phone calls had been made, favors called in. The interagency cooperation that was supposed to have come into effect following 9/11 had never really materialized, despite the recent development of the Terrorist Threat Integration Center located just a few short miles away. Harper had been one of the few to recognize beforehand that this would be the case.

"Well, we still have no claim of responsibility for the attack on Senator Levy, which in and of itself is highly unusual. Iran is denying all involvement, but I don't think we can take that at face value, especially since they officially announced that they're starting up their weapons program again. The timing is just too damn convenient. Besides, they had a better reason than anyone to take out the senator. He was their most vociferous opponent on everything from the acquisition of nuclear material to human-rights violations. One thing we do have is a tentative ID on the man who carried out the attack, and we can link him directly to Al-Qaeda. I sent that up to you earlier."

Director Andrews nodded slowly, his lips pursed. "I find this a little hard to believe. Why would they trust an American enough to bring him that far into the organization?"

"Maybe they know what happened in Syria."

Andrews looked up sharply. "You said the ID was verified by this guy Kealey. Where is he?"

"He just got back this morning. He's looking at cell phone intercepts with Davidson and Kharmai right now."

"I thought he was retired."

The deputy director shrugged. "He gave it a shot. I think he knew it wasn't going to last, though."

"Keep an eye on him," Andrews warned. "I read the file, and I know what he did in Bosnia. We're not trying to generate any publicity here, John."

"That was never proven, sir." The director shot him a skeptical look, which immediately made Harper regret the words.

"Just keep him in line, John. I appreciate what he's done here as much as anybody, but we have our hands full as it is. I don't need the Senate Oversight Committee jumping into the fray as well, okay?"

Harper nodded and stood to leave, but Andrews waved him back down into the seat.

"One more thing. I hear you have an analyst asking a lot of questions about Kealey. By that, I mean the same analyst you just mentioned." Harper tried to contain his surprise, but the director noticed his incredulous look and gave a small, reluctant smile. "There is a reason I have this job, John."

Harper nodded. "Naomi Kharmai. She's been with us for four years. She had clearance for the personnel file, so I gave it to her just to keep her happy. I told her not to take it any further, but I don't know if she'll listen. She's pretty stubborn."

The DCI considered his response for a long moment. Finally, he said, "If you think it's worth keeping her on this, then make sure she stays busy with the relevant stuff. As in, what happened in Syria is *not* relevant. Those soldiers officially died in a training accident . . . We need to be able to work with the military, and if that piece of misinformation comes out on our end, then they won't trust us with anything else. And frankly, I wouldn't blame them," Andrews added.

Harper was about to respond when the heavy mahogany door was edged open by a secretary. "Excuse me, sir, but you might want to turn to Channel 3. It's about Senator Levy."

The confusion was evident on the faces of both men as the director scrambled for the remote control. An image appeared on the screen of a high-rise apartment complex that Harper recognized immediately.

"If you're just joining us, we're here outside the Kennedy-Warren, an exclusive residential building on Connecticut Avenue, where officials from the Justice Department have tracked down the man suspected in providing information that led to the cold-blooded murder of Senator Daniel Levy last week. The man has been identified as Michael Shakib, a Congressional staffer with strong ties to the Iranian American community, who has—"

"Jesus Christ!" Andrews screamed, his voice drowning out the excited anchorwoman. "How the *hell* did this get past us, John?"

"The FBI is supposed to be keeping us up-to-date on these kinds of developments, but—"

"Bullshit!" Andrews took a few deep breaths, resting his hands on one of the few empty spaces on his cluttered desk. Seconds passed, and the anger fell from his features. "Sorry, John, that's not meant for you. I can see that they fucked us on this."

The DCI thought for a long moment before continuing. "You know, it might even work out better that we're not obviously invested. I don't see this ending well, not with all those reporters out there. All the same, get someone down there without making a lot of noise about it. Send Kealey, if you want."

Harper was in awe of the man's self-control. "If I know him, sir, he's probably already on the way."

"Make sure we have a part in this, John. Bring us into the loop. If we don't know what's going on, it'll be easier for them to hang the blame on us."

It was a dismissal. Harper left the room quietly, grateful to leave behind the now-fuming director of Central Intelligence.

* * *

Ryan had driven his BMW down from Maine rather than risk being stuck in an uncomfortable rental for the duration of his stay in Washington. He decided that it had been a good decision as the powerful 4.4-liter engine pushed the car north along Connecticut Avenue. He was quickly approaching the Dupont Circle underpass, a cell phone pressed to his ear as he expertly navigated the busy street with one hand on the steering wheel.

"I got it, John. Talk to the guy on the scene, don't make any noise . . . Fine, I understand. Here, talk to your girl." He handed it over to a pale-faced Naomi Kharmai, who had to unclench her tightly balled fists to accept the outstretched phone.

"Don't let them brush you off, Naomi," Harper said. "We need to know if this is on the up-and-up. If Shakib is the leak, then we're getting somewhere. Don't worry that we didn't get ahold of this first— it's what we do with it now, okay?" The DDO broke off to speak with someone else momentarily. "Call me when you have some details."

The phone went dead in her ear before she could respond. As Ryan shifted into fourth gear and punched the pedal, she slunk back down in the seat as far as she could go, absolutely positive that they would be dead long before reaching their destination.

Connecticut Avenue outside the Kennedy-Warren was filled to capacity with emergency-service vehicles, fire engines, and the unmarked government sedans that belonged to the FBI personnel on the scene. Piles of dirty ice had accumulated at the curb, and the pavement beneath their feet was slick. A stiff wind whipped between the vehicles, making the temperature seem even lower than it really was. Ryan thought it was probably less than 30 degrees, making him wish he had brought more protection from the harsh weather than a worn, black-leather jacket. To make matters worse, he and Kharmai were forced to wait for five minutes while their identification was confirmed by the ponderously slow police officers maintaining the perimeter.

Naomi was staring at an unmarked Chevrolet transport van that was at least 25 feet long. The rear doors were open, and Kealey could easily make out the switchboard inside, as well as a gasoline-powered generator bolted to the floor. The vehicle was surrounded by men in blue coveralls and body armor, each holding an HK MP10 down by his side, except for the few who carried shotguns chambered with entry rounds. The men were quietly conversing among themselves; some chewed gum rapidly, fingers tapping impatiently on the trigger guards of their automatic weapons. They tried to hide their tense faces, mostly failing in the effort.

Ryan recognized the stress-relieving rituals and knew immediately that they would get the job done. He hoped it wouldn't come to that.

"Do you think they're going in already?" Naomi asked.

"Jesus, I hope not," he replied, gesturing in the direction of the news vans held beyond the perimeter. Satellite dishes were attached to the roofs of the vehicles. "If he's actually up there, he can see everything we're doing. This can't get any worse than it already is."

Naomi spotted a heavy, angry-looking black man wearing a blue FBI parka over a white dress shirt and suit pants. He was shouting at a small cluster of agents, jabbing his finger into the air emphatically. She caught his eye and walked in his direction, Kealey trailing behind her. The agents scattered on their approach.

"Naomi. I thought you might turn up," the man said warily. She smiled pleasantly, ignoring the tone of his voice.

"Luke Hendricks, Ryan Kealey. Luke here is the ASAC for the Washington field office. Why didn't we hear about this?" she asked bluntly. The generous smile was gone from her face.

"Hey, you said it. I'm the *Assistant* Special Agent in Charge; that means there is about a billion people telling me how to do my job. I'm not the guy who decides what we share with other agencies," Hendricks responded.

Naomi was looking around. "Where's the ADIC?" she asked. She was referring to the Assistant Director in Charge, who runs the field office in major cities such as Washington, D.C., and Los Angeles.

"In the hospital, believe it or not. Double-bypass surgery—pretty convenient, huh? I think he must have seen this one coming."

Kealey appraised the FBI agent quickly, approving of what he saw. Hendricks had a right to be angry; he had been placed in a difficult situation with very little oversight, and the unexpected presence of the reporters only compounded the problem. All the same, Ryan thought that he looked like a man able to make quick decisions under pressure.

"What do you have at this point?" Ryan asked.

"Not much. Confirmation that he's in there, of course. The desk manager saw him go up twenty minutes before we walked through the door. We haven't started a dialogue yet, and I'm beginning to think it won't happen. I'm under pressure to send those guys in," Hendricks said, waving vaguely in the direction of the SWAT team standing by. "Personally, I'd like to exhaust all other possibilities before I give them the go-ahead. My guys are pretty pissed off, but you'd never know it looking at them. Right now, I don't see this man coming down alive unless he gives it up—if he eats a bullet, then we'll never figure out what he was up to."

Ryan looked up at the towering building, then back to Hendricks. He didn't say anything. Personally, he thought that it was a mistake to assume anything about the man on the eighth floor of this apartment complex, Congressional staffer or not.

"How did you get a line on Shakib?" Kealey asked.

Hendricks focused his attention on the man standing slightly behind Naomi Kharmai. Kealey was of medium height, with black hair on the long side, a lean, muscular build, and dark gray eyes that were somewhat unnerving in their intensity.

More than a decade earlier, Luke Hendricks had served as an infantry squad leader in the 82nd Airborne out of Fort Bragg. He had seen action in the Gulf, and had been awarded the Soldier's Medal for pulling two young privates out of a minefield close to the end of his tour. Hendricks rarely talked about the experience, but he knew the difference between a soldier and someone who had served in the military. He could recognize a soldier when he saw one.

"Obviously, we looked at nationality first. It made sense to check out anybody affiliated with Iran working on the Hill. That only took us so far before someone came up with the idea to look at travel plans. Shakib vacationed annually in Valencia. After a day or two, he'd charter a flight to Bucharest under a different name, and then on to Tehran. It was a low-risk strategy with minimal contact, suggesting the possibility that he was a sleeper. Who knows what else he's given up over the years? A lot of heads are going to roll when the whole thing goes public."

After Hendricks stated the obvious, he paused for a moment. "He knows we're out here. If we were completely off track, then he would have given it up a long time ago. This is the guy."

"And you couldn't keep this quiet?" Naomi asked.

"I didn't leak it, if that's what you're suggesting. A lot of people had access to this information," he responded angrily.

"Not us," she muttered.

High above the commotion, Michael Shakib was kneeling motion-less on a prayer mat facing east. His head was bowed in supplication facing Mecca, a place he had not visited, nor would ever visit, al-though the hajj was specifically required by the fifth pillar of his faith.

Shakib's features were distinctly Arabic, which was not surprising as he had been born in Qom before his parents emigrated to California in 1979, despite the immense difficulties associated with leaving the country after the Revolution. All his life he had been ex-posed to the prejudice and animosity felt toward Islam by his adopted homeland, but had never once considered leaving the faith. He was painfully aware that his appearance alone inspired distrust in the faces of the people he passed each day. This particular prejudice was largely imagined, however, for Michael Shakib was not an unattrac-tive man.

The sharp green eyes flecked with brown were his most notice-able characteristic, framed by perfect olive skin. Thick black hair was set off by his straight white teeth, a feature most uncommon in the poverty-stricken areas of Iran from which he had risen into the world.

In reflective moments, Shakib could concede that he had been bestowed certain benefits denied to many of his peers. He was grate-ful for these advantages, yet despised them at the same time. What had given him the right to be so successful, to enjoy the wealth and privilege usually accorded to only the most elite of America's youth? On a warm, still night in Barbados four years earlier, he had met someone who would change his path in life, who would give him purpose. It had not been a chance encounter, but that fact had never been revealed to Michael Shakib. Until that first meeting, he had survived on his instincts and innate intelligence alone. It had been a useless existence. Despite his undeniable success, Michael had welcomed the opportunity to further such a grand cause, and was now prepared to make his greatest contribution.

He was not disappointed.

"They don't know what they're walking into," Ryan said quietly. It was not his nature to press his opinion, although his every instinct was humming at the moment.

Only Kharmai heard, and turned to face him. "What do you mean?"

"Who do you think called them?" Ryan asked, waving at the reporters. As the wheels turned rapidly in her mind, Ryan pulled Hendricks to one side.

"Listen, I have no authority to back this up . . . It's just a suggestion, but I think you ought to expand the perimeter as far as you can. I know you can't get rid of the reporters, but that might give you a little breathing room. Also, you might want to have someone check these cars, verify the owners," he said. He noticed the other man's questioning look. "I didn't spend my whole career in Washington."

Luke nodded in agreement and understanding, then moved off to speak with the chief of the D.C. Metro PD. Kealey was grateful that Hendricks was open to suggestion, and could see that his first instincts about the man were correct. After several minutes had passed, he noticed agents checking vehicles and calling in license plate numbers. Ryan felt a tug at his arm.

"What did you say to Luke?" Naomi asked, brushing a stray lock of jet-black hair away from her eyes. Looking down at her, Ryan studied her face for the first time. She wasn't quite beautiful, but there *was* something undeniably attractive about her. Certainly, the bright green eyes and flawless caramel-colored skin would set her apart in any crowd. He took in the perfectly groomed hair and eyebrows, her expensive clothes, and could tell that she put a lot of effort into her appearance.

And she hadn't backed down from Hendricks either. He liked a woman who could stand up for herself. He angrily shook the intruding thoughts from his mind, telling himself to stay focused. Naomi had asked him a question, and he had to scramble to recall it.

"Just to have his people check the cars. He listens . . . That's a good quality in an SAC. How do you know him?"

"We've worked together before," was her tart reply. She did not offer further insight.

Ryan could see the corner of her mouth turned up in a bemused smirk. He hoped that she hadn't misinterpreted his look. His life was already complicated enough as it was.

The venetian blinds in his apartment were closed, denying access to the prying eyes of the snipers located on the rooftops across the street. Shakib moved slowly, almost gracefully, through the drafty rooms, past the luxurious furnishings and other trinkets acquired over the course of a lifetime. None of it mattered to him.

On the other end of his expansive living room, a flat-screen Sony television was mounted on the wall. Behind the glass, CNN was running silent images of the Kennedy-Warren apartment complex. He was pleased to note the mobile command unit set up in the courtyard below, the agents swarming around it like bees around a hive.

After the plans for the assassination of Senator Levy had been examined and confirmed, the American had brought many materials to Shakib's three-bedroom apartment overlooking Cleveland Park. When he had described to his visitor the expensive restoration of the building and the fact that it had been recently named a National Historic Landmark, the man had smiled and nodded, clearly pleased by the news. The American had demanded solitude while he poured over blueprints and floor plans. Michael went out for sandwiches and coffee while his guest walked through the rooms examining the walls, ceiling, and door frames. A great deal of time had been spent on the balcony, as the man inspected the intricate ironwork combined with cement emplacements that kept the heavy structure secured to the building.

After many hours, his visitor had settled on a single pillar, 4 feet in diameter tucked halfway into a wall. Although he had previously despised the oversized intrusion into his living space, Shakib listened while his guest explained the importance of this single load-bearing structure, how it supported the three floors above him. He had listened while the man described the properties of the heavy marble and stone used in the construction of the building, and the quantity of SEMTEX H that would be necessary to cut through such material.

Shakib had appreciated the patient explanation, and absorbed the information attentively with few interruptions. Although the American understood nothing of Islam, his technical expertise accorded him some measure of respect. Shakib admired diligence in one's chosen profession. In the end, the months of preparation had come down to this one moment.

It was time.

Eight floors down, the reporters were angrily berating the police officers pushing them farther down the street. The nasty edge to the elevated voices carried high above the crowd, adding to the collective tension. New barriers were erected and more men stationed behind them. Luke Hendricks was holding a cell phone in each hand, barking orders into each as lesser agents hovered around him, vying for his attention.

Ryan and Naomi had been pushed aside by the agents milling around the command vehicle, so that they were now on the perimeter, almost as far away from the action as the buzzing reporters. This was moving too fast. Kealey wouldn't breathe easy again until Shakib was on the ground in handcuffs, and everybody was clear of the area. Instinctively, he began looking around for potential cover, his gaze settling on the heavy transport van located just a few feet away. Far above his position, a sniper from the FBI's Hostage Rescue Team spoke into his headset.

"All ground units, this is Sierra Three. The doors to the balcony are open, over."

On the ground, eyes shot skyward in unison. Hendricks lifted a radio to his mouth, walking away from the crowd of people surrounding him. "Sierra Three, this is Command. Do you have a shot?"

"That's affirmative, over."

"Okay . . . Okay, sit tight. We need to—"

"Hold on," came the sudden interruption. "Command, he's got something in his hand. I can't identify—"

Luke briefly wondered what it could be as various scenarios raced through his mind. When he hit upon the worst possibility, he was shouting into the radio, "Sierra Three, *take the shot*, I say again, take the shot *now!*"

Special Agent Mark Silverstein peered through the Leupold Vari-X scope mounted to his custom-made Remington 700P LTR rifle. The cold wind whipping across the top of the building scraped at his nerves, but he had already adjusted his sights accordingly. There was nothing more he could do, except to put his faith in his training. At such a short distance, he elected for a head shot, and was surprised to see the target smiling in his direction as he eased back on the trigger.

As the .308 round violently exited the back of Michael Shakib's head in a pink cloud, the spasm caused by his sudden death caused his right hand to squeeze tight around the electric detonator it contained. It could have gone either way, but the fist was squeezed tightly . . . The circuit that his visitor had carefully constructed less than two weeks earlier was finally completed.

Before Hendricks even issued the order to fire, Ryan Kealey was already pushing his way through the crowd of agents and police officers who were staring at the top of the building. He was dragging Naomi behind him and screaming at Hendricks to evacuate the area, and then at the crowd: "GET DOWN, GET DOWN!" Even as the words left his mouth, he knew that they wouldn't make a difference. He pulled Naomi toward the transport van, his eyes locked onto the open rear doors of the vehicle.

Far above, a brilliant white light erupted from the side of the building, immediately followed by an ear-splitting crack as the cutting charge ripped the pillar in half. Before the loudest part of the explosion reached them, the crowd below was momentarily blinded by the initial flash. Fortunately, many were spared the sight of the eastern face of the building collapsing out toward them.

*   *   *

Assistant Special Agent in Charge Luke Hendricks had been distracted by the figure racing through the crowd. His vision was not obscured, and so he was able to watch in disbelief as death rained down from above. Falling awkwardly to the ground, he pressed his face into the freezing asphalt, covered his head with his hands, and opened his mouth to scream.

The thunderous roar of the explosion echoed in Kealey's ears as he threw Naomi into a corner of the armored vehicle and covered her body with his. Her muffled screams vibrated through his chest as thousands of pounds of cement, marble, and iron from the building's façade crashed down onto Connecticut Avenue. He could hear no other sound of human life, only the deafening sound of the world falling down around them. A sudden impact crushed the opposite end of the vehicle, flipping the van onto its side like a toy. He felt something sharp tear into his face as the walls caved in, the wheels ripped from the axles, the polycarbonate glass crumpling in the windshield and passenger doors. Then the noise was gone and everything went black.

CHAPTER 8

WASHINGTON, D.C.

"Connecticut Avenue was a scene of devastation this morning as an explosion tore apart the eastern face of the Kennedy-Warren residential complex. Although the building was evacuated prior to the explosion, officials fear that the death toll will continue to climb as many people at the scene are still unaccounted for. The explosion appears to be terrorist related, and is thought to have originated in the eighth-floor apartment of Michael Shakib, the man who allegedly provided information that led to the assassination of Senator Daniel Levy, the chairman of the Senate Armed Services Committee, here in Washington almost two weeks ago. We'll have more updates on the way. I'm Susan Watkins, for CNN."

Katie Donovan hurried past the disbelieving crowd gathered round the television in Terminal A of Dulles International, barely taking the time to glance at the ruined building on the screen. United Airlines Flight 213 had just landed after leaving Bangor less than ninety minutes earlier. She had gripped the armrests tightly the entire flight, struggling to maintain the self-control that had been gradually slipping away since she first heard about the bombing earlier that morning. A sick fear had taken root and blossomed in her chest as the hours crept past.

Ryan had given her a cell phone number for emergencies, but she reached only his voice mail each time she tried to call. Then she attempted to reach him by calling Langley direct, but they refused to give her any information, instead referring her to a hotline set up to handle calls from friends and relatives of the victims. *Victims.* The word echoed in her head. It was hard to imagine Ryan being victimized by anything, but she couldn't shake the fear, and the panic threatened to consume her—if he was okay, he would have called. She *knew* he would have called. By the time she reached the Avis counter, it was all she could do to keep from screaming.

Forty-five minutes later, Katie's rented Taurus screeched to a halt outside Georgetown University Hospital. A uniformed police officer yelled at her as she ran through the assembled crowd of reporters and into the building, leaving the car unattended with the keys still in the ignition. A preoccupied nurse absently waved her toward surgery care, which led in turn to a large room decorated in a failed effort to project cheer. Katie could not imagine a more despairing sight. The room was filled to capacity with frightened-looking people. She was dimly aware of quiet whispers of support and low, muffled sobs.

With weak knees, she squeezed through the crowd to the desk and tried to speak to the woman on the other side, but the words were slow in coming.

"Are you okay?" the attendant asked with a genuinely concerned expression. The young woman standing before her looked terrible, hair plastered to her face, the skin around her eyes red and puffy. "Take your time, honey. It's going to be fine."

Katie took a deep breath and rested her shaking hands on the counter for support. "I'm looking for my fiancé, Ryan Kealey. Ryan Thomas Kealey."

The nurse looked down through the list, shaking her head. "I don't see anyone by that name." Katie felt her heart sink, but there was a glimmer of hope. Maybe he hadn't even been at the Kennedy-Warren. But if he was okay, why hadn't he called? It just didn't make sense . . ."Hold on, honey, let me double-check." As the nurse turned to question a harried surgeon, Katie squeezed her eyes shut and willed herself to breathe again.

"Katie?"

She looked up to see him standing in the doorway, a large bandage covering the left side of his face. She could see long tears in his leather jacket, streaks of dried blood on his stained jeans and the backs of his hands. He hadn't called . . . It didn't matter, because he was there, alive. Her right hand flew to her mouth, the other reaching out for him as the tears streamed down her face.

"So you're both okay?" Harper asked. Ryan was pressed uncomfortably into a booth just outside of the hospital, a pay phone held to his ear. He needed to be outside for a while. The thin wall housing the phone rubbed at a long stripe of raw skin on his left arm, and the pain worked with the bite of the air to remind him that he was still breathing.

"We'll make it. A lot of other people didn't," he replied. "Naomi's right arm was banged around pretty bad. I was sure it was broken, but the X-rays came back negative. They gave her a sedative; she's asleep now, I think. Suicide bombers in D.C. The audacity of these bastards. John . . . I don't know how to fight that."

"We just got the first numbers." Harper paused for a moment, beats of silence filling the empty space. "As of 5:00 PM, 64 dead, 121 injured. Obviously, that's going to climb tomorrow when they finish going through the rubble."

Ryan didn't respond. There didn't seem to be much to say.

"Listen, you've had a long day. If it hasn't caught up with you, it will. We'll talk in the morning." A longer pause this time.

Harper sounded tired. Tired and weak. The combination served to gently ease yet another yoke down onto Ryan's shoulders, the burden of uncertainty. He wondered how much more he could carry before he crumbled under the weight.

"It's good to hear your voice, Kealey. I was worried there for a while. Give my regards to Naomi—the department already sent flowers to her room."

"That was good of you, John. I'll see you tomorrow."

After hanging up the phone, he leaned against the cold brick wall

facing the hospital, looking up into the black emptiness. Ryan noticed that his hands were shaking, but he couldn't will them to stop.
He had seen many awful things in his life, far more than most, but
knew that he would never forget the images that had confronted him
through the choking dust after pulling Naomi out of the crushed
van.

Now those terrible scenes reminded him of others, and he rushed
to quickly push the thoughts from his mind. Searching frantically for
something else to focus on, anything else, he found himself thinking
about what he had overheard Katie saying earlier. *My fiancé . . . I'm
looking for my fiancé, Ryan Kealey.*

They had never talked about marriage, and at first glance the idea
seemed completely implausible. They had barely known each other
six months, and he had never even met her family. Now that he
thought about it, she had never mentioned them. In truth, though,
he was more than ready to leave this life behind and start a family of
his own. There had been women in the past, of course, but none that
he cared about so much. If pressed, he wouldn't have been able to
say exactly why.

Although extremely intelligent, she was ruled by emotion, a fact
that Ryan found both fascinating and a little overwhelming. There
was nothing petty in Katie Donovan—for her, feeling decided what
happened next; it was real, and could be trusted. Sometimes, the
passion she exuded was almost frightening in its intensity. When she
cared about something, she threw her whole heart into it. She had
thrown her heart into him, he could see that now. For a woman who
would jump on a plane and travel hundreds of miles to be by his
side, Ryan thought he would give anything.

He walked back across long shadows in the street, to the woman
he had saved and the woman who might yet save him.

CHAPTER 9

IRAN

The icy, intertwined limbs of the oak and conifer trees climbed high above the narrow side street running north from Niyavaran Park. The very highest points of the branches dangled heavily before yellow sodium lights that spilled down onto wet pavement shining in the cold drizzle. The light did not spread too far, as if it knew that the darkest corners of the city were best left to their own devices, alone and unrevealed.

Except for the hypnotic sound of the gentle rain, the streets of Tehran were silent as the night grew deep.

Ali Ahmedi, twenty-eight years old, six-year veteran of the *Komiteh*, the Iranian Secret Police, was hunched in the doorway of a dimly lit restaurant. The hood of his anorak was over his head, his breath steamed in the air. By his side, he held the Kalishnikov that could be bought for less than thirty American dollars in the markets at the city center. His weapon was better maintained than most, the bolt free of rust, with a light coat of oil. As soon as he was permitted, he would find a warm, comfortable place on the floor inside and clean the weapon again. Ahmedi took pride in his work, a deep pride that left little time for his wife and infant child. He was particularly pleased with his current assignment, despite the inclement weather. Across the street, a second guard was well concealed in a dark alley.

The young officer counted himself fortunate; the alley had no over-head cover, and his friend would be well soaked by now.

Behind Ahmedi, past the grimy windows set in stout wooden frames, beyond the tables and chairs of rough-hewn oak, two men enjoyed a simple meal of lamb kebab and boiled rice.

A third guard drifted through the seating area in the foreground, an Uzi submachine gun slung carelessly across his chest. His eyes, though, were constantly moving over the dark shadows of the room, paying particular attention to the swinging door that led to the kitchen in the rear of the building. The two men and the guard; other-wise, the restaurant was empty.

Saif al-Adel pushed his plate away and leaned back in his chair, a contented expression settling over his narrow features. His face was almost feminine in appearance, with full lips, a long, straight nose, and pale, flawless skin pulled taut over high cheekbones. He took his time speaking, as was his custom; in the dangerous business that was his, one did not last by making rash comments or hasty decisions.

Hamza watched the man carefully. He was ever cautious of his fel-low Egyptian's volatile mood swings. They were difficult to catch; the signs could be as subtle as a small inclination of the head, a narrow-ing of the eyes. For Saif al-Adel, the word volatile held a different con-notation than it did for the vast majority of humanity. Hamza had personally witnessed what the other man's silent rage could lead to. Thinking about it now, he was brought back to an incident that had taken place nearly two years earlier. . . .

The sands of the endless desert south of Kabul burned be-neath the fiery orb above. Late in June of 2002, the morale within the organization was low, tempers flaring easily in the extreme temperatures that accompanied the rising and setting of the sun. The Afghans were afraid, and they tried to hide the fear with aggression and blus-ter. The fear could be attributed to the Americans, and to the MH-60 helicopters that would come low over the desert at night, and to the Special Forces soldiers that would fast-rope down to the desert floor below. Because of the fear, discipline was almost nonexistent in the flat expanse stretching in every direction. Young members of the organization congregated in large groups outside the caves, firing their weapons wildly into the air with complete disregard for the Western satellites that passed overhead. Hassan Hamza, while taking inventory of American Stinger missiles in the cool hollows of the stone outcropping, was drawn to the light outside by elevated voices.

Saif al-Adel, the recently installed commander of the military wing of Al-Qaeda, passed a small cluster of vociferous young volunteers. He heard the name of Muhammed Atef, his predecessor—until the day the Americans had come with their stolen coordinates and laser-guided bombs. He heard the sarcasm in the young voice, the snarled insults, and the derision that can be shown for the dead without fear of reprisal.

This is what Hamza saw: A junior member of the Taliban, maybe twenty years of age, held court at the center of a small group. His rifle was more than an arm's length away, half-buried in the sand, forgotten by the soldier. The men surrounding him roared their approval at the vicious humor, laughed at his biting tongue, but al-Adel was ignored at the periphery of the group. His head was turning, the expression on his face did not change as he slipped the Makarov pistol free from his belt. Then the head of the young soldier was pulled back and to the right, the crowd scrambling away abruptly, startled shouts filling the air. The muzzle was jammed into the soft flesh beneath the jawbone, brown eyes wide in surprise as the trigger was squeezed, and the top of the boy's head exploded up into the shimmering heat.

Saif al-Adel stood facing the stunned group of Taliban soldiers, the pistol loose in his right hand. There were armed men at his back, but he did not turn to track their movements. He was unafraid, and the statement had been made . . . The aggression faded from the eyes of the young men, replaced by a muted fear. Hamza had seen it all.

And could see it still. The hatred was gone at the moment, displaced by the rapture that always followed a successful operation. Hamza could feel it slinking just below the surface, though; for Saif al-Adel, pleasure and murder were born in the same bottomless pit.

"Hassan, my old friend, you are to be congratulated." The words were soft and sincere. Despite himself, Hamza felt a strong swell of pride at the compliment. "The American is amazingly proficient." A brief pause. "He is also obstinate, sullen, and evasive. I do not trust him at all."

The older man could concede that these descriptions were accurate. He had arrived at the same conclusions long ago. He pulled at his ragged black beard while he framed a response.

"He is useful for what he can accomplish, and for what he can tell our soldiers. He is a gifted teacher; I have seen it with my own eyes. A man who is Western in appearance and mannerisms, but can speak numerous foreign languages with local dialects. A man who is able to instruct our fighters on the use of improvised explosive devices, who can demonstrate sniping techniques out to 500 meters without the benefit of a telescopic sight. Most importantly, a man who does not boast, does not condescend when given the opportunity . . . What would you call such a man?"

The commander drank hot tea and averted his eyes. The answer was clear, but he did not want to acknowledge the truth of it, because if it was true . . . If it was true, then he was no longer really in control.

"He is an American," he spat. "He can only be against us."

"That is not so, Saif."

"He cannot be trusted."

"What more can he do?" Hamza asked reasonably. "How many citizens of his own country must he kill before you place your faith in him?"

Silence for a moment, save for the easy footsteps of the guard moving past empty tables.

Hassan did not want to openly challenge the young commander. To do so would be to invite a bullet in the early-morning hours, when he was curled tight against the cold. Loyalty did not carry far when anger was stirred, and one man finally succumbed to heavy eyelids and the pressure of commanding unruly boys who were not yet men. Maybe it would be the knife, held tight against his throat with his arms pinned tight to his body; the end could come in any number of ways. He did not want to take the chance.

"My friend, I understand your skepticism, because I share it." Hamza studiously avoided the word fear. "However, there comes a time when you must accept your good fortune, and use it to your advantage. It is a dangerous weapon we use, but with care it can take us far. He was a soldier, he was disgraced; that much is obvious . . . I know what you want. You want a complete history, you want to know this man inside and out. I tell you now, that is not possible. He is an enigma, by definition. We must accept what Allah chooses to give us, and be grateful."

A small smile, followed by another sip of tea. This was the dangerous time, when the smile could mean anything. Hassan knew why Saif was suspicious. He had questioned the American for three hours, and was told nothing. At one point, the commander held a pistol to the man's head and denounced him, accused him of spying for the West, but still had elicited no reaction. As dawn approached, he had finally given up in frustration. Hamza could see the man's mind working quickly now, cheek muscles twitching as al-Adel pondered his friend's opinion.

The older man thought that his considered statements had been well received.

"Hassan." The arms spread wide, the palms open in a gesture of reluctant capitulation. "You are correct, as always. I was wrong to doubt a man that you saw fit to bring into the organization. I have always respected your judgment." This last sentence was delivered deliberately, Saif's eyes burning into Hamza's face. They were genuine, reassuring words, and his subordinate felt the trust that was given him.

"With your approval, I want to give him full control of the operation in Africa."

"No, no." The commander's long arms waved the idea away quickly. "We have exhausted our ability to operate in that region. Since the bombings in Nairobi and Dar es Salaam, the Americans have considerably enhanced security at their embassies in the region. Most of their buildings are at least 100 meters away from the street, and the exterior windows are now coated in mylar. There are additional personnel and vehicular searches—in short, another attempt would result in far fewer casualties. I won't waste the infidel on a fruitless endeavor."

"I agree completely," Hamza said. It was true; the attacks in 1998 had resulted in the deaths of 213 people in Nairobi. It would be difficult to achieve that success again, and any members of the organization involved in the attack would almost certainly be killed by the marines guarding the perimeter.

"There is much to be gained from this strike, my friend. The support of the Iranians will be invaluable in the future. We will have safe refuge, access to new training camps with decent equipment. We will have money, weapons, volunteers. It is a new beginning for us. There is much to be gained. It cannot fail . . .

"It might interest you to learn, Hassan, that the American was far more forthcoming with information not related to himself."

Hamza's brow furrowed as he considered these words. He had not been present for the entire interrogation. "What do you mean? What kind of information?"

"Evidently, our friend Shakib stumbled onto some very sensitive material just after the senator's death. All of his documents are now in our Westerner's hands."

A small smile played across Hamza's face as he lifted his cup. "And these documents are of interest to us?"

"The American says that it is extraordinary information . . . He believes that we should take advantage of this opportunity, and I am inclined to agree.

"Take, as an example, the idea of a garden. To keep the garden clean, pure, the weeds must be removed. To destroy a weed, you can burn what is visible, pull at the surface growth, do whatever you wish to no avail. It is necessary, always, to kill the root. The root is protected on all sides, but when the soil has been removed, the root is vulnerable. It is possible, my friend, that the soil has now been removed, and the path is clear . . ."

Hamza watched as a maniacal glint sparked in the flat brown eyes of the man seated across from him. He knew that, as committed to the organization as he was, he would never come close to matching the fanaticism of Saif al-Adel. For this, he was grateful.

". . . for the American believes that in just under a month's time, we will have an opportunity to kill the president himself."

CHAPTER 10

BROOKS COUNTY, GEORGIA

In spite of her frequent complaints, University Hospital in George-town insisted on keeping Naomi Kharmai two extra days for observation. That was two days too long in her opinion, but the additional time did give her a chance to run down some information about Peter Hale, the man who had signed Kealey's discharge papers. Through discreet inquiries, she was able to find out that he had retired in 2001 despite having been offered command of the Eighth U.S. Army, which was based out of South Korea. It was a three-star position and would have meant a promotion for Hale, a major general at the time. Naomi wondered how the general's retirement might tie in with Ryan Kealey's sudden departure from the military.

It had not been difficult to convince the deputy director that she needed a few days of convalescent leave. Although she hated to appear weak in front of Harper, she needed the time if she wanted to speak to Hale in person. Finding his home address had been a little trickier, but she was eventually able to track it down through an acquaintance at the IRS.

Naomi suspected, rightly, that Jonathan Harper would not give her any additional information about Kealey or March. She wanted to know more about both men, though, so that she could draw her own conclusions. From an early age, Kharmai had been able to recognize this need within herself, the desire to place people and things into neat compartments with clearly defined labels. Often, she was able to convict others based on their actions alone, and when it was done, it was done; a judgment reached by Naomi Kharmai had all the permanence of the sun's place in the universe.

If General Hale wanted to be left alone, he certainly picked the right place for it, she thought. She had missed the turnoff once, and had to backtrack along the rutted dirt road that was bordered on both sides by ragged trees and bushes. After about ten minutes, she located the dented black mailbox marked only by the house number. Hale's driveway had been recently paved, but was still almost as overgrown as the main road. The branches scraped against the side of her vehicle as she drove deeper into the dense vegetation.

Suddenly the trees were gone and Naomi's rented Explorer broke into a vast field of wild grass. At the very center stood a large antebellum mansion. The front was dominated by a white portico that reflected the red light of the fading sun. The portico was held above the ground by four towering Doric columns, which led in turn to a gabled roof sweeping down to end chimneys that occupied both sides of the house. High windows were shadowed by a trellis overrun with fading vines of blue wisteria, Confederate jasmine, and Lady Bankshire roses. Despite the onset of winter, the pleasant smell of the flowering plants was heavy in the air as Naomi parked the Explorer and walked up to the front door.

Her first knocks went unanswered, and trying the door, she found it locked. Moving around to the rear of the house, she noticed a mud-caked red Chevy pickup parked on a bare patch of ground. Walking over to the vehicle, she placed the palm of her good arm on the hood and felt that it was warm, the engine ticking as it cooled.

"What are you doing?"

She whirled at the voice. Standing before her was a large man wearing a faded-red flannel shirt, brown corduroy pants, and muddy hiking boots. His hair was white and his shoulders stooped with age, but his vivid blue eyes seemed to compensate for the physical toll the years had obviously taken on his body.

"I said, what are you doing?" he asked again.

She smiled and stuck out her hand. "Hi, my name is Naomi

Kharmai. I'm looking for General Hale." The man looked her up and down quickly, and then swallowed her small hand in his. She could feel rough calluses running over her own smooth knuckles.

"Well, you found him. What can I do for you?" he asked.

Naomi held out her credentials, which Hale quickly examined.

"I'm with the Agency, and I wanted to ask you a couple of questions about some soldiers that were under your command at Fort Bragg," she said.

Immediately, his face clouded with suspicion.

"I understand completely if you want to call for verification. The number for the switchboard is—"

"I'll get the number. Follow me."

He walked around to the rear of the house, a shaded, white wooden porch coming into view. Naomi trailed awkwardly behind, the spiked heels of her knee-high leather boots sinking into the muddy ground.

Hale noticed and laughed heartily. "You picked the wrong shoes for Georgia, Ms. Kharmai." He reached the screen door of the porch and, to her amusement, held it open for her.

"Why don't you have a seat here? I'll be back in a few. Can I get you anything?"

"No, I'm fine, thank you," she said. Holding her identification by his side, he walked into the main house, disappearing from sight. She turned her attention to the view before her. The sky was something to see after the heavy clouds moving over Washington; ripples of purple, red, and gold were smeared across the orange sky, the sun dipping low on the horizon. The fields behind the house were empty, but far in the distance she could make out several low-slung clapboard buildings framed against a line of gnarled, ancient trees.

She was startled by the sound of the screen door squealing open on rusty hinges. Hale reappeared with a bottle of beer in one hand. He handed Naomi her credentials and eased his weight into a chair of wrought iron across from her.

"Well, you checked out, young lady. I'm a little confused, though. Seems like you could get any information you needed from John."

"You know Deputy Director Harper?"

"Oh, sure," Hale responded, an easy grin spreading over his worn features. "He sent us a lot of good people for some operations we ran in Kosovo and, before that, Iraq. Hell of a guy to have in your corner."

She nodded respectfully and pointed to the buildings in the distance. "Are those part of your property?"

The general nodded in affirmation. "They used to be the slave quarters. What you're looking at is just a little piece of the land attached to this house. There's over a hundred acres beyond those trees there, mostly empty fields. They used to hold corn, cotton, tobacco, anything that would turn a profit. The plantation was built in 1857 by a Confederate colonel who died at Shiloh. It was actually in my wife's family for over a century, until she passed away three years ago."

"I'm sorry to hear that," Naomi said, with as much sympathy as she could muster. Hale nodded his head sadly.

"I sure do miss her. This is a lot of space for one person."

Naomi waited the decent interval, but the general beat her to the punch. "So, what kind of information are you looking for? Is this about Kealey?"

Once again she was surprised. "How did you know?"

"It was just a guess. You've seen the file, I imagine. Everything you need should be in it."

"Not quite everything," she said. "Why did he leave? I mean, he made major in eight years. Isn't that good, even for a Green Beret?"

Peter Hale laughed and took a long pull from his beer. "First of all, they don't like to be called Green Berets. That's what they wear, not who they are. And to answer your question, yes, that *is* damn good. Ryan Kealey was going places." The amiable expression faded from the general's face as he looked out across the fields. His voice lowered, as if to reveal a confidence. "It's a damn shame what happened to him. Was there anything in the file about Bosnia?"

"No. Please tell me," she said. The tinge of desperation in her own voice was disappointing to Naomi Kharmai, but she knew that Hale was probably her only chance for answers.

"To understand," he said, "you have to have some idea about what was going on at the time. The Serbs were killing the Muslims indiscriminately, without regard to age or gender. It wasn't just murder, it was torture, mutilation, and gang rape. It was genocide on a grand scale. In 1995 alone, it's estimated that 7,000 Muslims were slaughtered, and that's a low-ball figure. The full measure of what happened there never really made its way into the international press, but Europe hasn't seen anything worse since the Holocaust. So you can imagine, it was a very dangerous time for the American soldiers who were stationed there as part of the NATO peacekeeping force."

Naomi nodded slowly, her gaze focused on the dark buildings in the distance. "Please, go on."

"Kealey was there in an advisory capacity only, working under the ground commander, General Wilkes. He was a first lieutenant at the time, if I'm not mistaken, based at Camp Butmir in Sarajevo with the NATO contingent.

"Occasionally, Kealey would go out with the SFOR patrols. There was a young Muslim girl who took a particular shine to him; she might have been twelve or thirteen years old. I can't remember her name; someone told me once, but I've forgotten it now. Of course, I wasn't in Bosnia at the time. This information comes from the soldiers who were on patrol with him. Anyway, there was this girl, a pretty little thing from all accounts. She would bring him chocolate, flowers, that sort of thing. I guess it was a schoolgirl crush. Ryan would always stop to talk with her for a little while. The other soldiers used to kid him about it, said he was leading her on. One day, the girl's mother came out of the house crying, screaming at the soldiers. Turns out the Serbian militia found out that the girl was talking to the Americans. You can guess what happened from there."

"They killed her?"

"If that was all, then it wouldn't have been so bad. They raped her repeatedly, beat her face in so that she couldn't be recognized, and then disemboweled her while she was still alive. Her mother identified her by a birthmark on her leg, and even then she had to look at the body twice to be sure."

Naomi shivered once, but it was just the cool breeze coming through the screened walls of the porch. The story did not bother her.

"So Kealey started to ask around. The leader of the local militia was a man by the name of Stojanovic. In truth, he didn't count for much at the time, didn't hold a lot of power. Kealey didn't care; all the fingers were pointing in the same direction. In the end, Ryan went to see the man by himself, against the explicit orders of the unit's commanding general.

"They found Stojanovic two days later. He was sitting in a chair, his throat cut from ear to ear. There were three dead bodyguards in the house, each shot twice in the head."

The tingle started to ease its way up the taut muscles of her back, but it wasn't the story. The story did not bother her, could not break through her defenses. "And this was in 1995? I thought he didn't leave the army until 2001."

"He didn't. There wasn't enough evidence to court-martial him, and there wasn't a lot of support for it, either, let me tell you. There *was* a preliminary hearing, but it didn't go far. All the soldiers that were interviewed covered for him. Up until that point, Kealey was a hell of a soldier; his evaluations were nothing less than stellar. There was already talk about giving him a company command, but that incident fucked it all up." Hale laughed, shaking his head. "Excuse my language. You spend enough time around the troops, that's what happens."

Naomi gave an understanding smile and pointed at his beer. "I think I will have one of those, if you don't mind."

The old soldier hopped to his feet. "Sure, I could go for another myself." When he went into the house, she was left alone with her thoughts. *My God, what kind of man is he?* He had risked his life, thrown away a promising career, all over a little girl who he didn't even know . . . *Who would go to those lengths?* Although she couldn't appreciate the sentiment in his actions, she recognized that Kealey had risen once more in her regard.

Hale was back out the door, handing her a beer. Reclining in his chair, he took another long pull and looked out across the grassy field. Only the very tip of the red sun was visible; it almost looked as though the horizon was on fire. Turning to look at him, Naomi noticed a thoughtful expression on the man's face.

"You know, Bosnia was Ryan's last assignment before he came under my command at Bragg. Obviously, the rumors about him had already drifted my way before he first came into my office to report for duty. In the military, everybody has a story and everybody likes to embellish the facts. It's easy to conjure up some history because no one knows if it's a lie or not, and there's no way to find out. But I wanted to know, so I asked him straight up—'Did you kill those four people in Bosnia?' "

Naomi waited expectantly. "And?"

The general turned toward her. His face was hard to read. "Ryan didn't say anything. He just stood up, saluted, and walked out. That was when I knew it was true."

Naomi shivered again, but the air was still . . . She was glad that she had taken the time to see Hale. The deputy director would never have given her access to this kind of information. For some reason, she really wanted to know the name of the little girl. It seemed important.

"General, there was something else, wasn't there? Something that happened between March and Kealey—"

The general's head whipped around. *"Where did you hear that name?"*

"It came up between the deputy director and Kealey," she said quietly. "In connection with the death of Senator Levy and the bombing of the Kennedy-Warren."

Hale's eyes were closed, his face pale. Naomi noticed that his hands were gripped tightly around the edge of his seat. For a panicked instant, she thought he might be having a heart attack. Then his breathing eased and his iron grip on the chair loosened.

"I'm sorry," he said. "It's just been a long time since anyone's brought it up . . ."

"Who is he, General?" she asked softly.

"Please, call me Peter." His hand moved to wipe the shocked expression from his face. It seemed like an eternity before he spoke again. "Ryan Kealey became part of my 3rd Special Forces Group just after he left Bosnia, in November of 1995. It was nearly two years before he was sent into the field again. During that time, he was the CO of ODA 304."

"ODA? What does that mean?" Naomi asked.

"Operational Detachment Alpha. It's Special Forces nomenclature—almost everything in the army has some type of acronym.

Anyway, he was honing his skills as a leader, getting the troops ready. Everything was great for a while, I had no trouble with anyone in his company. They were the best I had, even though Kealey bitched all the time because I wouldn't deploy his unit. I wanted him to get his head right, though; that's why I kept him at Bragg. After a while, he came to me with a complaint about one of his sergeants."

"The sergeant was March?"

Hale nodded. "He was the platoon sergeant. At first, I was a little skeptical, because he couldn't point out what the specific problem was. I mean, Jason March was a hell of an NCO. He didn't have a college degree, otherwise I would have pushed him kicking and screaming into Officer Candidate School. He was a little arrogant, but all leaders have self-confidence . . . Anyway, I just didn't buy into what Kealey was saying. Even he was embarrassed to bring it up, because it didn't sound like much."

"What did he say?" Naomi's voice was a gentle probe, almost seductive in cadence and tone.

The general hesitated for a moment. "He said that March never showed any emotion." He registered Naomi's reaction and recognized it as his own eight years earlier. "I know, I know. It doesn't sound like a serious problem. That's what I thought at the time. But if you think about it, you might understand what that means. For a young soldier in peacetime, the military is not a difficult life. You do what you're told, show a little respect to your superiors, and take some interest in your job. Anyone can do it. As you gain rank, though, the responsibility grows exponentially, while the pay does not. Now you find yourself held accountable for the lives and well-being of the soldiers under your command . . . With the responsibility comes stress, and with the stress comes the occasional outburst. Anything else is unnatural."

"Obviously, I've never been in the military, but that doesn't sound like enough," she said.

"No, you're right. It's not enough. Ryan also told me about the strange expressions that would come over March's face, and about the fact that he lived off base but no one had ever seen his quarters. To be honest, my opinion of Kealey dropped after this little speech. I mean, it sounded paranoid and more than a little unsubstantiated."

Naomi could see the pain flicker in the man's eyes.

"He was right, though. I should have listened to him. I finally deployed Kealey's unit in the fall of 1997. It was in response to the bombing of the Khobar Towers in Dhahran in 1996. If you remember, nineteen U.S. airmen were killed in the attack and Hezbollah claimed responsibility. It took a while, months of gathering intelligence, but we were finally able to pinpoint the architect of the attack: Mohammed Khalil. He had been granted political asylum by Syria, and was shacked up in a house on the Mediterranean coast.

"I needed the best because we only had one shot at it, so I gave Ryan's unit the go-ahead. It's called direct action, a mission that results in the capture or death of enemy combatants. It's usually the last thing SF is called in to do, but it's important. March was in an overwatch position. He was the only one on the squad to have completed the sniper school at Benning, so he was up on the ridge with the next-best marksman in the unit. It was going to send a message, it would have counted for something . . . March was supposed to take out the car with Khalil inside, and then notify the team on the ground. Instead, he shot the second sniper and fired on the unit as they came down the hill."

Naomi couldn't believe what she was hearing. "They were all killed?"

"All except the captain. The extraction team, which was the other half of the twelve-man detachment, arrived twenty minutes after they lost radio contact. They didn't know what had gone wrong until later, but they pulled Kealey out with a bad chest wound and a punctured lung. It's a miracle he survived as long as he did. They found a lot of blood at March's position, decided that he would probably bleed out, and that was it."

"So you just assumed he was dead?"

"There was pressure on us to do it that way. With no witnesses, nobody to dispute our version of events, we avoided a potentially huge problem. Until now, that is."

"Until now."

Naomi could hardly see Peter Hale, the dark having eased through the tiny holes in the screened walls, discreetly covering the porch with a black shroud. His disembodied voice reached out to her through the cool night air, along with the gentle chirps of crickets hidden among the long blades of grass.

"If Harper is sending you after him, then I hope you're ready. If you miss him once, he won't give you a second chance. You should count yourself lucky to have Ryan on your side, but remember what you're up against . . . Whatever happens, don't let March get his hands on you. Believe me, that's the last thing you want."

She felt a distinct ripple of fear run through her body in response to the general's last words. The fear pushed through her imagined wall of stoicism and touched her deep enough to leave her with a cold feeling that lingered in the pit of her stomach. For Naomi Kharmai, the fear was a new and unwelcome sensation.

Thanking him quietly for the beer and the information, she rose and pushed past the screen door. It squeaked angrily on its rusty hinges as she disappeared out into the empty space beyond the elevated porch.

CHAPTER 11

WASHINGTON, D.C.

Jonathan Harper's elegant brownstone was located in DuPont Circle on historic General's Row. The line of town houses had been constructed in the late-1800s and given to former Union army generals in lieu of a pension, the federal government finding itself somewhat short on funds at the time. The buildings had admirably withstood the ravages of time, towering over the narrow street below, just as they had more than a hundred years earlier.

Surprisingly, it was not difficult for Ryan to find a place to park his car on the street. As he walked with Katie up the front steps, he found himself wondering if Harper took advantage of his influence to ensure that the Metro PD kept the curb in front of his home clear of vehicles. Ryan knew that he would do the same if he were in the DDO's position. They were greeted warmly at the door by Julie Harper, a short, slightly overweight woman whom Ryan had known and liked for as long as he had her husband. He introduced the two women and moved gratefully into the warm interior of the house. Jonathan was waiting for them in the dining room.

"Ryan, that face looks terrible." Turning to Katie, he said, "It must be embarrassing for you to be seen with him."

Katie smiled and hooked her arm into Ryan's, pulling against him playfully. "Absolutely," she said. "I've started walking a few steps behind so people won't know we're together."

Harper laughed as Kealey sent a rueful grin in his direction. "John, this is Katie Donovan. Katie, John Harper. He's the deputy director over at Langley—my boss, in other words."

Jonathan shook hands with her warmly. "Thank you for coming. Ryan talks about you all the time. It's starting to affect his work, not that he ever did too much in the first place."

Katie laughed as Julie emerged from the kitchen with the first of several steaming dishes in her arms.

The food was delicious, a light meal of grilled lemon chicken with baked potatoes, a fresh salad, and French bread, all served with cold white wine. The talk across the table became easier and more animated as the night wore on and another bottle of wine was consumed. Long after the meal concluded, the two women wandered off to the living room with Julie clutching a third bottle, giggling softly at a shared joke.

Jonathan laughed as they walked away, shaking his head. "They certainly seem to be getting along." Kealey smiled in agreement. His host lifted his glass and stood up. "I need to go over a few things with you," he said. "Let's talk upstairs."

Ryan followed Harper up to the second-floor study. The walls were paneled in dark mahogany, a large part of the space consumed by an immense desk of burnished wood centered on a fading Persian rug. Taking a seat in one of two comfortable leather armchairs, Jonathan noticed the look on his friend's face and smiled knowingly.

"I know, it's a lot different from the rest of the house," he said. "I needed at least one room without floral décor and rose-patterned wallpaper. You might have the same problem if you're not careful."

Ryan laughed. "You might be right about that."

"She seems like a great girl. I'm glad you brought her."

"It was the least I could do. She flew in from Maine just to see me after the bombing. It's been four days, though; I think she's starting to get tired of being cooped up in the hotel all day."

"It's the safest place for her, Ryan. They bumped up the threat level again, you know; we're at red now, a 'severe' risk of terrorist activity, whatever the hell that means. You should probably just send her home."

Kealey shrugged. "I like having her around, and I'm worried about her being at the house all alone. Besides, she already called the university and dropped her classes for the semester. I tried to talk her out of it, but she said she needed a break anyway. I can hardly send her back to Maine now."

"Yeah, well . . ." All of a sudden, Harper looked uncomfortable. Ryan wondered why, but the other man had already changed the subject. "Listen, I want your opinion on something. What do you think about adding March to the Bureau's list of Most Wanted Terrorists? The idea keeps popping up."

The younger man shook his head immediately. "You said it yourself, John. That would cause a huge uproar in the media and it probably won't get you any closer to catching him. There's no way you can do that quietly."

Harper took a sip of wine and nodded thoughtfully. "The president agrees with you." Ryan looked up sharply and Jonathan continued: "The director was asked—and by that I mean ordered—to appear before the National Security Council two days ago. You can probably guess that it wasn't for a pat on the back."

"I'll bet."

Harper shrugged. "To be fair, he wasn't singled out; the top people over at Customs, Homeland Security, and the Bureau got the same kind of chilly reception. Nevertheless, our mandate puts us in the spotlight on this one."

Ryan thought about that for a second. "I don't see how," he finally said. "The fact that March managed to sneak himself and 50 pounds of SEMTEX H into the country can hardly be blamed on the Agency."

"You're missing the point, Ryan. Discovering the link between March, Al-Qaeda, and Iran *did* fall on us, and the consensus on the Hill is that we should have done it a lot sooner. Either way, the NSC advises that we are now the lead agency responsible for tracking down Jason March. Moreover, they want it done quietly."

"Oh, well, that's all right, then," Kealey said drily. "I thought they might be asking something difficult."

Harper ignored the sarcasm. "I've been batting some ideas around with Director Andrews. The only thing we can agree on is that March is the closest thing to a weak link the organization has. After all, he's the only one going back and forth, leaving a trail with every step he takes—"

"Which we haven't been able to pick up on," Ryan reminded him.

Harper tilted his head slightly, seemingly conceding the point. "That's not entirely true. As far as Senator Levy goes, we still have nothing. You're right about that. The vehicle was rented under a fake name, of course, and the FBI hasn't been able to dredge anything up on the launcher that March dropped in the Haupt Garden. The rain washed away any prints there might have been on the weapon, which is why we didn't get a positive ID right off the bat. We might have something in the bombing, though. I got a call this morning from Virginia. A DEA agent based at the Norfolk office was trying to crack a drugs-for-guns ring being run out of a waterfront bar, of all places. Anyway, his informer sees Michael Shakib's face spread all over CNN and tells the agent that he'd seen Shakib meeting with someone in the bar two weeks earlier. He said he only remembered because they got into an argument, and the owner told them to take it outside."

"Who was Shakib talking to?"

"Guy by the name of Elgin, Thomas Elgin. He's a piece of shit— his sheet makes for extensive, if unimpressive, reading. Even worse, he's a registered sex offender. Raped a thirteen-year-old girl back in 1990, did ten years in Marion for it. You have to wonder why March would deal with a man like that, directly or indirectly."

"If you're looking for someone to move explosives into the country, you can't be too picky," Ryan said.

Harper had noticed the expression that came over Kealey's face when he mentioned the rape part. He was well aware of how Ryan dealt with such people. "March must have been pretty confident. I wonder why he didn't just try to get the explosives here."

"There's a lot of risk associated with the entire process if you go that route," Kealey said. "First, you have to find what you're looking for in the quantities you need. If you want C4, the best bet is going to be a military facility or a construction site. Either way, security is going to be tight, and the theft is going to be reported immediately. If you try to buy it through a third party, you could be walking into an ATF sting. On the other hand, port security is almost nonexistent in places like West Africa. Then you only have to worry about U.S. Customs and the Coast Guard on our side of the pond. The risk is confined to one part of the operation. No, I think he definitely had to bring it in."

"Well, this guy Elgin might be able to tell you more. He's a loadmaster at the Norfolk International Terminals, working directly with the cargo coming off container vessels. It's the only lead we've got."

"It sounds weak. What do you mean, 'tell me more'?"

"It means I want you to go to Virginia," Harper said. Ryan started to speak, but the other man lifted a hand to stop him. "I know, I know. Let me explain something to you. The president is out of options. The U.N. won't support an air strike, but the public is demanding a response. He's in a tight spot, so he was pretty receptive to new ideas when the director showed him your file. Ryan, the president is scared of Jason March. He's scared of the man's capabilities, his connections, and his willingness to kill Americans. Brenneman wants somebody who can work fast and get results. The logic is flawed; he thinks that if March can be found, then Al-Qaeda's ability to operate will be seriously hindered. He also thinks that March might lead you right down the snake hole. It's unrealistic, I know, but Director Andrews is willing to humor him. They want you to go after him." Kealey didn't say anything for a moment. His face was empty as Harper waited for a reaction. "Ryan—"

"I remember when you asked me to look at some videotapes, John."

Now it was Harper's turn to fall silent as he stared into his empty wineglass. He could hear sounds of laughter from the two women downstairs, but it seemed much farther away than the actual distance allowed. "Listen—"

"No, you listen. You know I'll do it—that's why I'm here. We've known each other for a long time, ever since I was in the service and running jobs for your department. That's too long to bullshit each other. You should have told me the way it was from the very start. Barring that . . . I mean, come on, John. At the very least, you should have known that I would figure it out on my own. What I don't appreciate is you trying to mislead me. I don't ask for much, but I think I deserve better than that."

"You're right." A brief pause. "I mean that. I have to deal with a lot of people, Ryan. Most don't have the drive. Everything has to be spoon-fed to them . . . Sometimes I get caught up in that. I'm sorry."

Kealey waved away the apology; he didn't want to make a big speech, but the point had to be made. "Don't worry about it. I just want you to be straight with me. That's all I ask."

That last statement caused a little smile to work its way across Harper's face. "You're looking for straight talk . . . I want you to work with Naomi Kharmai on this."

The deputy director was surprised when Kealey did not immediately refuse. "In what capacity?"

"I don't want her waving a gun around, if that's what you're worried about. She's capable, Ryan. Her Arabic is better than yours, and I know you don't have any Farsi. Besides, she's . . ."—Harper was searching for the right word, but couldn't find it—"a more acceptable representative of the Agency. She might be able to open some doors that are closed to you."

"That's an interesting way to phrase it." Ryan was laughing, and Harper couldn't help but join in. "I could be acceptable. Give me a suit and a badge, see what happens."

"That would be a first," Harper said. The smile was broad across his face, but it faded with his next words. "There's one other thing, Ryan . . . Technically, you *are* retired from the Agency. As far as this situation is concerned, you're working as an independent contractor. That's straight from the director."

"He's covering his bets, huh?" The younger man frowned. "Is this because of . . . ?"

"No," Harper said. Then he hesitated. "Maybe. Bosnia might have had something to do with it. You know about the bad press we got in connection with the torture of prisoners in Iraq. Andrews is desperate to avoid more of the same." The other man started to speak, but Jonathan held up a hand. "It's not about him, anyway. *I'm* asking you to do this, and I know that I don't have to convince you, so let's not pretend otherwise."

Kealey didn't say anything. After what seemed like a very long time, he nodded, almost imperceptibly.

Harper let out a long breath and said, "Great. And thanks, Ryan. I hate to put you in this kind of position, but I really appreciate it. And believe it or not, the director appreciates it, too."

"I appreciated dinner. Julie's a great cook." Both men stood and moved toward the door. "One more thing." Harper turned to look at his guest.

"After this, I'm out. All the way. It's getting serious with Katie, but she wouldn't be able to handle it if I stayed at the Agency. She deserves more, and she's going to be angry enough when she finds out that I'm going to Virginia. Besides, I don't want to push my luck."

A look of understanding came over the older man's face. He had once served in the field as well, and knew what his friend was talking about. "You've done enough, Ryan. More than enough. I never thought I'd see you settle down, though."

"That makes two of us," was the amused reply as the two men went back down the stairs. Ryan collected Katie from the living room and walked with her to the door.

"Thanks again for dinner. It was so nice to meet both of you," she said.

Her golden-brown hair seemed to glow in the warm light of the foyer. Ryan couldn't take his eyes away from her.

Julie gave her a warm hug. "You too, Katie. Bring her back soon, Ryan, okay?"

He smiled and gave Julie a quick kiss on the cheek. "Absolutely." Turning to Jonathan: "Naomi's back tomorrow, right?"

"Hopefully."

"I'll talk to you in the morning. We'll probably leave for Norfolk in the afternoon."

"Sounds good. It was nice to meet you, Katie." He leaned forward to peck her cheek.

"Careful, John," Kealey said, a grin spreading across his face.

There was general laughter as they went back down the stone steps in the frigid night air, but the car was cold in more ways than one as Ryan turned the key and the engine purred to life.

They were halfway back to the hotel before he ventured an attempt at conversation. "So, it seems like you got along well with Julie."

"She's great." He could tell that she meant it, but the words were sharp.

"What's wrong?"

"Ryan, if you need me to tell you . . ."

"Katie, I really don't need this—"

"You know what I don't need? I don't need to be scared to death every time you walk out the door. I don't need *that*, okay? You almost died four days ago. I thought you *were* dead. To be in that position, not knowing . . . Do you have any idea what that feels like? Of course you don't. Now you're taking off again, right after I dropped my classes so we could—" She stopped herself, but not before Ryan figured out what she had been about to say. *So we could spend more time together.*

He sighed in exasperation. He didn't mean to, and it was barely audible, but she caught the implication immediately. "And who's Naomi?"

"Katie—"

"Is she pretty? I'm sure she is . . . You don't need to answer that."

Ryan looked over at her. From high above, streetlights positioned along the road occasionally cut deep into the shadowed interior of the car. Passing under one now, light flickered through the windows and clearly illuminated the expressions within. He briefly saw tears welling in her eyes, but the anger and suspicion he expected were not spread across her delicate features. Instead, her face was clouded with fear.

The next exit was for Rock Creek Park, and he abruptly swung the car into the lane on the far right. The road hummed quietly beneath the tires as Ryan eased off the accelerator. It was not the way to the hotel.

"Where are we going?" she asked.

"You'll see." They drove on for a few minutes more until he parked the BMW on a road adjacent to the park. Getting out of the car, he helped her into her black woolen peacoat. He noticed that she walked by his side, but stayed several steps away as they moved deeper into the park. The distance was a gulf between them. The trees lining the footpath towered far above like sentinels keeping a silent watch on the troubled couple below.

Katie slipped twice, Ryan catching her on both occasions before she fell. After the second fall, he couldn't help himself: "You're a little drunk."

Despite herself, she smiled reluctantly. "I think you're right." They were approaching a bridge running over the partially frozen water. There were fewer lamps here, but the moonlight cast a serene glow over the park and glittered on the ice covering the low stone walls. The stars were bright in the clear sky. They were halfway over the bridge when Ryan stopped walking. He noticed that Katie was shivering and pulled her close, rubbing her slender arms beneath the heavy coat.

"You're freezing . . . I'm sorry to bring you out here like this, but I wanted to talk. Not in the car, and not in the hotel." She looked up into his eyes, and Ryan went on: "I *do* understand how you feel. I've lost a lot of people I've been close to. I'll tell you about it sometime, but not now. Not tonight.

"You asked about Naomi. I barely know her, Katie, but let me tell you what I do know. She's blunt, sarcastic, and ungrateful. She means nothing to me. Let me repeat that. She means *nothing* to me, and that's not going to change. I saved her life at the Kennedy-Warren and she didn't even thank me. Now I'm stuck with her for at least the next couple weeks when I want nothing more than to be here with you. I want you to be able to trust me, because I trust no one more than you." She opened her mouth to speak, but he held up a hand to stop her.

"Let me finish. I know that you're afraid. Tonight I told John that this is the last thing I'm doing for the Agency, and I meant it. A few more weeks at the most, and I'm done. I need you to be strong in the meantime. It's just a job for me. It's important that you see that. There's a lot I want to do when it's over, and I want—no, I *need* you by my side.

"Katie, I love you more than anything and I have to know: will you marry me?"

Ryan pulled a small burgundy box out of his pocket and opened it. He was scared to death, but Katie's mouth dropped open in amazement, her bright blue eyes sparkling with surprise and happiness. She flung her arms around him, causing the box to tumble out of his hand. He laughed and they kissed deeply. He had been terrified to ask, almost certain that she would refuse him. Now, breathing in the fresh, clean scent of her, he knew that he would never regret his decision. He was only angry that he had to leave the next day.

"I take it that's a yes?"

Katie kissed him again in place of an answer. They held each other for what seemed like an eternity until Ryan finally broke away.

"Now," he said with another relieved laugh, "let's find that ring."

CHAPTER 12

LANGLEY • NORFOLK, VIRGINIA

It seemed like much earlier than seven when he woke the following morning, his eyelids tight against the light slanting through half-closed curtains. Despite the early hour, Katie was already up and moving about, a dizzy smile spread across her face. Both were pleasantly exhausted after having made furious love deep into the night and early-morning hours.

Ryan went about his normal routine in preparation for the day ahead. Every few minutes he would catch Katie staring at the diamond on her left hand and she would look up with a sheepish expression on her face. He knew how she was feeling, though, as it was his first time being engaged as well. It was an unusual confluence of emotions: pride, that he was good enough for a woman like this; anxiety, because he could still screw it all up; anticipation, thinking about the family that they would make together. Most of all, he just felt fortunate, recognizing how lucky he was to have her in his life.

By eight they were both ready to leave. He checked out of the hotel while Katie had the valet bring the car around. She drove south toward Langley because Ryan wanted her to take the BMW back to Maine, but she wasn't experienced driving a stick shift and needed the practice. They both burst into laughter when the car stalled at numerous stoplights and the vehicles behind erupted into a cacophony of horns and loud curses. For some reason, none of that seemed to matter.

It was almost an hour later when they arrived at headquarters deep in the wooded hills of Virginia. Harper had clearly made arrangements, as the security guards manning the gate waved them through following only a cursory inspection. The heavy sedan slowed to a halt outside the entrance.

"I hate this."

"I know." He gently touched her cheek. "I'll miss you."

"Me, too," she said. Her long fingers came up to wrap around his. Ryan leaned in for a quick kiss, but it went on for several minutes until he reluctantly pulled away.

"John's probably pissed already, I'm really late. I'll see you in a week or two—I'll let you know. I'll call you, okay?"

"You'd better," was her quiet response. "I love you."

"I love you, too." He looked into her eyes for as long as he could until he bumped into someone and was forced to turn around as he went up the steps toward the main entrance. At the doors, he turned once again and laughed when the BMW pulled jerkily away from the curb. Clearly, she was having trouble adjusting to a third pedal.

Ryan had always been intimidated by the immense hall that marked the entrance to CIA headquarters in Langley. The space was dominated by the Memorial Wall dedicated to those field officers who had died in the line of duty. Due to the clandestine nature of the Agency, the names were not listed; instead, a star was attributed to each fallen agent.

Ryan occasionally wondered if a star was waiting for him. It was not for want of recognition, because he knew about the wall. He also knew about his profession, and was realistic when handing out odds, even for himself.

In the hunt for Jason March, he didn't care to hand out odds of any kind.

Leaving the elevator, he walked toward Harper's office and was admitted on arrival. He was surprised to see that Naomi was already there, waiting with the deputy director. She was immaculately turned out in a white suit jacket with a matching skirt that ended at midthigh. He was struck by her appearance until he thought of Katie and felt a small twinge of guilt.

"Good morning, Ryan," Harper said. When he looked up, a strange little grin appeared on his face. "You're right on time, believe it or not; I was just about to tell Naomi what's happening. I've got you two booked on a 1:30 flight to Norfolk. The tickets are waiting at the airport, and I've made some arrangements for transportation when you get there."

"Sounds good. Who are we meeting?"

"Adam North is your liaison on the ground. He's DEA—the same guy who hooked onto this piece of information in the first place. They want to be kept up-to-date on this, probably so they can claim partial credit when you run March down."

"If, John. If I run him down."

The DDO gave a little smile. "I have a lot of faith in you, Ryan. In both of you," he said, turning to look at Naomi. "Anyway, you'd better get moving, especially if you plan to check your weapon. That plane is leaving with or without you. Good luck, and keep me updated."

Harper shook hands with them both. On their way out the door, Jonathan pulled Kealey back gently, whispering quiet words into his ear. "I want you to watch yourself with Elgin. I saw that thing in your face yesterday when I mentioned the rape part—The president is willing to break some rules, but there's a limit to what he can overlook. You're no good to me on suspension or in jail, Ryan. Just be careful, okay?"

Ryan nodded and they were out the door. He didn't see the look that Naomi gave him. It was partially bemusement, but also understanding. She couldn't help but revel in the knowledge that she wasn't supposed to have. Lost in self-congratulation, she didn't quite catch his question.

"Sorry, what was that?" she asked.

"Your arm. How is it?"

"Oh, it's fine, thanks. By the way, that's a nice shade you're wearing," she said with a smile.

It took him a second to catch on, but when he wiped the back of his hand over his mouth, it came away smeared with Katie's pink lip gloss. *So that's what Harper was grinning about,* he thought with a rueful shake of his head.

They didn't speak again until they got to the airport, but Ryan noticed that the little smirk never quite left Naomi's face.

Less than three hours later they were on the ground at Norfolk International. Ryan had checked weapons on domestic and international flights many times before and knew how to fill out the paperwork, so there was not a substantial delay in retrieving his gun case. Soon they were moving through the automatic doors of the passenger terminal, stepping out into the cool autumn air. He pulled a cell phone from his pocket and dialed a number. "Yeah, this is Kealey. We're at the entrance for United. Okay, we'll be waiting."

"When was the last time you fired one of these?" he asked Naomi after turning off the phone. He tapped the small metal case with his left hand.

"I have no idea. It's been a long time, though."

"I'll ask North to get you something."

She was about to decline the offer, but then she remembered General Hale's parting words: *Whatever happens, don't let March get his hands on you. Believe me, that's the last thing you want.* The memory sent another cold shiver running through her body.

It wasn't long before a large black Suburban with government tags pulled up to the curb and the driver jumped out. "Hey, Adam North, DEA."

"Ryan Kealey, and this is Naomi Kharmai. Good to meet you."

North didn't look like any law-enforcement agent Naomi had ever seen. He was huge; she guessed that he was well over 6' 4" and probably topped the scales at 270 pounds. He wore a black-leather jacket over a plain gray T-shirt and threadbare jeans. Her eyes moved down and noticed that his shoes were dirty Nike cross-trainers, scuffed and worn with age. The DEA agent caught her disapproval and grinned through a thick, unkempt beard.

"Don't look so disappointed," he said. "I've been trying to put these assholes away for three months, and it's a little hard to blend in with a suit and tie."

Ryan laughed as he tossed his little grip and Naomi's huge suitcase into the back of the truck. He sat in the front with North while Kharmai climbed into the rear seat.

"So," North said as he pulled away from the curb and into traffic, "where to begin?"

"First off, I want your opinion. What was it between Shakib and this Elgin guy? Was he moving in the explosives?"

"No, I don't think so," was the unexpected response. "Elgin's responsibilities all lie on this side of the ocean, and I highly doubt he has any real connections to speak of. Part of his job is to check the bill of lading against the actual containers on the ship. I think what happened is that he came across something he wasn't supposed to see, and he tried to make that work to his advantage. I would have to say he was successful, seeing as how he's still alive."

"Did you talk to the port authorities?" Naomi asked.

"I did, but only to get a grip on the loading and unloading procedures. If Elgin was trying to extort money from Shakib, then the people running the terminal aren't going to have any knowledge of that anyway. Besides, I wanted to keep this information close to the vest. If Elgin gets word that people are asking questions, he'll find a way to disappear. He's not very bright, but he's smart enough to know when to cut and run."

"Tell me about Elgin's job," Ryan said. "What are his responsibilities? If he found something, how could that have happened?"

"Okay, when a ship comes into port, it's issued a job number, a booking number, and the port of discharge. Elgin is responsible for assigning the job number, which in turn places the ship in a pre-assembly area. Basically, that determines when the cargo will be unloaded. Then a dock receipt is issued against the cargo, and responsibility of the load is transferred from the ship's captain to the marine terminal.

"While the ship is waiting to be unloaded, the bill of lading is checked against the actual cargo. That's our guy's primary job, to supervise the walkthrough of the cargo hold. Right now, there are still no effective measures in place to check each container. It's a huge problem for U.S. Customs because there is no way to verify the contents. Closed containers, which is basically every container aboard, are listed as S.T.C. That stands for 'Said To Contain.' The entire shipping industry is essentially run on the honor system. I mean, some of these ships can carry 7,000 twenty-foot containers. The amount of manpower that would be needed to check each one is completely unfeasible. It just can't be done."

"Then how would he run across illegal cargo?" Ryan asked.

Naomi spoke up from the rear seat. "If the container was damaged, then they would have the authority to open it and examine the contents, right?"

"Exactly." North looked back at her with a surprised expression. He was genuinely impressed. "It took me forever to figure that out, but you're right; that is the only way it could have happened. Indirectly, it was a huge break for us."

"So from there, it was just a matter of locating the receiving party, which in this case was Michael Shakib. Well, this is just great," Ryan said. A look of disgust came across his face. "This guy doesn't have anything to tell us. All he did was blackmail Shakib."

"That's not entirely accurate," North said. "Elgin can give you the ship's point of origin, as well as the person or company that consigned the container in the first place. I would say he has a lot to tell us."

"Well, let's find out. What do you call this place?"

"It's called The Waterfront. I guess the owner doesn't have a lot of imagination." He turned to Ryan with a look of incredulity on his face. "You're not thinking of going in now, are you?"

"Why not?"

"Well, the SAC at the Norfolk office is expecting you, first of all, and the deputy administrator came down from Washington to help supervise this little powwow. If you don't show up, that's going to be a problem. Second, I think we ought to decide how to deal with Elgin. I mean, he's not going to just hand over this information. He probably made a lot of money dealing with Shakib, so he won't be very forthcoming."

Kealey frowned. "Listen, I've heard about Elgin, and I can't say that I'm very impressed. I'm under orders to move quickly on this, orders that came down from the president. I'm pretty sure that supercedes the authority of the deputy administrator for DEA. The only problem I see is that you can't be involved in this if you're part of an ongoing investigation."

"Actually, that's not going to be an issue." A huge grin spread across North's face. "My boss got a personal call from the national security advisor. All domestic operations take a backseat to your little mission. She even threw out your name. I guess you must carry a fair amount of pull."

Ryan didn't answer. He opened the metal case to reveal the components of his personal firearm, a Beretta 92FS. It was broken down into four pieces: the receiver, slide assembly, bolt group, and recoil spring. His hands moved in a blur as the weapon came together, the magazine checked and inserted, and a round chambered. The safety was on as he placed the pistol at his side and slid the metal case under the seat.

"That looks like military issue," North said. "Got some years on it, too."

"It's served me well," was the response. Ryan wasn't giving anything away.

Adam North smiled at that as he took the next exit leading down to the docks. He glanced back at Naomi. "Are you coming in?"

"Well, I wouldn't be very helpful sitting here, would I?"

"I'm just saying . . ." The DEA agent flushed slightly as he turned to look at her again. "This is not exactly a friendly place, and what you're wearing isn't going to make this any easier."

Naomi followed his gaze to the white skirt riding high on her thighs. She tugged it down self-consciously as Ryan choked back laughter.

"Then we'd better stop so I can change," she said, struggling to keep the anger out of her voice.

North pulled the Suburban into a gas station. Naomi jumped out and opened her suitcase at the rear of the vehicle, pulling out several items before storming off toward the ladies' room.

"Don't worry about it," Ryan said as they both laughed. "She doesn't like me either."

"Pretty cute, though," North said. Kealey was surprised; Kharmai didn't seem like the bigger man's type. "British?"

Ryan shot him a look. "That obvious, huh?"

"Well, you know." North looked embarrassed. "I don't deal with that a lot. Uh, why isn't she working with . . . What do you call them? You know, the guys on her side of the water . . . ?"

"MI-6, you mean? I don't know. It's their loss, I suppose." It was a good question, one that he hadn't thought to ask her, but Ryan wanted to get back on track. "Anyway, tell me about this place. What kind of layout are we looking at here?"

North quickly turned back to business as he hunted for a piece of paper and a pencil. He drew a diagram on the center console as he spoke. "Okay, it's pretty straightforward. There's only one front entrance, but the interior is surprisingly large. As soon as you go in you have a seating area on the right, four pool tables on the left. Past that is the bar, facing the door. I know for a fact that the owner keeps a sawed-off shotgun under the counter, double-barreled." Ryan didn't like that piece of information, and the DEA agent registered his concern. "I know, I know. I'll watch that. There's no need for you to announce yourself. I'll go in loud and let them know who I am. Since they've seen me before, they'll be less likely to come up firing."

"What are you carrying?"

North pulled a long case out from behind his seat and opened it halfway.

"Jesus, what the hell is that thing?"

"It's an M4 Super 90. Benelli only makes them available to law enforcement. Pretty imposing, huh? The telescopic stock helps to compensate for the size, and it fires on semiautomatic. The drawback is that it only holds five rounds, but I'm loading slugs. If I have to pull the trigger, nobody's going to lift a finger afterward. I tried to get my boss to spring for a custom version chambered for seven, but the number crunchers over at Justice didn't like the cost."

"I think what you have will do the job. Naomi needs something. Do you have a backup piece?"

North looked concerned. "Yeah, but that's it. Without it, you can only count on me for five rounds."

"Believe me," Ryan replied, "if you need more than that, we're already in trouble."

Naomi emerged from the restroom, the anger gone from her face. Kealey was relieved; she was going to need her mind clear in a few minutes. She had changed into a tight T-shirt and a pair of low-slung jeans. The new outfit was more practical, but did nothing less to show off her admirable figure. As she got back into the truck, North went on with his explanation.

"So that's the only front entrance. You see what I'm talking about, Kharmai? Okay, good. Now, the bathroom is over here adjacent to the bar, so you can keep an eye on both at the same time. The door to the stockroom is shielded from view, but you should have time to react if anyone comes out. There are no windows in the bathroom, so you don't have to worry about our guy getting out that way.

"Here's what I'm thinking: I'll go in first unarmed to make sure that Elgin is there. If he is, and he should be, then I'll come out to collect my weapon. Naomi, I already explained to Ryan that I'm going in loud. You don't need to say anything. You head to the front and keep an eye on this blind spot." He pointed to the diagram and she nodded her head in understanding. The DEA agent turned to Ryan. "You want to get him out of there quick. Like I said, this is not a friendly place. I've spent a lot of time in there recently, and even I can't always tell who's carrying. You should make it clear that we are only there for Elgin. Otherwise you'll get some asshole with a warrant out in Idaho pulling down on you from behind." He searched their faces. "Are you sure you want to go ahead with this?"

"Definitely. The longer we wait, the greater the chance that he catches on and we lose him. It's now or never," was Kealey's decisive response. Naomi looked a little less eager.

North grinned. "My kind of man. Let's go."

He put the heavy truck into gear and they drove on down to the docks. North dug out his backup piece and handed it to Ryan, who in turn checked the chamber and passed it to Naomi, butt first.

"This is a Glock 29. You have nine rounds plus one in the chamber, okay? It doesn't have an external safety. All you have to do is squeeze the trigger." Turning to North: "That's your backup?" He made a show of looking around the interior of the truck. "This thing is like a mobile armory. Where do you keep the grenade launchers?"

That earned him a brief laugh. It was Ryan's way, and had been ever since he was a young platoon leader, to try to ease the tension before heading into harm's way. A certain amount of stress and fear was useful, because it kept you sharp. Too much, though, could cause even the most experienced people to freeze up at the worst possible time. Looking back, he could see the tension in Naomi's face, and hoped that she would keep it together long enough to do what was needed.

"That's it," North remarked. They were rolling slowly past a low, cinder block building. The exterior hadn't seen new paint in many years, the white coating cracked and missing entirely in some sections. Blocklike letters in black paint spelled out THE WATERFRONT across the uppermost part of the building's face. The windows were streaked with dirt and covered with rusting steel mesh.

There were only three other cars in the litter-strewn parking lot as North pulled in on the second pass.

"Do me a favor, Kealey. Pull out that shotgun while I check it out. I'll be back in a sec." North hopped out and ambled toward the entrance. Ryan reached behind the seat and pulled out the soft case. Keeping it below the passenger window, he opened it and withdrew the Benelli. It was 3 ½ feet in length, the barrel alone accounting for almost 19 inches. Looking back, he noticed that Naomi's eyes were wide at the sight of the weapon.

"Don't worry," he said as he checked the breech to verify that it was fully loaded. He turned awkwardly in his seat to face her, but her eyes were darting away. "Naomi, look at me."

She finally met his gaze. When she reached up to brush her hair back from her face, Kealey saw that her hand was shaking. "You're going to be fine," he said. "I need you to be focused in there. Just watch the bathroom door and my back, don't worry about Elgin. I know what I'm doing, okay? You have to trust me."

"Hey," she said, her eyes suddenly flaring. "I'm not scared, Ryan, and I don't need your help. I can bloody well take care of myself."

Kealey lifted an eyebrow, but didn't say anything in response.

North came out of the bar moving slowly at first, then faster as he approached the vehicle. Ryan pushed the door open.

"We're good to go. He's sitting at the bar, blue jeans and a black long-sleeved shirt. You've seen a picture?" They both nodded in the affirmative. "Okay, let's move."

Kealey handed him the Benelli, and North checked the breech instinctively. That small gesture gave Ryan added confidence in the ability of the young DEA agent as they moved quickly forward, Ryan's Beretta low by his side as he trailed behind the bigger man.

They were inside.

North moved to the left as soon as he cleared the doorway to make room for the two CIA officers following a half step behind. His shotgun was up, traversing the room and he was shouting: "DEA! Get on the ground! I said, GET ON THE GROUND!"

Most of the people in the room froze at the sight of the big agent and the semiautomatic shotgun that he held. Then they were falling to the floor as Ryan came up low between the tables. The bartender's hands dropped under the counter as he watched the approaching agents.

"Don't do it!" Ryan shouted. "This is not about you! Get your hands in the open!"

He could see the hesitation in the old man's grizzled face as he reached the bar. Naomi was facing away from Elgin as she approached, her attention entirely focused on the bathroom . . . And then Elgin was up and moving fast, but Ryan couldn't take his aim away from the bartender. Elgin with a knife out, turning Naomi around and the knife tight against her throat, her body between the two men.

Elgin whispering into her ear, the eyes cold and empty.

Naomi, the Glock loose by her side, her eyes wide and locked onto Ryan's.

No time to decide as the bartender brought the 12 gauge up and Ryan dropped to the ground, the Beretta swinging left across his body as he fired. The bullet plowed a shallow furrow across Naomi's thigh before it ripped into Elgin's left kneecap. Over his head, the shotguns booming in unison, glass shattering into thousands of pieces behind the bar. Elgin screamed in agony as the knife moved away from Naomi's throat and she turned, dragging him down by the hair, the muzzle of the Glock pressed against his head.

Then they were both on the ground, Naomi turning him so he lay facedown as she straddled him from behind and kept the pistol jammed into the base of his neck. The bar erupted as the small group of people rushed for the front door. Ryan stood up to look over the counter and could see the bartender on the ground, a half-inch hole in his chest, the body surrounded by thousands of shards of bloody glass. Turning, he was relieved to see that North wasn't hit, the shotgun dangling in his right hand as he walked up.

"He got a round off?"

"Into the counter, I think. He didn't get it up all the way," North replied. Ryan turned his attention to Naomi. The pistol hadn't moved from Elgin's head. Her eyes were glazed over, her face pale.

"Naomi, it's over," he said in a soft voice as he gently pulled the pistol from her outstretched hand. Her leg was bleeding badly, but she didn't seem to notice the pain.

"Get some pressure on that, North. I think she's in shock. I need to talk to this bastard." Ryan grabbed Elgin's shirt collar and dragged the injured man toward the stockroom, ignoring the screams of pain as he pulled him over the floor littered with broken glass.

The rear of the building was a large, dark room stacked floor to ceiling with crates. Ryan propped Elgin up against the cool stone wall next to the door and searched him quickly but thoroughly. Satisfied that he had no other weapons, Ryan moved back into the bar and picked up the man's knife.

"What the hell are you doing?" North demanded. He had located a first aid kit and was working on Naomi's leg.

North's eyes moved up from the weapon in the other man's hand to Ryan's face. The young DEA agent, several inches taller and 90 pounds heavier, abruptly shut his mouth and looked away. Ryan walked back toward the stockroom, his knuckles white around the rubber grip of the knife.

Thomas Elgin was leaning against the wall just as Ryan had left him, his breath coming in short, fast spurts. He looked up as Kealey entered the room, eyes defiant as he clutched his ruined leg.

"*Fuck* you want, asshole?" he snarled.

Without saying a word, Ryan crouched and pushed the first inch-and-a-half of the knife into Elgin's chest. He was rewarded by a shriek of agony as he twisted the handle to make the wound more difficult to close and to encourage blood flow. Ryan was well aware that he didn't have a lot of time, and guessed that Elgin would be more motivated to talk if the hole in his chest was leaking at a steady rate.

In a low, menacing voice, he said, "I need some fast answers from you."

"*What do you want, you sick fuck!*" Elgin screamed, twisting his body, desperately trying to get away from the knife. Kealey obliged and pulled it out of his chest. The injured man's words didn't seem to have any effect on him, though. This time, the serrated edge scraped across the protruding bone of Elgin's mangled kneecap.

In the other room, Special Agent Adam North of the DEA shuddered as another unearthly scream echoed throughout the building. The howl of pain almost managed to drown out the sound of the approaching sirens as North finished applying the improvised pressure bandage to Kharmai's thigh. She was starting to come around now, a spark visible in her large green eyes as her mouth moved in an attempt to speak.

"Take it easy," he said. "You're okay now. You did a great job." It was a sincere compliment. For an intelligence analyst to be thrown into this kind of situation and react the way she did was an amazing thing. The sirens grew louder and the door burst open, paramedics swarming into the building. They were followed closely by officers from the Norfolk and Portsmouth police departments and a number of Virginia state troopers. As soon as they came through the front door, Ryan emerged from the stockroom, his face an impassive mask.

As the police officers secured the building, several returned from the back room with pale faces and immediately looked in Kealey's direction. Confusion seemed to rule the day, but it wasn't long before a consensus was reached, and a nervous officer put handcuffs on Ryan Kealey at the behest of the person now in charge, Captain Gina Nolan of the Norfolk Police Department.

CHAPTER 13

NORFOLK

★ ★ ★

"What the hell were you thinking, Ryan?"

Kealey and Harper were seated in the sterile interrogation room at Norfolk Police Headquarters. The irony was not lost on Ryan as the DDO questioned him from across the cold metal table. "I had to pull a lot of strings to get you out of this. I thought I told you to use kid gloves. Does that phrase mean anything to you?"

Kealey's gaze drifted across the bare walls as the other man glared in his direction. "I realize it didn't turn out the way we—"

"Ryan," Harper's voice lowered, even though the door was closed and there was no one else in the room. "Elgin had a lot to say about you. If he starts talking to the press, even the director won't be able to contain the shit storm. Rightfully, this operation should have landed on the DEA's doorstep. You went too far with him."

Kealey looked to the upper corner of the room and saw that the camera used to monitor interrogations was disconnected, the wires hanging loose against the wall. He wondered why he had checked. "You said that the president cleared this, John. I did what was necessary."

"Bullshit!" Harper tossed several photographs onto the table. "Pictures don't lie. The Bureau can't pressure Elgin because we have this hanging over our heads. In other words, we can't force his hand because you took away our only leverage."

"John—"

Harper held up his hand to silence the younger man. He stared at Ryan intently for a moment before quickly looking away. "Ryan, you went too far," he repeated. The anger was gone from his voice, replaced by a weary resignation. "The director wants you out, and he's going to get his wish if Elgin doesn't open up. The State Department sent some people over to talk to the little bastard, but so far they're coming up empty. I need you to give me some good news, because I've called in all my debts."

"The boat that the explosives came in on is called *Natalia*; it's a 25,000-ton container ship registered in South Africa. It has a regular route, making stops in Marseille and Rosslare in the south of Ireland before heading over to our East Coast." Ryan looked up to catch Harper's incredulous expression. "Jesus Christ, John, I didn't go in there to make idle threats. This is what we needed, and now we have it. We don't have time to waste with gentle persuasion, you said so yourself."

"Well, why the hell did you keep me hanging on? This might be enough to save you—did he identify March?"

Kealey sighed and shook his head wearily. "I knew he wasn't going to be able to. If Shakib had told March about the situation, then Elgin would be in a dirt-covered hole somewhere and we wouldn't have gotten this far. I told you before, March is not given to making mistakes. He doesn't believe in loose ends."

The irony of this statement was immediately apparent to Jonathan Harper. Clearly, Jason March's biggest mistake to date was not killing Ryan Kealey on that Syrian hilltop seven years earlier. But that thought had come unannounced, and it was incredibly disloyal. He felt ashamed that he had identified with a killer, even if only for a moment. It went against everything that he valued.

Ryan watched a myriad of emotions cross the other man's face and wondered what he was thinking.

With Kealey's contribution, the tension was gone from both men. It was still an interrogation room, though; the cold gray walls felt closer by the second, the scarred metal desk screamed confessions, and the disconnected camera seemed to watch over everything with an unwavering eye. Ryan was tired of it. He thought of Katie and for a moment felt better, lighter.

"I think I've done enough for today, John. Can you get me out of here, or did you just come down for the conversation?"

A sly grin eased itself across the older man's face. "Who do you think you're talking to, Junior?"

They departed the Norfolk Police Department less than a half hour later, both men down low in the backseat of a Chevy Suburban almost identical in appearance to Adam North's. The heavily tinted windows shielded the occupants from the view of the few reporters savvy enough to stake out the department motor pool.

"I should have asked before, but how's Naomi doing?"

"She'll be fine," Harper said. "North ran her over to the De Paul Medical Center. They stitched her up okay and gave her something for the pain. She's checked into the Marriott Waterside. That's where I'm taking you."

"John—" Kealey started to protest, but was cut off just as fast.

"Ryan, you got what we needed. I want you to get some rest, because you'll probably be moving out again tomorrow, depending on what we dig up. Everything else that needs to get done today is on my side of the fence, and if I show up at the DEA division office with you in tow, it's going to cause more problems than it will solve. They aren't too happy with you right now." Kealey nodded his head in reluctant agreement as the vehicle turned onto Waterside Avenue.

"I'll call for you tomorrow morning," Harper said as the vehicle slowed to a halt next to the hotel. Ryan moved to climb out, but the other man stopped him with a hand on his shoulder. "You got what we needed, Ryan, and all three of you walked out. That's the important thing. Go talk to Kharmai; North said she looked pretty down when he left her."

"What happened today wasn't her fault, John. It was mine. I told her she could trust me, and then that bastard got to her with a knife . . . She has a right to be upset."

"Hey, she's only alive because of what you did for her in

Washington, okay? Keep that in mind. She should be grateful to have you around. Go get some sleep."

Ryan gave a mock salute and Harper couldn't help but smile as the Suburban pulled away from the curb. As he went through the process of checking in, Ryan began to realize how tired he actually was. It was hard to believe he had woken up with Katie just twelve hours earlier.

The elevator stopped on the third floor and he got out, looking down at the scrap of paper that Jonathan had pressed into his hand. *Room 305.* There. He looked down at the dirt on his ragged jeans from where he had hit the floor in the bar, and realized that he probably looked like hell. *Oh well,* he thought, *at least I have a decent excuse.*

Naomi Kharmai was curled into a tight ball on the bed, a white cotton bathrobe loose against her bare skin. The room was completely dark, but her eyes were wide open, staring fixedly into the empty space. After North had taken her back to the hotel, she had showered once, then again, and then a third time, the hot water beating down as it burned over the closed wound on her left thigh. Now, with nothing left to distract her, the scene played over and over in her mind. She was moving toward the bar, confidence in her stride, the Glock steady in her hand. She could see her own face from a distance, the fierce determination, the set of her jaw. Then she was facing Ryan, the sharp blade biting into her throat as Elgin whispered filth into her ear: *I'm gonna cut you and fuck you, bitch.*

Cut you and fuck you . . . She sobbed once, a loud, dry sob that vanished into the empty room. There was a knock at the door.

"Naomi, it's Ryan." She didn't answer. "Naomi, just let me talk to you for a minute."

The door handle jiggled, but she didn't get up to let him in. After a minute or so, she heard a strange clicking sound. Ryan pushed his way into the room and turned on the light.

She sprang up, hurriedly wiping hot tears from her eyes. "What the hell do you think you're doing?" she yelled angrily. "If I wanted you to come in I would have opened the fucking door!"

He raised his hands in surrender. She took in his dirty jeans, the black T-shirt tight over his chest and arms, and the most recent addition: a thin, looping scar that ran down the left side of his face. He must have come straight from the police station. She felt something that only heightened her anger and confusion.

"Look," he said, "I just wanted to check on you. I'm glad you're okay."

"No thanks to you," she sneered. "Nice job shooting me, by the way. No harm done . . . Maybe they'll give you another medal." Sarcasm usually came easy for her, but it didn't feel right this time, and she felt a small tinge of regret as soon as the words left her mouth.

He stared at her in disbelief. The catlike green eyes were wide in anger, but he could see the glistening tracks down her cheeks and the red irritation at the corner of her eyes. For all of that, he couldn't help himself. "What do you mean, another medal?" he asked slowly.

From the expression on his face, she knew that she was caught. He moved toward her slowly until he was standing only a few feet away. His face was as blank as it had been when he emerged from the stockroom at the bar.

"Listen to me," he said in a low voice. Naomi took a step back involuntarily. "I'm sorry for what happened to you today, but stay the hell out of my personal life. You have no right to dig into my past. Keep it up, and I'm done looking out for you."

Then he was gone, disappearing into the hallway. She didn't move for a few moments as a number of emotions passed over her face. Finally, she went to shut the door after him.

CHAPTER 14

IRAN • NORFOLK

Southeastern Iran, on the Makran Coast overlooking the Arabian Sea.

Far to the north, the peaks of the Zagros can be seen towering over the arid landscape. Apart from the size, the mountains and the land below are almost indistinguishable.

He stood on the black tarmacadam that was sticky beneath his feet. Now easing into November and almost 95 degrees Fahrenheit, the air thick in his nose and mouth. His frustration was exacerbated by the people standing in the near distance, the air force colonel sent by Mazaheri, and the aides who smirked and stood with jutted chins and arrogant eyes as they basked on the fringe of his power. There were the two young members of the *Komiteh* as well, the ever-present AK-47s slung across their chests. Hassan Hamza stood with them, speaking in quiet tones to the colonel, his eyes moving with ill-concealed disdain over the young men who surrounded the senior officer. They had been talking for twenty minutes, and there appeared to be little progress.

The impatience was not visible in March's face or the carriage of his lean frame. He stood quietly and stared out to sea as the argument carried on behind him.

They were in the port city of Bandar Beheshti, less than a 100 miles from the Pakistani border. The men stood in the shade of one of the open warehouses. It was not a large harbor, with only four berths and four jetties, each of which held two mobile cranes. There was an electric evacuator for the discharge of grain from a container ship, and the chain-wheel cranes, of which there were two, rolled well in from the edge of the macadam. A pair of ancient forklifts also occupied the broad expanse of black asphalt.

Besides the four open warehouses, there were two sheltered structures and the harbormaster's office, which was little more than a shed of corrugated iron. Surrounding the port, nothing but razor-sharp strands of concertina wire and empty space.

He heard voices rising, and he turned toward the group of men. Hamza was stalking angrily in his direction, the colonel shouting at his back. The Egyptian wiped beads of sweat from his brow as he approached, his mouth curled into a snarl beneath the heavy mustache.

"Those bastards!" he hissed. "They understand nothing. In Tehran, everything is a phone call away. It is not that easy here."

"What's the problem?" March asked.

"There is no truck. There is no way to move the cargo, but we cannot leave it, not even in the closed warehouses. It is many miles to Arak, it is a mountain pass . . . We must have a truck."

"Did you speak to the harbormaster?"

Hamza waved his arms in frustration. "I asked if there was a vehicle in the secure buildings. He would not say . . ."

Hamza stopped talking. The laughter of the colonel's aides was shrill in his ears. The gleaming eyes had moved away from his face and were focused on the office that lay across the stinking heat of the asphalt.

Less than five minutes later, Jason March emerged from the dull metal structure. He was wearing a faint smile. A small silver object caught and reflected the sunlight as it dangled from the fingers of his right hand.

"A key. So there *is* a truck," Hamza said as he joined March at the locked sliding door of the second warehouse.

"If there was not a truck, then that is what he would have said," was the flat response.

Hamza stared at the harbormaster's building and noticed that the colonel and his aides were doing the same. The laughter had stopped, and the aides silently sulked around the Iranian officer like scolded children. The heavy door was lifted to reveal the vehicle, an International 4900 4x2. March hopped into the cab and began to dismantle the plastic housing surrounding the steering column. The engine roared to life a few minutes later.

"Unfortunately, he only had the key to the warehouse," March explained. "It will be an inconvenience, but only a minor one."

Hamza did not reply, only turning once more to look at the office that was like a mirage in the heat of the afternoon.

A technician had accompanied the group, a former dockworker who was skilled in the use of a mobile crane. The 20-foot container waited patiently on the second jetty, the ship having departed many hours ago. The truck was reversed onto the jetty, the container was loaded. It would be a long journey, but they were not expected for several days. They had all the time in the world.

Ryan Kealey woke to the ringing of the phone on the nightstand. Rubbing the sleep out of his eyes with one hand, he picked up and answered with the other. Looking out of the window, he could see dark clouds hanging over the bay and hear the low rumble of thunder in the distance.

"Ryan, it's Harper. I'll meet you and Kharmai out front at ten. Be ready for the airport—we got a hit. I think you're going to like this."

"Okay, I'll be downstairs." He hung up and went into the bathroom. He had fallen asleep almost immediately after entering his room the night before, but after showering and shaving, he was beginning to feel halfway human again. There was a tap at the door just as he finished getting dressed.

Naomi stood in the hallway. Her face was nearly contrite, but not quite. She looked almost as stunning as she had the day before, wearing a thin cashmere sweater and a pair of dress slacks to cover the bandage on her thigh. Her face was drawn, though, and her eyes shadowed as though she had slept poorly. She started to speak and then hesitated. "Are you hungry?" she asked. "Come on, I'll buy you breakfast."

He couldn't tell if that was supposed to be some kind of apology, but he shrugged and followed her down to the ground floor. The restaurant seemed to be pretty decent, and he was surprised to see that it was almost completely empty. They took a seat as far away as possible from the other guests, and soon he was enjoying a full breakfast of eggs, bacon, toast, and coffee. When she ordered only a blueberry muffin, he smiled and she caught it.

"What's that look for?" she asked. "I'm on a diet."

He shook his head. "You know a diet is the last thing you need," he pointed out. "And I resent you making me say that, by the way. I'm engaged, you know."

She grinned and pushed her plate away. Leaning forward in the chair, her long fingers moved uncomfortably close to Ryan's as she spoke. "Listen, I apologize for last night, but only to a certain extent. I don't think I'm getting fair treatment here. It took quite a bit of digging for me to get up to speed on information that you and the deputy director should have been willing to give me up-front." He didn't answer and she went on. "The whole point of this is to track down Jason March, but you haven't told me the first thing about him. I know that you were a soldier, Ryan. I know what he did to you and your men."

He closed his eyes and tried to contain his reaction. *How did she find out?* It was immediately clear to Ryan that he hadn't given Naomi Kharmai enough credit. The only question was what to do about it now. He opted for conciliation.

"It seems like you know everything," he said. It was a struggle to keep his voice light. "What else can I tell you?"

Naomi thought she was fairly adept at gauging mood, and sensed that now would not be a good time to mention Bosnia. Shrugging her shoulders, she reached over to steal his glass of orange juice. "Well, I'd like to know what we're trying to accomplish. Clearly, March is associated with the Iranians and Al-Qaeda, so they're definitely working together. We know what the Iranians want. What about Al-Qaeda—do you think they're going after the same thing?"

Ryan shook his head and took a sip of coffee. "If they use a nuclear weapon, or even manage to acquire one, then they're finished. They'll lose most of their state-sponsored support due to fear of sanctions imposed by the U.N. or, even worse, American military retaliation. I'm sure these thoughts wouldn't readily occur to Al-Qaeda's leadership, but that's the reality of the situation. They've made a lot of contradictory statements about their attempts to purchase nuclear material."

"What about Iran?"

"Well, if we find out that Iran has a weapon, they can just claim it's for national defense. Then they'll make some minor concessions to make it easier to swallow. The OSCE and the U.N. won't like it, and neither will we, but the North Koreans have already discovered that we're willing to let a lot slide as long as you keep it on your side of the fence. That's why Brenneman is so intent on stopping them before they get that far. Once they have a weapon, our options obviously become more limited."

She smiled and popped a piece of muffin into her mouth. "It's pretty clear that you're not an expert on foreign policy," she said.

"That's true enough," he replied with a grin of his own. "But the fact remains that Al-Qaeda is more likely to retain their grassroots support and the flow of small arms and money into the organization if they stay away from the biological and nuclear side of things. Otherwise, they'd be asking for more trouble than they can handle. If I had to guess, I'd say that they're helping Iran with *their* nuclear ambitions."

"In exchange for what?"

"It's hard to tell. They might not even have come to an agreement yet," he said. "It could be money, political asylum, arms—it might even be something as simple as safe passage through the country. For that kind of help, though, I would say that they'll expect a lot in return."

"That makes sense." Naomi finished her juice and peeked at her watch. It was almost ten. "How do you think March fits in?"

Ryan didn't answer as the waiter approached with their check. He waited until the bill was settled and they had collected their coats before picking up the thread. "You read the file, so you know what he is." She hadn't read the file, but didn't stop to correct him. "His appearance and training allow him to blend in perfectly here. He might even have been able to bring some international connections to the table. For any stateside operation, March is going to be their best bet for success. Also, he has a lot to teach the young recruits. They won't use him unless there's a high probability that he'll come back alive. Believe me when I say that Al-Qaeda gets stronger every day he's involved."

"That's a scary thought," she murmured.

Ryan nodded his head in agreement. "I know."

The black Suburban was parked along the curb, a gentle mist of rain falling around them as they hurried from the hotel entrance into the warm interior of the truck. Harper was waiting in the front passenger seat. As soon as the doors were shut, the vehicle moved off into traffic. Ryan handed the deputy director a carryout cup of coffee from the hotel's restaurant, and the older man nodded his appreciation.

"We came up big on the *Natalia*, Ryan," he said. "It belongs to a man by the name of Stephen Gray. Does that ring a bell?"

Kealey scanned his memory. "Vaguely. Owns a shipping company, right? He got into some trouble when one of his boats was picked up on the way to Northern Ireland with a cargo hold full of weapons."

The DDO tossed the file he was holding into Ryan's lap. "One and the same. It caused a lot of problems because the weapons were high grade, a thousand 40mm automatic grenade launchers still in the packing grease, eight thousand rounds of ammunition, crates full of Vektor 7.62mm tripod-mounted machine guns. All of it was manufactured by a division of Denel Arms, in which the government holds a majority share. As you might expect, the Brits were furious. There was a lot of speculation that Gray was stockpiling weapons to sell to the highest bidder, but he beat the charges on a technicality."

Naomi's eyes opened wide and Ryan looked up sharply. "That's a problem," he said. "If any of that is true, then there's a good chance that Al-Qaeda has access to some serious firepower."

"I'd say it's more than a chance," Naomi put in. "I mean, look at the facts. Gray owns a shipping company that was used to smuggle arms. One of his ships brings explosives into the States, which in turn are used in a terrorist operation by Al-Qaeda. There must be some direct connection."

Harper was nodding slowly. "And I'm willing to bet that Jason March is that connection." He picked up a second file from the floor at his feet. It was a dark brown folder with no markings that Naomi could see. He handed it back to her. "It's about time you got a look at this, Kharmai." Kealey shot her a questioning look, but she ignored it and began to peruse the contents as the DDO explained: "That is a complete history of March . . . everything we know, to be more specific. There isn't much more than a 201 file. His records were good enough to get him into the military, and once you're in, no one looks much further."

She looked up curiously. Ryan was staring out into the rain. "What do you mean by that?" she asked.

"I mean that he didn't exist until he joined the army," Harper said. Her mouth hung open as she searched his face.

"That can't be right," she said. "The military looks at your birth certificate, your driver's license, even your secondary-school records, right? How could he just—"

"Every piece of documentation that he submitted was an invention." It was Ryan speaking, and she turned to look in his direction. "Filling out the initial paperwork was the risky part, but even then they don't look too hard—the army has always been desperate for warm bodies. Once he was in, it was all taken as fact. Airborne, Ranger School, Air Assault, Sniper School, the SERE course—that's Survival, Evasion, Resistance, and Escape—SF Assessment and Selection . . . He got into all of it by the strength of his military record, and he succeeded in everything he did. He was a model soldier. There was no reason for the generals signing off on it to doubt any of his personal history before he came into the service."

Naomi detected a bitter edge to Ryan's words, and her conversation with General Hale came flooding back once again: *I just didn't buy into what Kealey was saying . . . It sounded paranoid . . . I should have listened to him, though . . . I should have listened . . .* She was looking through the file. If anything, March's achievements were even more staggering than his commanding officer's. The first page listed his MOS as 18 Charlie, or Special Forces engineer sergeant. In addition to the schools that Ryan had mentioned, Sergeant March had completed EOD (Explosives Ordnance Disposal) and was qualified in both Scuba and HALO—High Altitude, Low Opening freefall parachuting.

When it came to the list of awards and achievements, though, the DD214 was noticeably bare. The highest award that March had earned was the Meritorious Service Medal. Aside from that, there wasn't much to speak of.

"If he was such a great soldier, why didn't he receive more commendations?"

Ryan had to think for a minute, as it was a good question. "He did okay; he received all the standard medals as you move through the ranks, and any decent E-7 gets the MSM. It's just that he rubbed a lot of officers the wrong way, and they're responsible for approving the awards. He was always separate from his peers, never wanted to be a team player. A lot of people didn't like the way he acted . . . It made them nervous."

Including you, she thought. But Ryan Kealey had looked deeper into March's mind, had seen what was truly lurking there long before anyone else. He couldn't be blamed for what Jason March had done seven years earlier, or for the crimes he had committed since. She handed the file back to the deputy director.

"Now you have an idea of what you're going after," he said.

She managed to keep a straight face, but thought she saw the corner of Ryan's mouth lift in amusement. Clearly, Harper didn't know what kind of investigator he had brought into the fold.

"I want you two in Cape Town to see what Gray has to say. He has a converted warehouse there that he uses as an office and base of operations. He also owns shipping operations in Durban and Richard's Bay, but Cape Town is the base."

He pointed back to the file sitting on Kealey's lap. "That should contain all the information you need. As you can imagine, Stephen Gray is not a favored citizen since he beat those charges. We have unofficial support from the South African government to conduct this operation. Translated, that means that they will overlook something, but not anything. You got me this time, Ryan?" His voice was steel as he stared at the younger man.

Kealey nodded deferentially, which was a source of some amusement to Kharmai until Harper fixed her with the same sobering gaze.

"Let me also tell you that the local police force hasn't been brought into the loop, and it's not going to happen anytime soon. They don't know who you are . . . It's worth keeping that in mind. They won't hesitate to shoot if they think you're a threat. I'm not saying this for my own health, okay? The nearest U.S. embassy to Cape Town is in Pretoria, which is over 600 miles away. That doesn't give you a lot of room for error, so you can't afford to fuck up, because no one has your back."

Jonathan Harper turned in the seat to point something out to the driver as they approached the departure gates for Norfolk International, the wet street hissing beneath the tires as the skies finally opened and rain hammered down onto the roof of the vehicle and the approaching road.

"I almost forgot." Harper turned back around over the back of his seat to hand them each folders. "These are your passports and driver's licenses. Congratulations, you now work in Silicon Valley. It should be a substantial salary increase for both of you, if only on paper," he said with a grin. "Put anything you need on expenses, but don't forget who's ultimately accountable, okay?"

The smile faded from his face as he turned back to business. "There is a reason that I'm sitting here instead of my comfortable little office in Langley. This situation has the full attention of the director and the president, so it has to have our full attention as well. I'm counting on both of you."

The small convoy had been traveling northwest for almost eight hours. They were crossing the Dasht-e Lut, the great salt desert that seemed to stretch endlessly in every direction. When the foothills of the Zagros had finally appeared in the distance, the sight had inspired the young policeman seated in the passenger seat of the second Land Rover to murmur a brief prayer of gratitude. In front of the policeman was the vehicle carrying the man from Al-Qaeda, the air force colonel, and two of his aides. Behind him was the International 4900 driven by the American, carrying the metal container that was bound for the plant at Arak.

They had passed through the towns of Nikshahr and Bampur, small groups of children waving excitedly as the vehicles carefully navigated the narrow streets. Four hours later, the city of Bam could be seen to the north, causing a man native to the sprawling municipality to cry out excitedly from the backseat. They had traveled only 50 additional miles since the city outskirts had faded from view.

Earlier in the day, the startling contrasts of the desert had come as a welcome surprise to Ali Ahmedi, who had, until now, spent every one of his twenty-eight years in the streets of Tehran. His views of the Iranian landscape had always been limited to the jagged peaks of Mount Damavand, the highest point in Iran just north of the capital city. He had never experienced the desert until the trip to Beheshti, the immense white cumulus clouds bright against the brilliant blue backdrop of sky, falling down to the razor edge of the horizon where the sand, stone, and dried-out mud of the *kavirs* began.

Now the air was cool, and Ahmedi rolled down the window for the breeze as the stars settled in overhead. Soon they would stop, as travel over the sucking mud of the *kavir* salt marshes was dangerous enough in the daytime, when the path ahead was visible and a judgment could be made.

His friend and fellow officer of the *Komiteh* drove the vehicle. In the rear seat were three of the colonel's aides. As the hours passed, Ahmedi had listened to them with amusement, at first. Then growing impatience, and finally, outright annoyance.

All they could speak of was the American.

Their conversation was littered with wild supposition and theory; the American was not an American at all, but a European mercenary; the American was a spy for the Great Satan; the American was a killer of the highest distinction, without peer.

The last one had some merit, he thought.

Ahmedi had watched the American fix the man of Al-Qaeda with his movie-star good looks and snake eyes, and then move off easily toward the harbormaster's office. He recalled that the harbormaster had shouted that the warehouse could not be opened, that a truck must be acquired elsewhere. The American had entered the building of corrugated iron, and the harbormaster had not been seen again . . .

No one had dared to enter the office afterward. Ahmedi would have said that the man from Al-Qaeda was afraid of the American, and that the colonel and his aides shared the fear.

The headlights flashed from the truck behind, and the policeman at the wheel of Ahmedi's vehicle flashed his in turn. The convoy stopped and the engines died. Sleeping bags were pulled from behind the seats as a cool breeze lifted the loose sand into the black night. It was twelve more hours to Arak. They would resume at first light.

CHAPTER 15

CAPE TOWN, SOUTH AFRICA

Founded in the mid-seventeenth century by Governor Jan van Riebeeck, Cape Town was first given life as a supply station on the Dutch East India Company's sea route to the East. Over the years the city flourished, occupied first by the British, and then returned to the Dutch in 1803. By 1806, the port was once more in British hands, and soon became the capital of the Cape of Good Hope Colony. When the Union of South Africa was established in 1910, all administrative proceedings were moved north to Pretoria, but the coastal city continued to expand as the diamond and gold mines of the Transvaal provided enormous and lucrative quantities of raw exports. Now, as both the legislative capital and one of the largest maritime ports in the world, it was easy for Ryan Kealey to understand why Stephen Gray would choose to base his company in the thriving commercial and industrial center that marked the gateway to the African continent.

They arrived in Cape Town at three in the afternoon after traveling almost 8,000 miles, the sun sweltering overhead as Ryan drove their white Nissan X-Trail deep into the heart of the city. Naomi sat in the passenger seat, a large map spread out across her lap as she navigated the way west on the Strand toward the waterfront. Judging from the expression on her face, Ryan knew she was occupied by more than the directions she was giving.

"Come on," he finally said. "You're driving me crazy with that look. What are you thinking about?"

She turned in the seat, the concern obvious in her face. "I'm worried about how we're going to handle Gray. I mean, don't you think we're just a bit shorthanded here?"

Ryan shrugged, his attention focused on the road ahead. "He owns one of the largest shipping companies in the country, so he's obviously an intelligent man. We'll try to reason with him. I highly doubt he wants to face extradition; it's a tough sell, but I'm sure the State Department will make the request if Brenneman makes a point of it. I don't see the South Africans trying to get in the way, do you?"

"I guess not," she said. "What if he doesn't listen to reason? Turn here."

Ryan swung the jeep around a corner, swearing under his breath as he narrowly missed sideswiping a smaller vehicle. He was still adjusting to driving on the left side of the road. "I don't think that far ahead," he finally replied, turning to give her a small smile.

They were driving slowly down the narrow streets of the Victoria and Albert Waterfront, known to the locals simply as the V&A. As one of the Cape's premier tourist attractions, the streets were lined with expensive stores and their patrons, sunburnt tourists trudging along the sidewalks as they struggled under a common load of cameras, daypacks, and shopping bags. The Waterfront had been restored in the late-1980s, and although many of the buildings had been modernized, some still bore the remnants of Victorian industrial architecture left over from years of British rule. Overall, Naomi thought the effect was quite pleasing as the jeep crested a low hill and the sparkling waters of Table Bay came into view.

"Slow down," Naomi said. She looked back down at her map. "Take a right here."

Ryan turned onto the next street. They were moving away from the bustling center of the commercial district and into the industrial area. The change was subtle at first, marked only by the diminishing number of people on the streets. It wasn't long, though, before towering warehouses of red brick and cracked gray cement completely replaced the exclusive restaurants and boutiques of the commercial sector.

"What are we looking for?" he asked.

She consulted her map once more and nodded slightly toward one of many identical structures. "That," she said. Parked outside of the warehouse was a silver late-model E class Mercedes.

"Kind of telling, isn't it?" Ryan said. "There can't be too many of those around." He looked for guards secreted in the alleys bordering each side of the warehouse, but none was visible. "Do you see anything?" he asked her.

Naomi shook her head, and Ryan accelerated down the street.

"What do you—"

"Hold on a second, I'm thinking," he said. Although the street was well behind them now, the shapes and orientations of the buildings were held perfectly in his mind as he thought about what he would need to begin a loose surveillance . . . It was some time before he realized he still had an audience.

"Sorry, Naomi. What were you saying?"

"It's not important," she said. "I'm more interested in what *you* were just thinking."

He sighed heavily as they moved back through the streets bordering Table Bay. "I was thinking that it can't be that simple. For a known arms dealer, he doesn't seem to take a lot of precautions. That's not realistic, though; he has to have protection, and that means an unknown number of armed guards inside the warehouse, plus some kind of alarm system. The best way is to hit him in transit, but that would never fly with Harper—we're supposed to do this without making a lot of noise."

Naomi didn't respond for a while, the darkening waters of the bay holding her attention as Ryan drove back into the commercial district, the well-lit storefronts passing by on the right, with an impressive view of the water on the left. She absently watched navigation lights move up and down as a number of ships bobbed on the gentle swells of the Atlantic. "Maybe it *is* that simple," she said on reflection.

"What do you mean?"

"Gray beat the government at their own game—he was caught

red-handed and still managed to stay out of jail. Now he's even richer than before. He might just be arrogant enough to think that he's beyond their reach."

"It's a thought," he said. "But we have to be sure." His eyes involuntarily moved to Naomi's throat, and he suppressed a shudder at what might have been. "I think we've already taken enough chances."

She didn't respond as Ryan pulled their rented Nissan into the Victoria and Albert Hotel's parking lot. They checked in and opted for a light meal on the patio overlooking the bay. Although both were exhausted, they did not refuse when the waiter brought out a wine list along with the menu.

The meal was excellent, and made all the more so by the sweeping view of the bay below. It seemed as though the water would have gone on forever were it not contained by the fiery red of the sky and the flat tableau of Mount Table held in silhouette against the fading sun.

Conversation was uneasy at first, but after a while Ryan began to overcome his initial distaste for Naomi Kharmai. He knew that it was partly her looks and partly the wine, but he found himself gradually warming to her as the night wore on. When he thought about the smirk on her face outside the Kennedy-Warren, he considered her lightning reflexes in the bar in Norfolk. When he recalled her lack of gratitude, the memory was quickly followed by an image of salt-stained cheeks and a hurried swipe at warm tears in a brightly lit hotel room. Despite the contradictions running through his mind, he couldn't help but hold her liquid green eyes when they met his across the table.

Long after the meal was done, the waiter brought them a second bottle of Bordeaux. Naomi drank one glass very fast, then savored another. They spoke about the flight over, and their first impressions of the African continent. As the light receded over the warm stones of the patio, they found themselves talking about their early years in the Agency, although Ryan was more interested in her years in general.

"I know it's impolite to ask," he said with a boyish grin, "but how old are you, anyway?"

"You don't have any cards to play," she responded with a smile of her own. "I already know how old *you* are."

"That's true," he conceded. "You seem to know a lot."

"That's why I'm here instead of my little cubicle at Tyson's Corner," she said, her eyebrows arching wickedly. "The director thought one of us should know *something*."

He laughed as he lifted the bottle to pour them both another glass.

"And how old is your fiancée?"

"Her age for yours."

An amused expression came over her face as she set down her glass and considered. "Okay," she said, "I'll just have to trust you on this one. I'm twenty-nine. Your turn."

"Twenty-nine?"

Her smile faltered. "Thirty. But, God, twenty-nine sounds so much younger, doesn't it?"

He laughed again and held up his end of the bargain. "Katie's twenty-four. I know that makes me sound bad, but—well, I don't really have anything to say in my defense. She was my student, which only makes it worse, I guess."

"You were a professor?" she asked with some surprise. "Aren't you a bit young for that?"

"I'm only a lowly associate professor. I probably still have a job if I say all the right things and grovel a little. Why? I don't seem the type, right?"

"No, that's not it," she said. "My father taught at Cambridge. He was really well known, a leader in his field. Most people wouldn't have thought he was the type either."

"Is that why you moved to the States, because of his teaching?"

She nodded, and Ryan watched an unhappy look come over her face as she stared down at the table. "He was offered a position at Harvard when I was eighteen. He did really well . . . wrote a few books, secured his tenure. When they offered me a full ride and I turned it down, he was so angry that he didn't speak to me for a month." She hesitated before speaking again. "He wanted me to follow in his footsteps, I guess. He was even more disappointed when I joined the Agency."

"Why did you turn it down?" he asked gently. She finally looked up to meet his gaze.

"I had to earn it, you know? I didn't want my future handed to me. It seems stupid now, but I really felt strongly about it at the time. He could be stubborn, too, so we didn't get along too well. It wasn't like I wanted much. I mean, if he would have talked about me just *one* time the way he talked about my brothers—"

She stopped in midsentence, pushing back from the table and standing up quickly, her chair tipping back and over in the process. Ryan rose to his feet almost as fast.

"What is it? What's wrong?"

She was shaking her head, clearly amazed and angry with herself. "Nothing," she said. "Nothing, really. God, I just prattle on sometimes. I'm sorry, forget it—"

"Naomi." She was grabbing her coat, turning away from him. "Naomi," he repeated. He caught her arm as she started to walk away. "If he wasn't proud," Ryan said, "then he was wrong."

She searched his eyes quickly and saw that he meant the words. She hesitated and then moved in close, leaning up to kiss him lightly. She pulled away only slightly afterward, her soft lips close to his like the promise of something more. Then the moment passed and she was walking away, the tap of her heels light against the rough stone as she moved past empty tables toward the hotel.

Ryan was stunned. He stood alone on the terrace, the taste of her sweet on his mouth as the darkness moved in across the bay. God, for that not to have happened. He couldn't take it back, though, and he had to work with her for a long time yet. Only now did he think about Katie, and that just wasn't good enough. He forced a mental image to punish himself, and when she appeared, it was on the rocky bluff overlooking Cape Elizabeth, a strong inland wind sweeping her hair back from her face as she looked out over the ocean. Even in his mind, jumbled and confused as it was, the clarity of her features was breathtaking. Then the image shattered into a thousand pieces, and he knew at once that he was responsible.

He shook his head as he walked away from the table. For that not to have happened . . .

The next morning began early for Ryan. He showered and dressed before the sun came up, stopping on his way down the hall only to slide a scribbled note underneath Naomi's door. It said nothing about the previous evening, just a few lines to let her know that he was taking the jeep out for some supplies. She had consumed more than her fair share of wine the night before, and he didn't see the harm in giving her a few hours to recover. He stopped at the hotel's restaurant to pick up a cup of coffee, then at the front desk to get directions to the stores he needed to visit.

The air outside was brisk, a gentle purple-orange dawn easing the Cape into another day. He knew that it was too early for the shops on the Strand to be open, but he couldn't take seeing Naomi again just yet. *She's a strange woman,* he thought absently. *So smart and stubborn, so afraid to show any weakness.* He had to let her know that it wasn't going anywhere, but he still had to be able to work with her afterward. It was a difficult situation. Would it be better, he wondered, to leave it alone? To see what she had to say? She might regret it as much as he did.

Then again, there was that long moment before she had pulled away from him . . . Ryan wondered if she had waited in her room after leaving the terrace, listening for his knock at the door, a robe slipping down low to reveal her bare shoulders. The image stuck in his mind as he drove the Nissan west toward the industrial section of the city.

The silver Mercedes was there, but in a slightly different spot. Thinking back to Harper's file on Gray, Ryan remembered that the businessman also owned a town house on the Buitengracht, in addition to numerous properties farther north; there was a good chance that he had spent the night at one of those locations before driving back to the warehouse in the morning. Ryan looked at his watch. Only eight minutes past seven, and the man was already at work. He filed that fact away as he got out of the jeep and took advantage of the empty street to survey the arrangement of the buildings surrounding Gray's renovated warehouse. The sidewalk opposite was very narrow, almost nonexistent before it rose up into the face of yet another industrial complex.

Ryan's eyes followed the lines of the building up to the flat roof, and then on an imaginary path cutting down diagonally to the metal-framed door on the other side of the Mercedes. He walked down a litter-strewn alley, the straight cement walls towering on either side of him, and was pleased to find an aluminum fire escape hanging over a Dumpster, which was coated in flaking brown paint.

By standing on the Dumpster, he found he could reach the base of the fire escape. It pulled down easily when he tugged on the lowest rung. It was all he needed for the moment. Satisfied, Ryan returned the retractable ladder to its original place and hopped down from the container, walking back down the narrow space between the buildings toward the jeep. He still had a lot to do before nightfall.

Naomi woke just before ten, the sheets in a tangle at her feet. Crawling out of bed, she was startled to see the sun halfway into its climb through the African sky. She could hear happy shouts of children beneath her window, and she wondered why Ryan had let her sleep for so long. Thinking his name forced her to recall the night before. Sitting on the edge of the bed, her mind scrambled to recollect the events that had transpired.

Oh God.

I can't believe I did that, she thought. *I can't believe it.* Naomi knew she felt something for Ryan, but also knew instinctively that it could never work. He was engaged, and . . . Well, that was all that was wrong, really, but it was enough. He hadn't pulled away, though. She could remember that clearly now. She'd given him the opportunity, but he didn't pull back. All the same, he couldn't think too much of her after what she had said. Rambling on about her father, feeling sorry for herself. There would be no more of that, she decided. No way in hell.

CHAPTER 16

IRAN

They arrived much earlier than expected, just as the sun was beginning its downward descent over the highest peaks in the
mountainous Khondaub region west of Arak. The convoy had picked
up speed upon reaching the highway running northwest from Ker-
man through Yazd and Isfahan. Once the last city faded from view,
the surrounding landscape gradually became less populated as the
hours passed and the low-lying foothills gave way to rocky escarp-
ments towering far above the desert floor.

There were no private homes within 30 kilometers of the complex, at least none that were occupied. The interior ministry had
forced the families out when construction was first started on the
heavy-water reactor. They received no compensation for their loss,
but they were fortunate enough to have left with their lives. The current regime would have been far less generous.

The facility lay nestled in a shallow valley, the flat tan buildings
blending into the surrounding granite walls that served as natural
protection against inbound missiles. The complex was encircled by
twin chain link fences topped with razor wire. To the untrained eye,
security would have appeared weak, almost nonexistent, but it was
there. It could be seen in the weapon-clearing barrels that marked
the entrance to each building, and in the camouflage netting that

shielded the truck-mounted SA-8 Gecko SAM system. It could be seen in the phase array radar bolted to the command vehicle, and in the bunkers that dotted the perimeter, complete with ammunition stores and grenade sumps. The unmarked minefields that were scattered throughout the open ground south of the facility would have been harder to pick out, as would the early-warning sensors that monitored mountain passes as far as 20 kilometers away.

The convoy was expected, and was not forced to contend with these extensive security measures. Once cleared through the main gate, the vehicles cut an erratic path through the complex. First they passed the four-story structure that served as a barracks for the soldiers, and then the largest building on the compound: the prestressed concrete structure that housed the twin reactors and the smaller steam generators. Beyond the reactor building was the immense cooling tower that served, unbeknownst to the base commander, as a reference point for the NSA satellite control teams at Fort Meade, Maryland.

The vehicles finally slowed to a halt in front of the administration block, a cluster of identical buildings linked by narrow corridors that comprised the northernmost part of the compound. The weary men descended from the vehicles, each stretching in the cool mountain air as a truck-mounted crane was pulled alongside and soldiers were called for to assist in unloading the container. March did not stay to supervise the procedure, instead turning to follow Hamza and the Iranian officer into the cool interior of the administration building.

The hallways all looked alike to March: spotless white walls and freshly waxed pale tile floors, no paintings, no windows. He noticed that the building was missing the usual procession of harried file clerks and overworked administrative personnel. In fact, they passed no one at all on the lengthy walk into the heart of the structure. The silence would have been overwhelming were it not for the gentle, irregular tap of their shoes on the gleaming floor. Finally, the colonel stopped at an unmarked door. He knocked softly, and was granted permission to enter. "Wait here," he said, and the door closed behind him.

The officer was gone for five minutes. Hamza avoided the other man's eyes, but knew instinctively that the American was watching him. He found it difficult not to flinch under the penetrating gaze. His mind kept returning to Beheshti, to the mocking tone of the colonel's voice, to the contempt in the American's eyes, to the solitary shuttered building that was the harbormaster's office.

Hamza thought of the sun beating down, cooking the sheets of metal and whatever lay within. He wondered if the flies had yet to find the harbormaster.

The door was pulled open and they were beckoned inside. The interior of the room was a marked difference from the sterile halls. Small, tastefully framed paintings decorated the walls. The carpet was maroon, deep and soft, and expensive-looking armchairs were scattered throughout the space. March noticed that his companion stared as though he had never seen such luxury.

Saif al-Adel was seated on one of the several couches. He stood as they entered the room, the thin smile taut over his narrow features. Hamza was relieved to find him in good humor.

"Welcome, my brother. We were afraid that the desert might have swallowed you whole, along with our American friend here," he said.

Hamza chuckled nervously and looked to the other man in the room, the Iranian minister Mazaheri. He was wearing full clerical robes, the corners of his eyes crinkling beneath the elaborate turban as he offered his greetings. "You have the container," he said. It was not a question.

Hamza nodded, and the minister's smile grew. "You have performed an invaluable service to my country. I have made the other arrangements, as promised. Our South African friend has already delivered your package. You are to be congratulated." Mazaheri cast a sideways glance at al-Adel, and then focused his attention on the other Egyptian. "Come, my friend," he said, placing a friendly arm around Hamza's shoulder. "Share a meal with me. You've traveled far, you should rest before the transport arrives."

Hamza looked to his commander, and received a smile and an approving nod. "He's right, Hassan. You deserve more than a good meal, though. I would say that it is time to reevaluate your place in the organization. Your reward is long overdue."

Despite his best efforts, Hamza could not contain the small smile that spread across his lips. He would be made a commander, he would be Saif's equal . . . After all these years, it was now a certainty. He went easily, following the minister out of the room, standing tall as he considered the new powers that would soon be his. The smile stretched as an image presented itself to him—it was his name, in large print next to those of al-Zarqawi and bin Laden in the Western newspapers. The image grew in his mind, clouding out all other thought. He would be known, as al-Adel was known. He didn't hear the minister's idle chatter, and he did not notice that the American walked far behind with Saif, far enough that they could speak privately.

"You know who I am," the commander said.

It was a blanket statement, and March did not think it required a response as they moved back through the clean white halls.

Finally, al-Adel continued: "Everything about you concerns me. I make no secret of that. Hassan will only speak well of you, but I am not so easily convinced. I ask of you a single question: what has the West done to you, one of its own, that you would see it burn?"

March considered the question, but only briefly. "You asked me this before, and my answer is the same. Yes, I know who you are. On the other hand, you know what I can do. I ask nothing in return for my actions, only that you provide me with the basic materials that are required for success. What I've done in the past, who I am, is not your concern. We will either proceed on that basis or not at all. The decision is yours to make."

Saif al-Adel looked up as the steel-and-glass doors approached. Hamza and the minister pushed out first, their backs instantly bathed in a red glow from the sun sinking low over the mountains. "You are a brave man to say such things to me," he said absently. "If I didn't know differently, I would say you were a fool. You should know that the air force colonel had many good things to say about you. His assignment was not a random choice. He was impressed, and so Mazaheri was impressed. I want to show you something."

They followed the other two men out into the rapidly cooling air. The minister and Hamza were walking toward the dining facility, leaving twin trails of dusty footprints in the thin sienna topsoil that covered the granite stone of the valley floor. A small group of soldiers stood outside the open doors, laughing and talking as they waited for the meal line to advance.

"I have known Hassan for fourteen years. He is a fellow Egyptian, and has always served the organization well. Two years ago he saved my life in an American ambush, and he wept with me when we were denied the privilege of burying our less-fortunate comrades. For that, and for his service, I love him as a brother."

March watched as the minister spoke to Hamza, patting him on the shoulder and pointing to an adjacent building as though offering an explanation. March watched Hamza nod in agreement, and Mazaheri began to walk away as the other man continued on toward the dining hall.

"The colonel was impressed with you, but not with Hassan. He was described as 'poorly prepared,' and 'weak when confronted by a lesser man, a man with no authority.' The colonel is Mazaheri's son-in-law, and as such has the minister's ear and his respect. I would gladly cut the man's throat and watch him choke for breath, but Mazaheri is the key to Al-Qaeda's future, and so he must be humored . . ."

March saw the arrogance in Hamza's walk. Mere words, a false promise had given the man steel in his backbone when before there was none. He watched the soldiers lift their weapons as one. There was the terrible moment of comprehension as Hamza extended his arms, desperately throwing his palms out at the rifles pointed in his direction, screaming that it was a mistake. There was the distinctive crack of a single Kalishnikov, followed by the steady rhythm of automatic fire. There was the sight of flailing limbs as bullets ripped through his outstretched hands and into his face and chest.

The firing stopped. Hassan Hamza lay dead on the ground, streams of blood already running out from underneath his body in thin rivulets, seeping down into the cracks of the stone as the soldiers cleared their weapons and resumed their conversation. Mazaheri was still walking. He hadn't turned at the sound of gunfire, nor had he flinched when the reports echoed back over the mountains.

When al-Adel turned to look at Jason March, there was no evidence of grief in the commander's face. "To ensure the future of the organization, I would let these animals kill my brother. When you came to us, it was as a volunteer. You had neither my trust nor my respect. Now you have my respect. You've earned that much. Bear in mind, though, that you can only fail me once . . . Remember what happened here. It is a good lesson."

Peering into the American's eyes, he saw nothing that might hint at fear or indecision. Instead, he saw a strength that rivaled his own. Saif al-Adel knew that the man would not take the words personally, and was pleased.

What he heard next, though, shook the commander to his very core.

"You want what I can achieve. In return, I want you to take me north."

A lengthy silence ensued. "Why?"

"You know why."

CHAPTER 17

CAPE TOWN

They began watching the warehouse just before dawn on the third day.

With only two people, it would have been impossible to follow Gray away from the building. Kealey knew that their faces would too quickly become familiar, and security around the businessman would be heavily increased if they were spotted. He wanted the chance to isolate Gray if at all possible. The lost hours in the man's schedule grated at Ryan, but he was reasonably satisfied with their coverage of the warehouse. It was secluded and quiet. Approaching vehicles could be heard long before they turned onto the narrow street running through the maze of industrial buildings that marked this forgotten district of the Cape.

The previous day had been well spent. The shops on the Strand had provided Ryan with better equipment than he could have hoped for. At a small sporting-goods store he had found a good set of Rigel 2350 night vision binoculars. These he purchased, along with two cushioned sleeping bag mats and a backpack. He also stopped at the local CNA grocery store to pick up a case of bottled water. For the other items that were needed, Ryan put in a call to Pretoria. From there, the request was forwarded to Langley and approval was given. Just past three in the afternoon, as Ryan and Naomi were finishing lunch in awkward silence on the terrace, the delivery was made by diplomatic courier. The parcel, opened in the privacy of Ryan's hotel room, contained the Tait Orca encrypted radios and earpieces that he had specifically requested.

It also contained a P22 Walther handgun complete with a 5" modified barrel, the extended muzzle threaded for the heavy Dalphon suppressor that lay next to the weapon.

Ryan didn't need the radios or the pistol yet. They had parked the Nissan several hundred meters away and approached from the north, winding their way through a labyrinth of buildings before reaching the aluminum fire escape of the building opposite Gray's. Naomi was shivering violently as they climbed the ladder and settled in on the roof, sliding their way forward to find the best view of the warehouse below. The sun was just peeking over the horizon when the silver Mercedes glided up next to the curb. Ryan checked his watch: 7:15 AM. Gray seemed to be fairly consistent in his habits.

They watched as the driver got out of the vehicle and walked around the car, looking up and down the street as he moved. He was a large white man with a shaved head, a neat goatee, and more fat than muscle. His poorly fitted suit stretched at the seams, and even at a distance, Kealey could spot the bulge beneath the man's left armpit. The passenger door was opened and the second occupant of the vehicle stepped out onto the street.

It was Ryan's first look at Stephen Gray. He was small and neat, deeply tanned, and clean-shaven, with a full head of closely trimmed silver hair; the man wore his wealth well. Ryan watched the driver walk several steps ahead of his charge, the right hand held beneath his jacket as his eyes searched the surrounding buildings. The front door to the warehouse was pulled open, and Ryan could see the big man pause inside the threshold as though disarming a security system. It was clear that the driver knew his job. It would be better if he was poorly trained, but Ryan knew that it could have been worse. He was relieved that Gray didn't seem inclined to travel with a large entourage, as was the habit of so many other rich men.

Once the door closed behind the two men, the warehouse was still for hours. No movement could be seen through the small metal-framed windows at the front of the building. As the sun rose and beat down on the pebbled surface of the roof, Naomi began shifting her body impatiently and casting little glances in his direction. Finally, she sidled over next to him slowly.

"Can I talk?"

"Quietly," he said.

"How long are we going to stay here?" Her body was very close to his.

"Until nightfall."

Ryan heard her mumble something under her breath, and turned to look in her direction. She was drinking bottled water, and a few drops spilled down onto her chest. His eyes involuntarily followed the path of the drops, moving down from her face to the thin sheen of sweat on the graceful curve of her neck, and then over small, firm breasts straining against the damp cotton of her T-shirt. He caught himself and looked away quickly, forcing his attention back to the warehouse below. He angrily wiped sweat out of his eyes and drank from his own water bottle.

Naomi was watching him carefully. She edged a little closer, so that their legs were touching and her shoulder was pressed lightly against his. "Listen," she said in a low voice. "I'm sorry about what happened the other night. I was way out of line, and I probably drank too much . . . It didn't mean anything, okay? It won't happen again, I promise."

Her tone was anything but apologetic. He eased his body away from hers slightly in turn. "It was as much my fault as yours. I'm sorry if I gave you the wrong impression." He looked up into her face, inches away from his own. "You're right. It didn't mean anything, and it's not going anywhere. That's all that has to be said."

She held his gaze for a few seconds longer, as if measuring his sincerity, then slowly slid her mat back to its original position as Ryan turned back to focus on the building below.

Just after one in the afternoon, a battered white scooter screamed up to the entrance of the building. A young African male hopped off and kicked hard on the door. It was cracked open slightly. A large bag was thrust in through the opening, and the delivery boy received a fistful of rand in return. The money was stuffed down into his dirty jeans before the tires spun in the street and the scooter whined away.

The hours continued to pass as the vibrant sounds of the Malay Quarter drifted over the rooftops from the east. After the few words spoken earlier in the afternoon, Ryan cast two more quick glances in Naomi's direction. Both times he could see clearly the anger and hurt in her face. He was beginning to regret capitulating so easily to Harper's request that she be brought along.

Finally, the air began to cool as dusk settled over the weary city. Ten minutes after the streetlights came on, the heavy door of the warehouse was pushed open. The big man emerged first, the right hand once again shielded from view inside his jacket. He surveyed the street, then turned and nodded as Gray followed him out, pausing only to set the alarm once more. Ryan checked his watch again. It was just after 8:00 PM. He waited for five minutes after the Mercedes had driven off before standing up on the rooftop, gratefully stretching sore muscles as he shook out a day's worth of inactivity.

"Well, that was time bloody well spent," Naomi said. Kicking at her water bottle, she watched as it bounced over the surface of the roof, scattering small rocks along the way. Ryan looked over as she leaned down to rub at a cramp in her thigh.

The sarcasm rubbed at his nerves, but he held his temper as he rolled up his mat and packed it neatly into the backpack. "You're right. It *was* time well spent," he said in a neutral tone. She threw him a withering look and he rose from his crouch to point down at the warehouse. "Now we have some idea of what we're looking at. Gray only has one guard, but he's a professional. Did you watch him get out of the car? He kept the door open and the engine running while he checked the street, and his eyes didn't stop moving the whole time they were in the open, which was about fifteen seconds."

She looked a little less certain of herself as he went on, seemingly speaking more to himself than to her. "They're careful about setting that alarm. We can't get in at night and wait for them unless I ask Harper to send me somebody from Technical Services. Somehow, I don't think he'll jump at the idea."

"So what do you think?" she asked.

He shook his head absently as he picked up her belongings and added them to the pack. "We'll keep looking, for now. Time is a factor, but we need to do it right. We'll get an opportunity sooner or later."

Standing up, he began to walk over to the fire escape, Naomi trailing along dejectedly as she pondered days on end of lying in the heat looking at nothing more than bricks and mortar. She didn't see the small smile that played over Ryan's face as he swung his leg over the edge of the roof.

"You know something?" he said. "I think I'd like to see what's on the other side of that building."

CHAPTER 18

IRAN • CAPE TOWN

Almost 2 miles above the desert floor east of Tehran, the Mi-26 cargo helicopter swept toward Mashhad at speeds approaching 170 miles an hour. Mashhad, however, was not its destination. Instead, the helicopter would set down at the makeshift airfield south of the Atrak from which March had first entered the country almost three weeks earlier. On arrival, the four auxiliary fuel tanks would be replaced, and the helicopter, designated as HALO by the Soviets who had so thoughtfully provided it, would continue northeast over the border and deep into the sparsely populated floodplains of Turkmenistan.

Jason March, sleeping lightly in a seat reinforced with ceramic plating, was one of two passengers on the flight. The other passenger sat across the wide, empty aisle, and stared out into the impenetrable night as a number of thoughts churned through his mind.

Saif al-Adel was, if nothing else, a pragmatic individual. This mindset had been constantly reinforced by his discovery of many years ago: that whispered words of friendship could solve almost any problem. Especially when those words were followed by a bullet. Over the years he had taken more lives than he could count, both directly and indirectly. Now, for the first time in his life, he was imbued with the idea that his own future might rest in another man's hands. The thought did not sit well with him.

If he was to choose poorly here, all of his past achievements would quickly be forgotten. The accomplishments were many, and he was proud of each in different ways. He recalled his early years as a volunteer in the fledgling Islamic Jihad movement, one of many ignorant youths shouting slogans in the dusty streets after the assassination of Anwar Sadat.

That he could see the truth of his world at twenty years of age was a constant source of pride for Saif al-Adel.

After that came deeper involvement and growing responsibility as the lesser candidates returned to the mundanity of everyday life that was children, work, and fastidious saving so that they might pretend to be something other than sheep for one week a year on the overcrowded beaches of Quseir.

Saif would rather die than be commonplace. Time and time again he had proven his courage and leadership. He remembered a crowded storage facility on the Indus River, nervous laughter as the command wires were routed up toward the driver's seat on a warm November afternoon. He remembered embracing his subordinate, the man who would drive the vehicle into the embassy at Islamabad, and he recalled the silence that hung over the room with the harsh smell of cigarette smoke as they waited for word of his success.

Thirteen dead on that attempt, but they missed the ambassador to Pakistan. A minor victory, nothing more. In 1996, a major role in the bombing of the Khobar Towers complex, which set the stage for his greatest personal accomplishment to date. After Khalil's unexplained death on a dusty mountain road in Syria, an opening higher in the organization had become available. The success in Dhahran brought the name of Saif al-Adel to the Director's attention. Word filtered down that he had been noticed, that he was to be given operational command for two simultaneous strikes, attacks on foreign targets that would bring the West to its knees.

At first he had made a show of his doubt, and used it to shield his personal desire. Like any man without a conscience, he was a natural actor. *I am far too young,* he had said. *The chance will go to a proven leader.* The commanders quietly praised his modesty and self-effacement. Then the summons came, and it was in his nature to view the choice not as a reward, but as an opportunity. For almost two years afterward he had made the preparations. The painstaking acquisition of almost 1,300 pounds of TNT, the rental and false registration of the numerous storage facilities where it would be stored, the training and motivation of the bombers who would meet Allah without knowing what they had accomplished. All of it lay on al-Adel's shoulders, and it had been a major victory against the infidels. The operation had resulted in 224 dead, including dozens of Americans.

His mind snapped back to the present as the helicopter shook with the power of the twin Lotarev D-136 turbines that drove the massive, eight-blade rotor overhead. All that he had accomplished would mean nothing if the American was not what he seemed. Despite the narcissism that rose to dizzying heights within his own mind, al-Adel was not immune to his own faults. He could see that he wanted to impress the American by granting him the audience he had requested. For that, al-Adel could stand to blame himself. The Director did not appear on a whim; he was constantly on guard against the U.S. soldiers creeping east over the parched landscape, the newest brood of Afghan soldiers loyal to the West, and the inevitable traitors within his own organization. To ensure his presence, a valid reason must be given to justify the risk of exposure.

This he had explained to the American, and the reason was a plan. For Saif, that simple explanation was enough. He had been stunned when the news came that 92 lay dead outside the Kennedy-Warren, and knew at once that he had underestimated the man's capabilities. Al-Adel had greater faith in the American than he would have admitted to.

He believed that the man could get to the president. He also knew that an operation of that magnitude would require the Director's approval. It was on the hinge of this knowledge that al-Adel made his decision. If the plan was not worthy, and the American was not congratulated for his brilliance, then Saif would personally drag him out of the camp and shoot him before receiving his own bullet.

With this comforting thought, Saif al-Adel joined his fellow passenger in a dreamless sleep as the helicopter cut fast through the
night toward the shimmering waters of the Caspian Sea.

Goddamn Ryan Kealey. Naomi was on the roof once again, and
the sun was just as merciless as it had been the day before. There
wasn't a cloud in the sky. She had spent most of the morning cursing
Ryan under her breath, while periodically checking to make sure that
her radio wasn't transmitting. He had rented the 20-foot catamaran
early in the day, but then relegated her to the roof once more after
explaining that it wasn't enough to cover one side of the building.

Easy for him to say, she thought. *He's out on the water with a decent breeze and I'm stuck baking up here.* The silver Mercedes had
arrived on cue in the morning and had not moved since. Even the
delivery boy had failed to make his sole contribution to the day's
events. Naomi felt her body growing numb from inactivity as the
minute hand on her watch continued its endless circle.

The hours of silence were painful to her. It would have been better if she'd been able to talk to Ryan, but his orders had been strict:
stay off the radio unless you have something to report. She knew
herself well enough to admit that Ryan's imperious behavior was not
the real reason for her current mood.

She forced his face out of her mind and tried to concentrate on
the building below. She felt herself drifting as the hours passed, and
it was with a start that she looked up to see the heavy doors of the
warehouse crack open. The night had moved in, and a full moon cast
a brilliant light down over the empty street, clearly illuminating the
face of only one man.

One man. It was the guard, and Naomi watched as he carefully
pulled the door closed and locked it behind him. He walked quickly
to the Mercedes, unlocked the door, squeezed his heavy frame into
the car, and drove away. Naomi felt the excitement rise in her chest
as she groped back across the rough surface of the roof for the radio.

The cold gray waters of Table Bay lifted the large boat on the gentle swells as Ryan stood at the helm, staring toward the line of warehouses jutting up from the rocky shore. His attention was focused on

the only building still illuminated at this late hour, although no motion could be seen from the brightly lit interior.

He was startled back to reality by a sudden burst of static from the radio resting on the instrument panel inside the covered cockpit.

"Ryan, pick up." He heard the urgency in her voice and reached quickly for the handset.

"Go ahead."

"The driver's gone," she said, her excitement penetrating through the harsh static. "He just drove off by himself . . . Did you hear me? He's gone. What do I do?"

Ryan's mind moved rapidly as he considered the options. "Okay, listen carefully. Go get the jeep and pull it around to the front of the building. Wait in the front seat and pull out the map like you're looking for something. If the driver comes back, hit the Selcall button twice. The radio won't make any noise on your end, but I'll get the message. Then get the hell out of there." A beat while he thought. "Make sure you bring that pack down with you. You got all that?"

"Got it."

Ryan slid the radio into his coat pocket and moved quickly back to the stern of the boat. Ripping the tarp off the small rubber dinghy, he hooked up the power cord to the portable crane and started the generator before undoing the tie-downs that secured the smaller craft to the catamaran. Looking up and across the water, he could see that the incongruous French doors tucked into the rear of the renovated warehouse were still open to the cool night air. They'd never get a better chance, he decided.

Naomi was racing through a tangled web of dark alleyways, her pounding footsteps echoing loud in the narrow space between the buildings. She fumbled for the keys as she reached the Nissan, tossed her pack into the back of the vehicle, and slid onto the cold leather of the driver's seat. The temperature had dropped rapidly after sunset, and she found herself shivering as she started the engine and pulled the jeep out of the secluded alley.

The dinghy bounced over the gentle waves, Ryan wincing at the loud rumble of the 40 hp outboard motor churning up the water behind him. He shut down the motor after a few hundred meters and let the momentum of the boat carry him into shore. Jumping out, he pulled the dinghy up behind him, almost slipping on the wet rocks beneath his feet as he moved up the beach toward the open doors.

Naomi turned off the headlights as she turned the corner and braked to a gentle halt on the street opposite Gray's building. The road was still clear as she unfolded the map and nervously fingered the radio lying by her side. *Hurry up, Ryan.*

Kealey passed through the double doors, the Walther up as he moved into the warehouse. Light from the fluorescent bulbs positioned far above erupted over the white-painted brick walls, reaching down to touch and illuminate a shining floor of lacquered oak.

Stephen Gray, seated behind an immense desk in the center of the room, was reclining comfortably in his chair, sipping at a cut-crystal glass of Chivas. He was startled by a shadow moving over the mirrorlike surface of his desk, and looked up as the dark figure entered the room.

He immediately knew that he would not survive the encounter. His buildings had been raided by the authorities many times before, but this was not how the police came, through the back entrance with silenced pistols and shadowed faces. He began to tremble as his right hand inched toward the second drawer of his desk.

He tried to recall if the revolver it held was loaded.

Ryan moved quickly to control the situation. "Stephen Gray," he said in a low, calm voice. *Reason,* he thought. *Reason with the man.* "It's nice to finally meet you. I have a few questions, if you don't mind. Stay still and keep your hands on the desk."

"Fuck you." Gray's face was twisted in anger and defiance. He started to get to his feet.

Kealey saw that reason wasn't going to get him anywhere. He moved fast around the desk before Gray could stand and put his foot hard into the man's chest.

The chair flipped backward and Gray fell violently to the floor, the air crushed out of his lungs. Gasping for breath, he got to his hands and knees before Kealey's foot slammed up into his stomach.

Gray felt his ribs crack on the second blow, and tried to curl himself into a protective ball as his vision blurred. Despite the nauseating pain, he could feel the barrel of the pistol being pressed into the base of his skull.

"I *want* to pull this trigger," Ryan snarled. "You have one chance to save yourself." He reached into his jacket pocket and pulled out a wrinkled picture, dropping it unceremoniously in front of the businessman's face. "How do you know this man?"

The silver Mercedes came fast around the corner, screeching to a halt right in front of the Nissan 4x4. The air caught in her lungs as Naomi reached for the radio and furiously punched the Selcall button. She tried to focus on the map, but the heavy driver was already out of the car, holding a bulging sack of takeout in one hand and tapping on her window with the other. The suspicion was plain in his face before she even began to lower the window.

"I swear it's the truth!"

"I don't believe you." Ryan's finger tightened on the trigger as he pressed the cold metal harder against the man's head. "That's the only name he's ever used with you?"

"I knew his father personally. You can look for yourself. Jesus, look . . . Look, just let me up. I'm not going anywhere." Any distraction would do, Gray thought to himself. *The gun is loaded, I know it is. If I can just get to it, I might have a chance.*

Ryan grabbed him by the shoulder and pulled him up roughly. Immediately, Gray moved for the desk. "It's right here, I have a file on him—"

The fist tightened around the back of Gray's shirt, pulling him back and away. "Sit down," Ryan said. He moved to the desk and started opening drawers. Turning to face the other man, he held the Smith & Wesson revolver up toward the light. "Is this what you were looking for?"

Opening the cylinder, he spilled the bullets out of the gun, the rounds rattling and rolling away across the polished floor. Casually tossing the revolver onto the desk, he moved forward in a smooth motion and slammed the butt of his own pistol into Gray's face. The impact reverberated along the length of his arm. As Ryan pulled back to deliver a second blow, the radio tucked into his pocket bumped the corner of the desk, inadvertently pressing the transmit button.

"No, I have absolutely no idea," Naomi was saying. "I think I made a wrong turn coming out of the Malay Quarter . . . I'm just trying to get back to the Commodore. Can you point it out to me? I mean, if you don't mind."

The doubt had faded slightly from the man's blunt features. Leaning forward and through the window, he began to trace a line along the map, snapping out directions in heavily accented English. His finger was tracing through the map and along her leg . . . She held the map tightly in both hands, her arms straining so that she almost ripped the thin paper in half. Her mind was moving at the speed of light. *Keep him occupied, Naomi.*

She placed her hand on the man's forearm and gave him her best smile. "I can't thank you enough. You're a lifesaver." She hit the tone perfectly, and watched the grin spread over his face as his eyes scoured her body for the first time . . .

There was a burst of static from the radio.

The driver saw something change in her face and he pulled back quickly, the lascivious smile fading fast, replaced by a sneer as he dug for the weapon in his jacket.

Naomi's hand moved down in a blur to the space between the seats, pulling up on Ryan's Beretta. She got there first. Her mind was blank as she pointed the gun at his chest and fired twice, the shots ringing in her ears as she watched him fall back, shock carved into his face.

She stumbled out of the jeep, the radio forgotten behind her. She was reaching down, searching for the man's keys, only to realize that they were in the still-running Mercedes. Naomi didn't notice the lack of blood on the driver's chest as she pulled the keys out of the car and ran to the front door of the warehouse.

The shots were audible from inside the building. Stephen Gray looked up and smiled in Ryan's direction, a bloody, awful smile. Something feral slithered into his eyes as he spoke. "You may know his name, but it won't change anything."

Ryan stepped back, still aiming the Walther at Gray's chest. "What are you talking about?"

"The shipment has already landed in Washington. It's too late to stop him. Do you understand what I'm saying? He's going after all of them. *He already has what he needs.*"

Ryan was about to respond when the door burst open. He swung his pistol and then stopped when she moved into view. Naomi ran into the building . . . All she could see was Ryan.

Gray reacted immediately. With astonishing speed he turned the corner and hit Naomi head-on, the pistol flying out of her hand and across the floor. She was stunned by the blow, struggling to stand when Gray reached past her, his fingertips brushing against the Beretta. Then it was in his hand, and he was turning up and around . . .

Kealey shot him twice in the chest. Stumbling backward, Gray hit the wall and slumped down against it. He glared up at Ryan, a thin trickle of blood running out of his mouth and down onto the clean white cotton of his shirt. He summoned the last of his strength and lifted the pistol in Naomi's direction.

Ryan had no choice. Taking two steps forward, he leveled the Walther and fired a third bullet into Stephen Gray's forehead.

He breathed a soft curse. This was going all wrong . . . His first priority was to get out of the building. Moving forward, Ryan lifted the Beretta out of the dead man's hand and slid it into his coat pocket. Naomi was crouched against the wall, staring up at him with horror in her face. Leaning down, he grabbed her arm and yanked her roughly to her feet.

"Where's the driver?"

"I shot him," she said in a low monotone. Ryan's eyes were moving fast around the room. There was a wall full of file cabinets and papers strewn across the man's desk. He thought about sending Naomi out to the boat while he looked through the papers. He thought about the probable response times for police units heading out of the commercial district, and about what they would find when they arrived. He knew instinctively that Gray wouldn't keep records of any illicit dealings in these file cabinets.

His deliberations had taken three seconds. It was too much of a risk. Besides, he already had what he came for. He grabbed Naomi's hand and pulled her hard toward the open doors leading out to the bay. A scuffling sound behind him, movement on unsteady feet. A moment of shock as he considered . . . No, it couldn't be. He didn't turn to look.

They were running hard, out through the back as a long burst of automatic fire followed them, ripping through the French doors and sending jagged splinters of glass and wood spinning out onto the beach. Ryan felt like he was barely moving as his feet pounded over the sinking sand, Naomi like dead weight behind him, her hand tightly gripping his. Another long burst of fire, and then a shouted curse in Afrikaans as the bolt locked back on an empty magazine. Ryan pushing the dinghy out over the rocks, pulling her roughly in and the engine roaring to life. The boat was going hard over the waves, slapping against the rubber floor as they jumped each swell. Two minutes later they were out of range of the driver's submachine gun, and Ryan cut back on the motor as they eased up to the rear of the catamaran.

Ryan finally forced himself to turn and look at Naomi. He was almost certain that she had been hit. He felt an overwhelming wave of relief when she didn't appear to be wounded, but it was difficult to tell; he could see only her back as she crouched facing away from him, her upper body leaning over the side as she was violently sick into the black waters of Table Bay.

CHAPTER 19

TAJIKISTAN • CAPE TOWN • PRETORIA, SOUTH AFRICA

The journey had been long and arduous, but they were now closing in on their final destination.

The most difficult part for al-Adel had been in securing more auxiliary tanks for the helicopter. It had taken shouted curses and threats of retribution in fractured Farsi over the encrypted radio, but the promise had been made and kept. The fuel tanks were waiting in a covered truck bed just off an abandoned highway north of Repetek. From there, they were free to continue on the third leg of the flight. The sky began to darken once again as the Mi-26 headed northeast, skirting the jagged western edge of Tajikistan that led toward the lush and fertile floor of the Ferghana Valley.

Saif al-Adel noticed that the American had not spoken for the entire duration of the flight. He wondered whether this was a sign that the man regretted his earlier demands, but soon dismissed the notion when he examined the other passenger's face and saw nothing but quiet confidence. Clearly, the American had unshakable faith in his own abilities.

It was some time before they banked east over the valley floor 3,500 meters below. The descent took the heavy aircraft shuddering down through dark gray cumulus clouds, a light rain washing over the armored plating as the weight of the helicopter settled onto the struts of the landing gear. The monstrous blades continued to slice the air overhead as the passengers climbed down from the elevated cabin. Al-Adel gave a hand signal to one of the two pilots through the cockpit glass, and both men moved away from the craft as power to the engines was increased and the helicopter lifted once more into the air. Then it vanished into the black clouds and they were alone.

March pulled the hood of his anorak up to shield against the freezing rain that had already seeped its way down his neck and under his thin pullover. A vehicle was waiting for them, a Russian-made UAZ-3151. Al-Adel had his rucksack on the muddy ground, his hands buried deep in the bowels of the pack until he found what he was looking for. His eyes were bright when he lifted the Garmin handheld GPS receiver for March to see.

"The Americans would dearly love to get their hands on this. I imagine they would pay a great deal of money for the information it contains. Tell me, what would that money mean to *you*, my friend?"

Jason March fixed his steady gaze on the other man before speaking. "If you think I came this far to betray you for money, then you are the fool, Saif."

"We shall see." A smile spread over the Egyptian's face as he held out his hand. "Give me your pistol."

March hesitated, and the smile turned into an impatient sneer. "Give me your pistol or I'll shoot you where you stand. Even if you survive the bullet, you won't last long—the temperature is already below freezing, and the wolves are always hungry in the winter."

Reluctantly, March handed over his Beretta. "And your pack." March gave him that as well, and watched as the other man perused the contents. Satisfied, Saif al-Adel stood and gave him a questioning look. "Food and water? Where are these plans you speak of?"

March smiled and tapped his own head gently with two fingers. An incredulous look spread over the commander's face, but it was quickly replaced by a cold gaze. "Then I hope you have a good memory, my friend. A very good memory indeed, because your life depends on what you have to say today." He threw the rucksack back toward the American, but held on to the Beretta. "Get in the jeep."

"And where are we going?"

Al-Adel turned east toward the jagged spires of the Tian Shan mountains. "Up there," he said.

Ryan had called the embassy in Pretoria from the catamaran with a request for transport. There would be hell to pay when Harper found out, but it was the only option open to him. He had briefly considered making the trip without Agency assistance, but knew that the consequences would be far worse if they were intercepted by the police without official cover. In that situation, he wouldn't have put it past Langley to completely disavow any knowledge of their presence in South Africa.

In fact, he wouldn't have expected anything less.

Despite the fact that they had nowhere else to go, Ryan realized they couldn't stay out on the water. The first police officers on the scene would take in the vehicles left on the street and the shattered doors leading out to the beach, and then rightly conclude that an escape had been made by boat. Police cutters would be dispatched with orders to board every small craft in the vicinity, and the larger docks around the bay would be sealed off. Even now, approaching the private dock of the Victoria and Albert Hotel, he could hear the sirens screaming on the other side of the bay.

Looking down at his watch, he estimated that they had at least seven hours to kill, even if the embassy car carried diplomatic plates and traveled south unimpeded as fast as possible. After docking and securing the catamaran, he found blankets in a storage compartment beneath a seat at the stern. These he stuffed haphazardly into his backpack along with more bottled water, sacrificing space for speed. Finally, he turned his attention to Naomi.

She was sitting on a hard wooden bench just aft of the cabin, hugging her knees against her chest and watching him intently. As he walked toward her, though, she pulled away from his outstretched hand.

"Naomi," he said, impatience in his voice. "There's no time for this. If you don't follow me right now, we're both going to spend a lot of time in a South African jail. You know I wouldn't hurt you. Gray had a gun—he would have killed us both without thinking twice."

After a moment she held out her hand without speaking. Ryan pulled her up off the bench and they stepped onto the dock, walking hand in hand past the bright lights of the V&A hotel and into the empty streets beyond.

The steep roads leading out of the valley gave them the most trouble as the jeep, lacking 4WD capabilities, continued to slide toward the precarious edge of the path. Several times March felt his heart in his throat as the jeep drifted in the deep mud toward the brink and a plummeting drop of several hundred meters to the valley floor. He was terrified of mountains and precipitous slopes, a fear that dated back to his childhood. He felt the cold sheen of sweat on his body and hoped that they didn't have far to go. Fortunately, they soon moved away from the lip of the valley. The route smoothed out when they reached the cut-granite roads leading into the mountains.

Although the heater was going full blast, the air was bitterly cold in the higher regions, pushed along by a howling wind that whipped over the stone outcroppings and drove the frigid gusts through unseen apertures in the vehicle's frame. As the elevation continued to climb, the rain turned to sleet, and then to a driving snow that made progress even more difficult.

"Do you see that?" March followed al-Adel's finger to a small stone structure perched on a rock outcropping at least 100 meters above the road. The building blended into the surrounding mountains so well that he would never have seen it on his own. "It is one of our observation points—only one of several. This is the only passable mountain road for 10 kilometers in any direction. That is why this place was chosen. If the Americans come, we will have ample time to evacuate the camp."

"It's a good location," March conceded. He could see that there were other advantages as well; even those cruise missiles with the greatest range, the Tomahawks and the Harpoons, would not be able to reach the landlocked base from the North Sea. Additionally, incoming aircraft would be forced to cross the airspace of numerous countries in order to mount an attack. It would be difficult to get the consent of each government to do so. "It must be hard to direct the organization from here, though."

Al-Adel nodded in agreement. "The unit commanders have been delegated a great deal of responsibility. Approval for missions is now granted by myself, or by Abu Fatima. You would know him as al-Zawahiri. He is a great man—I have known him for almost twenty years."

The Egyptian fell silent as he consulted the Garmin navigation system once more. "We're almost there," he said. The space between the jagged rocks bordering the path began to narrow, and March could faintly hear the low rumble of a diesel engine over the screaming wind. Soon the outline of a track vehicle appeared through breaks in the snow, and then the formidable sight of a 100mm turret-mounted main gun pointed down the road in the direction of the approaching jeep. Al-Adel slowed to a stop and waited as a young man climbed out of the rear hatch and trudged heavily through the snow toward their vehicle, holding an AK-74 rifle and a portable radio. Several words were exchanged between the guard and al-Adel in rapid-fire Arabic, and then the young soldier spoke into his radio.

After the guard had completed a cursory inspection of the jeep, the BMP-3 infantry carrier was rolled back to allow them to pass. The road led into a small clearing contained on three sides by towering granite walls that kept out much of the inclement weather. The clearing was dominated by a large canvas tent powered by a command vehicle and its generator, both of which were miniscule by comparison. Two more soldiers of the Taliban stood guard outside the imposing shelter, but otherwise the clearing was devoid of human life.

After leaving the jeep, al-Adel and March approached the tent slowly, careful to keep their hands in plain view. One soldier checked them for weapons, taking both of al-Adel's while the other stood back and covered the two arrivals with his rifle. Once again a quick conference was held by radio, and then the tent flap was pulled back to allow both men to enter.

Ryan and Naomi walked for twenty minutes before he found a suitable location just opposite the predetermined collection point. The alley entrance was just below a recently installed streetlight, and the glare of the bulb made all but the first few feet of the black corridor impenetrable to the eye. The space between the brick walls of the buildings was perhaps 4 feet wide, and dominated by the smell of rotting garbage in close proximity. The stench was slightly quelled by a cool breeze that felt like an arctic wind in the narrow confines of the alleyway.

He moved deep into the dark space before pulling one of the two blankets from his pack and folding it into thirds. He placed the neat square of material on the litter-strewn ground and pulled Naomi down onto the makeshift seat. Then he reached for the second blanket and draped it over her, watching with satisfaction as she pulled the coarse wool around her body. After taking his own seat on the rough cement several feet away, Ryan focused his attention on the road adjacent to the alleyway and tried to ignore the biting cold.

After a few minutes he turned to check on Naomi and found her watching him, the luminous green eyes clearly visible even in the shadowed confines of the alley. He could also see that she was shivering hard, the thick material having fallen down from around her shoulders. Sliding over, he wrapped the blanket even tighter around her, and then pulled her shaking body close to his. After another moment she relaxed and rested her head gently on his shoulder.

"Ryan?"

"Hmmm?"

"When you shot him, did you feel anything?"

"What do you mean?"

"Is it hard for you? I mean, killing someone?"

"Yes."

"That's a lie," she mumbled after a moment. He did not respond. "I watched your face when you pulled the trigger . . . There was nothing there."

Her eyelids were growing heavy, and she pushed herself tighter into his body as the sleep began to wash over her like a warm sea. "What was the little girl's name, Ryan?"

He felt his muscles stiffen with apprehension. He did not want to remember that, to remember what they had done to her. It had taken so long to forget . . .

"It's not right, you know. It's not right that you feel nothing when you take a life . . ." A long pause. "The girl in Bosnia. What was her name?"

"Safiya," he finally said. Her head was dipped, her face hidden from view. She could not have known the pain it caused him. "Her name was Safiya."

"Thank you." The words were so soft that he almost missed them.

Once again he stayed silent, and after a few minutes heard her breathing settle into the soft rhythm of sleep. Looking down, Kealey found her features hidden by layers of lustrous hair falling about her face. Only her nose was visible, the very tip peeking through the black waves. Instinctively, he pulled her even closer, turning his head away from the alley's entrance just as a police car screamed past.

He willed the hours to pass and waited for the image of a young girl's torn body to fade from his mind.

The air was warm and thick inside the tent, the combined effects of an overworked space heater and the trapped odor of men who had not bathed in weeks. There was a section separated from the sleeping quarters by a threadbare blanket hung from a wooden pole. The makeshift curtain was not pulled all the way across, and March could see the communications gear set up on a wooden fold-out table. A soldier wearing a headset was seated before the array of equipment. *Monitoring the radio net,* he thought. He'd done the same thing many years before.

There was a flurry of activity in another cordoned section and two men emerged, one with a rifle in his hands. The other carried no weapon, and wore a thick woolen sweater over a linen shirt and wrinkled dress pants. The eyes behind the simple steel-frame spectacles were bleary with lack of sleep, but March could still easily identify the distrustful gaze that was aimed in his direction. The younger man with the rifle watched March carefully as his superior pulled al-Adel aside and began speaking rapid French in forceful tones.

March was fluent in the language, a fact that he had never revealed in al-Adel's presence. He clearly understood that the older man was angry with Saif for bringing him into the mountains. Abruptly, the man turned to speak to March in cultured English. "Do you know who I am?"

"Of course."

"Why have you come here?"

"To speak with the Emir." March tilted his head a fraction to the left and appraised the man who stood before him: Dr. Ayman al-Zawahiri, the Director's private physician and closest confidante. March knew it was widely suspected in Western intelligence circles that this man had died several years earlier in an air raid over southwestern Afghanistan. "I thought Saif would have explained this to you. I do not think it is too much to ask, considering what I have contributed to your organization."

"What you have contributed," the physician repeated, an edge to his voice. A short, barking laugh as he turned to al-Adel in amusement, and then back to the American. "What have you done that is so special? I was fighting the jihad from an Egyptian jail when your mother was dressing you for school. The death of a politician, the destruction of an empty building . . . These are your grand accomplishments? That is all you have to offer?"

"It is more than your entire organization has achieved in four years," March pointed out. He watched the arrogant smirk fade, slowly replaced by a strangely indifferent expression.

The older man turned to the junior soldier with the rifle and issued a command in French. Before the last word left his mouth, March had taken three lightning-fast steps forward to deliver a vicious blow to the young man's throat. The soldier's iron grip on the rifle slipped as his hands shot to his neck, groping at his crushed windpipe, his eyes bulging wide. March pulled the weapon out of the air, ejected the magazine, and snapped the round out of the chamber before the clip hit the ground. Only then was al-Adel screaming for security. The American's hands were out and open, the rifle disarmed at his feet as the two soldiers standing guard outside pulled back the flap and moved quickly into the tent.

March ignored the muzzles held to his head and the violent Arabic curses. He ignored the tortured choking sounds of the dying soldier. He stared straight into the shock-ridden face of Ayman al-Zawahiri before speaking again.

"I won't let you give that order," March said, making no attempt to hide the snarl in his fluent French. "I didn't come this far to lose my life at the hand of some pimple-faced child. You would be the one dying now if it pleased me to see it happen. I am here to give you an opportunity, perhaps the greatest of your life. Trust me when I tell you to take it. If nothing else, I should have your trust by now."

The rifles did not waver. There was complete silence in the room. Finally, the physician gave a hand signal and the soldiers slowly lowered their weapons. "Check him again," he said, waving absently at one of the fighters. He studied March intently, his face wiped clean of any emotion. "My trust is not so easily won."

One of the young men stepped forward nervously and patted him down at arm's length. The boy on the ground was moving slower than before, the spastic movements coming less frequently now that he was almost out of air. The nineteen-year-old fighter conducting the search saw that the American did not once look down at the destruction he had caused. He finished as quickly as possible and retreated into the communications room, immediately pulling the curtain back behind him.

Al-Zawahiri lifted his chin in March's direction and said, "Follow me." March was surprised when the man turned toward the entrance leading back outside. He was so surprised that he did not immediately take note of Saif al-Adel's body next to his, the pale face moving in close, hissing words and flecks of spittle into his ear.

"You are a dead man, American. *Dead.* I swear it to you."

There was nothing he could say. He ignored Saif and followed al-Zawahiri across the bleak clearing toward a cavernous opening carved deep into the mountainside.

"Mr. Kealey? Ms. Kharmai? The ambassador will see you now."

Ryan stood with Naomi and followed Gillian Farris, the deputy chief of mission, through the large, oak-paneled doors leading into the ambassador's spacious office. Henry Martins stood up from behind his desk politely as they entered, but there was no trace of a smile on the broad, weathered face. Martins had nearly thirty years of experience in the Foreign Service, but had never before dealt with a situation quite like the one he currently faced. He did not relish the opportunity to do so now.

"Please, take a seat," he said. He walked around the desk and joined them in the small seating area, easing his weight wearily into one of the several comfortable armchairs. Ryan watched in surprise as Martins poured them each coffee from a small carafe on the low center table. Finally, he looked up to study them from beneath hooded eyelids.

"I received a call thirty minutes ago from the Minister of Foreign Affairs. He's been on the phone with the chief of the South African Police Service . . . Evidently, the only vehicle found outside of the warehouse was a silver Mercedes sedan leased three years ago by one of Stephen Gray's holding companies. That will go on the police report, by the way."

Ryan breathed a soft sigh of relief and saw the tension drain out of Naomi's shoulders. The Nissan must have been taken by Gray's injured bodyguard. It was definitely a break; the vehicle would have linked them directly to the scene. Although they were traveling under assumed identities, it was one less thing that might come back on them at a later date. "What about the driver?" he asked.

The ambassador raised his thick eyebrows and settled back slightly, the chair creaking in protest against his shifting weight. "Nowhere to be found. The police won't be looking too hard, either." He took a long sip of coffee before continuing: "It should be said that this won't come cheaply. President Mbeke will be leaning on us for favors in the months to come, and he'll get much of what he asks for. You were under orders to question Gray quietly, as I understand it."

"That's right. He wasn't very forthcoming."

"Clearly. I've spoken with Jonathan Harper as well—he'll have some choice words for both of you when you hit stateside. He's not a happy man. Director Andrews is coming under heavy fire from the president. Privately, of course. It's a miracle that this little debacle escaped notice of the press. I hope you at least got what you were looking for."

Ryan nodded in the affirmative. "I have a name for you, sir: William Paulin Vanderveen. I know I'm in no position to be making requests here, but I really need your best people working on this. I need family history, anybody he might still have contact with. If that looks promising, then I need surveillance. Most of all I need photographs; I have to verify that March and Vanderveen are one and the same."

Ambassador Martins was nodding slowly, his gaze alternating between the two CIA officers. "You two were placed in a difficult situation there. I can sympathize with that, but you're asking a lot."

"Sir, the South African government has a good reason to pitch in here," Naomi pointed out. "No offense, but the embassy's resources just won't cut it. We've got to put the SA police to work. Vanderveen is a citizen of this country, and responsible for the murder of more than a hundred people. You might want to make sure they understand what that headline would look like on the front page of the *New York Times*—we really need all the help we can get. Besides, they won't be getting any favors at all if President Brenneman has to carry all the weight for these attacks."

There was the hint of a smile at the ambassador's mouth. "You don't pull any punches, Ms. Kharmai. But I agree, they do have a certain responsibility in this matter. I'll push for you on one condition: you don't leave this embassy unless you're getting on an airplane. Deal?"

"You'll have no argument there. I think we're both ready to get back to Washington," Ryan said.

"Good. I'll start making some calls."

Martins stood up, indicating that the conversation was over. Both CIA officers rose to their feet as well, moving toward the door, which the ambassador graciously opened for them.

"I want both of you to get some rest," he said as they moved out into the anteroom. Farris was waiting for them along with Aaron Jansen, the ambassador's private secretary. "We found a couple spare beds—Gillian will show you where to find them. Oh, and the deputy director wants to hear from you, Kealey. Anything more from Washington, Aaron?" Ryan watched the young man shake his head. "Okay, good. Ms. Farris will find you a secure telephone. I should have some information for you later in the day. We'll get you a change of clothes and the basic necessities as well."

"Thank you, sir."

The ambassador acknowledged Ryan's gratitude with a slight nod and retreated back into his office, closing the door softly behind him.

"I bet you two could use some sleep," Gillian Farris said with a smile. "Follow me. Aaron, Minister Zuma wants some time this afternoon. Can we clear the ambassador's schedule for an hour at three?"

"Sure, Ms. Farris." The secretary smiled pleasantly. "I had the head of embassy security penciled in, but I can bump him back to tomorrow."

"Okay, great." She left Jansen behind in the anteroom and led them through the building toward the staff temporary quarters. "This used to be the press room, but we converted it to make space for the additional security personnel after the bombings in Tanzania and Kenya," she explained. "It's not much, but it's all we have available at the minute. Anyway, here are your keys—I'll come and find you in about five hours."

"Thanks," Ryan said. "We appreciate it."

The DCM smiled and turned back toward the main building, leaving them alone in the brightly lit corridor.

"See you in a few, Naomi." He pushed into his room without looking back down the hall. A moment later he heard her door open and then slam shut. Sitting down on the edge of the hard mattress, he shook his head and reached for the receiver of the secure telephone.

Aaron Jansen had served as the ambassador's private secretary for ten months. It was his first posting and a good one; most Foreign Service officers found themselves in obscure locations filling out low-level paperwork for the first few years of their career. Jansen owed his success to a Yale degree earned magna cum laude and his father's wide-ranging influence. Despite his privileged upbringing, Jansen was used to the long hours and the heavy responsibility of his current position. He was accustomed to planning the ambassador's schedule down to the most minute details. Jansen was young, handsome, and affable. He always had a joke or a kind word for his coworkers, especially the women. He was popular within the embassy walls, and he enjoyed his work.

The gate guards were well acquainted with the secretary's strolls into the city center. He never came out of the embassy at the same time, owing to the ambassador's unpredictable schedule. Sometimes he would walk across the broad expanse of cement in late afternoon, when the heat swelled and the air-conditioning was going full blast in the gatehouse. Other times he would make an appearance in the evening, when the sun had dipped behind the pale stone of the city's skyline and the air was cool and inviting.

On only one morning each week did the secretary leave the building at precisely 8:30 AM. The young marine stationed outside the embassy watched as Jansen ambled across the circular driveway, the polished shoes shining in the hazy morning sun. The corporal, young and impressionable, snapped to attention as Jansen approached.

"Good morning, sir."

Aaron Jansen smiled easily and shook his head in mock disappointment. "Corporal, I'm only about two years older than you are. I keep telling you to cut that out. How are you doing?"

"Just fine, sir, thank you."

Another rueful smile. "Well, I guess there's no convincing you. I'm just going to get some air . . . Give me about twenty minutes."

"Sounds good, sir. Do you have your identification with you?"

"Always."

"Okay, I'll call it in, then." The corporal was attentive to detail, which was how he'd earned his position in the first place. He called in the departure time to the operations center and made a note in his log before opening the electronic gate reserved for pedestrian traffic. "See you in a few, Mr. Jansen."

"Catch you later, Corporal." The secretary passed out into the busy street. He turned left from the embassy and walked down Pretorius, trying his best to avoid the crowded mass of humanity that lined the main artery running through the heart of the city.

The interior of the cave was tall and wide, but not deep. The only lighting was dim, emanating from oil lanterns that hung from the wet stone of the walls. It was also surprisingly warm, perhaps owing to the large number of young Taliban soldiers who were gathered in the dark space. They cradled small arms in their laps and listened intently, apparently oblivious to the discomfort of the rough dirt floor on which they sat. Each weapon had been cleared before they were allowed into the cave. Their collective attention was focused on the man who stood before them, his voice shaking with emotion as the words echoed in their ears:

"Praise be to Allah, that he has delivered you, the sons of Mohammad, into my welcoming arms. We ask that Allah forgive our wrongdoings, for He in His Greatness knows that the jihad cannot be fought by one man alone, and that we challenge an immoral enemy whose sins are far greater than ours. We bear witness to the atrocities that have been wrought at the hands of the Zionists and those who seek their alliance . . ."

"*Omin!*" The thundering voices were as one, rippling back over the man who beseeched them in a calm, measured cadence.

"Have our brothers and sisters not suffered? The children of Palestine, persecuted by the murderous Jews, have they not suffered? And where is the outcry, why is there no fatwa issued? The time of Western imperialism is at an end, my friends—"

"*Yaum al akhir! Omin!*"

March pushed his blond hair up under his raised balaclava and sneaked a glance at the men who flanked him. Al-Adel's lips were slightly parted, the eyes blazing. He was staring wondrously at the man who held the crowd in the palm of his hand. Turning to his right, March saw that al-Zawahiri was wearing a similar expression.

It was just beginning to dawn on him that he was in an exceptionally dangerous place.

"They seek to spread their poison, and their arm grows longer with each passing day. We have been chosen by Allah to crush that arm . . . We have seen the slaughter in Burma, Fatani, Chechnya, and Bosnia Herzegovina. We have seen our homeland run red with the blood of innocents. They have turned their backs on our holy crusade, my brothers—"

"*Aiwa!*"

"They spit their laughter as though we are nothing—"

"*Aiwa!*"

"We ask Allah to guide us in this time of peril, in this time of hardship. He alone knows what we have endured, and He calls out for vengeance, He seeks to incur His Wrath—"

"*Aiwa! Al Baseer, wa tayyibato!*"

"We place our fate in His hands, for He is the Most Capable, and the Light that we seek. My brothers, Allah wept tears of joy when the

Americans lost their twin pillars of debauchery in New York, their monuments to greed and the suffering of His chosen people—"

"*AIWA, SHAYKH!*"

March felt a surge of adrenaline at the man's words, and the quiet assurance with which they were delivered.

"My word is the truth, and you will hear it now. We will not rest until our Palestinian brothers have driven the Jews into the sea, and the infidel armies have been routed from the land of Mohammad, peace be unto him—"

"*As salamo alaina.*"

"And this is the only path, for it is said, '*If you meet those who reject, then strike the necks.*' It is Allah's will, and He stands behind you in all His glory. There will be much rejoicing by our people when the heathens in the West feel the full measure of His Fury, and so it will be until all Muslims live together as one in His Kingdom. Praise be to Allah."

"*Subhana Rabbi yal A'la.*"

"Go in peace, my brothers."

The gathered fighters jumped to their feet, their shining eyes locked onto every movement of the man as they burst into wild applause. They watched in pure adoration as he climbed down painfully from the elevated stone outcropping at the back of the cave, waving to them like a visiting dignitary, and was immediately surrounded by a cluster of bodyguards, trustworthy veterans whose service dated back to the Soviet occupation of Afghanistan.

The applause continued to grow even after the speaker had turned a corner and was swept from view. Soon it was an incredible wave, the clamorous noise reverberating from the jagged granite walls like thunder.

Saif al-Adel wiped tears from his eyes and turned to the American. It was a new look, a side of the Arab that he had not yet seen . . . In this place, March wore the face of the enemy. He braced himself, waiting for the pain of a knife or a bullet from behind, but there was nothing. A surge of relief coursed through his body as he decided that he was safe for the moment. Belatedly, he pulled the balaclava down to hide his face from the crowd.

"Remember what I said, American. He has no love for you or your kind. Is that not obvious now? Maybe you begin to understand the risk you have taken in coming here."

"You brought me, Saif," March whispered gleefully. "It's your neck, too." He did not stop to watch the color drain from the Egyptian's face, turning instead to follow al-Zawahiri into the hidden depths of the cave. March had waited for this audience for three years, and now he was within minutes of meeting, in his eyes, the greatest man on the face of the earth.

Aaron Jansen was not in a hurry, and it was a beautiful day. He walked slowly east through the clamorous streets, enjoying the vibrant sounds of a busy city. He stopped at a coffee shop painted a brilliant white; the sun was so bright off the shining surface that it hurt his eyes just to look at it. He sipped at the warm coffee as he continued past the Caledonian Sports Ground, stopping once more to briefly watch the last few minutes of a vigorous soccer game played out between two groups of young men.

The jovial shouts of the players followed Jansen as he passed under the canopy of jacaranda trees that had sprung up alongside the playing fields. The cool shade felt good on his back as he waded through the riotous color of the purple blossoms that had fallen from the trees above. With his customary consideration for his host country, Jansen tossed his empty cup into a trash receptacle and stopped at a cluster of pay phones facing away from the fields.

He had long since memorized the number, a fifteen-digit monstrosity that had given him some trouble during the first tentative months of his treachery. Through a quick check on the Internet, he had discovered that the international calling code placed the receiving line somewhere in the Paraná province of Brazil. That was as far as he dared to take his inquiries, though. For Jansen, ignorance was bliss, and ignorance was a numbered account in a Zurich bank that had been growing steadily for the past six months.

The line was picked up after a single ring. "*Quem você se está chamando para?*"

"I'm calling for the Rodriguez Holding Company."

The voice on the other end abruptly changed from rapid Portuguese to flat, unaccented English. "Go ahead."

"One name, two descriptions. This is in relation to the shooting death of Stephen Gray . . . the name is Kealey. Male, five foot ten inches to six feet, one-hundred and seventy pounds, black hair, gray eyes. No name for the woman, but she's a British national of Indian descent, five foot four inches or five foot five inches, slim, black hair, and green eyes. Best guess: CIA, based out of Langley. They're due back in Washington today. I would have more, but—"

"Your information will be passed on. Thank you for calling." The voice was gone, the phone dead in his ear. Jansen replaced the receiver with a shaking hand and smoothed his hair. The entire exchange had taken nine seconds.

The money was nice. The money was very nice, but he knew he would not sleep that night at all. Aaron Jansen turned in his tracks and began the long walk back to the embassy.

Ryan had called Jonathan Harper first. It had been a brief conversation, not that there was much back and forth. He had given the deputy director the name of William Vanderveen, and then listened to a barrage of angry denigrations. After five minutes, Harper had run out of steam and reluctantly congratulated Ryan on a job well done.

The next call had been to Katie back in Cape Elizabeth. That one had been a little bit trickier, since he didn't really have a good excuse for not calling in six days. There was no screaming or accusations from her end, though in some ways, it was far more painful to endure her quiet disappointment. He vowed that he would make it up to her once he got back to the East Coast. It would piss Harper off even more if he went straight back to Maine after a brief appearance at Langley, but Ryan knew where his priorities lay.

It had just taken him a while to figure it out.

There had been no mention of Naomi, from her end or his. He hoped that Katie had enough trust in him not to worry about it, but that sounded stupid, even in his own head. He had kissed her . . . No, that wasn't right. Naomi had kissed *him*. But he hadn't exactly stopped it in a hurry, had he? Ryan cut the thought off quickly and decided to get some sleep.

*   *   *

It seemed like only a few minutes later when he heard a knock at the door. Gillian Farris poked her head in, her fiery red hair in sharp contrast with the plain white wall behind her.

"The ambassador would like to see you in twenty minutes, Mr. Kealey," she said. "I've already woken Ms. Kharmai—can I tell him you'll be there?"

Ryan laughed and rubbed the sleep from his eyes. "Call me Ryan, Ms. Farris. And yes, you can tell him I'll be there. It wouldn't be a good idea to keep the ambassador waiting, would it? Any chance of some breakfast?"

"It's more like lunch now, but we'll find something for you." Her eyes drifted over his bare chest and washboard abs. "You might want to put a shirt on too, Ryan. The ambassador probably doesn't appreciate those long hours in the gym as much as I do," she said with a wink and an engaging smile. She pulled back from the open door and closed it behind her.

As her footsteps receded down the hall, Ryan snapped his open mouth shut and burst into laughter, shaking his head in amusement. That *was* a story he could tell Katie, if only to get a laugh out of her jealous reaction. He stepped into the adjoining bathroom and showered quickly, then shaved and brushed his teeth before dressing in the clothes that the embassy staff had left for him earlier in the day. He decided that the DCM had probably picked the clothes out herself, since they were in good taste and fit remarkably well.

There was another knock at the door just as he pulled his shirt on. Naomi was waiting for him in the hall.

"Hey," he said. "Sleep okay?"

"No," was her blunt response. He locked the door behind him and they began walking toward the embassy's main building. "What did the DDO have to say?"

"He wanted to know how I got the Beretta through airport security. I told him to go and ask the guys in Science and Technology. Apart from that, he bitched for a while, then said we did a good job."

She laughed without mirth. "That sounds about right. I don't think we really accomplished anything, though."

He turned to look at her in surprise. "Why do you say that?"

"Well, what do we really know now that we didn't know before? His real name? It's not like that'll be the one he's using. And I don't buy into this surveillance business—I'm pretty sure that someone who's managed to avoid capture for eight years won't be going home to see his nieces and nephews just for the hell of it. He's too smart for that."

Ryan didn't respond as they approached the ambassador's anteroom, and Naomi relented a little bit. "I'm sorry, it *is* something. We might be able to—"

"No," he said, waving her apology away. "You're right." He fell silent for a moment. "You know what the last thing Gray said to me was?"

"No, I didn't hear."

"He said, 'The shipment has already landed in Washington. It's too late to stop him. He's going after all of them.' "

She turned to look at him. "What do you think that means—'all of them'? All of who?"

"Think about it, Naomi. Senator Levy was killed because he forged an alliance with the French and the Italians. Who's coming to Washington in November?"

"Chirac and Berlusconi." Her eyes opened wide as she caught on. "Oh my God, do you really think . . . ?"

Ryan shrugged. "Why else would he take the risk? It would have to be something big. Like I said before, he's a huge asset to Al-Qaeda. They wouldn't chance losing him on a minor operation."

"But it's suicide," she objected. "It's impossible to kill the president of the United States—let alone two other national leaders at the same time—and just walk away."

They reached the anteroom and Ryan pulled the door open for her. "Naomi, Jason March is one of the most dangerous men the U.S. military has ever produced," he said. "If anyone can get away with it, it's him."

They moved deeper into the bowels of the cave.

The wind rushing over the razor peaks of the Tian Shan mountains was only a distant roar in the black tunnels that continued down in a seemingly endless circle. The air was far colder away from the cave's entrance, and March found himself shivering violently as he blindly followed Ayman al-Zawahiri. He kept his hands slightly out in front of him to avoid running into any walls, but was more concerned with the fact that Saif al-Adel was less than two steps to his rear. He could not help but wonder if he was being led to his own grave.

His fears, however, were somewhat abated by the appearance of a dull light in the distance. As they moved closer to the opening, al-Zawahiri turned awkwardly in the narrow space and murmured brief instructions.

"Wait here. I will call for you when he is ready."

March nodded and leaned back against the damp wall as the physician disappeared through an entrance carved into the earth. To his surprise, al-Adel did not take the opportunity to issue more muted threats. He wouldn't have had much of a chance, in any case, as the older man returned a moment later, his considerable girth outlined in the opening by the faint light at his back.

"He will see you now, American. Saif, you are needed above. Your presence is not required here."

March did not turn to humor himself with al-Adel's stunned expression, although he dearly wanted to. Instead, he took a deep breath to calm his shaking hands and took his first tentative step toward the light.

Ryan was instantly wary when he and Naomi sat down across from Ambassador Martins. The man was clearly disturbed about something.

"I hope you two slept well." They both watched as the ambassador poured coffee with a shaking hand. "I apologize," he said, "but the inquiries I put out this morning have not yielded positive results."

He cleared his throat and went on. "That is not to say we have not learned anything. The problem is that we've underestimated just how dangerous this man really is. I've already forwarded copies of the information we gathered to the FBI and the Justice Department. I thought they needed to see it right away." The ambassador pushed a folder across the table, which Ryan immediately picked up and opened. "Those are photographs of William Vanderveen as a young man. There aren't many—apparently he was somewhat camera shy. We couldn't find many people to corroborate that statement, though, because . . ."

Ryan could see right away that March and Vanderveen were the same person. He was so lost in the photographs that he almost didn't catch the ambassador's awkward pause. "Because what, sir?"

"Because everyone in his immediate family is dead."

Naomi choked on her coffee, but Ryan didn't notice. His attention was completely focused on Martins.

"Don't jump to any conclusions," Martins continued. "There was never any concrete evidence that Vanderveen was responsible. Our closest guess is that he fled the country in 1981. I can't tell you what he did after he arrived in the States, but the South African government has been very cooperative in piecing together their records. Their only stipulation was that the information didn't go public, and I said we were more than happy to agree. This story could be extremely embarrassing to the army, not to mention the country as a whole."

"I need to hear it all, sir."

And so the ambassador began.

The bolt-hole was small, far too small for three people to stretch out comfortably. The two men inside were each seated on an olive green military cot. The two cots were positioned next to a small space heater, and al-Zawahiri pointed to a third when Vanderveen entered the room. He took a seat and waited patiently. It was not his place to speak first.

The physician pulled a thermos from a pack on the hard dirt floor. He proceeded to pour hot tea into a metal canteen cup, which he then handed to his superior. Vanderveen watched as the cup was gratefully accepted by unsteady hands.

The man took a sip of the warm liquid and smiled weakly, finally looking up at his guest. "We find small pleasures here . . . They are the only kind to be had."

Will Vanderveen nodded his understanding, but did not speak. Al-Zawahiri was looking at him with something approaching approval. Vanderveen wondered what had caused the sudden change of heart.

"I trust no one more than Ayman. I have heard on the radio of your victories, and he tells me what you have done. He says there is an arrogance in you . . ." The Director waited for the American to speak, and seemed pleased when he did not. "That is immaterial to me, in any case. By your actions you have demonstrated your loyalty. Allah's blessings and salutations be with you, my brother."

"And with you," he said automatically.

The infamous half smile appeared at the Director's mouth. "Do you make a mockery of my faith, American?"

A sharp intake of air, but the awkward moment was free of panic. Vanderveen understood fear, even felt it on very rare occasions. Fear of other men, though, had never entered into the equation. "No, Emir. I only wanted to demonstrate my respect. I apologize if I offended you."

The apology was ignored. "You speak my language well, but there is something of the Helabja Valley in your accent . . . or perhaps not. Perhaps I am mistaken."

A long hesitation, which peaked the interest of his inquisitors. *Only the truth,* Vanderveen decided. *They may know more than they're letting on.* "I trained Kurdish insurgents in the Helabja when I was with the army."

The Director savored another long sip of tea, and gestured from his canteen cup to the American. Immediately, al-Zawahiri poured another cup, handed it to Vanderveen, and then poured a third for himself.

"I understand that you are reluctant to speak of your past. This is the habit of men who have things to hide."

"I cannot deny that, Emir. However, the things I have seen, the things I know . . . They could only prove useful to you."

This sentence was received with a sudden spark of interest. The Director leaned forward slightly, grimacing at the pain in his chest. He caught the American's reaction.

"Don't be concerned, my friend. Your countrymen came close three years ago. Too close, but I have changed my ways since then."

"They are not my countrymen," he spat.

The Director lifted an eyebrow in amusement. "No? You fought with them. Is that not so? You killed for them. What else could they be?"

Vanderveen ignored the question. By doing so, he knew that he took a tremendous risk. "I assume al-Adel has told you about our friend Shakib?"

The tall man stared at him for a long time before answering. *So the arrogance is there, after all.* "I was told that he had some information. Nothing more."

Vanderveen smiled in satisfaction. "It is much more than information, Emir. It is a means to an end. I have in my possession a two-month advance itinerary for the president of the United States, as well as presidential briefings compiled by the American Secret Service."

Both men stared at him in shock, unable to conceal their amazement. Al-Zawahiri's head was swimming with the enormity of the statement. It was a few moments before he could put his finger on what was bothering him: it was the way the man referred to "Americans" with detachment, as though they were a separate breed from himself. But this man *was* an American, was he not? "Why have we not already heard about this?"

A shrug. "It is not the kind of information that can be passed on lightly. Complete security can only be guaranteed in a face-to-face meeting such as this one."

"You fail to understand, my friend, that these plans would have been changed after Shakib's death . . ."

The physician's words trailed off when he noticed that the American was shaking his head in disagreement. "These documents were neither found nor suspected to be in his possession at any time. They were returned to their rightful place after Shakib made copies, and the originals were never reported as lost or compromised. Give me a sheet of paper, please, and a pencil."

Al-Zawahiri dug for the items, which he then handed over. Vanderveen propped the paper on his knee and drew a crude calendar, circling the specific dates as he spoke: "As I said, it is a two-month itinerary, beginning in the month of October. As of last week, the president has continued to meet every major obligation outlined on the schedule. We are now in the first week of November. Unfortunately, circumstances have left us with very little time to act. However . . . I believe that two-and-a-half weeks will be sufficient, *if* I move quickly. With your approval, of course."

"And what is it, exactly, that you intend to do?" the Director asked.

Vanderveen looked up into the calm brown eyes of Osama bin Laden and smiled. "On November 26th, President David Brenneman will be hosting formal negotiations with the French president and the Italian prime minister in Washington. I'm going to kill them all."

CHAPTER 20

TAJIKISTAN • PRETORIA

Deep in the cold bowels of the Tian Shan mountain range, the man known as the American held his audience rapt with the plan that he had carefully conceived over the previous few weeks. It was a plan that would establish Al-Qaeda's dominance over world events, as well as providing them with a sponsor nation in Iran.

The plan appealed to his audience for these reasons and more.

The three men who sat in the cave shared a sickness. It was a disease that was never spoken of in plain terms, but once disguised as revolutionary fervor, it became a topic of discussion that could hold their collective attention for many hours. The disease could be seen in their shining eyes, and in the rapturous smiles that creased their faces when they talked about the technical difficulties of destroying a city block and murdering the president of the United States, as well as the leaders of two other nations, all at once.

"The most difficult part of the operation is already accomplished," Vanderveen said. His Arabic was nearly flawless. Eleven years earlier he had been sent to the excellent Defense Language Institute in Monterey, only to be returned to his unit after three months when his proficiency surpassed that of the program's director.

At the time, he had modestly accepted the man's praise and a syrupy letter of commendation. Now, deep in the hellish caves, he made no effort to hide his arrogance. "The Iranian is my only concern . . . Can he be trusted?"

Al-Zawahiri nodded, staring sadly into his empty cup. The thermos had long since run dry, much to his disappointment. "I do not believe Mazaheri would cheat us, especially after what you have already done for him in escorting the container to Arak. He has my confidence."

"Is it what I asked for?"

"Actually, it is somewhat more: 545 bricks of SEMTEX H. The *plastique* is out of the Czech Republic. Each brick weighs 2,500 grams. The total weight of the shipment, if I am not mistaken, is—"

"About 1,360 kilos, or a little over 3,000 pounds. I believe that will be enough."

Al-Zawahiri was vaguely impressed with the man's rapid calculations. He would have been stunned to learn that the American could have done the same math in his sleep at five years of age.

"The challenge comes in creating a kill zone wide enough to encompass the entire convoy," Vanderveen continued. "Despite Shakib's contributions, there are things we don't know."

"For instance?"

"How the recent attacks will affect Brenneman's security situation, for one thing . . ."

As the American explained the numerous factors that might prevent a successful strike, a very different conversation was taking place 750 miles to the southwest.

The Vanderveen family history, as described by Ambassador Martins, was sketchy at best. There was a fading birth certificate, he explained, a wilted document from the eastern Transvaal dating back to 1964. For their purposes, it was worthless.

For the time being, the first ten years in the life of William Vanderveen would remain a mystery.

There was also documentation dating back to 1975. These were medical records held at the Rand University in Johannesburg. They verified that a young man, accompanied by his mother, had visited the psychology department in February of that year. The boy's scores were astronomical; well beyond the top 1 percent of the population, and yet his family had declined numerous requests for follow-up testing.

According to the file, the psychologist who had administered the exams, a Dr. Wilhelm D. Klerk, had expressed bitter disappointment that the woman and boy had never returned to his department. This disappointment had been tempered when the doctor discovered that they belonged to Francis Vanderveen, the famed South African general; it was only to be expected that the family would seek privacy in such matters.

Ryan Kealey made an effort to listen dispassionately, but soon found himself consumed by conflicting emotions; deep down, he wanted nothing more than to kill the man who had betrayed and murdered five of his fellow soldiers. At the same time, he felt a desperate need to understand, as though understanding might erase some of the lingering pain and guilt. Ryan listened to the ambassador intently, but was fast with the questions: "Who was this General Vanderveen?" he asked. "Why was he so important?"

Martins answered this to the best of his ability. He talked about South Africa's policies during the apartheid years, and he explained that the military was often the first line of defense against African uprisings in the capital and major cities such as Johannesburg and Cape Town.

"When Daniel Malan took power in 1948, he immediately dismissed several high-ranking army officers who were known to be unsupportive of his policies. At the time, Francis Vanderveen was a captain in the 11th South African Special Services Battalion. He survived the purging of the ranks, though, mostly because it was widely rumored that he had been collecting damaging evidence for years, files that tied many of the National Party's most prominent figures to the Nazis during the second World War."

"In other words," Naomi said, "Vanderveen was untouchable."

The ambassador nodded. "Precisely. However, that is not to say that he disagreed with Malan's views. In fact, he had long been noted for his support of the Afrikaner *Broederbond*.

"In 1959, Vanderveen established a liaison between the South African Defense Forces and the Bureau of State Security. This position gave him the authority to oversee both military *and* police matters in South Africa. By that time he was a colonel, and responsible for enforcing the Pass Laws and Section 10 of the Black Urban Areas Act of 1945. I won't bore you with the details, but this was legislation that served to confine black Africans to demarcated areas in remote parts of the country, thereby providing the illusion, if not the reality, of a white South Africa."

"How could one man oversee that kind of operation?" Kealey asked.

"He didn't," was the ambassador's reply. "He had a huge staff on hand, not to mention the army itself. Nevertheless, there *is* evidence that Vanderveen led many of the raids himself. In the 1960s alone, it's estimated that he orchestrated the removal of almost two million black Africans."

Naomi considered this piece of information for a moment. "You know, I took a course last year at GWU where we looked pretty closely at apartheid and its role in South African history. I don't recall seeing this man's name anywhere."

Martins sipped at his coffee and nodded slowly. "You wouldn't have. You see, Francis Vanderveen was very effective at his work, but his tactics were something of an embarrassment to the government, even a government as ruthless as Malan's. As he went about enforcing Section 10, the colonel didn't always wait until the houses were vacated before moving in with the bulldozers. Worse yet, there were rumors that he had a hand in the Sharpeville massacre of 1960."

"I *did* read something about that," Kharmai interjected. "The security forces opened fire on a group of African protesters outside a police station. The officers later reported hearing shots, but no weapons were ever found on the bodies."

"That's right. Sixty-nine people died in the square, with another hundred or so wounded. Vanderveen had quite a reputation by this time. No one was foolish enough to accuse him outright, but everyone knew who had given the order to fire. Incredibly enough, Vanderveen's career wasn't damaged in the slightest by that incident. In fact, he was promoted to brigadier general in 1964. That was the same year of his son's birth."

Ryan settled back a few inches in his chair. *Finally, we come to it.*

"William Paulin was the second child of Francis and Julienne Vanderveen. Their first, Madeline Jane, was born in 1961. As the general was gone the majority of the time, the children lived with their mother on the family estate in Piet Retief, a small town in the Assegai Valley. By all accounts, Julienne was a very beautiful woman, and wholly devoted to her children." Martins hesitated. "What follows is largely conjecture, but as I said, we had a difficult time finding reliable witnesses.

"You've already seen the transcripts. William scored 184 on the Stanford-Binet when he was eleven years old. He also scored off the charts on the Weschler Scales and the Slosson Intelligence Test for Children. His brilliance was undeniable, but his sister was another matter entirely. She was better known for her . . . well, for her promiscuous behavior. In 1975, it was widely rumored in the village that she was seeing one of the Africans working a nearby farm. A young man in his early twenties."

Naomi did the math quickly. "She was *fourteen?*"

Martins nodded. "It didn't last long, though. Madeline died that same year. Apparently, she suffered a fatal fall in the mountains surrounding her home."

Kealey thought he saw where this was going. "The general?"

But Martins shook his head. "No. He would have had ample motive if the rumors were true, of course, but Francis Vanderveen was 100 kilometers away on the day his daughter died, supervising the destruction of an entire village in the Natal. He was not responsible."

A brief silence ensued. "Surely you're not suggesting that William—"

The ambassador held up a hand to stop Naomi. "I'm just giving you the facts."

"But he was so young," Kharmai protested. "It doesn't seem . . . right, somehow."

"There's nothing right about it," Martins agreed. "But the story doesn't end there. A month after the girl was buried, the young man she had been seeing went missing from the farm he was working. They found him a week later in the first hills leading out of the Assegai. The body was virtually cut to pieces."

"And the girl's father?" Ryan inquired.

"Was 1,100 kilometers away at the time, supervising a troop buildup on the Angolan border."

Another silence, longer this time. "Needless to say, Julienne was devastated by the loss of her only daughter, but I'll get back to that in a moment."

The ambassador shifted his weight in the seat and flipped through the file he had been given earlier in the day. "Francis Vanderveen was promoted to major general in the spring of 1975, four months before Madeline's death. Up until this time, South Africa's white population was protected from hostile African lands by a ring of buffer states that fell under *Afrikaner* control. Two of those states were Mozambique and Angola, both of which were governed in the early 1970s by Portugal.

"In 1974, economic instability led to a military coup in Lisbon. This effectively cut off all funds to Portugal's foreign interests, including the army. When the Portuguese commanders in both colonies realized that they were about to lose control of the coastal territories, they agreed to set dates for independence: June of 1975 for Mozambique and November of that same year for Angola."

"Sir, what does this have to do with Francis Vanderveen?" Kealey asked.

"Hold on, I'm getting to that. Some level of authority over these two states was deemed necessary at the top levels of the South African government. After all, their very vision of a white South Africa was at stake. An agreement was quickly reached between the prime minister, John Vorster, and Samora Machel, the rebel leader in Mozambique. Angola was less receptive to the South African proposals, so the land was up for grabs. There were three main parties vying for control of the territory: the rebel-led MPLA, which was backed by the Soviet Union and the Cubans; the FNLA, headed by Holden Roberto and supported primarily by the United States; and UNITA, a centrist organization under the control of a Swiss-educated lawyer named Savimbi."

Naomi was visibly surprised. "I thought the U.S. government was pretty adamant in its criticism of apartheid. Why would Washington intervene?"

"From our point of view, the South Africans were the lesser of two evils," the ambassador explained. "The MPLA was well funded by two Communist governments, and there was a good chance they were going to come out on top. We wanted to limit Communist exposure on the African continent, and to do that, we were forced to deal. But it wasn't actually Washington that stepped in. I'll explain in a moment.

"Anyway, once Vorster decided to invade, he was offered support by both the French and the Americans. In late 1974, the French government organized a meeting between Savimbi's UNITA and the South African Bureau for State Security. Francis Vanderveen was one of the first officials invited. Once in Paris, he accused the French foreign minister of trying to ride his army's coattails into Cabinda, which is an oil-rich enclave of Angola. He was right, of course, but he ruined any potential alliance with the French."

"So he was stuck with us," Ryan offered.

"Exactly," Martins agreed. "And it didn't seem like such a bad deal at first. The CIA had purchased radio stations and newspapers to run propaganda against the MPLA. The Agency certainly seemed to be doing its part. Vanderveen was selected to lead the invasion force. The prize, of course, was the capital, Luanda. His armored column crossed into Angola on the 23rd of October 1975, and he easily won the first battles at Sa da Bandiera and Namibe, encountering almost no resistance at all. As his forces pushed north toward Benguela, though, things began to change."

Ambassador Martins stood up and moved to his desk. Unlocking one of the drawers, he came back to the seating area with a small tin box in his hands. Placing it gently on the coffee table, he took his seat once again.

"After our meeting this morning, my people began tracking down William Vanderveen's surviving relatives. Only one could be found on his father's side: Deborah Poole, neé Vanderveen, the general's sister. She's well on in years now, but she was more than willing to talk with the young man who came out to interview her. And she gave him this."

The ambassador produced a small silver key and unlocked the box. Then he turned it so that Naomi and Ryan could see the contents.

Kealey leaned forward and picked up the first document. After unfolding the stained, torn paper, he began to read.

> *My Dearest Julienne,*
>
> *We are now entrenched in a muddy field outside Novo Redondo. What you would see, if you were here, would not resemble much of an army at all. We have almost no ammunition or fuel due to our waffling politicians. The men are down to one meal a day, and lucky to get that. In all my years as a soldier, I have never felt as unappreciated as I do now.*
>
> *A man from the American CIA came to look at our maps and give us his educated opinion. I told him that we needed supplies more than anything else, and he laughed in my face. I was told that it is a lost cause, that reclaiming Angola is no longer "politically expedient." I said that he would feel differently if he had fought over hundreds of kilometers to protect his country.*
>
> *Julie, I would say this only to you, but I think that we must have them if we are to reach Luanda. It is more than physical supplies: Vorster needs the U.S. after the war as well, and he can't afford for this campaign to go on. If the Americans were to give him their full support, we would have victory and I would be back at home, where I belong.*
>
> *That they would abandon us now is unspeakably treacherous to me.*
>
> *I miss you and William very much. I'll see you both soon.*
>
> *Love always,*
Francis

Ryan finished the letter and handed it over to Naomi. Selecting another from the box, he read through it quickly. The content was much the same.

"My God," Naomi murmured after a moment. The ambassador cleared his throat gently, causing both his guests to look up.

"Needless to say, the American support never arrived. It was an Agency operation from the start, black on black. Washington was never involved. Of course, once Congress found out about it, they quickly put an end to things. Officially, the Senate voted to stop all U.S. aid to anti-MPLA forces on the 18th of December 1975. In truth, however, the damage was already done. Once Vanderveen's column reached Benguela, the MPLA launched a massive counterattack. The rebels had Cuban troop reinforcements and Soviet artillery on their side, whereas Vanderveen was struggling with unreliable supply lines and political indecision in Pretoria. He was forced to pull back his army on the 10th of November. During this time, his letters to Julienne became increasingly bitter, particularly with respect to the Americans.

"Five days later, the general's helicopter was hit by small-arms fire as it left a camp just south of Cubal. Francis Vanderveen and twelve other soldiers died in the ensuing crash."

"Unbelievable," Naomi said softly. Ryan said nothing. He could guess what was coming next.

The ambassador paused for a moment to let the information sink in. Finally, he said, "There were some communication issues that made notification impossible. It wasn't until two weeks later that the widow was informed. The defense minister broke the news himself, I'm told, in light of Vanderveen's rank and stature. I suppose it turned out to be too much for Julienne. As I said, she was already devastated over her daughter's death. Losing her husband must have been the final straw. She committed suicide that same night. According to Mrs. Poole, it was also the last time anyone saw young William in Piet Retief."

Naomi shook her head slowly. Ryan remained silent. He was beginning to put the pieces together in his mind, but he wanted to hear the ambassador say it first.

Martins studied them each in turn. "Unfortunately, this is where the facts end. Anything else is pure speculation, but I have an opinion, if you'd like to hear it."

Naomi nodded once. "Please, Ambassador."

"I think there's a good chance that William Vanderveen saw these letters," Martins said, gently resting a hand on the small tin box. "I also think that he probably had something to do with his sister's death, not to mention what happened to the young man she was seeing. I believe William may have taken what he wanted from his father's words, because doing so would have been a good deal easier than shouldering the blame himself. In my opinion, Will Vanderveen found exactly what he was looking for in the United States: an outlet for his rage. And he's not going to stop until everyone knows how he feels."

CHAPTER 21

PRETORIA • TAJIKISTAN • LANGLEY

For Ryan Kealey and Naomi Kharmai, South Africa had yielded its secrets, and had nothing left to offer. As their meeting with the ambassador drew to a close, Gillian Farris began to make the arrangements for their return to Washington. When the embassy car was ready to depart for Johannesburg International late that afternoon, her hand rested in Ryan's for a very long time. Gillian was sorry to see him go.

Naomi fell into a deep sleep on the short ride south, leaving Ryan alone with his troubled thoughts. He wasn't sure how to proceed. As his mind struggled for answers, Naomi's words came back to him, but with a taunting edge that had been absent in her spoken voice: *"What do we really know now that we didn't know before? His real name? It's not like that'll be the one he's using . . ."*

The name was important to Kealey because it offered some small measure of relief from the feeling of impotence that had plagued him for years. Now that he had the truth, though, he wasn't sure what to do with it.

It had become clear to Ryan during the ambassador's recitation that William Vanderveen blamed the West—or more specifically, the United States—for what had happened to his family. It was also clear that Vanderveen had joined the army of a country he hated for only one reason: to learn the skills that he would ultimately twist to use against his unsuspecting benefactors.

With this thought, Ryan found his thoughts drifting back to Vanderveen's intentions in Washington. Needless to say, it was a huge risk for the man to return to the city, so whatever he had planned would have to be worth that risk. Stephen Gray's final words echoed in his ears with the steady rhythm of a dripping tap: *The shipment has landed in Washington . . . He already has what he needs.* The last shipment to arrive in Washington was an unspecified amount of explosives. Would he be arrogant enough to try the same thing, perhaps sneaking it ahead of the increased security at the ports?

Could it have come in on the *same* shipment as the first explosives that were used?

In his former life, Vanderveen had been a highly skilled Special Forces engineer. As such, he had the patience and the specialized knowledge to carry off a successful attempt on the president's life. Ryan thought the man would fall back on what he knew, despite his sniper training at Benning. He decided that he could only trust his instincts, since he had no proof either way.

He tried not to think about what might happen if he was wrong, or if he was right but not fast enough in putting it together.

As he leaned back in the comfortable seat and tried to follow Naomi's example, Ryan decided that it was time to pay Thomas Elgin another visit.

As the Boeing 747 carrying the two CIA officers lifted into the clear night sky above the lights of Johannesburg, Will Vanderveen emerged from the depths of the Tian Shan mountains, following Ayman al-Zawahiri into the quiet hollows of the surface caves. The ground was littered with cots and sleeping men. The stench from their unwashed bodies filled the air, despite the cold and the open space.

"You will get 45,000 U.S. dollars for expenses, then," al-Zawahiri said in a low voice. "In five installments of 9,000 dollars each, all to the same account." A small frown moved over his face. "We will need Mazaheri to move it."

Vanderveen continued as though he hadn't heard. "Make sure

that the funds are routed through Western Europe, preferably England or France. American banks are required to report lump sum deposits of 10,000 dollars or more to the government. By keeping the deposits under that amount, we remove some of the risk, but there is still some danger in using the one account. Unfortunately, I have very few complete identities. Creating a full legend takes time, which is the one thing we don't have. In less than a month's time, the itinerary will be useless."

They moved out of the caves and into the clearing, walking quickly through the cold night air toward the massive canvas tent and the steady hum of the generators.

"Will he keep to the schedule?"

"He has so far."

"And you think it can be done?"

"There are no guarantees, but we will never have a better opportunity. I believe it can be done."

The Egyptian did not respond as they moved gratefully into the stale warmth of the tent. The radio operator pulled back the curtain and waved for his commander's attention. A moment later, al-Zawahiri was calling for the American.

Vanderveen walked into the cramped room and took the proffered sheet of paper. He scanned it quickly, but one name stood out from the rest. He stared at it in disbelief.

"Kealey."

"You recognize this name?"

"Yes," was the strained response. "Where did this come from?"

"The information came out of South Africa. We have somebody in the embassy there."

"Is he reliable?" Vanderveen asked.

"Completely. He works for money . . . They are usually the best," al-Zawahiri said. A brief pause. "Does this present a problem?"

Vanderveen did not respond for a long time. "No . . . no problem."

"Perhaps it would be better for us to remain in contact, so that we can inform you of his movements." This was said with some insistence.

"No, he won't be staying in Africa. Besides, it's too dangerous. We can't risk everything on a phone call—I can't even begin to guess at the NSA's capabilities, especially in the D.C. area. You won't be hearing from me until it's over."

Al-Zawahiri did not respond. Instead, he turned to stare at the radio operator, who quickly stood up and stepped outside. Only then did the physician turn his attention back to Vanderveen. "That is unacceptable. We need Mazaheri's people to move the funds. He will want assurances."

"There are no assurances." Vanderveen was growing impatient. "We've been over this already—"

The other man held up a placating hand. "You will be given a number to call. The minister has an asset in Washington who will handle the finances. We have few people skilled in that area since Zouaydi was taken in Madrid. It is not a question of the money, you understand. It is a question of trusting you with an operation of this magnitude. Mazaheri will never relinquish total control . . . The Iranians have a great deal at stake here. Even if you are successful, we will have accomplished nothing if they can be directly linked to the assassinations."

Al-Zawahiri fell silent for a moment, a thoughtful expression passing over his blunt features. Finally, he said, "You will make contact twice a week from the time you return until the day of the operation itself. You will be told when to call before you leave. I can negotiate nothing less than that. You will not be expected to divulge your specific movements, but they must know of any problems you encounter. This contact will benefit you as well: they will arrange for additional funds and documents should the worst come to pass."

Vanderveen knew that was a lie. The Iranians would deny everything if his cover was blown. They wouldn't lift a finger to help him if it all went bad, but he needed their help now, and he needed safe refuge when it was over. He had no choice but to play along.

"Fine. Is Mazaheri's man in Washington?"

Ayman al-Zawahiri smiled gently. "Who said anything about a man?"

Surprise registered briefly in Vanderveen's face. It was almost beyond belief that Mazaheri would entrust something as important as operational funds to a woman.

"She is a valuable asset, and she is trusted," al-Zawahiri continued.

"That is all you need to know." The smile faded. "This is not a request. If you fail to call at the specified times, it will not matter if you succeed. Do you understand?"

Vanderveen nodded once. "I will do as you ask. And I will succeed."

There was a long, awkward silence. It was difficult for the physician to believe that the American was willing to commit such an act against his own people, especially for nothing more than a secure place in the organization. In the end, though, he had no choice but to support the man. It was the Emir's wish, and carried no less authority than a command from Allah Himself.

"Good. Tonight, you rest. The helicopter will return in the morning. And then, my friend, it's up to you."

Ryan Kealey had been in Washington for only two hours when he was called back to Virginia to the director's office at Langley. He was sore and tired from the long flight, and his anger was exacerbated by the fact that he wouldn't be getting back to Katie anytime soon.

Jonathan Harper was already waiting in the spacious room, reclining in one of the chairs scattered around a low table. The DCI was sitting opposite him, and the two men stopped their conversation when Kealey stepped through the mahogany doors.

The director stood and extended his hand, a stocky man whose considerable girth was well concealed by the tailored Ralph Lauren Purple Label suits that he favored. "Bob Andrews, pleased to meet you."

Kealey returned the handshake. "Same here, sir."

For his part, Andrews dubiously eyed the man who stood before him. He'd heard many things about Kealey, and the man's appearance seemed to coincide with his reputation. He wore heavy Columbia hiking boots, dark jeans, and a threadbare crewneck sweater of marled gray cotton. His face was deeply tanned from the African sun, even more so than usual, and the jet-black hair was a little wild. Taking all of this in for the first time, the director had to remind himself again of the man's achievements.

Andrews gestured to one of the empty chairs. "Take a seat, Ryan. Congratulations on your results in Africa."

"Thank you, sir."

"I appreciate your coming in to see me today," the director said, as though Kealey had had a choice in the matter. He gestured to the cups resting on the table in front of him. "Coffee?"

Kealey nodded his thanks and moved to pour coffee and dump cream into one of the cups. Meanwhile, the director had lifted what Ryan thought to be his personnel file and was skimming through the contents. "Let's see . . . eight years with the army, retired as a major. DFC, three Bronze Stars, two Purple Hearts. Impressive. Action in Kosovo and the Gulf. Two years in the 1st SFOD . . ." Andrews looked up from the file with a questioning look. "Delta?"

Ryan nodded as he sipped at his coffee. Andrews lifted an eyebrow and turned his attention back to the file. "Then you were on the army's Security Roster, is that right?"

"Yes, sir. I signed a waiver when Director Harper recruited me. Otherwise, my 201 would probably still be buried somewhere at Bragg." He knew that the DCI would understand what he meant. Although the army keeps the vast majority of its personnel files at Human Resources Command in St. Louis, the 1st SFOD-D is given special dispensation to store records pertaining to its operators in a highly secure facility at Fort Bragg.

Andrews closed the file and tossed it onto his desk. "And an Intelligence Star, to round it all out. These pages show you've racked up quite a few achievements, Kealey," he said, drumming his fingers on the closed file. "Unfortunately, this means that I have to take your opinion seriously."

Ryan looked over to Harper, whose face remained expressionless.

"You brought down a lot of heat for that stunt you pulled with Elgin, you know. That still hasn't blown over, but I'm willing to put it aside for now," the director continued. "You think Vanderveen's going after the president. Tell me why."

Kealey shifted uncomfortably in his seat, then went on to relay his brief conversation with Stephen Gray, and the man's final parting words.

"I admit that it sounds worrisome, but is that all you've come up with?" Andrews asked, the skepticism heavy in his voice.

"Sir, we know for a fact that Vanderveen is tied in with the new Iranian regime. He's been linked to Al-Qaeda as well. I mean, we have tape of him meeting with some of the highest ranking people in the organization. It doesn't get any more ironclad than that. Now, consider these facts: Senator Levy, Iran's biggest opponent on the Hill, is assassinated in broad daylight after assuring the Washington press corps that the weapons program in Tehran will be shut down. Then we have Michael Shakib, a known Iranian affiliate whose cell phone records show that he placed a call to a cloned phone less than three minutes before the rocket attack. After the Justice Department tracks him down, he blows himself up rather than risk being taken alive. Why?"

Andrews glanced at Harper, a perplexed expression moving over his face. "Because that's what they do, Kealey. It's part of the conflict for them. Killing as many people as possible, spreading fear, and creating terror are their primary goals—"

Ryan held up a hand to stop him. "Maybe so, sir. But think about this: what if Shakib did it, at least in part, because *he couldn't risk breaking under interrogation?*"

Harper shot an inquiring look at Kealey, but Andrews didn't notice. "You're saying he passed on information we don't know about? Something related to the president?"

Ryan shrugged. "I'm just saying it's a possibility we should look into. God knows it's happened before. Remember that State Department laptop that went missing four years ago? It contained highly sensitive code-word material, and they never found it. The same thing happens over at Justice all the time."

"Jesus," Andrews breathed. He turned to the deputy director. "John, I think we ought to bring the Service in on this. We'll advise them to run an internal audit, see what they can come up with."

"I agree," Harper said, but the expression on his face did not match up with his words.

"Unfortunately, I'm going to be tied down for the next few days with Homeland Security. I can't get out of those meetings, John, but I'm going to set up an appointment with you and Brenneman. I want you there as well, Kealey," Andrews added as an afterthought. "Maybe you'll be able to convince him to cooperate with us on this."

"It would be a big help, sir. I just hope that I'm wrong."

"So do I," was the director's heartfelt response. "So do I."

*   *   *

Less than five minutes later, Harper and Kealey were out of the DCI's office and heading down toward the first floor. They walked slowly, speaking in short bursts when the hallway was quiet and clear of people.

"Jesus, Ryan," Harper said with a smile on his face. "If you show up at the White House looking like you do now, I'm going to run out of the building and never look back."

Ryan laughed and glanced down at his clothes. "I guess I'll have to invest in a suit."

"Is that how you dress when you lecture in Orono?"

"My students are even worse than I am, John. It's all a matter of degree."

They fell silent as a tall, trim woman with a flowing mane of auburn hair passed them hurriedly in the hall carrying a stack of files. She flashed Ryan a little smile as she brushed by.

Harper noticed and stuck his elbow in the younger man's side. "If I got half the attention you do, my friend, I would die a happy man."

"Not if Julie overheard you saying that. In fact, she would probably kill you herself."

Harper smiled at the retort, but soon turned serious again. "That shit you just gave Andrews . . . You don't really believe any of it, do you?"

"No. I guess it *is* possible that Shakib leaked something other than Senator Levy's route, but it's not likely. Andrews is just new enough to the job to believe something like that, though, and he never would have listened to me if all I'd had to offer were Gray's final words. This way, he gets to throw some accusations at the Secret Service for failing to control their information, and we get what we want; some real help in tracking Vanderveen down. Unfortunately, now we have to sell it to the president." Kealey smiled to himself. "That might be a little bit trickier."

Harper shook his head incredulously. "I always said that you would be a star at headquarters, Ryan. You're the most naturally deceptive person I know."

The younger man grinned. "Don't worry, John, I'm not out for your job. I'd never have the patience for all the ass-kissing you have to do."

Harper laughed. "It's that ass-kissing that keeps you out of jail when you pull shit like you did with Elgin."

"Speaking of Elgin, I think the man knows more than he's saying. I want to work with Adam North on this, the guy from DEA. He kept it together when it counted. My problem is going to be getting access. Do you think you can arrange that?"

Harper nodded slowly as they crossed the open lobby toward the security desk. "It'll be tough, but I can get you in there. The worst part will be avoiding the press. I believe they're holding him in Alexandria. Don't leave any marks on him this time, Ryan. You shouldn't have done that in the first place."

"Don't worry, I know how to handle it."

As they pushed out into the cool Virginia air, Ryan looked down the long rows of stone steps to see a dark blue BMW waiting at the curb. Katie was standing next to it, shivering a little in a short black dress. She looked incredible, her light makeup artfully applied, diamond drops hanging from her ears. Her hair was up, and a few loose locks of golden brown fell down around her face. She smiled up at him, and Ryan's heart skipped a beat.

He turned to Harper, who was wearing a sly grin. "You clever bastard . . ." He put his hand on the other man's shoulder and squeezed. "Thanks, John. I owe you one."

"Take her somewhere nice, Ryan. She deserves it. I'll see you tomorrow."

Ryan let go of his friend's shoulder and hurried down the steps, wrapping her up in his arms before they shared a lingering kiss. Harper watched from the top of the steps with a rueful grin, laughing a little at the strange compatibility of the couple. Ryan with his unkempt hair, tattered sweater, and heavy boots, while Katie looked like she had just stepped off a runway in Milan.

Harper thought of Julie and his smile grew. As he walked toward the parking lot and his own waiting car, he decided that they would enjoy a night out on the town as well. After all, life was too short for anything less.

CHAPTER 22

ASHLAND, VIRGINIA • WASHINGTON, D.C.

Nicole Milbery had been in the real estate business for sixteen years, and had never wanted to do anything else. Now, at thirty-seven years of age, she was a slender woman of medium height, well known and highly respected in her community. Her shoulder-length honey-blond hair was layered in the latest style, and her soft, doelike brown eyes belied the dogged determination and intelligence that was a hallmark of her character and the reason for her considerable success. She was the sole proprietor of Milbery Realty, an agency based in the northern reaches of Virginia that catered primarily to upscale clientele.

The person sitting across from her now did not fall into that category. He was looking for something far more modest, 120 acres at the most, and only to rent. Although her profit on the deal would be marginal at best, she found herself unwilling to hurry the proceedings along. He was a strikingly handsome man. The dark brown hair was streaked with gold, and she noticed that it drifted over his forehead into his eyes, which were the most amazing color of green she had ever seen. His full lips were perfectly centered beneath a long, straight nose; the clean-shaven jaw was square and firm, and his skin radiated a healthy glow.

He had come into her office just forty-five minutes earlier. When they shook hands he had smiled, revealing boyish dimples and a set of perfect white teeth. Her breath had caught in her throat, and ever since that moment, her professional poise had seemed an arm's length away, just beyond her grasp when she needed it most.

"So, Mr. Nichols," she said, deliberately emphasizing the seductive quality of her voice. Her eyes were locked onto his. "I think we've made some good choices here. When would you like to take a look at these properties?"

He covered his mouth and faked a cough to hide his sudden grin. Just hearing her say it made him want to laugh. He had chosen it on a whim three years earlier, and in retrospect, he knew it had been a mistake. The very name itself occasionally drew attention, something that he was definitely not looking for.

Still, it was amusing.

He moved his hand away, once again in full control. "As soon as possible, Nicole," he said with another charming smile. "I have time today, if you do. And please, call me Tim."

He thought the third house would suit his needs perfectly.

It was a farm, really, 97 acres situated on earth that would now be teeming with hundreds of rows of red winter wheat if the fields had been seeded in early September. Because they had not, the recent rainstorms had washed away much of the topsoil, leaving behind what could only be described as a lake of mud.

The property was located just off Chamberlayne Road north of Richmond. It was a rural community; the closest house was a half mile away, but Interstate 295, which ran east and west, was less than 3 miles away, and I-95, which ran north to Washington, was not more than 4 miles to his west. He turned his attention back to the one-story red brick house as they walked away from Milbery's Ford Escape and up the hard-packed dirt of the driveway.

"As you can see," she was saying, "the house itself is somewhat modest, but really quite lovely. I know it looks small, but the basement is finished and quite extensive. Perhaps the best part of all is the privacy."

They were inside, moving steadily through the small structure. "This is the den. Hardwood floors in every room." She stamped her heel lightly as if to prove her point. "Plus, a cozy little fireplace for the cold nights that we've been getting. Perfect for you and . . . Is there a Mrs. Nichols?"

Will Vanderveen held up his left hand, which was missing a ring on the third finger. When he winked at her, she blushed and turned her face away.

He looked around at the depressing surroundings. *What a shit hole,* he thought. He would never have been caught dead living in such a place voluntarily, but for less than a month, he could suffer in silence. Besides, he was interested in the property for other reasons.

"Nicole, do you think we could take a look at the barn?"

It was far more impressive than the house, a solid structure with staggered floors that followed the contours of a gently sloping hill. Vanderveen looked around, pleased by what he saw. From the road, only the very top of the barn could be seen, as it was located behind the house. The interior was dry and warm. It offered an entrance on only one end, but there was a large sliding door with a heavy lock. More importantly, the single entrance was wide enough to accommodate a large commercial van. He kicked aside some of the straw to reveal a hard concrete floor.

It couldn't have been better.

He turned to ask a question and found her facing away from him, leaning over to pluck a wayward piece of straw from the top of her shoe. He thought she had timed it well. His eyes moved over her ass, firm beneath the short red skirt, and down the long, taut legs to the three-inch heels she was wearing.

She removed the offending article and stood up quickly. Turning to face him, she immediately caught his wandering gaze. A small smile played over her glossy red lips. "Do you like it?" She was trembling with anticipation. "The place, I mean."

He wasn't embarrassed at all. He held her eyes and said, very quietly, "It's perfect."

"So you'll be taking it, then?"

"I think you could say that, Nicole." He was already walking toward her, slowly working the buttons loose on his shirt. "You could definitely say that."

* * *

It had been two days since the meeting with Director Andrews at Langley. Ryan spent the mornings at Headquarters, but the afternoons were reserved for Katie alone. They went window shopping in Georgetown, and for long walks hand in hand through the stark winter contrasts of Rock Creek Park. They ate at ridiculously expensive restaurants on the Hill, and even took in a play at Ford's Theatre, something she had wanted to do for a long time.

It was late in the evening on the third day when they arrived at the Capital Grille, a small, elegant restaurant on the corner of 6th and Pennsylvania. As always, Ryan felt a pleasant little jolt at the way heads turned to follow Katie's passage through the crowded dining area. She was wearing a slinky black dress that ended at midthigh, and sling-back heels that perfectly accentuated her long, slender legs. Her usual glossy pink nail polish had been replaced by a clear lacquer, and her hair was swept up into an impossible pile that she had somehow secured with a number of silver barrettes. Ryan thought she had never looked more beautiful.

The meal was delicious and the surroundings nothing less than spectacular. Katie was amazed when Senator John McCain came walking through the door, immediately followed by a phalanx of junior staffers. Ryan almost had to restrain her from jumping up to point and scream like a giddy schoolgirl; Katie followed politics with the same degree of enthusiasm her peers reserved for musicians and celebrities.

He wondered how she might react to the fact that he was meeting with President Brenneman in less than a week, but decided that the reserved atmosphere of the restaurant was no place to find out. He pictured her probable response: *You're kidding, right? You're so full of shit, Ryan!"* All of this in a loud voice, overheard by the horrified waiters as they tried to figure out what to do. The image caused him to laugh out loud, as did the questioning look that she shot him across the table.

When they returned to the Hay-Adams just after midnight, the warmth of their suite was a pleasant reprieve from the damp snow that was drifting over the city. Katie collapsed onto the bed without kicking off her shoes, still floating from her Congressional sighting and the excellent '94 California chardonnay they had consumed with their meal.

"God, that place was great! This hotel is great, too. I think we should move here. There's nothing to do in Maine anyway. What do you think?"

"I don't think you mean that. Besides, there's plenty to do in Maine. You could take up fishing."

She pouted her lips and gave him a skeptical look. "Do I look like a fisherman?"

He smiled and joined her on the bed, propping himself up on one elbow as he began to remove the silver clasps from her hair. "No, you don't look like a fisherman. That's a good thing, by the way . . . I've never found them very appealing." She laughed a little at that. His voice took on a different, more serious tone when he spoke again. "As long as you're still marrying me, we can do whatever you want, Katie."

She looked up at him in amazement as the last clasp came free and the honey brown waves tumbled down around her face. "Are you serious?"

A brief pause, and then he grinned. "No, I just thought it would be a romantic thing to say."

She slapped him hard on the arm as he laughed. "I really *do* hate you." But she didn't mean it, and couldn't help but respond when he leaned in to steal a kiss. A few minutes later she was sliding the straps of her dress off her shoulders as he began to explore her body, his strong fingers running slowly down the lean curves of her back.

She moaned as his head dropped and she felt his lips grazing her breasts. She tugged at his pants as he unsnapped her bra in a practiced motion, sliding the black lace down until it caught for an instant on her hard nipples. Her dress slipped from the side of the bed to the floor, her fingers wrapping tight in the sheets as she felt his mouth move on her flat stomach. She sucked in her breath and squirmed as he kept going down . . .

A sound penetrated the waves of pleasure, and it took her a second to realize that it was Ryan's cell phone. He got to his feet and reached for it. She whispered an expletive under her breath as he hit the TALK button and turned away from her.

"Kealey here. Yeah . . . Good, it's about time. Okay, that works for me. I'll see you then."

She was sitting up on the bed, pulling the sheets around her body and staring at him as he cut the connection. "Who was that?"

He hesitated, and that said it all. "Oh, I get it." Her face changed. "It was that Naomi, right?"

"Yes, it was. Listen, I need to head out early, Katie. I might be gone when you wake up."

"Why?" She gazed up at him with worried eyes. "Where are you going?"

"Just to Langley. It'll be a long day, though. I might not make it back tomorrow night." He set the phone down and moved to join her once again. As he leaned in to kiss her, though, she turned away. "What's wrong?"

"Nothing," she said. "I'm fine, really." But Ryan couldn't see her face or read her thoughts, and had no way of knowing how hard his words had hit her: *I might not make it back tomorrow night.*

The unfortunate double meaning of the statement served to remind her of the fear she had been living with over the past several weeks. It had been hard enough to deal with in the first place, but now that they were engaged, it just seemed like she had that much more to lose, because there was the implied promise of a family and a life together that seemed so close she could almost touch it.

She wanted to tell him how she felt, to try to make him understand. At the same time, she didn't want to be a burden. Katie sensed that whatever he was involved in was much more dangerous than he was letting on, and she couldn't help but think that the less she bothered him with her concerns, the clearer his mind would be if he was headed into harm's way.

Ryan was confused by her sudden change in demeanor, and automatically assumed it had something to do with Naomi. *Jesus*, he couldn't help but think. *How many times do we have to go over this?* She still had her back to him. Realizing that she obviously didn't want his company, he wandered aimlessly over to the French doors that led out to the balcony. Pulling them open, Ryan stepped out into the cold night air wearing nothing more than his boxers. The view below was spectacular, as the Federal Suite overlooked Lafayette Square and St. John's Cathedral, the lights below illuminating the fresh white powder that blanketed the streets.

The scene was lost on him. Instead, he was remembering something that had occurred more than five months earlier.

They had still been getting to know one another at the time, enjoying the thrill of a new and exciting relationship, too caught up in each other to notice any flaws. She spent the night at his house on the Cape more often than not, although she kept a small apartment in Orono. On one particular night, some of Katie's friends had come over for what she called, with an impish grin, "margaritas and a movie." Evidently the emphasis was on margaritas, because after at least four of the sweet frozen drinks, her best friend from Orono had made some highly suggestive remarks about Katie's new boyfriend, with Ryan in clear and obvious earshot.

Katie had tried to brush it off, but once her friends had gone, it was clear that she was still upset. When he asked her what was wrong, she refused to talk about it. Finally, after a great deal of gentle coaxing on his part, she had tearfully confessed that she didn't think she could compete with that particular friend for Ryan's attention.

That incident summed up everything he loved about her: she simply didn't know how beautiful she was. The friend, while remarkably attractive in her own right, was plain in comparison. Strangely enough, a large part of Katie's allure was her complete disinterest in her own appearance; he could count on the fingers of one hand the number of times he had seen her stand in front of a mirror for more than a few seconds. What made her modesty so remarkable was the fact that it was completely unfounded. She was a goddess in every sense of the word, but no matter how many times he told her so, she just scowled and told him to quit teasing her.

He loved every inch of her, from her delicate toes to the strands of gold in her hair—caught and brought out by the sun, a rare-enough sight in Maine. The way her full lips felt on his own, the way her cheeks had flushed when he found a book of her poetry and proclaimed it to be, with complete sincerity, "really good," and in response to her skeptical gaze: "Seriously!"

What really held him, though, were her eyes. They were the perfect shade of cerulean blue, beautifully framed beneath long, dark lashes, and they changed dramatically with her mood. Lighter when she was amused or happy, turning to deep, dark pools of indigo in moments of concern or anger, and at the precise moment of climax . . .

Damn! Ryan shook his head angrily. If only she wasn't so touchy when it came to Naomi, or just about every other woman he had ever met, for that matter. As he emerged from his thoughts, the scene below suddenly came into focus. In the dim light, the snow swirled furiously around the statues of Andrew Jackson and the Comte de Rochambeau, as if struggling to breathe life into the marble figures. All in all, it was a breathtaking sight.

But it was incomparable to the view that greeted him when he walked back into the room. The woman he loved was still turned away from him, but it didn't matter; she was beautiful from any angle. He could not help but admire the way her skin glowed in the soft light of the suite, as the stunning curves of her body seemed to perfectly complement the elegant atmosphere that suffused the room.

Seeing her in this way, Ryan came to a sudden realization. He would put up with these petulant tantrums forever. He didn't care if she grew out of it or not. If that was the price of knowing her, then it was a small price, and he would pay it gladly.

A few minutes passed. Katie tried to push the worry out of her mind and go to sleep, but her skin was still tingling from his touch. Her gaze drifted down to the diamonds that twinkled on the third finger of her left hand. The last of her resolution disappeared, and when she turned over to face him, her heart lifted when she saw that his attention had not wandered. That was all it took. "Well, come on," she said with feigned impatience and a precocious grin. "You're not going to give up that easily, are you?"

His smile lit up the room. Three steps later he pounced on her, and she was shrieking with laughter until his attention became too much, and her cries of ecstasy spilled out into the night.

CHAPTER 23

NORFOLK • WASHINGTON, D.C.

When Will Vanderveen arrived at Norfolk International Terminals late in the afternoon to collect his consignment, the last-minute rush in the container yard rendered him almost invisible to the workers who hustled over the broad expanse of rain-slicked cement.

It was how he had planned it. The change in shift allowed him to blend easily into the crowd, and it was not a coincidence that his navy blue coveralls, steel-toed boots, and wool knit watch cap closely resembled the outfit worn by many of the lower-level NIT employees.

The cement was littered with hundreds of 20- and 40-foot containers, stacked four high and seven deep, as port regulations required. Towering above the identical metal boxes were the rail-mounted gentry cranes that were in constant motion, depositing one container after another onto an endless procession of flatbed trucks.

As he crossed the open space, he approached three men standing next to a row of containers. One was holding a clipboard and a Styrofoam cup of steaming coffee, and his uniform identified him as a captain in the Virginia Port Authority.

Vanderveen studied the captain, an older man with iron-gray hair cut close to the scalp and hard ridges carved into his face. His pale blue eyes were almost unnaturally clear. Vanderveen was almost certain that he was an ex-Marine, most likely an upper-level NCO.

" 'Scuse me," Vanderveen said as he approached. No one noticed him, and he gave it a minute before tapping the man on the shoulder. " 'Scuse me, sir."

The captain turned with an annoyed expression on his face. "Yeah, can I help you?"

Vanderveen set his jaw, narrowed his eyes slightly, and carefully added a generous measure of hard Southern inflection to his own voice. "Sorry t' butt in." Fishing some paperwork out of his folder, flashing the captain a sincere but unapologetic smile. "I need to get m' consignment, but I've never used NIT before. Can I bring m' own truck in here?"

"No, I'm sorry, son," the man drawled. He paused. "Well, hold on jes' a sec. Yer gettin' it l.c.l?"

"Yes, sir, I sure am."

"Well, now, that's another story. They might let you bring 'er in." He pointed to a barrier in the distance. "Other side a' that fence, there's an access road to the l.c.l yard. You jes' show 'em your ID and ya bill a' ladin' and you'll be set."

Vanderveen nodded his thanks. "Well, I 'preciate it, sir. Hey, where can I get me some a that?" he asked, pointing to the man's steaming cup.

The captain laughed and spit noisily on the ground. "Hell, you don't want none a this, son. Tastes like shit."

Ten minutes later, Vanderveen was pulling a rented U-Haul cargo van up to the gatehouse outside the smaller yard reserved for l.c.l shipments, otherwise known as less than container loads. These, as the name implied, were exports that did not require the use of a whole container. It was an excellent way for small companies to save money on shipping.

It was a very useful tool for people in certain other lines of work as well.

The gate guard stuck his head out the sliding window when Vanderveen pulled up.

"Help ya?"

"Jes' here to collect some crates." Falling straight back into the role. "Got m' license if ya need it."

"Gotta see ya bill of lading, too."

Vanderveen frowned. "I ain't got one a them, buddy. Got m' way-bill, though. They tole me that was good enough."

"Yeah, that'll work. Lemme see it."

When he was satisfied that everything was in order, the guard turned to his computer and pulled up the Yard Management System. Then he handed back Vanderveen's ID and waybill, both of which identified him as Timothy Nichols. "Okay, sir. Ya already been cleared through Customs. They got yer crates in Warehouse Three. Can't have no personal vehicles in the yard, though."

"Aw, come on now." He was laying it on thick. "How else am I gonna get m' stuff out?"

The guard nodded sagely. "I hear ya. They don' tell people shit around here. Happens all the time." A brief hesitation. "Tell ya what. You jes' go on ahead . . . I'll take care of it fer ya."

Vanderveen allowed a relieved expression to slide over his face. "I 'preciate it, buddy. Jes' down here, ya say?"

"That's it. Two rows down, then take a left. Can't miss it."

"Gotcha." The thin wooden barrier lifted and he drove through, following the guard's directions until the warehouse came into view. He pulled up next to the enormous metal structure and hopped out of the van, ambling into the brightly lit interior of the building.

Almost immediately, he was approached by a slightly overweight, middle-aged woman, wearing a hard hat and a frown. Looking her over, Vanderveen's eyes drifted down to the identification badge pinned to her clean chambray shirt: Bobbie Walker, Warehouse Manager.

"Sir, you can't be in here without a hard hat. Can I help you?"

She was clearly not a Southerner, but he couldn't stop now. There was no way of telling how well she knew the captain and the gate guard. He gave her a rueful grin. "Sorry 'bout that, ma'am. Man at the gate tole me t' come on up here and get m' crates. Didn't say nothin' 'bout the hard hats."

Her face softened a little bit. "Well, that's okay." She took a few steps and snagged one from the top of a nearby locker. "Put this on, please. Now, you have your documentation on you, Mr . . . . ?"

"Nichols, ma'am, Tim Nichols. I sure do." He handed her his driver's license and the waybill. Her forehead creased as she considered the name, but her mind couldn't quite make the leap.

They walked across the warehouse floor past heavy piles of aluminum girders and rolls of wood pulp. She was checking numbers against her list when they stopped in front of a stack of small wooden crates.

"Here we go: forty crates, seventy-five pounds each. That's a heavy load." She looked at him curiously. "Whatcha got in here, anyway?"

"Jes' some computer stuff, far as I know." The lie rolled effortlessly off his tongue. "Can't really tell ya, t' be honest. Company just puts m' name on there for convenience. I do what I'm told, Ms. Walker. Nothin' more, nothin' less."

She laughed, her small blue eyes glittering with amusement. "Everyone works for the man, Mr. Nichols. That doesn't surprise me at all."

Vanderveen was looking around the warehouse. He didn't spot any watchers, but they didn't get the job by being obvious. If they had a line on him, they would make their move in the next few minutes. "So, Customs already through with me, huh?" He tried to pass it off as a casual question, but he watched her reaction carefully.

"Yeah, they just do a spot check most of the time."

"So they didn't open 'em up, then." *She'll lie to you. If she lies, kill her. Do you have your knife?* His hand involuntarily drifted back to an object hooked to his belt. *Yes, there it is. Use it now. Now. NOW NOW NOW NOW NOW.*

She was shaking her head. So was he, but for very different reasons. "Things have been crazy around here lately, what with the terror alert and all. We got people from OSHA and Customs all over the terminal. Cause more problems than they solve, you ask me. They don't bother too much with us, though. Spend their time looking at the dry-bulk and open-top containers on Pier Two. Government don't got time to be looking through everything that comes out of our little yard."

She seemed sincere. He breathed a very soft sigh of relief and nodded along with her. "They's troublemakers, all right. Ms. Walker, you think I might pull m' van in here t' get this stuff? Only take me 'bout twenty minutes, tops."

She looked reluctant. "I don't know . . . It's against policy."

Another smile. "Come on now. Think I don't know a woman in charge when I see her? Hell, you're th' one makin' the rules around here anyway, right? Anyone gonna break 'em, might as well be you."

She blushed very slightly and touched his arm. "You're a charmer, I'll give you that. Okay, you bring it on in. Twenty minutes, though, and that's it. Fair enough?"

"I'll be in and out b'fore ya know it."

She giggled like a teenage girl at his choice of words. "I don't think so, Mr. Nichols." Her face was a deep scarlet now. "In fact, I highly doubt it."

Twenty-five minutes later Vanderveen rolled out of the gate. A cold can of Coke rested in the cupholder next to him, a parting gift from the blushing Bobbie Walker. A brief wave to the gate guard and he was leaving Terminal Boulevard, taking the right turn onto Hampton, a smile on his face and 3,000 pounds of SEMTEX H in the cargo hold of his rented van.

Eight days to go, he thought. In eight days he would change the world.

David Brenneman watched as a gentle rain drifted over the gardens spread out before him. He was seated in a simple chair in the Blue Room, sipping steaming coffee from a delicate china cup. For once he was alone, and he took advantage of the solitude to admire the beauty of his surroundings.

Brenneman knew that many of his predecessors had grown tired of the mansion's elaborate trappings, thinking it more like a museum than a home, but he had become only more fascinated with the history of the place as time wore on. The Blue Room was his personal favorite by far—a large, oval space that offered a sweeping view of the South Lawn. The center of the royal blue carpet was dominated by a marble table purchased by James Monroe in 1817. Hanging above it was an elaborate French chandelier dating from the early-nineteenth century. When he closed his eyes, he was pleased to hear only the gentle tap of the rain against the lead-lined windows.

The brief reprieve would have been much more enjoyable, though, if he didn't have to return to the situation brewing on his doorstep.

A week earlier, the FBI's Explosives Unit had finished its analysis of the residue collected at the Kennedy-Warren blast site. The explosives were identified as SEMTEX H, originating from the Czech Republic. When these results coincided with the findings of an independent lab, it became clear that the main charge had been smuggled into the country, which meant that Customs was first on the firing line.

Of course, there was plenty of blame left over for the man in charge of it all. His approval ratings had dipped six points in one week, and supposedly there had been quiet talk from the new Senate Majority Leader about pulling support for the incumbent in the upcoming election year. Brenneman believed the rumors to be true, and was astounded and angered at the speed with which his own party had dismissed his chances for reelection.

He was startled from his thoughts by a Secret Service agent standing at one of the entrances to the room. "Excuse me, Mr. President. Deputy Director Harper is here to see you."

Brenneman waved a hand absently. "Thanks, Dan. You can send him in. Oh, and could you call the kitchen and have them send some more coffee over?"

"Of course, sir."

The agent withdrew, and Brenneman stood as Harper entered the room. "John, good to see you. How's Julie?"

"She's fine, sir. Thank you for asking." Harper never ceased to be amazed by the man's prodigious memory and sheer graciousness, especially considering the pressure he was currently under.

Brenneman gestured to the seat opposite his own and glanced at his watch. "Take a seat. I'm supposed to be at a meeting with Patterson from Treasury, but you've got my full attention for the next twenty minutes."

"I'll get right to it, then, sir," Harper said as he sat in a mahogany chair. "You're familiar with the file on Jason March?" He received a brief nod in return. "Then you'll know that March is not his actual name. Two of our officers have just returned from Pretoria, where they were able to discover his true identity."

The president leaned forward with interest. "And?"

"His name is William Paulin Vanderveen, a South African national, thirty-nine years old." The deputy director handed him a briefing folder, which the president immediately opened. The pictures were the first thing to catch his eye. "The South African authorities believe that he was responsible for the murder of one Joseph Sobukwe in 1975. Vanderveen was eleven years old when Sobukwe was killed. Vanderveen's sister died under unusual circumstances as well, but he was never officially tied in with that."

"Jesus Christ." Brenneman leaned back in his chair and perused the contents of the folder. The picture began to unfold over the next several minutes: Francis Vanderveen, a South African general even more ruthless than the policies he enforced; William, the general's brilliant, misguided son, wholly devoted to his father; a broken promise of American money and support; a fiery helicopter crash on a warm December morning. The president was absorbed as a Filipino steward glided into the room and poured coffee from a silver carafe. The room was silent until the man was gone and the door closed behind him.

"So this man, William Vanderveen. He blames us for what happened to his family, is that right?"

"That would appear to be the case, sir. We found evidence in South Africa—letters—that suggest William Vanderveen knew plenty about the general's antipathy toward us in the last days of the Angolan campaign. Then you have his sister's death and his mother's subsequent suicide . . . It doesn't take a great stretch of imagination to see how this might have played out."

"And we trained him."

"Yes, sir."

"Jesus Christ." The president leaned back in his chair and closed the folder. "So what are we dealing with here, John? How can we use this information?"

"Sir, to be perfectly honest, this kind of information is useful for shoring up a case against him when he's caught, and that's about it. There's a reason the Department of Transportation keeps coming up empty on the airport surveillance tapes. Vanderveen probably has at least two airtight identities, everything from driver's licenses down to birth certificates. That's the only way to explain his ease of movement in and out of the country."

The president nodded slowly as he lifted his cup. "I'm sure you've heard that some of my advisors are pushing me to reconsider the military option. They think Tehran's involvement is clear enough to justify air strikes."

Harper lifted his open hands. "Sir, we know who is directly responsible for these attacks, and we know that he's not hiding out in a training camp. It would be a—"

"So where is he?" Brenneman interrupted. "What are your people saying? This, uh . . ."—he looked around for his briefing folder—"Kealey. Is that right?"

"Yes, sir. He was one of the officers involved."

"What does he think?"

"In his opinion . . ."

Brenneman lifted an eyebrow. "Out with it, John."

"He thinks that Vanderveen is coming after you, sir."

The rain beat against the windows, but there was no other sound in the room. The president shifted in his seat, but the expression on his face did not change. "May I ask how he came to that conclusion?"

Harper hesitated once again. "Vanderveen hasn't failed here yet. Kealey thinks he's going to set his sights higher."

"That's it?" Brenneman looked skeptical.

"No, sir." Harper went on to tell him about Gray's final words, and the same confluence of facts that Ryan had pointed out during their recent meeting with Director Andrews.

"So where is Kealey now?"

"Something came up that he could only take care of today. Naomi Kharmai, the only other officer directly involved in this case, is with him, if I'm not mistaken."

Brenneman ignored the circumspect answer. "What exactly do you need from me, John?"

"Sir, I've got my best people working on this, as does the Bureau.

It's just a matter of time, really, but any adjustments that could be made to reduce the threat to your own security would be—"

"You want me to hide in a corner, is that it?"

Harper hesitated, unsure of the other man's reaction. "As a precautionary measure, I believe—as does the director—that it would be a wise decision to cancel any high-profile events for the next couple of weeks. Especially those for which details have been released by the White House press secretary."

"If I'm hearing you correctly, most of your argument stems from this man Kealey's instincts. You must have a lot of faith in him."

Harper leaned forward in his chair. He sensed defeat, but he wasn't going down without a fight. "Sir, Ryan Kealey has risked his life several times in the past few weeks tracking down William Vanderveen. I've known him for eight years, and I trust his judgment. It's only because of Kealey and this other officer, Kharmai, that we can even put a name to the face. Believe me, I know we don't have much right now, but we're getting closer, and the threat is very real. Vanderveen has serious backing and financial support from Al-Qaeda, and there is solid evidence that the Iranians are involved as well. They have a clear motive here, sir. Kealey knows this man, and he's our best chance at finding him. When you look at it that way, we're not asking you for much. The reason for the change in schedule doesn't even have to be released to the press."

Brenneman nursed his coffee and stared out at the rain clouds moving over the gardens. It was several minutes before he spoke. "John, I respect your judgment . . . I always have. Nothing you've said just now has disabused me of that notion. At the same time, I can't afford to change my schedule without something more concrete. I'm not trying to prove anything; this isn't about reckless bravery. I'm meeting with President Chirac and Prime Minister Berlusconi early next week. If we can come to some agreement for compensation of lost oil contracts, that meeting might very well result in the dismantling of Iran's weapons program without one American soldier setting foot in the country." There was a brief pause. "It'll be historic, John, the best thing I've done in four years in office. I just won't cancel that meeting without good cause."

The president stood, signifying that the conversation was over.

Harper rose to his feet as well, and the two men looked at each other in silence as the rain streamed down the large windows beside them.

"I'm sorry you feel that way, sir, but I respect your decision."

Brenneman reached out to firmly shake hands with his deputy director. He thought about the steel wires protruding from the torn remains of the Kennedy-Warren, and he remembered the mangled vehicles that had lined Independence Avenue less than a month earlier.

"I want you to find the bastard, John." Brenneman's voice was low, but the anger it held cut through his calm demeanor. "Find him and put him down."

"You have my word on it, Mr. President."

CHAPTER 24

ALEXANDRIA, VIRGINIA

It was early evening when Ryan finally pulled into the Alexandria Detention Center's parking lot after having battled the reams of rush-hour traffic on I-95. He locked his car and walked toward the building's entrance. Adam North was already there, waiting on the steps and smoking a cigarette. He smiled as Ryan approached, and the two men shook hands.

"It's about damn time," North said. "What happened?"

"The traffic around here is a killer. I don't know how people put up with that every day."

"Hey, the money's in the city. People will suffer anything for a paycheck every couple of weeks. Listen, I have bad news."

"Tell me."

"Elgin's found himself a lawyer, and he's recanted on waiving his Miranda rights."

Ryan closed his eyes and shook his head. "I should have seen this coming. Court-appointed, right?"

North took a final drag on his cigarette and flicked the butt into the gutter. "No, he's actually managed to get somebody decent, probably on the smallest retainer possible. Elgin's assets have been frozen, and I guarantee that his attorney isn't aware of that little fact."

The DEA agent paused and turned his face up to the dim light, breathing in the damp, heavy air. "The government's moving fast on this one. He's already been indicted, and the A.G. is seeking three Federal counts. Conspiracy to murder U.S. nationals tops the list. Maybe if they weren't in such a hurry . . . I don't know. Doesn't matter, anyway. He'll never talk to you one-on-one now. You want to leave it, see if we can cut a deal?"

"We don't have time for that. Besides, he had a knife to Naomi's throat, Adam. He'll give us the information, one way or another, and then he can rot in jail. What does the conspiracy charge carry, anyway? Twenty years? If he doesn't feel like talking, he'll be lucky to see day one of that sentence."

With most people, Adam would have dismissed these words as an empty threat. Instead, he was immediately reminded of Elgin's screams in the dark back room of the Waterfront Bar. "Where is she anyway?"

"Naomi? I told her it got pushed back a few days. I'm hoping that she doesn't call me on it until then."

A small smile replaced the bigger man's uneasy expression. "I wouldn't want to see her face when she finds out . . ."

Ryan caught the intentional change in subject and sensed North's lingering apprehension. "Listen, you've seen this guy's sheet, right?" He received a hesitant nod in return. "Elgin raped a thirteen-year-old girl, okay? Not to mention that ninety-two people died at the Kennedy-Warren, and he could have stopped it. Think about that, Adam. Ninety-two dead, hundreds of lives ruined, all so Elgin could clear . . . what? A couple thousand dollars, maybe? He doesn't deserve any sympathy, especially from us."

They were asked to turn in their weapons. North obliged, handing over his Glock, but Kealey shook his head and held up empty hands. After they moved through a metal detector, North signed the register while Kealey looked on impassively. Ryan was required to show the deputy identification to get a temporary pass, but that was all. It was the one thing on which he had insisted, and Harper had come through for him; there would be no record of Ryan Kealey's visit to the prison.

He wondered if Harper had already realized his mistake. For

Kealey to be held responsible for any unfortunate incident that might befall Thomas Elgin, there would have to be an official record of his arrival at the detention center.

The interior of the structure was not at all what he had expected. Most of the walls were painted powder blue, and the floors were covered by cheap government carpet, but carpet nonetheless. He thought that was an unusual thing to see in a prison. The most surprising thing, however, was the lack of noise. It took him a while to notice the absence of sound, if only because it was such an obvious disparity.

North noticed his confusion. "This is what they call a 'New Generation' prison. Everything is controlled from a single operations center, and the deputies move freely among the prisoners. Inmates who get loud or try to fight are removed immediately, and noise suppression was taken into account when they chose the building materials."

"It seems like all that would be pretty expensive," Ryan said.

"I guess the benefits outweigh the cost. Anyway, I don't know what you know about the Bureau of Prisons, but Elgin has already been placed into the CIM system. I thought it would happen eventually, but—"

"Hold on, you're going to have to explain that to me."

They were passing through an open lounge, filled with wooden tables and comfortable-looking armchairs. Several inmates were crowded around a television, set at a low volume, absorbed by a basketball game while a deputy sheriff looked on with a bored expression. Ryan was struck by the guard's casual stance, and he couldn't get over the relaxed atmosphere that seemed to blanket the detention center.

His attention snapped back to North as the acronym was explained: "CIM is the Central Inmate Monitoring System run by the Feds. It applies to pretrial prisoners as well, and Elgin earned a place due to the publicity his case is already getting in the media."

A small frown spread over Kealey's face. "I hope he's not getting any special treatment."

North shook his head. "No, nothing like that. He is getting some special *attention*, though. That's what I'm saying . . . I can't guarantee that I can get you in the room alone with him."

Ryan gave him a sharp look. "I can't do this without your help,

Adam." A moment later he spoke again, but in a much lower voice. "More to the point, I need you to keep your mouth shut when it's done. We've already talked about this. If you want out, just say the word."

The tone of his voice left North with little doubt that leaving was no longer an option. "I'll get you in there," he said.

Ryan smiled with relief. "Good."

They were cleared through an electronic door that led into the operations center. Seconds later, the watch commander walked up and extended a large hand.

"Louis Jackson. Pleased to meet you, gentlemen." Jackson was a heavily built black man who looked to be just shy of fifty. His bald head gleamed in the low light of the watch center. Despite his age, Jackson's strength was clearly visible beneath the immaculately pressed uniform that he wore. Ryan didn't need to see it to know it, though; his hand was still stinging from the man's powerful grip.

"You boys carry a lot of sway," Jackson said in a low rumble. "I got a call this morning from Harper over at Langley, as well as Nance at DEA. Both of 'em told me they'd have my balls in a vice if I didn't get you access to Elgin."

North gave a friendly chuckle. "We're not trying to cause you any inconvenience, sir. Believe me, if we had it our way, we wouldn't have to talk to this piece of shit again."

Jackson laughed as well. "Yeah, he *is* a piece of shit, all right." The watch commander quickly turned serious again. "All the same, he's a high-profile prisoner under my roof, and the man's counsel could make trouble for me. The lawyer is even more annoying than Elgin, but she knows her business."

"She?" Kealey asked with obvious surprise. *Why the hell would a woman want to represent Elgin?* "Who's the lawyer?"

"Her name is Alex Harris," Jackson said. "This isn't the first time I've dealt with her. She runs her own little firm in Richmond, and her track record is pretty damn good. Tell you the truth, I'm amazed that Elgin was smart enough to hire her."

He held out his right hand and punched a warning finger in their direction. "Anyway, the point is this: I'm happy to accommodate you, but if Harris decides to bring down heat on my command because you two fucked up somehow, then my attitude's gonna change real quick. Just so we're clear."

North and Kealey nodded contritely, and Jackson waved over a deputy standing by the door. "This is Matthews. He's gonna show you boys the room we've set aside for this little venture. He'll wait outside while you talk with the prisoner."

Ryan didn't want the guard, but he sensed that Jackson's cooperation was sketchy at best. More to the point, the watch commander looked like he wouldn't mind dismissing orders from a higher authority. Kealey didn't want to push his luck.

He saw that North shared his apprehension, and shot him a restraining look. "Thank you, Lieutenant. Let's get this over with."

As they walked several steps behind the guard, Ryan saw lingering concern in the DEA agent's face. "I know," he said, leaning in to speak in a low whisper, "it's not ideal. Get the lawyer out of there, Adam."

"What do you mean, 'Get the lawyer out of there'? Where the hell am I gonna—"

"Just get her out of there. As soon as you can."

They stopped at an unmarked door with a Plexiglas window tucked neatly into the gray steel. Matthews turned to face them. "Okay, gentlemen, I was told—"

"Hold that thought, Matthews. I'm going to go grab a cup of coffee. You guys want one?" Ryan asked.

North shook his head, discreetly shooting him another questioning look. Matthews nodded his head in the affirmative.

"Right back." Ryan moved off down the hall as North pushed his way into the interrogation room and Matthews took up station outside the door.

"I still don't understand why this meeting is necessary," Alex Harris said. She was glaring angrily at North while Thomas Elgin slouched in his chair, fingers interlaced with his hands resting on his paunch. He made no attempt to hide the smirk plastered on his face.

Adam ignored the prisoner, choosing instead to focus his attention on Harris. She was a stunningly attractive woman who tried very hard to play down her looks. Her efforts were largely unsuccessful; her figure was draped in a formless gray business suit that ended in a long skirt, but shapely calves hinted at what lay beneath the uninspiring attire. Her glossy auburn hair was tied back haphazardly, and she wore heavy glasses that kept slipping down her long nose. The thick lenses could not hide her bright blue eyes, though, or the anger that they currently contained.

"What are you staring at?"

A small grin played over his face. "Nothing."

"I'm sure you've already been made aware of this, Agent North, but my client has offered his statement to the Attorney General, and that offer was declined. So unless—"

"Did you really expect the A.G. to grant immunity for a statement that may or may not lead to additional arrests?" North asked her. The amiable smile was gone, replaced by a level stare that reduced most people to silence. He was surprised when it failed to faze the experienced trial lawyer. "I mean, let's not forget that part. It wasn't a free offer. In our opinion, your client is seriously jeopardizing any chance of cutting a deal by withholding information."

"Hey, buddy—"

"Shut up, Thomas." Harris held out a warning finger and managed to cut her client off before he got started. She met North's penetrating stare, but it was several moments before either of them spoke.

It was Adam North who finally broke the silence. "Could we speak in private, Ms. Harris?"

She shook her head violently, several strands of hair coming loose and drifting around her face in the process. "My client has the right to hear anything you have to say."

He stood abruptly and started toward the door. "Then it looks like I'll just have to report to the A.G. that your 'client' has once again failed to cooperate with this investigation. If you're pushing for a deal, lady, you're gonna be pushing for a long time."

He had the door halfway open before she called out. "Hold on, Agent North."

A moment later she was following him out of the room, closing the door emphatically behind her. She turned to the guard standing by the entrance.

"I don't want anybody coming in or out of this room until I return. Is that understood?"

"I got it, ma'am . . . No one in or out."

Satisfied with that response, Alex Harris stalked toward the visitors' lounge with Adam North following reluctantly behind.

It took nearly five minutes of wandering around, but Ryan finally found what he was looking for.

The registration desk was built in a large semicircle with an elevated counter facing out toward the lobby, much like the reception area in a hotel lobby. Four computers sat behind it, as did a number of telephones. An open doorway could be seen beyond all of this equipment, but the person manning the desk was nowhere in sight.

He leaned over the counter and studied one of the phones, taking the time to scan the handwritten markings beside each button. When he found the right one, he looked up at the fire plan posted on the wall. The faded paper provided a vague description of the facility's layout. Ryan pressed the button and lifted the receiver as the intercom crackled to life.

"Deputy Matthews, please report to Processing. Deputy Matthews to Processing."

Matthews looked up and frowned as the message was snapped out over the public address system. *Damn* . . . Processing was on the other side of the building, and he didn't have the keys to the interrogation room. At the same time, he couldn't afford to slip up with the watch commander. Jackson had already cut him down three weeks earlier for what he had done, or rather, for what he had *not* done in breaking up a fight in the housing unit that left one man slightly wounded and another in critical condition.

He weighed his options carefully. He knew that the big man was with the lawyer, and Elgin wasn't going anywhere in leg irons. Jackson had instructed him to remain outside the door, and countermanding one of the lieutenant's orders was usually grounds for termination.

However, Matthews also knew that Jackson and the head of Processing played basketball together in Arlington Mills on most Saturday afternoons. He was largely dependent on his knowledge about budding alliances within the prison hierarchy to counteract the effects of his own ineptitude. Matthews was keenly aware of his lowly status at the detention center.

The last of his indecisiveness melted away. He couldn't afford another poor fitness report in his file.

The smaller visiting agent, the quiet one with the black hair and gray eyes, was already forgotten.

Matthews moved away from the door and down the long hall toward Processing.

"So what exactly is on offer here anyway?"

Harris waited impatiently as North stirred his coffee and counted the seconds.

"I'm waiting . . ."

"Ms. Harris, we both know that your client is looking at some serious time here. Even if you somehow manage to get the conspiracy charge dropped, we still have him for supplying materials to Al-Qaeda and for assault on a Federal officer."

"This isn't news to me, North. What's your point?"

He took a deep breath and a long sip of coffee before answering. "The assault charge is a lock, okay? I'll testify myself, if the prosecutor asks. Hell, I'll probably volunteer my services. But I can deal on the other stuff. You know who the key witness against Elgin is, right?"

She nodded. The impatience began to dissipate, replaced by a mild interest. "Your CI."

"You got it. He's pretty sharp, a hell of a lot more reliable than most of the people we're forced to work with. And I think he'll make a good witness. That said, his memory could get a little fuzzy if your client decides to cooperate."

Alex Harris spread her hands out on the table, palms up in a conciliatory gesture. "I think we have something to build on here, but that just isn't good enough. I need a retraction from your informant, and I need it in writing. That's the only way that Elgin is going to talk."

North didn't respond immediately, but his mind was working away. *You might be surprised, lady. Your boy might be talking sooner than you think.* His eyes involuntarily moved to the clock mounted on the wall of the lounge. Five minutes had elapsed since they left the interrogation room.

Never before had five minutes felt so long to the young DEA agent.

Ryan was walking away from the desk when a voice reached out behind him. "Sir? Excuse me, sir . . . What were you doing in here, just now?"

He kept walking, and the voice got a little louder. "*Sir*, please answer my question."

Ryan turned his head to answer but kept moving forward. He wasn't really concerned; the words were authoritative, but the voice itself was tinged with indecision. It was a woman speaking, and not in the tone typically used by a deputy sheriff hardened from years of guarding prisoners. "I'm a Federal agent. Take it up with Jackson, he's the one who ordered the call."

Ryan realized that his last sentence didn't really make any sense, but it did what he intended. The receptionist was confused as she stared after him with worried eyes. She reached for the phone. She knew about Lieutenant Jackson, had heard in the break room the whispered rumors of his legendary temper. Why bother him without good cause? Besides, the man walking away from her desk was obviously not a prisoner.

What harm could be done?

The receiver was returned to its cradle as the receptionist sat down at her desk and resumed her work.

After three hallways and two turns, Ryan was once again standing outside the door. He was relieved to see that Matthews was gone, but felt a sudden streak of anger, mostly directed at himself, when he realized that the guard had probably locked the door before leaving.

If so, then that was it. He didn't have time to get through the lock; it was only a matter of minutes before North and the lawyer came back down the hallway, or before Matthews realized what had happened and returned with reinforcements. If only the guard was as stupid as he looked . . .

And it appeared that he was. Kealey breathed a soft sigh of relief when the knob turned easily in his hand.

He pushed the door open and stepped inside.

"You have to be realistic here," North continued. He was hunched over the table, staring intently at Alex Harris. "A full retraction in writing is not going to happen, because that translates into immunity on the conspiracy charge *and* providing aid to a foreign terrorist organization."

"I thought that's what you were pedaling," she said in exasperation. "You just expect me to take your word for it and then get Elgin to hand over his statement? Is that it?"

He stared at her for a long time. Seven minutes had passed. He hoped that Ryan was moving fast. "Ms. Harris, are you aware that the Treasury Department has already frozen your client's assets?"

Her face changed, and she tried to hide it by lifting her cup and taking a long sip of cold coffee. From the way her cheeks burned, North knew that the news had come as a surprise to her. He decided to tighten the screws.

"There's no reason you should have known about it, since it wasn't initiated by the presiding judge. From what I hear, you run a pretty small firm. I don't imagine that you have a lot of time for pro bono work—"

"So what are you saying?" she asked, cutting him off in midsentence. Her voice followed her temper and began to rise. "That I should file a motion for withdrawal? Hand it off to a court-appointed attorney fresh out of night school? If that was your plan, Agent North, then you're wasting your time. And mine."

She stood up and snatched at her briefcase, angrily pushing up on the bridge of her glasses as they slipped down her nose. As she moved to leave the lounge, he called out to her one last time.

"Why *are* you representing him then?" She stopped in her tracks and turned to face him. "You're not getting any money out of it, and this is a pretty reckless way to earn a reputation as a defense lawyer, because he's looking at twenty years any way you cut it." A lingering pause as North debated whether to ask the next question. The in-

decision resolved itself quickly, though, as he was genuinely interested in her response. "You have access to his criminal record. You
know what he did. As a woman, why would you want anything to do
with helping a man like that?"

When she finally smiled at him, North saw a cold, detached intelligence that gave him the answer before she even opened her
mouth. "Come on, Agent North. Don't be so naive. This trial is going
to be headline news all the way up until the verdict. For that kind of
attention, I think I'm willing to set aside the feminist agenda, at least
temporarily. After all, principles can't buy air time, can they?"

She winked at him, actually *winked* at him, and then spun on her
heel to leave the room. North leaned back in his chair. Well, that was
that. *Good luck, Ryan. Better you than me, pal.*

Especially if you have to deal with her.

When he stepped into the room, Ryan didn't say a word. He didn't
even look in Elgin's direction. He shut and locked the door behind
him, then checked for a camera in the upper right-hand corner near
the ceiling. Seeing nothing but bare walls, he turned to face the prisoner. Elgin was already up and cowering at the far side of the room.
His movements were awkward because of the handcuffs and leg
irons that bound him, as well as the heavy brace on his left knee that
served as a reminder of their last encounter. The smug look was long
gone, replaced by a mask of pure terror.

"*What the fuck!* What are you doing here, man? Where's my
lawyer at?"

Kealey advanced with startling speed, kicking a metal chair out of
the way before reaching the prisoner. His right fist moved in a blur,
slamming up into Elgin's solar plexus. As Elgin slumped and choked
for breath, Ryan lifted him up and pinned him against the wall, wrapping his left hand around the man's windpipe and squeezing hard.

"I don't have time to fuck around anymore, Tommy. You told me a
half truth once. It won't happen again. There was another name on
that bill of lading, wasn't there? You're going to—"

"*I don't know! I don't know anything, I swear!*"

Pulling back a few feet, Kealey pushed his weight forward and
slammed the injured man hard into the wall. This was immediately

followed by another violent blow to the stomach. The second was less powerful than the first, as Ryan struggled to keep the man upright and maintain his own leverage at the same time.

All the same, it was enough. Elgin retched and continued to slump to the ground. Ryan let him go, then reached around and pulled an object from underneath his jacket at the small of his back.

Elgin's eyes grew wide when the knife was produced. He leaned away from the weapon, which only made Ryan's job easier as he reached to pull Elgin's head back by grabbing a handful of greasy hair, leaving the man's throat unprotected.

"Do you remember this?" Kealey waved the ceramic knife in front of Elgin's bulging eyes. "I'm sure you do. That was a bad move, by the way. You really pissed me off with that little stunt. She still got the drop on you, though, didn't she? I guess you're not as tough as you thought . . . There was another name on that bill of lading, wasn't there? Otherwise, it wouldn't have gone missing from the harbormaster's office at NIT. Last chance—*What was the name?*"

Another violent shake of the head. Ryan's fist was like a stone around the tape-covered handle. He was taking it too far, and he knew it. The knife was on Elgin's throat, and he pushed it down until the blade began to sink and a thin red line appeared, little rivulets of blood running down and pooling on the cold tile. Elgin was screaming, muffled screams until Ryan realized that he was holding his hand over the man's mouth. He pulled it away and tried to collect himself. He realized that his hands were shaking.

"I'll tell you! I'll tell you anything! Please stop! Just . . . Jesus, just stop!" Elgin continued to ramble on, although the words were twisted and made incomprehensible by fear and pain.

"The name, Tommy. *Right now.*"

It was a long hallway, but Alex Harris was in no particular hurry, still fuming at the DEA agent's arrogance and her own wounded pride. His jab about money was especially painful because it was true. She had spent the better part of the last decade in a prominent Chicago-based firm, but her own firm was in its fledgling years, and she didn't have the time or resources to represent a client who couldn't pay, even a client whose case enjoyed broad publicity.

Despite what she had said in the lounge, she had no choice: she would have to file a motion for withdrawal. As she walked, she found her anger at this new development focused on the agent who had brought her the news. *What a waste of time,* she thought. *That guy pulls me away to offer something that he can't possibly have the authority to deliver, and then—*

The realization hit her with the force of a sledgehammer: *It was a sham. That guy couldn't have been more than thirty, and he clearly had no legal training whatsoever. Why would they send someone to deliver a phony offer, though? There was nothing to gain from it, unless . . .*

She realized with a start that the guard was no longer stationed outside the interrogation room. In fact, she couldn't see anyone in the hall, though she could hear a distant conversation to her rear. She began to run, the heavy briefcase banging against her leg, 100 feet away and closing. The deputies trailing her called out in surprise at the sudden movement.

Ignoring them, she reached the door and burst into the room, looking down into her client's panicked eyes.

Down until she saw that the blood followed the cracks in the tile beneath her feet.

She stumbled back and screamed in fear and shock, and then in rage as the deputies rushed toward the room.

Ryan turned the corner toward the exit, cursing inwardly when he saw what awaited him. Naomi Kharmai was arguing in loud tones with Adam North, who was sliding his pistol back into its holster after receiving it in exchange for his pass.

Naomi saw him and turned her fury away from the DEA agent. "What the *hell* are you doing here, Ryan? I was supposed to be part of this, remember? This is *bullshit!* Just you wait until the deputy director finds out . . ."

She went on and on as Ryan flashed his identification and slapped his pass down on the counter. The deputy who scooped it up was wearing a wide smile, clearly amused by the scene Naomi was making.

Ryan was less enthralled. Seconds from now he knew there would be a sharp crackle of static, followed by an urgent radio transmission. This would result in a second call to the watch commander, who would quickly determine what had transpired.

The door to the parking lot was less than 15 feet away.

"You have to stop, Naomi. Okay?" Ryan grabbed her outstretched wrist and pulled her close, whispering harsh words into her ear. "We need to get out of here *right now*."

She pulled away, but her face was still only inches from his. She fell silent as he guided her toward the exit. North was already stepping out into the freezing air. He held the door open as they followed him over the threshold.

Ryan was paying attention to everything while he held the door open, Naomi's hand warm in his own, sounds assaulting him from every direction: a distant conversation in the street, a car horn sounded by an angry motorist. The scrape of their shoes as the tile gave way to damp asphalt, and the crackle of the deputy's radio as the door eased shut behind them.

CHAPTER 25

WASHINGTON, D.C. • HANOVER COUNTY, VIRGINIA

The apartment was not, by any stretch of the imagination, a desirable place to live. The space was cramped and sparsely furnished. Tattered white curtains hung over the grimy windows. The counter, when cleared of half-eaten takeout, which was not often, was irreparably stained. The place stank of stale cigarettes and sweat, a smell that had been with her for the past six months. She guessed that most of it drifted up from the rooms below, and the rest emanated from her minder. Now, seated in a worn leather recliner, she could hear him as he moved around in the adjoining room.

Fatima Darabi leaned back in the seat, her dark brown eyes intensely focused on the flickering television in front of her. A cell phone rested on the end table next to her, as did a 9mm Makarov pistol. Both the phone and the gun were never more than a few feet away from her body. Her left hand was propped up beneath her chin. She watched . . .

It was amazing to Darabi that they would repeatedly show the atrocity on national television. She was even more surprised by the fact that the government allowed it. The collapse of the Kennedy-Warren was by no means a pleasant thing to see, even for someone who hated America as much as she did. Nevertheless, she knew that the footage had come at considerable expense to the networks, and had long ago learned that everything in this country was defined by its monetary value.

It was at times like this that she relished her role. Here she was, in the heart of the nation, with intricate knowledge of the man who had squeezed the trigger at the Kennedy-Warren, and yet the Americans knew nothing of her existence. To have such a privilege . . . !

The rage that drove her did not begin as her own, but it had been bred in her from the start. When the U.S. Navy cruiser *Vincennes* shot down Iran Air Flight 655 over the Atlantic in July 1988, the admirals in the Pentagon had called it an accident, pleaded their innocence even as U.S. munitions continued to pour into Baghdad. Her brother had been on that flight, returning to American University in Dubai after two weeks at home.

In the years preceding her brother's death, her parents had been peaceful people, warm and caring. They had the capacity to hate, though, and when they discovered the same quality in their daughter, they nurtured it as carefully as they nurtured her body and her mind . . .

Fatima was pleased by her current assignment. She had been briefed on few specific points, but she was astute, and knew that the money she had dispersed through more than fifty foreign accounts was going to someone important. The name itself could tell her nothing, as it was obviously not his own. The man's voice told her little more; it was not difficult to detect the French lilt on the other end of the line, but she suspected the accent was affected for her benefit. She was not trained in such matters, but it did not matter. It would not pay to delve too deeply. She had received her instructions from the minister himself, a fact that she was quietly proud of. She would not live forever in this hole. Soon, she would be brought back to Tehran to assume her rightful place at Mazaheri's side.

But for now, she was waiting for the next call. When it came, it would be a few clipped sentences, most likely a murmured request for additional funds. The man wasted no time in conversation. It was a character trait that Darabi appreciated.

She stirred in her seat. The cell phone was ringing . . .

*   *   *

The day wore on like it was never going to end, but the long hours in the office were not the source of her mood. They only compounded the problem.

Nicole Milbery pulled her eyes away from the telephone and tried to concentrate on the seller's agreement she was filling out on her computer. She was trying to understand why he hadn't called. She thought that the two hours they had spent in the barn had been incredible, definitely worthy of a follow-up performance, but it was becoming apparent that her most recent client didn't feel the same way.

She felt cheated and humiliated, emotions made worse by the fact that she still wanted him, wanted him to call, wanted again what they had experienced only a few short days ago.

It was not her way to be patient, to let things fall into place. *If he doesn't call by tomorrow,* she decided with finality, *he's going to regret it. No one treats me like this.*

She realized she was staring at the phone again. She tried hard to ignore the little pinpricks behind her eyes and went back to angrily punching at the keyboard that rested on her desk.

Frank Watters watched with thinly veiled interest as the sole customer moved through the rows of household appliances and electronic gadgets. The man who moved without pause past heavy refrigerators and elaborate stereo systems did not fit in amongst his regulars. At the same time, he wore clothes unmarked by the dirt of a building site, unstained by the remnants of a hurried lunch eaten from the tailgate of a truck.

Watters, the elderly owner, was pleased by his own observations, and did not hesitate in making them; there was very little else to do on a quiet Thursday afternoon.

Located just south of Ashland in Hanover County, Watters's Electrical Supply was a haven for housewives and electricians from three counties in any direction. His business was not hurting for customers, but the store was busy in the early morning hours alone, when his regulars came in to purchase what would be needed for the day's work.

The sole customer had been in the store for almost twenty minutes, absently fiddling with the big-screen televisions, when he finally brought his list to Watters. As the paper was pushed over the counter, the old man noted with a small twinge of satisfaction that his earlier observations had been correct. The tanned knuckles were missing the scrapes and scars that were particular to an electrician or an independent contractor. The fingers were long and slim, but still retained some appearance of masculinity, as did the man's broad shoulders. Watters, with his insatiable curiosity, thought the hands more appropriate to a writer, or a pianist, perhaps . . .

The customer knew what he wanted, though, and any lingering doubts that Watters might have had concerning the man's expertise were soon dispersed. The order was not unusual, and so the old man was easily able to fill it from his stock: Number 18 AWG copper wire on a 50-foot roll, a single-pole toggle switch with two exposed terminals, wire cutters of good quality, several screwdrivers of various sizes, and electrical tape.

Watters gratefully accepted cash for this small purchase. He had no way of knowing that his only customer of the afternoon would later visit two other supply stores to complete his requirements, nor could he know for what purpose these materials were intended. Any suspicions he might have had were dampened by the man's polite manner and the easy smile that was offered as the customer pushed open the door and stepped outside.

In the true heart of the state, far from the bustling cities of Richmond and Norfolk, beyond the comfortable rurality of the Blue Ridge Parkway and the scenic views offered by winding ribbons of road, lies the heavily forested land of rolling hills that remains largely untouched by the time and wallets of transient tourists.

At night, the air is pierced only by the gentle songs of birds and crickets, or the rushing wind as it follows the jet stream and pushes northeast through the uppermost branches of leafless trees.

For November, Virginia is experiencing a certain anomaly. The state has earned a dubious honor by surpassing the prior record for most days with measurable precipitation in any month of the year. It has rained for eighteen days and nineteen nights, and Will Vanderveen, as he sits hard at work in the steeped shelter of the barn behind his modest home, is beginning to understand how Noah must have felt.

When he thinks of the ark lifting in the great flood, he is buoyed as well, but not by the prospect of salvation.

The interior of the barn has undergone no grand revisions in the short time that he has occupied it; in fact, it remains largely the same. There are only a few noticeable differences: A large swath of broken straw has been cleared from the cement, pushed to the sides to make room for the white Ford Econoline van that now dominates the open space. Against the far wall, on the opposite side from the sliding door, a large wooden table has been erected. A myriad of tools and materials can be found on the rough surface, patiently awaiting his ministrations.

In addition to the materials purchased at Watters's Electrical Supply, Vanderveen has managed to find a portable workstation with a lamp and optical magnification, which will be crucial for the more delicate parts of the job. The workstation sits on top of the table next to a soldering gun, rated at 20 watts, accompanied by two ounces of Antex solid wire flux.

Beside the soldering iron rests a digital ammeter and 30 feet of pliable conduit. All of this equipment combined would be useless without the pair of Verizon cell phones that Vanderveen has purchased on the outskirts of Richmond, along with three months of nationwide service. He will not need more than a few weeks from the phones, but to deviate from the plan is to attract notice, to attract attention . . .

Sitting in his hard wooden chair, listening to the gentle patter of rain on the roof overhead, Vanderveen's mind is far away as his hands move with speed and confidence. Far from the intricacies of solder joints, far from the strained relationships between voltage, current, and resistance through a circuit.

He is troubled by the fact that the money was not routed directly to him. They could have easily routed it through the Caymans instead of their own intermediary. It would have cut out a great deal of unnecessary risk, although the woman has done well so far in making the funds readily accessible.

For the most part, though, his mind is occupied by the other woman, the realtor.

On reflection, he can concede that it was a mistake. Deep inside, a small voice tells him that he is making a great many mistakes these days. A sweaty afternoon spent in the straw of the barn was not worth even the slightest chance of detection. By giving her what she wanted, by easing the quiet desperation, he had granted her access. Access to him, and access to what he is doing. Now, it was not inconceivable that she might choose to stop by unannounced.

He was grateful for the lock on the sliding door. At the same time, he recognized that it was a temporary impediment.

He thought that he was weak because, before Washington and Mashhad, he had spent two weeks with Sadr's advisors in Najaf, and before that, seventeen weeks in the fear-drenched killing grounds of Ramallah. If he had been trusted in those places, he would have been given a woman. As it was, he was tolerated but not accepted. He was only recognized later, when he was gone, when he was no longer a danger to the respective organizations.

After all that time, five months of forced abstinence, the night with the realtor was like salve on an open wound.

And now it was a serious threat to his freedom and his life. Afterward, with her naked form wrapped around him in the soft straw of the barn, she had spoken with undisguised contempt of her husband. He had recognized a need in her, a need that would not be satisfied at home.

If he could satisfy that need, as he had done once before, then the woman was a threat to his freedom and his life.

Vanderveen pushed those thoughts aside. It was done, and he could not change it. If it was a weakness, to need a woman, then it was a weakness he thought he could live with.

The copper wire turned in his hands. Back to the task at hand, he ran through the schematics in his mind. It would begin at the power source, running from the battery to the terminals on the switch. The battery would not be hooked up until the last minute, though. He still had to determine how long the circuit could remain closed before the battery was drained of power and unable to provide the requisite 12 volts. That would come later.

From the switch, the two-cable copper wire would run out to the exposed circuitry of one of the cell phones, and then on to the number 6 blasting caps.

For the moment, the copper wire hung limp over the side of the wooden table.

Vanderveen surveyed his equipment with satisfaction. The crates that had been retrieved from the Norfolk Terminals were well hidden beneath the straw in the barn, but the inquisitive mind of the realtor was always in his thoughts, as was the scheming mind of his former commanding officer.

Kealey . . . Vanderveen did not often think of him. He had discovered, through a discreet inquiry, that the man had been present at the Kennedy-Warren just before it blew. *How much more convenient it would have been if Kealey had died in the explosion,* he mused. Vanderveen did not think it likely that his old friend posed a serious threat to his plans.

All the same, he knew that the problem of his former commander's involvement would have to be addressed. His work could not be compromised because his work, at any given moment, had the unlimited potential to instill fear, to feed the paranoia that was spreading like a plague throughout the American public.

When the towers crumbled on 9/11, it was as if he had been reborn. The weeks after the attacks had seen blame thrown toward every corner of the globe, but it was bin Laden and his organization that received the brunt of it. And when it was narrowed down, when it was a certainty, only then had Vanderveen sought to expand his own horizons.

At the time of greatest danger, when new volunteers were considered with the greatest unease, Vanderveen had slipped effortlessly into the organization, because the hatred that he felt toward his adopted country could not be feigned, and the hatred was not satiated by the death of three thousand Americans.

Ever so gently, he touched the grounded tip of the soldering iron to the mechanical joint on the single-pole switch. In its final state, the two-wire annunciator cable would form a parallel circuit. It would be necessary to check the current moving over each detonator, because he knew that a single cap would require between 2 and 10 amperes to function correctly. The voltage would not be a concern, as that was the only common parameter in the circuit he had devised. He had decided on four detonators; only one cap was actually required, but he would not risk the chance of a misfire.

He worked into the early-morning hours, his hands moving steadily, the device taking shape. Six months ago, it was a dream. Four months ago, the glimmer of an idea. Two months, a working plan. Now it was a certainty. The wire was warm beneath his fingers, running in its predetermined path until Vanderveen decided otherwise. It was his creation, and he had little doubt that it would function as intended. Still, there were days to go, and no limit to what might go wrong.

North was the first to leave the parking lot, his mud-spattered 4Runner bouncing out onto Mill Road, followed soon thereafter by a spirited squeal of rubber as he took the sharp right turn onto Eisenhower Avenue. Ryan turned the key in the ignition as soon as Naomi clambered into the passenger seat. Then they were pulling out of the lot in another squeal of tires, Ryan making full use of the car's six gears as the engine roared in approval. First he headed south, navigating his way down Huntington until it merged with Route 1. Then he pushed the vehicle back up to the Jefferson Davis Memorial Highway, which he followed for several miles as he threaded his way back into Washington.

"What the hell was that all about, Ryan?" She was turned in her seat to face him, the anger glowing in her eyes and cheeks.

"We needed results, Naomi. The way you had it planned wasn't going to work—"

"How would you know *that*?" she asked, her voice rising again. "You didn't give *my* way a chance, did you?"

"He gave it to me, Naomi. Elgin gave me the name. He took the waybill from the terminal because he wanted something to deal with later, just in case. He didn't know at the time how big this was going to get. The name was insurance, that's it."

"How did you get him to tell you?"

"That's not important. The second person on that missing waybill was George Saraf. Judging by the surname, I think you'll find it's another identity for Michael Shakib. Not as good as a direct line to Vanderveen, but it's still something."

"How did you get the name, Ryan?"

A light drizzle had returned to the city, the gentle touch of a storm system that was lingering over central Virginia. There were very few other cars on the highway, and he was glad of the open road as the distinctive white markers of Arlington National Cemetery flashed by in the dark.

Ryan turned to look at her, knowing that she wouldn't stop until he said the words. She would know soon enough anyway. "I beat it out of him, Naomi."

Her eyes widened, perhaps a millimeter or two, but she did not respond. It was what she had expected to hear.

A lengthy silence ensued. She settled back in her seat, glad of the truth, thinking that the explanation was over. She was startled when he continued speaking, almost as though he hadn't stopped in the first place.

"But he still wouldn't talk, you know? When it's a piece of shit like Elgin, you think it'll be easy, but sometimes they surprise you. Sometimes they surprise themselves . . ." Ryan told himself to let it go, to spare her the details, but the words kept coming, seemingly of their own accord. "I only had a few minutes, Naomi. We were at a standstill. You know it, and I know it. I have piles of paper at Langley, you have even more, but sitting behind a desk isn't going to get us any closer to Vanderveen."

There was an edge to his voice. She turned to stare out the window, but he wasn't done. His left hand dug down between his back and the warm leather seat. She didn't see what he was doing until the knife was extended at arm's length, handle first. "You wanted to know, right? You asked the question . . . This is how, Naomi. This is how I got him to talk."

She recoiled at first from the proffered weapon, but a strange curiosity took over as she watched her own hand reach out to accept it. She could see that Ryan had dismantled the wooden grip, presumably because the rivets would have set off the metal detectors inside the building. To make it a usable weapon, he had wrapped electrical tape around the exposed handle. The slick black surface was still shiny and damp with sweat.

Turning it over in her hand, the light from the streetlamps caught and illuminated the blade.

She saw a streak of red on her palm.

The knife fell out of her hand and away from her body, the light weapon bouncing once before coming to rest on the floorboard at her feet.

"I had to convince him, Naomi. I had to show him I was serious. It was the only way. Naomi?"

"Take me home, Ryan." The words were small and pitiful. She *felt* small and pitiful. The blood was sticky and wet on her hand, and she was looking around desperately, but there was nothing in reach with which to remove it.

He couldn't see her hand, or her face in the shadows. He hesitated, unsure of her reaction. "I need you to follow up on this. I'll probably be out of the loop when Harper—"

"I know." The words were almost inaudible. She was kicking at the weapon with her heel, pushing it back under the seat and out of her sight. "Just take me home."

She lived on a crowded row of town houses on M Street, uninspiring structures with crumbling brick facades and weathered Georgian detail. When the heavy sedan glided up to the curb, she pushed the door open quickly without saying a word. Ryan watched her run through the gentle mist of rain and disappear into the house as a number of emotions fought for room on his face.

Ryan believed that he had shown her something new, and he was not proud of it. It might make her stronger, smarter in the end, but there was a price to be paid for the experience: despite what she knew of his past, she would never again look at him in the same way. Knowing that he was now less in her eyes irritated him, rubbed at his emotions like sandpaper on sunburnt skin, and he wondered why that should be when they had known each other for less than a month.

The anger was a slow burn as he turned the BMW back into the heart of the city. He picked up the cell phone lying on the passenger seat and tapped out a number from memory. Katie answered on the first ring.

"Hello?" For some reason, they did not often use their cell phones to keep in touch. He was not surprised that she didn't recognize his number.

"Katie, it's Ryan."

"Hey! God, I've been so worried! When are you coming back? I'm starving, so I thought we might—"

"Listen, I need you to get your stuff together and check out of the hotel right now." The urgency in his voice was hard to miss, but she asked it anyway.

"Why? I have to—"

"Don't ask questions, Katie! I'll tell you later. Just get your stuff and go, okay? It's important."

There was a long silence. When she finally spoke again, the words carried a toneless resignation. "Where will you meet me?"

"I can't stop in front of the hotel. Turn left out of the front doors and walk three blocks. Only take what you can carry. I'll replace whatever you leave behind."

"I don't want you to replace my things, Ryan. I *want* you to tell me what's going on. I've been waiting here all day, and now you just—"

"I'll explain it to you later, I promise. Fifteen minutes, okay?"

He absently snapped the phone shut without waiting for her response, and then cursed under his breath when he realized that he had hung up on her.

Ryan didn't know how bad it would get. The room at the Hay-Adams was reserved under his name, and he knew that once the story got out, reporters would be cold-calling the local hotels to get a sound bite and video for the morning news. He didn't want his name in print *or* his face on television, and he didn't want Katie to suffer those indignities either. Refuge might still be found at Langley, but he wasn't yet ready to face Harper or the man's recriminations. Kealey needed time to frame his words, time to shape an adequate explanation as to why he had nearly killed a prisoner in Federal custody.

The prize was a name, but it was not a guarantee. In this case, he didn't think the prize would be enough to salvage his short-lived career at the Central Intelligence Agency.

That was fine by Ryan; he had made a promise to Katie, and he intended to keep it.

Through the thin veil of rain, the glittering facade of the Hay-Adams appeared in the distance. He hoped that she had managed to find a raincoat in the small store in the lobby, but knew that it wouldn't do him any good either way. Whether she reached the car dry or drenched with rain, he was almost certainly in for another argument.

Without thinking about it, he took the knife out from under the passenger seat and slid it under the floormat beneath his own feet. Naomi Kharmai, as prepared for it as anyone could be, had been exposed to violent death twice in the last month. In the case of Stephen Gray, the death had been one of necessity. Some might have said, and he thought a case could be made, that it was actually one step behind outright murder. If it *was* murder, though, then it was understandable, even justifiable. What could not be rationalized was the random, senseless death she had been forced to confront in the broken remains of the Kennedy-Warren.

Ryan could do nothing for her now; she had touched the cold, sharp edge of reality and would sink or swim in her own time. He thought he recognized in her the strength to set it aside, to push it away and carry on with the task at hand.

If he could have kept it away from her altogether, he would have done so gladly.

It was his strongest desire that Katie should never have to endure the same. It was the reason he wanted her out of the hotel, and it was the reason he pushed the knife under the mat. If he was hard on her, if he told when he should ask, it was done out of fear that she might one day be forced to carry the same burden, year in, year out, until it crushed her spirit and her life with its weight.

Just as he would give anything to have her close, he would give anything to protect her innocence.

He would never have expressed these thoughts to her; it wasn't in his nature and the words would have come out awkward, clumsy, and wrong.

He hoped she knew it, though. He hoped she felt it. To Ryan, only one thing took precedence, and soon, Katie would be everything, the only thing. When that day came, he knew that he would finally be able to put the past to rest.

CHAPTER 26

WASHINGTON, D.C. • LANGLEY

A day trip to Washington, to look at the route and consider the options.

It was a fine day for the journey. Away from the clouds that hung over central Virginia, away from the monotonous calculations and mind-numbing work with the soldering iron. He took his most recent acquisition, a four-year-old Honda motorcycle, a VT1100 Shadow, all chrome and glistening metallic paint. He preferred not to use the van until it was absolutely necessary. Had he driven it into the heart of the city and been stopped for a traffic violation, the vehicle would have become useless to him.

He pushed the bike north on I-95, turning onto Exit 170 before racing through the western edge of Alexandria. As he crossed the Potomac, reflections from the river below scattered shards of sunlight over the polished curves of the motorcycle.

I-95 was, for the most part, a seemingly endless stretch of empty road bordered on both sides by towering stands of pine. He had been tempted to open the throttle, to get some fun out of the ride, but the desire was tempered by an unusually heavy police presence and the Virginia State Police Cessna 182s that drifted far overhead. Still, the open air was a huge relief from the confines of the barn, where the locked door and the threat of the realtor seemed to bring the walls closer each day.

He made the turn onto US Route 50, also known as New York Avenue. Vanderveen left Prince George's County at the same time he crossed the Anacostia, pushing west into the southeastern edge of the District. As the Washington Convention Center loomed large in front of him, he turned left onto 7th Street, the Honda's big engine ripping through the calm air and bringing some of the more complacent tourists to life. He grinned at their startled expressions as he crossed Independence going south, turning his head ever so slightly to look down the length of the road.

The sight failed to stir any emotion. The debris had long since been cleared, the burnt-out hulks of the vehicles currently resting in a disused airplane hangar at Dulles, where teams from the FBI's Forensic Unit and the National Transportation Safety Board continued to scrape at the scorched surfaces in vain search of evidence.

Vanderveen's interest was nothing more than that of a curious motorist turning to peer at a roadside wreck. He turned from the scene even before the open space gave way to an endless procession of parked cars and building fronts.

The Gangplank Marina stretches from the Francis Case Memorial Bridge to the end of Water Street. Across the channel lies the close-clipped grass and brightly colored flags of the East Potomac Golf Club. The 310-slip marina, which is almost always full, is shadowed, as is the club, by the towering presence of the Washington Monument to the west.

There are boats of all descriptions docked at the marina: 29' Boston Whalers, a diesel-powered Catalina, smaller catamarans, sailboats, and a sleek, 58' fiberglass Fairline Squadron—one of the largest motorboats at the port.

One yacht stands out from the crowd, however, and it was this craft that held Vanderveen's attention as he perused the walkway next to the marina, skirting small groups of tourists while keeping his distance from the slips themselves. The USS *Sequoia* was slightly more than 100' long, with most of the main deck, including the pilot-house, enclosed by teak-and-glass paneling. It was his first look at the boat, but Vanderveen knew its history. He knew that Nixon sailed down the Potomac eighty-eight times on the presidential yacht, and that it was the setting for Eisenhower's meetings with Churchill and Field Marshal Montgomery on the eve of World War II. Vanderveen had also learned that the *Sequoia* was sold into private hands by President Carter in 1977, after which it deteriorated for several years in a shipyard until restoration began in 1984.

Now owned by the Sequoia Presidential Yacht Group, LLC, it is available for charter, but use of the boat by the president or the vice president takes precedence over arrangements made by private citizens.

Will Vanderveen knew all of this, just as he knew that President Brenneman had already reserved, through the White House Office of Public Affairs, use of the *Sequoia* on the 26th day of November.

At first, he knew far less about Brenneman than he did about the yacht, and was confused as to why the president would want to sail the frigid waters so late in the year. It was not until later that he discovered, by browsing microfiche at the Richmond County Library, that Brenneman was an avid sailor and the proud owner of a Thomason ketch, which is docked at his home in Boston Harbor.

Vanderveen guessed that Italian and French leaders would find the cold wind whipping over the Potomac far less enjoyable. He smiled at the mental image that accompanied this thought and studied the *Sequoia* through a pair of Ray-Bans, his face partially hidden beneath a faded baseball cap. At one point he had considered an attack on the presidential yacht itself. The assassinations could have easily been carried out with a single underwater mine such as the Swedish Rockan; he had seen the same device used effectively in the Strait of Hormuz and other places. He knew that the Secret Service had no protocol in place for dealing with such a threat, and that by close-tethering the Rockan's steel case to the *Sequoia*'s anchor, he could further reduce its acoustic signature and impede their obsolete countermine equipment.

At the same time, he was leery of the mine's sensitive electronic components, not trusting a remote device to function correctly unless he had devised it by his own hand. The principle, that he was taught so long ago and lived by still, was "simplicity equals success." By limiting the number of components, by testing the firing system over and over again, only then could he be sure of his work.

The waterfront made him nervous, too. The few roads leading away from the area would be manned by dozens of Secret Service agents, ready to instantly seal off the perimeter in the event of an attack. He couldn't abide the thought of being trapped in a tightening noose of Federal agents, even for the chance to see the *Sequoia* sink to the bottom of the Potomac. Supposing, of course, that he survived the encounter, the ensuing years spent rotting away in a Federal penitentiary would not be worth a few rapturous weeks of national anguish.

No, he much preferred to live through the event. With 3,000 pounds of SEMTEX H strategically placed on the motorcade's route, survival would be a definite possibility, and success all but guaranteed.

Walking back to the Honda, Vanderveen swung onto the leather saddle and turned the key in the ignition. Kicking the bike into gear, he gunned the engine and sped off down 7th, heading north toward Pennsylvania Avenue. There was still a lot to see and do before leaving the city.

"I can't fucking believe you, Ryan. Andrews came down on me like a ton of shit for your little escapade in Alexandria. You know what he called it? Untenable. He used that word at least a dozen times. Did you hear me tell you not to leave a mark on him? *Did you?*"

Once again, Ryan found himself seated across from Jonathan Harper, and once again, the conversation had taken a turn for the worse.

He decided to go on the offensive. There wasn't a lot to lose either way. "I'll go willingly, John. I already told you I wanted out, but I'm your—"

"What?" A grim smile played at the corners of his mouth. "You're my what? Best shot at getting Vanderveen? Is that what you were going to say? Because the director doesn't believe that anymore, and I'm not so sure of it myself."

"Nobody else has managed anything—"

"And nobody else has shot dead a well-known businessman on foreign soil, Kealey. Nobody else has assaulted a prisoner in Federal custody. Every time that I tell you to keep things quiet, you turn what should be a simple operation into a fucking spectacle."

Ryan thought that he had taken it too far this time because Harper was using his last name. It was a rare occurrence. Against his better judgment, he pressed on: "And ninety-two dead on Connecticut Avenue, John? Eight Secret Service agents and a U.S. senator dead? What do you call that?"

"It's because we don't play by their rules, Ryan, that we're better than them—"

"It's because we don't play by their rules that we're *fucking losing*." The words were spit out, along with the last of his self-restraint.

A long silence ensued as they stared each other down over Harper's desk, each waiting for the anger to dissipate in the other.

"You don't make my job any easier, Ryan." It was the last jab, and right that it should belong to the deputy director. "Undoubtedly, you're wondering why word of your late-night visit hasn't reached the front page of the *Washington Post*."

"The thought had crossed my mind."

"We cut a deal with Elgin. Full immunity, straight from the top."

Ryan flared, but Harper's hand was up to stop him. "You don't get a say in it, because it was your doing. The A.G. sent the offer directly to Elgin, because the attorney . . . You've met her?" A brief, angry shake of the head. "Well, the attorney is a high flier. She would have taken the publicity of a scandal over a deal for her client, but Elgin, dumb as he is, knew better. He said he would fire her if she broke the terms, and that would have looked worse for Harris than having her client walk away free and clear.

"In other words, Ryan, we got pretty damn lucky. Harris was the easy part—we're still trying to convince the watch commander that it would be better for all concerned if he just dropped the matter. He doesn't want the publicity either, so that might help us out a little bit. Only—and I want you to pay special attention to this," he said, jamming his index finger into the top of his desk to make the point clear—"only because we had something on Elgin are you still sitting across from me. Without that card to play, you would have been done, without question. You're making it hard, if not impossible, for me to watch your back. You have a name, fair enough. The name is different from the passport used in Valencia. Once again, fair enough. But you had better hope that this information turns out to be golden.

"Believe me," Harper said with a scowl, "nothing should be more important to you right now, my friend."

Naomi Kharmai leaned against the back of the third black Suburban, shivering hard despite the pale sun overhead and the thick woolen peacoat that was pulled tight around her. She was extremely pissed off, a fact that had been made abundantly clear to the SAC in the staging area. She had asked Harper if it could be kept in the Agency, had almost resorted to begging him, but he had mumbled something about "pressure for cooperation," and now she was essentially out of the loop. Despite being one of the first people on the scene, she had been told, in no uncertain terms, that she was now included only as a professional courtesy.

She listened to the banal conversations of the agents around her and the clatter of automatic weapons as the HRT operators pulled gear out of their trucks and shrugged into heavy bulletproof vests.

She was startled by the loud roar of a motorcycle racing down the road next to the parking lot. Turning toward the sound, she was almost blinded by the light reflecting from the bike's chrome pipes and bright blue paintwork. Squinting into the scene, she jumped again when a hand clamped down on her shoulder.

"Should be less than twenty minutes," the man said.

She turned to face Bill Green, the Washington field office replacement for Luke Hendricks. "What, exactly, are you waiting on?"

"Search warrant to come through," he replied. "I just got off the phone with one of my people at the courthouse. Evidently, the judge wasn't too happy about how you dug up the information. She had a long talk with Alex Harris, and that helped out a little bit—"

"You think she's dragging it out on purpose?"

"That would be my guess. We don't really have a choice either way, so we wait here until we get the word."

"Hey, boss." They both turned as another agent approached. It was one of Green's fawning aides, a tall, well-dressed prep-school type. He handed the SAC a thin manila folder. "This just came back from the courthouse."

Naomi waited impatiently as Green perused the contents. "Well?"

He glanced up and flashed her a smile full of straight white teeth. "It's a go." Before she could respond, he was running toward the lead vehicle, shouting orders at the HRT commander, and then back at her over his shoulder: "Pick out a vehicle. You can wait on the sideline, Kharmai, but the teams are full. You stay *off* the field, understood?"

He didn't wait for an answer. She glared at his back as he climbed into the passenger seat of the first vehicle, which pulled fast out of the parking lot.

She found what passed for room in the last vehicle, smashed in between two sweaty operators and their piles of gear. The Suburban swung from 7th onto D Street, racing east as the retractable stock of an MP-5A3 banged painfully into her knee for the third time. She gritted her teeth and, as she had done so many times in the past few weeks, silently cursed Ryan Kealey for putting her into this situation.

The apartment building on D Street was less than impressive. The outside looked respectable enough, with a four-story brick facade and worn stone steps leading up to a solid door of weathered oak. As soon as she stepped inside, however, the smell hit her like a slap to the face. The stench was a putrid combination of various cooking smells, which wafted up from beneath closed doors and permeated the filthy walls, and the lingering scent of spilled beer and what might have been the contents of a baby's diaper. She almost retched until she started breathing through her mouth, and then saw that the others were doing the same thing.

Above it all, the piercing cries of a child and screamed obscenities from a Korean couple at the top of the stairwell.

Naomi lingered behind as Green and the HRT operators moved rapidly up the first flight of stairs. She had been given a flat 9mm pistol, which hung loose from her hip.

"How are they going in?" she asked Green when she finally caught up with him.

"It depends on what they hear. If there's activity inside, then it's entry rounds. If it's quiet, they'll go with the ram." She nodded and started forward, but he reached out to grab her arm. "Hold on, let them get into position."

The SAC listened to something over his earpiece, then turned back toward Naomi. "Okay, we're moving up. Stay behind me."

Inside the cramped apartment on the fifth floor, Abdullah Aziz al-Maroub watched intently as the last two agents went up the stairs. If it had to happen on his shift, he was glad it happened early, before the monotony of the work set in. In another hour, his back would have been sore and his eyelids heavy. He might well have missed them altogether.

He thought about how remarkably easy it had been to satisfy the apartment manager in the spring of 1998, when their predecessors had first set up in the city. It had taken nothing more than a few crumpled twenty-dollar bills to gain her permission, and the camera had gone up that same day. Positioned just above the transom inside the doorway, it gave him a clear shot of everyone leaving and entering the building. There was no sound; a video cable alone provided the images on the 20" screen in front of him, but he knew who these people were, and he knew why they were here.

As he called out for Darabi, his eyes never left the monitor.

Arriving on the fifth floor, Naomi saw that the operators were already in their preassigned positions. She held back with Green, her heart pounding in her ears.

One of the men extracted a fiber-optic snake from his pack. Holding the miniature video monitor in his left hand, he kneeled and slid the unit's tiny camera under the cheap wooden door of Apartment 5A.

Vanderveen was on 12th Street heading south when his cell phone buzzed in his jacket pocket. He pulled the motorcycle over to the side of the road and answered immediately. Only one person had this number, and she had been instructed not to call except in case of an emergency. "Yes?"

"Listen carefully, I don't have a great deal of time. The authorities are coming up the stairs right now."

"How many?"

"Seven. Five are heavily armed."

He managed to stay calm, despite the fact that this woman had personally wired the necessary funds to his bank account and knew the name he was currently using. "What are you going to do?"

"Don't worry, I won't be around to tell them anything. The place we're using is clean. We're almost finished wiping the disks."

"What about the phone? They can track—"

"The phone was cloned. Believe me, you have nothing to worry about on your end. I've been doing this for a long time. Do you have the necessary funds?"

"I already have most of what I need, and money left over for the rest of it." He paused briefly. "So that's it, then."

"I'm afraid so. Good luck."

Fatima Darabi pressed END without waiting for a response, her hands shaking as she deleted the call log on the phone. She had known it could come to this, but she had never really expected the worst. Now that the worst had happened, though, she knew she would do her duty. She felt a sense of falling inside, and wondered if her brother had endured the same as his plane fell to the surface of the Atlantic. Her reverie was broken as al-Maroub emerged from the bedroom, cradling an automatic rifle. She looked up. "Is it done?"

He nodded. Darabi reached for her weapon.

Without turning around, the operator crouched at the door, lifted one finger, then a second. His eyes, focused on the small screen in his left hand, suddenly went wide. Naomi, in the stairwell just behind the SAC, was leaning forward to whisper a question in his ear when a hail of bullets punched through the door in front of the entry leader. The first rounds caught him full in the chest, pushing him back across the dirty tile as the assault team returned fire.

Kharmai dropped to the ground as the hallway erupted. Her hand was down by her side, tugging at the pistol, then groping for the strap that held it in place. The door in front of the fallen operator was being torn apart by bullets, as was the thin drywall on either side.

The operators were scrambling for cover, but three went down before they could get out of the line of fire. Bill Green was lying next to her on the stairs, trying to talk, his mouth filling with blood. His face was frozen in a look of disbelief. Naomi saw with horror that at least a dozen rounds had shredded his body armor.

In that paralyzing moment, fear was an iron fist around her heart. She was gasping for breath, her eyes welded shut. She could hear the whine of the bullets as they slammed into the drywall inches above her head. The downed operators were screaming in pain until one of the terrorists filled the hallway with another magazine full of 7.62mm rounds.

The two surviving agents finally pulled it together, one providing cover as the other tossed a flashbang through a gaping hole in the shattered door. Naomi, with her eyes closed, didn't see the blinding light that spilled out into the hallway, but the grenade's concussion left her senseless as the door crashed inward and the operators disappeared from view.

Sitting on the Honda at the side of the road, Vanderveen watched the traffic pass. His face was blank, but his mind was churning.

It was time to walk away. Despite the woman's words, he knew she would overlook something; it was inevitable. After all, they had somehow managed to track her down. He had a second set of documents that she had no knowledge of, a set that he kept on his body at all times. He had used them already, and needed them for the 26th, but they could serve him now in a different way. National Airport was just across the bridge, not more than a few miles to the south. From there, he could connect to an international hub and be out of the country in less than two hours.

But then what? There were certain truths he had to consider here. There would be no place for him in the organization if he walked away now, that much was certain. The Iranians were the bigger threat. They might give him the benefit of the doubt, but more likely, they would assume he had blown the woman's cover. Either way, his own future was now inexorably linked to the outcome of the operation.

More important than any of this, however, was his own personal desire to see it through. For many years he had delighted in the perverse irony that the country he hated was giving him the tools of its own destruction. It had not been easy to feign his loyalty, especially in the beginning, when he was required to live in the squalid barracks and forced to take meals with his supposed peers. When he had finally revealed himself in Syria, it was with one end goal in mind: to inflict his pain on as many of them as was humanly possible. What waited in the barn on Chamberlayne Road would, in a few short days, advance this goal considerably. He could not, *would* not waste it now.

He was dimly aware of a rising rage. He had to push it down; it would not serve him here, but the question remained: how could this have happened in the first place? They clearly didn't have his bank account, the one he had used for the house and the van, otherwise they would have moved on him in Virginia. It had to be an outside source . . . Shakib? If he had been given the location of the safe house, it was certainly possible. But he'd never know because Shakib was dead, blown apart in the Kennedy-Warren, with Ryan Kealey waiting in the street below.

Nothing changed in Vanderveen's face with this recollection. *Kealey.* There was no doubt in his mind that his former commanding officer had something to do with this unfortunate development. It was bad enough that the man had the audacity to survive what should have been a kill shot in Syria. Now he was really pushing his luck.

Something sparked behind his eyes. If Kealey wanted to be involved, then so be it. Vanderveen started the Honda and eased back into traffic.

When she came back to herself, Naomi was alone in the hallway. Standing up, she checked herself for injuries, afraid of what she would find. Miraculously, her body seemed to be intact. She walked on shaky legs toward the wrecked apartment. As she reached the doorway, the two remaining operators pushed out, oblivious to her presence, talking quickly but calmly into their lip mics.

"TOC, this is Alpha 4, I have four agents down. I need EMTs *now.*"

Naomi stepped into the devastation, slipping her pistol back into its holster. The cheap furnishings had been nearly destroyed, the carpet littered with splinters of wood and shards of shattered glass. One of the terrorists was lying spread-eagled on the floor. She felt bile rise in her throat when she saw what was left of the man's face. She looked away quickly and forced a few shallow breaths, briefly catching the voices behind her in the process: "TOC, make that five down. I repeat, five down. Two tangos out of play. Confirm ambulances en route."

Passing into one of the bedrooms, she was aware of distant sirens. The room was sparsely furnished, its most notable feature a desk that had been smashed by bullets, and what looked like the remains of a laptop computer.

Fatima Darabi was sitting against the wall where she had fallen. Her body was ruined, but her mind was still intact and all she knew was pain. She opened her mouth to breathe. When nothing happened, she realized that she had only a few seconds left. Through the rapidly encroaching darkness, Darabi watched as the dazed-looking woman wandered into the room.

Darabi's fading brown eyes flickered to the handgun lying next to her. One of the agents had kicked it out of reach just after he fired a half dozen rounds into her chest. It was a stretch, but she would try for it anyway. Her body was dying, but the hatred that drove her was as strong as ever.

As Naomi examined the contents of the desk, she sensed something move behind her. She turned to stare at the body propped up against the wall, thinking she must have imagined the sound—until the eyes moved. Then, to her disbelief, the woman's hand was reaching out for the Makarov that lay a few feet to her right. The operators had obviously assumed, in their haste to get back to their fallen team members, that the subject was dead. But she wasn't dead, at least not yet, and the gun was in her hand and rising as Naomi frantically groped for her own pistol . . .

Naomi was far too late. The dying terrorist leveled her weapon and squeezed the trigger.

The pay phone was on the far edge of the lot, shielded from the storefront by a row of dilapidated vehicles, climbing out of a small mountain of refuse and cigarette butts. The metal casing was dented and scarred, and the telephone book absent, having been ripped away from its metal wire a long time ago.

Vanderveen didn't need the book, as the number was already seared into his mind. It was the last thing he needed to do in the city. He could not make the call from his cell phone or from his rented home in Virginia. Nor could he have done it from the waterfront, despite the slim chance that it would be traced back to that location. He picked up the receiver and dialed the number.

"Hello, you've reached the U.S. Army Rangers Association. This is Pam speaking, how may I help you?"

"Hi, Pam. My name is Ryan Kealey. I'm a member of your organization and I receive your newsletter, the 'Ranger Register.' I haven't been getting it lately, though . . . I recently moved, and I was wondering if you have my new address on file."

There was only a minor risk in this approach. She might ask for his Social Security number, former address, date of birth . . . any number of things, none of which he could answer. If she asked, he would simply hang up and look for another way.

"What is your new address, Mr. Kealey?"

He breathed a soft sigh of relief. "It's 1662 Manor Drive, Springfield, Illinois." He gave her the zip code. "I wasn't sure if I sent it or not . . . Is that what you have?"

He could hear the distant sounds of a computer keyboard over the line. "No, sir, I have 1334 Village Creek Road, Cape Elizabeth, Maine. I'll go ahead and change that for you now."

"Thank you very much."

"Is there anything else I can help you with today?"

Vanderveen looked up in annoyance before answering. Several ambulances were racing past him on the Dwight D. Eisenhower Freeway, and he could barely hear the woman over the scream of their sirens. "No. You've been very helpful."

"You're welcome. Have a good day, sir."

Vanderveen hung up and walked back to the Honda. He remembered Kealey as a man with incomparable devotion to the units in which he served. Since he had served in a number of units, it had taken a number of calls. A lot of calls, in fact. Vanderveen had almost given up when it finally came to him.

In that glorious moment of epiphany, he remembered that Kealey had once gone to the commanding general at Bragg with a fund-raising idea for the Ranger Memorial Foundation. This recollection had then led him to the USARA, one of the leading organizations chaired by former Army Rangers.

Vanderveen felt a twinge of satisfaction as he crossed the Francis Case Memorial Bridge and left the darkening Washington skyline far behind. He had come to a decision. He was going forward with it. He had come too far, worked too hard to throw it all away now. To assume the woman had taken her own life before talking required a tremendous leap of faith on his part, but he was prepared to take that leap. There was too much to lose if he didn't.

It had been a productive day, and Vanderveen allowed himself a glimmer of satisfaction at the knowledge that he once more held the power of life and death over a man whose fate should have been sealed on a Syrian hilltop seven years earlier.

After the late-night dash from the Hay-Adams, Kealey had traded down to a far more modest hotel on the outskirts of Alexandria. He had paid cash in advance before learning that the Elgin story was already dead, thinking that if the reporters managed to track him down, they had probably earned themselves a story. He was drained— physically from the long hours and the constant stress, and emotionally from the protracted argument with Harper that had not managed to resolve itself.

Ryan had no illusions that his career would continue at the Agency, but he respected Harper, counted him as a friend, and it bothered him that he had walked out of Langley without trying to repair the rift between them.

He brought the BMW to a halt in the dying light of the hotel's parking lot. He breathed deeply and closed his eyes, allowing himself, just for a moment, a glimpse at what life might hold when it was all said and done. The teaching at Orono wasn't bad; it was boring, but he could live with that. Maybe he'd get more involved, take on some extra classes. Maybe they would move, find a place closer to the city. Katie had suggested it recently, but he wasn't sure if she had been serious or not.

They could go anywhere. Ryan had a great deal of money, mostly inherited from his grandfather on his mother's side. He tried not to flaunt it . . . There was the car and the fancy hotels, but the house on Cape Elizabeth, while comfortable, was nothing overly extravagant for the area, and retirement was still nothing more than a distant possibility. The engagement ring had been his biggest purchase by far of the past year.

At the same time, he wasn't cheap, and there were so many places they could go . . .

He got out of the car and walked toward their room. Maybe, for a while at least, it would be good to get away. He wondered what she would think of a ceremony at sunset on a beach on the Mediterranean, and a smile touched his face at the thought of her reaction. Suddenly, he couldn't wait to ask her.

Unlocking the door, he was greeted only by silence when he pushed into the room. "Katie?" No answer.

Looking around, his eyes moved to the bed. Her luggage was sitting on the bedspread, her clothes spilling out of it. Just then she emerged from the bathroom and, seeing him, stopped dead in her tracks. The look on her face said it all.

It's your fault, Ryan, a little voice inside told him. *You've been ignoring her for weeks. You should have expected this.*

Still, he had to ask it. "What are you doing? What's wrong?"

There was a long silence as she summoned up her resolve. When she did, her words hit him like a slap in the face: "I'm leaving, Ryan. I'm going back to Maine."

He had seen it coming, of course, but that didn't make it any easier to hear. "Why?" She didn't answer, instead moving forward to cram the rest of her clothes in the bag. "Katie, please, just . . . Will you stop for a second?"

Her movements slowed until she stopped completely and looked up at him. Even from across the room, he could see that she was trying hard not to cry.

"Why are you leaving?"

" 'Why?' " She was incredulous, staring at him with a strange combination of anger, disappointment, and hurt on her face. "Are you seriously asking me that? Ryan, I've hardly seen you in the past few days, and all I can think about is what you're doing and whether you're okay or not. Do you have any idea how hard that is? Do you even remember why I came down here in the first place?"

"Yes, I *do* know. I told you—"

"You're such a liar," she interrupted bitterly. The look in her eyes reflected the pain she was feeling. "You don't understand at all. If you did, even a little bit, you wouldn't be putting me through this. You would know how much it hurts."

He was beginning to realize how serious this actually was. "Katie, I'm sorry. God, I'm sorry. I didn't know, I swear . . ."

She was still staring at him. The disappointment had given way to a gaze of distrust, which was somehow far worse. "I love you, Ryan," she finally said. "I do. But I can't be here while this is going on, I just can't. Being here, so close but not knowing what's happening, wondering if someone's going to knock on the door in the middle of the night and tell me that you—" She broke off abruptly, unable or unwilling to verbalize the thought. "It's just too much for me."

A horn sounded outside. Katie swiped at her eyes with the sleeve of her sweater and picked up her bag. "That's for me," she whispered. "I called a taxi. My ticket is waiting at the airport."

Ryan didn't know what to do. For all the anguish he was feeling, the worst part was seeing her in pain. He thought about reaching out for her, trying to hold her back, but sensed that that would only make things worse. He was fighting for words. How often does everything come down to a few sentences? What could he offer that might limit the distance between them? *Say something.*

"Katie?" She turned at the door but refused to lift her gaze. "I hope you understand that what I said before, about needing you . . . I meant that, you know? I can't think of anything else, or say anything else that would be more true."

She let go of what might have been a choked sob, but she still wouldn't meet his eyes. "Don't call me, Ryan."

"What?" The panic started to rise inside. He took a step toward her. "Katie, listen—"

"No!" She held up a wavering hand to stop him. "Just . . . don't, okay? Not for a while. I need some time."

"Katie!" She was gone, the door closing softly behind her.

He stared after her in disbelief, wanting to follow but unable to move, trying desperately to figure out what the hell had just happened. Looking around, he was vaguely aware of sterile prints and stock furniture. This would be life without her, he knew. Flat surroundings and still air.

He couldn't go back to that, not after what she had given him. He needed time, time to think about it, time to figure out how to get her back, but something was piercing his thoughts. He looked around, dazed, still trying to get his mind around the disaster that had just transpired. His cell phone was sitting on the dresser where he had tossed it earlier. After staring at it for a good twenty seconds, he finally realized that it was ringing.

Ryan was running back out to the car less than thirty seconds later. The tires on his BMW left a 6-foot strip of rubber behind as he peeled out into the night, back toward the city lights, back toward Washington. He had taken his jacket and his phone. For the moment, decisions about Katie would just have to wait.

CHAPTER 27

WASHINGTON, D.C.

When Naomi woke, her return to the world was a gradual process. First she had a sense of shadows spread across the ceiling, separated only by fine threads of yellow light. As she gained a sense of her surroundings—*a hospital?*—the light seemed to bleed into the dark patches, so that she soon became aware of the faces staring down at her. She read them carefully as her vision cleared. When she saw concern and not dread in their eyes, she felt relief wash through her body.

Ryan took her hand as Harper went to look for a nurse. "Naomi, can you hear me?"

She tried to speak, but her throat was dry and she wasn't altogether there yet. "Mmmm."

"You're going to be fine," he assured her. "You took two rounds, but the vest caught both of them. I wouldn't move around for a little while, though. It's going to hurt."

Sure enough, she felt a crushing pain in her chest when she tried to sit up. Ryan eased her head back onto the pillow and smoothed her hair. "Jesus, I just told you not to move," he said in quiet exasperation. "I don't believe you sometimes. If I told you not to run into traffic, you'd probably do it just to spite me."

She smiled weakly. "How long have I been out?"

"About three hours. How do you feel?"

She tested her limbs and winced. "Sore. Can I have some water?"

As Ryan went to fill a cup from the sink, she said, "When can I go home?"

"We're waiting to see," he replied gently. He handed her the cup. "Try to get some rest." He squeezed her hand as she drank. Harper reentered the room, followed soon thereafter by a harried-looking nurse. The young woman proceeded to check Naomi's vital signs as Ryan pulled the deputy director toward the door.

Once they were in the hall, he leveled Harper with angry eyes. "What the *fuck* was she doing on that raid, John?"

"She's a grown woman," Harper responded quietly. "She wanted the chance and I gave it to her. Besides, you're in no position to question me, Ryan, not after the shit you pulled with Elgin."

The younger man looked away and tried to calm himself. Anger wouldn't help him here, and he knew it. "What was in the apartment?" he finally asked.

"Not much, but it's early yet. We're still trying to ID the occupants. The landlord had names, of course, but they were meaningless. It would have been nice to take one of them alive. The Bureau found a cell phone, still intact but cloned. We probably won't get anything useful out of that. The outgoing calls were deleted. There was a laptop, too, but someone put a half dozen rounds into it when the shooting began." Harper leaned back against the wall and rubbed his eyes. "It wasn't a good trade, Ryan. HRT lost four operators with another one on the way out. The SAC got clipped as well. We didn't get shit in return. The Bureau's in an uproar; that's two of their top guys on the East Coast dead inside of a month. The only positive thing is that we've been able to throw the press off track. They're carrying it as a high-risk arrest warrant that went bad."

"There was no kind of documentation anywhere in the apartment? I find that hard to believe."

"Well, believe it," Harper said. "They knew what they were doing." A thoughtful expression came over his face. "I'm interested in the woman. You know how the Iranian hard-liners feel about women in general. They would only use one if it was absolutely necessary. Whatever she was doing for them must have been special. The landlord said these two landed on her doorstep about six months ago, so we'll have people checking immigration records from early in the year. If they were meant to be long-term sleepers, they would have burrowed right in. It would have been Tehran to Western Europe, to break up the trail, then on to Washington. There's a good chance we'll pick them out sooner or later."

Ryan looked up. "What makes you so sure they were Iranian?"

"Naomi said she heard them calling out to each other in Farsi when the shooting started."

"That only narrows it down, John. Farsi is spoken in Afghanistan, Iraq, Bahrain . . . They could have been from just about anywhere in the Middle East."

The DDO frowned impatiently. "Given recent developments, Ryan, I think it's safe to say they weren't Iraqis. This lead originated with Shakib, remember?"

"Yeah . . ." Kealey sighed heavily. "Yeah, you're right."

Harper was looking at him curiously. "What's wrong with you?"

"Nothing." He realized he had snapped out the answer. "What now?"

Harper was still staring at him. "They'll be discharging Naomi in an hour or two," he finally said. "The Bureau's supposed to be faxing the apartment inventory over to Langley, so I want to get back and take a look. Can you wait for her?"

"Yeah, I'll wait." Ryan rubbed his face wearily. He was tired, and he didn't want to sit around for an hour or two and brood about Katie, but he couldn't leave Naomi alone in the hospital. "Not a problem. I have some things to think about anyway."

Harper nodded and clapped a hand lightly on Kealey's shoulder. As he began to walk away, Ryan hesitated, then called out to him.

Jonathan turned. "Yeah?"

"About the woman who shot Naomi . . ."

Harper shook his head slowly. "It wasn't Naomi who got her. Naomi managed to get off a few rounds but missed. It was one of the Bureau guys."

"Okay . . . thanks."

"You bet."

As Harper was walking away again Ryan felt something lift from his shoulders. It was the last thing Naomi needed right now, to live with that burden. He was glad she wouldn't have to.

He went back in to wait for her.

CHAPTER 28

HANOVER COUNTY • LANGLEY • WASHINGTON, D.C.

The storm system had finally dissipated over central Virginia, leaving behind damp earth and tree limbs made heavy by weeks of rain. A steady wind blew in from the southwest, pushing scattered clouds across the early-morning sun and beads of water against the weathered timbers of the barn.

Vanderveen was in the dark shadows of the house, visible only when the clouds left the sun behind and let hazy light stream in through the open windows of the kitchen. He was looking in the refrigerator for something to drink and thinking about his plans for the day.

He finally settled on a small bottle of Tropicana orange juice. He was extremely tired, having slept little the night before. On his return from Washington he had watched the house for nearly four hours, half-expecting to see some sign of police activity. By the time he had finally deemed it safe, the sun was already topping the trees in the east. The fact that the house had not been raided meant one thing: the woman had followed through on her promise. He didn't feel any sense of sorrow over her death, nor did he feel any gratitude for her sacrifice. In fact, he was glad she was dead; she had been the most dangerous link between him and the Iranians. With the woman out of the picture he was safe, at least for the moment.

Everything was on schedule. He would complete the main charge by early afternoon, securing the more fragile components of the device in the van before testing the circuitry again. In the evening he would begin the arduous task of arranging the heavy concrete blocks that, once lined up against the metal partition that separated the cab from the cargo area, would serve to direct the force of the blast out through the rear doors of the vehicle.

The screen door slapped shut behind him as he walked out across the black soil toward the barn, stopping dead in his tracks when he saw the realtor's Ford Escape parked next to the barn. The sliding door, which he had eased shut but not locked, was now open wide to the cool morning air.

He cursed low, under his breath. Lost in his thoughts, he had not heard her arrive, and the kitchen window did not allow a view to the main road, from which he might have seen the vehicle approaching the rear of the house. After a few brief seconds of deliberation, Vanderveen kept walking forward.

She was standing next to the van, on the bare cement surrounded by straw. He looked around quickly to see what she might have touched before examining her face, which was almost lost in the shadows of the barn.

She had come to please. He could tell that from her tight jeans and stomach-baring halter top, from the light touch of strawberry-colored lipstick to the way her honey-blond hair carefully framed her high cheekbones. It was also clear that she had seen too much.

"Hi." She was uncertain, he saw with some amusement, because her planned argument had been ruined. He tried to remember her name. *Nicole.* "I was just . . . I just wanted to stop by because . . . Well, you know."

"Hi, Nicole. You don't have to explain anything. I'm glad you came." He flashed a winning smile and moved forward without missing a beat. She took two steps back, but there was nowhere to go. Pulling her close, he kissed her on the lips and let his hands slide down the length of her back. She didn't respond to his touch, and he immediately registered that she was too afraid to move. *Interesting.*

Vanderveen pulled away abruptly and walked over to closely examine his worktable. He couldn't be sure, but he thought that the light to his optical magnifier had been off, and now it was on, clearly illuminating the contents of the desk. He felt a trickle of annoyance.

"I—I was only in here for a second. I ju—just wanted to see you again . . . If you don't want me to come back, I—I won't. I'm sorry, I really am . . ."

The words were getting farther away. He thought that the conduit had been resting in a wooden crate, and now several pieces were sitting *next* to the crate. The trickle turned into a steady stream of anger.

"I—I didn't touch anything. I'm . . . Well, I'm so sorry I just walked in here, I—I should have knocked. I should have come up to the house first, I know . . ."

He thought, and he was almost certain, that his detonators had been in a tight group of four, and now one was separated from the pack, resting on the other side of a .40 caliber pistol. The stream gave way to a river of rage. He picked up the weapon, feeling its reassuring weight in his palm.

She was almost at the door, walking backward and still talking. "I—I—I didn't see anything, I sw—swear . . ." Her voice began to rise when he turned and she saw the gun. "Please let me go. *Please! I'm sorry! I didn't see ANYTHING, I SWEAR TO GOD!*"

He lifted the pistol and shot her once in the stomach, then watched with satisfaction as she collapsed to the cement.

They were seated in Harper's seventh-floor office, lounging in the same chairs they had occupied a few weeks before. Naomi was at home recuperating, at Harper's insistence. She had shown up that morning at Langley, hunched over with the pain. Harper had ordered her home to get some rest, but her initial refusal to leave had impressed Ryan. He didn't want to think about what that meant.

The deputy director was in a glowing mood. The Bureau had already managed to track down a taxi driver who had taken the Iranian woman to National Airport several days in a row during the first week of November. Since she had never actually boarded a plane, it wasn't hard for the agents tasked with the investigation to figure out what she had been doing there.

"She was using a locker," Ryan said.

"That's right." Harper leaned back in his chair. He looked pleased with himself. "They never found any ID in the apartment, but the locker was under the same name she gave to the landlord: Theresa Barzan. They found Saudi passports for her and her minder inside."

"Did *those* names come to anything?"

Harper's jovial mood seemed to fade a little. "Not yet. The investigation is drawing a lot of resources, though. They're going to start looking at banks—that's a lot easier to do since the passage of the Patriot Act. The Bureau thinks she might have been moving money for Shakib."

Kealey looked skeptical. "It's going to take forever to go through the banks, John. They'll fight the Feds every step of the way. What about Vanderveen? Was she supposed to be moving money for him as well?"

The deputy director shrugged. "Who knows? It's certainly possible. Anyway, there's been a development you need to know about. The director has been stuck in meetings all week—one of the upshots is that the visit by Chirac and Berlusconi is getting the NSSE designation."

Ryan was not at all surprised. NSSE stood for National Special Security Event, and the Secret Service, under Presidential Decision Directive 62, was the government agency primarily responsible for security planning and implementation at such events. He realized they'd be completely sealing off the Gangplank Marina on the 26th and that the FBI, FEMA, and the Washington, D.C., Metro Police Department would all be called in to help.

"The only problem with that, John, is that the designation will find its way into the hands of the press. Vanderveen will find out about it and make adjustments accordingly. There's no way he's going to back out now."

Harper's face dropped a little bit more. "I don't see what else we can do, Ryan. I know the banks are a long shot, but we're running out of time. Besides, we still don't have definitive proof that he's even in the country, let alone Washington, D.C."

"He's here, John. I'd stake my life on it." Kealey was thinking hard. "What about property?"

"What about it?" Harper asked. Then he caught on. "You mean a stable base of operations."

"That's exactly what I mean," Ryan said. There was a long pause. "Listen, I think it's time to make some assumptions. I know it's risky to do that, but I don't see that we have a choice. We have a lot of little leads, but we're not tying them together fast enough. We have to assume that Vanderveen is definitely going after all three of them: Brenneman, Chirac, and Berlusconi."

Recollection flickered in Harper's eyes. "From what Gray said to you in Cape Town."

"Exactly. Vanderveen was trained as a sniper, but he is an engineer first and foremost. To take out all three of them at the same time, he would almost invariably use a bomb. So if we assume that that's what he's doing, the question becomes: where is he building it?"

Harper thought for a moment. "Not in the city."

"No." Ryan was shaking his head. "Not in the city. Too congested, too many potential witnesses. At the same time, he wouldn't want to be too far away. When it's done, he has to travel with it. That's a risk in and of itself."

"So, what then? Virginia, Maryland . . . ?"

"That's where I would start. Recent rentals would be a good place to begin. If we go with the idea that he's storing explosives, he's going to need access to a house. Of course, that's a huge area to cover, so we have to limit the search parameters. He'll need a decent amount of land, not to use, but to ensure his privacy. We have to look in rural areas; start from farms, then move out to the suburbs. He'll want access to escape routes, and that means major roads—anything more than five miles from an interstate highway won't be a consideration."

Harper was staring at him. "Where is all this coming from, Ryan?"

"It's called OPSEC—operational security. The whole point is to minimize the chance of discovery. Vanderveen understands it as well as I do, but there are no guarantees and it requires a lot of guesswork on our part. It's why I was hesitant to suggest this in the first place . . . If we commit resources and I'm wrong, we'll be giving him a huge advantage."

The deputy director was nodding slowly. "All the same, at this point I think we have to take the risk. I'll talk to Andrews about making this a priority at Tyson's Corner. Of course, that will serve a second purpose by getting the Bureau and the Secret Service involved." Harper smiled wearily. "I have faith in you, Ryan, but I don't want the Agency running solo on this. We don't want to be the ones left holding the bag if it all goes to hell."

Vanderveen was intently focused on the most delicate part of the process, hunched over the magnifying glass and carefully examining his mechanical joints. It would take only a touch of solder, but the wiring would have to be thoroughly tested to ensure that his heat sinks had functioned as intended. Otherwise, it was possible that the heat of the solder gun might have damaged the sensitive components of the cell phone's ringer.

Frowning, he turned when he heard a noise behind him.

Nicole Milbery was contorted in the fetal position, her arms clenched fiercely over the wound as if to squeeze out the terrible pain. She had managed to drag herself perhaps four feet. The route was marked by an erratic trail of blood leading back to the glistening pool, but she was still no fewer than five feet away from her cell phone.

Vanderveen had searched her soon after she fell, a task made much more difficult by the fact that she was slippery red, screaming, and writhing in agony. He found the phone almost immediately, then felt a sweet rush of relief when he checked her outgoing messages and saw that the last one had occurred more than three hours earlier.

He was safe, but she had almost ruined everything.

In his anger, out of spite, he had placed it next to the straw on the edge of the cement. As the pool of blood continued to spread around her, she had questioned him, begged him, screamed obscenities, but every word had been met with silence. Then, when the realtor was all but forgotten, he had turned again to watch in fascination as she pulled herself toward the phone, moaning in anguish as each little movement sent jagged spears of pain racing through her abdomen.

He shook his head. Where did she think she was going? Surely she must know that he would never allow her to actually reach the phone.

She was much stronger than he would have imagined, but it was clear that she had finally given up. The determination of the dying woman had given way to pitiful sobs almost ten minutes earlier. Now she hardly made any noise at all, and the light was already beginning to fade from her soft brown eyes.

Once approved by the National Security Council, the NSSE designation put things into rapid motion on Water Street and the surrounding area. Around the marina itself, wire fencing was rapidly installed by a company whose twenty-five full-time employees had been thoroughly screened by the Secret Service advance team, which was already on the scene and working hard. The *Sequoia* was scoured from top to bottom for hidden weapons and explosives, and background checks were ordered for the residents who lived in the buildings that lined the waterfront.

It was determined, after heated debate, that the White House press office would take care of developing and distributing passes for the event. The list of people with access to the presidential yacht was reserved to a few choice aides whose pictures, backgrounds, and fingerprint cards were sent by diplomatic pouch from Paris and Rome to the head of the advance team. She examined the pictures and made sure that her people saw them. Then they went back to their preparations.

He would not be satisfied without first test-firing the device. It was already laid out across the cement. Standing in the shadows cast by the late afternoon sun, he quietly examined the work that had cost him the better part of the morning.

From the battery, the bare copper wire separated into two distinct paths, then came back together at the exposed terminals of the toggle switch. Conduit would be used to insulate the wire from the sheet metal of the van, but it would not be necessary here, as the cement served the same purpose. The wire split from the switch and reunited after 10 feet at the exposed circuit board of the cell phone. From there, it began to resemble a ladder. There was nothing unusual about the rails, but each of the four rungs was covered by a five-pound sandbag. Each sandbag, in turn, concealed a number 6 blasting cap. He had wanted the number 8 caps: the seismic detonators were both more powerful at eight grains of PETN per cap, as opposed to six, and safer, with a lower chance of hydrostatic discharge. All the same, he was relatively satisfied with what he had. It would do the same thing in the end.

He hadn't taken any chances, though. He had used the digital ammeter for the first time that morning to check the resistance over each blasting cap. It came out to roughly 1.9 ohms per cap, and a little more than 2 ohms over the switch itself.

The calculations had appeared in his mind like a sudden gust of wind on a calm summer day. The reciprocal of the sum gave him the total resistance in the circuit, 0.384 ohms, which in a parallel circuit is always less than the resistance over each component. From there, 12 volts divided by the reciprocal provided him with the total current moving through the circuit: 31.26 amperes. This translated to a little over 6.31 amps moving through the legwires of each electric cap. Using the ammeter to check his calculations, he had allowed himself a small smile at the numbers that appeared on the LCD display. Everything was working out perfectly.

Vanderveen understood how dangerous a test fire could be. Even now, with nothing more dangerous than four blasting caps at his immediate disposal, he took all necessary precautions.

After all, he didn't need to see the detonation. He only needed to see the effects.

He stood behind the bulk of the Econoline van and pulled the second cell phone from his pocket. The number to the first was on his speed dial. His breath came faster than usual, despite the fact that nothing important was about to happen. His finger hovered over the button. All around him, still air and dust particles floated in the dim light of the barn.

There was no sound from the woman. *Why not?* He peeked around the corner of the van to examine her still form. He realized, with a start, that he had not heard her move for at least twenty minutes. She must have died when he first started to run the wire out over the cement.

He was a little surprised that she had gone so quietly, but it didn't really matter. He returned to his position, completely focused on what was about to occur. His back was against the cool metal of the van, the number was on his screen. He breathed deeply, felt the dry air of the barn enter his lungs.

He pushed the button.

Joshua McCabe, the assistant director of the Secret Service's Office of Protective Research, arrived at midday to confer with the head of the advance team. Jodie Rivers was a petite, pixie-faced woman with inquisitive hazel eyes and shoulder-length auburn hair. At thirty-two years of age, she was young for her position, but a sharp intelligence, combined with the ability to spot problem situations long before they developed into full-blown situations, had earned her rapid escalation through the ranks, along with the grudging respect of her superiors.

After instructing his driver to wait with the Lincoln Town Car, McCabe followed her along the gangplank as she pointed out the various implementations that had been made. The assistant director knew her reputation within the Service as a go-getter with unparalleled energy, but he thought Rivers now looked tired and overwhelmed by the magnitude of her task.

"As you can see," she was saying, "the security fencing closes off the end of Water Street underneath the bridge. It's a dead end anyway, but we're waiting on concrete barriers that will go up on the other side of the fencing. We'll have at least three, and probably five checkpoints for pedestrian traffic moving through the area—I haven't finalized those arrangements yet, but we're taking a hard look at the spots where 6th, 7th, and 9th streets run into Maine. Those areas worry me because they're so open. We've designated 4th Street as the eastern edge of our perimeter, and we want to use Arena Stage as the command post. I have to talk today with the artistic director to see if that'll work . . . The main thing is keeping vehicles out of the area. Explosives are the big concern, so that's where we'll focus our efforts."

"What about the background checks?"

An agent was calling for her attention. She gestured for the man to give her a minute, and then focused on the assistant director's question. "It's going well so far—nobody's come up on our radar yet. We still have a long list to run through, though. We started with the business owners, because they're the ones who are going to give us the most grief over the vehicle restrictions. From there, we'll concentrate on the people who have boats docked at the marina. We've already gotten a lot of cooperation from the GPSA . . . That's the Gangplank Slipholders Association."

McCabe nodded. "That was a good call, getting them involved. You've closed off the marina parking lot, right?"

"Of course." She hesitated. "Sir, pulling all civilian craft out of the marina is not a realistic option. In fact, that would crowd up the channel and work against us. We need to clear out all the slips within about a thousand feet of the *Sequoia*, though. Even a thousand isn't good enough to serve as a standoff, but we won't get much more than that. Keeping vehicles out is the easy part—it's these boats and the channel itself that have me worried."

"If you weren't worried, Rivers," McCabe said, "then I'd say you weren't doing your job." He gave her a little smile to show her he was joking. "Besides, that's the navy's baliwick. They'll bring in their mine-sweeping equipment tomorrow. One other thing I want you to do is coordinate with the Coast Guard. I want to see cutters positioned at the entrance to the channel and at least two other points on the *Sequoia*'s route, in addition to our own personal escort. Also, make sure we have a designated UHF channel on marine radio. Apart from that, everything looks good to me. What about the motorcade?"

With McCabe's words, she felt a little bit of the tension start to drain away. Jodie Rivers had always tried to place herself above the politics of her job, but praise from her superiors felt as good to her as it did to anyone else. "We're going to stay with the route we've got. If we take Maine through the tunnel to 12th and follow it north to Pennsylvania, we can limit the number of sharp turns and push the speed up. Furthermore, 12th will be a whole lot easier to close than 7th, and we don't have too many options; most of 14th and 12th north of Pennsylvania are shut down for construction, so we have to detour on 13th Street—"

"I'm aware of that," McCabe reminded her. "The construction was covered in the preliminary report."

Rivers shrugged off the momentary lapse in her memory. "The route will be shut down on the night before the event, anyway—that's when the crews are scheduled to weld the manhole covers and remove the mailboxes."

McCabe was genuinely impressed with what she had already managed to accomplish. He touched her lightly on the shoulder, careful not to make it seem like anything more than a friendly gesture.

"You're working too hard, Rivers," he said. "Let some of your people help carry the weight. Come on, I'll buy you a cup of coffee. You look like you could use it."

The explosion was nothing more than a sharp crack muted by the weight of the sandbags. When he pulled them off to examine the blasting caps, he was pleased to note that not one remained intact.

Vanderveen was slightly bothered by the delay that was inevitable when using a cell phone trigger. When the ringer on the exposed circuit board was activated, the circuit was closed and the power found its way from the wet-cell battery to the blasting caps. The process took time, though, and Brenneman's motorcade would not indulge him by stopping right next to the van.

He would have to time it well. The news of the recent security escalations surrounding the State visit had not given him cause for concern. Most of the changes would be made around the marina itself, but he would be far away from the checkpoints and rooftop observers when the bomb was triggered.

In fact, he already had a perfect seat for the show.

Will tossed the shredded sandbags into the straw, then cleared the cement before taking a seat at his worktable, which was now empty with one exception. The document that lay on the wooden surface was 134 pages long, double-spaced with diagrams.

The first page was titled, "Program Events and Protocol." It was stamped CONFIDENTIAL.

He had never asked Shakib where the document had come from, and had made a conscious decision to force the question from his mind. It would not help him to dwell on the fact that his success was entirely dependent on the accuracy of the information contained in its pages.

He knew that the report was authentic. He had seen the same economical wording and phraseology used in countless other documents in his former profession. What he didn't know was how the recent NSSE designation would affect the security arrangements, and with Shakib gone, he had no way of finding out.

His fingers tapped out an irregular beat on top of the document as he considered. It would be a shame if the report turned out to be worthless after all. There was a wealth of knowledge at his fingertips. Page four told him that there would be thirty-six cars in the motorcade. Pages five through ten gave him the order of the vehicles, and a circled paragraph on page seven informed Vanderveen that the sixth vehicle in the procession would contain the president of the United States. Brenneman's Cadillac would be neatly tucked in between a GMC Suburban carrying four Secret Service agents and a backup limousine. The fourteenth vehicle would carry the Italian prime minister, and the twenty-first would contain the French president.

Despite what he had told the Director while deep in the caves, Will did not think it likely that he would manage to include all three of the targets in the blast radius. In fact, he had come to realize that it was almost an impossibility. The separation between the vehicles was just too great.

At the same time, the devastation that would be unleashed by a 3,000-pound bomb on a crowded city street was completely unpredictable. Even Will Vanderveen, with his intricate knowledge of blast theory and physics, could not be certain of the final result.

He was looking forward to finding out, though.

Vanderveen walked toward the entrance to the barn and stared out across the fields. He absently studied the tree line in the distance and wondered if that would be a reasonable place to bury Milbery's body and conceal her vehicle.

CHAPTER 29

TYSON'S CORNER, VIRGINIA• CAPE ELIZABETH • HANOVER COUNTY

The Terrorist Threat Integration Center first started life at CIA Headquarters in Langley, Virginia, but was moved to a state-of-the-art facility in Tyson's Corner when construction on the new building was completed in spring 2004. As one of many changes made within the American intelligence community following the disastrous events of 9/11, the joint venture was initially staffed by more than 125 people from the FBI, CIA, Homeland Security, and the State Department. Although the people now assigned to the TTIC have full access to the resources of their parent agencies, the main goal of the facility is to sort incoming information into usable intelligence, as opposed to actually going out and gathering credible information in the first place.

It was this distinction that was troubling Naomi Kharmai as she slumped in her chair and stared at the pile of maps and papers lying before her. Despite the fact that the full measure of the center's resources had been dedicated to the search for Will Vanderveen, very little progress had been made in the past two days. She had first realized how difficult it would be during her own preliminary research, when she discovered that 381 farms under 180 acres had been sold the previous year in Hanover County alone. And that was just *one* out of the 135 counties in the state of Virginia. The worst part of all was the limits on their search parameters: if Ryan was mistaken about any part of Vanderveen's intentions, they could very well be looking in the wrong place entirely.

For the third time in the last hour, she swiveled in her seat to look for Ryan. The room was filled with people hovering over computer screens, talking into telephones, standing over fax machines, and generally trying their best to do the impossible: find one man who could be anywhere in three states with a combined population of more than 13 million people.

She saw Deputy Director Harper standing across the room in deep discussion with Patrick Landrieu, the director of the TTIC. Naomi couldn't be sure, but it looked like they were arguing about something. *That's not a good sign,* she thought to herself as she continued to scan the room for Ryan.

She finally gave up and tried to focus on her map of northern Virginia. Taking another sip of lukewarm coffee, she stared through bleary eyes at the myriad of roads. After much debate, she had finally decided to focus her efforts on the six counties directly north of Richmond: Caroline, Hanover, Spotsylvania, Stafford, Prince William, and Fairfax. Her specific interest was I-95 running north into Washington, and she had branched out her search according to Ryan's suggestions: anything more than 5 miles away from the interstate had been immediately removed from the list, along with any property larger than 180 acres.

What she was left with was a staggering list of 564 farms sold in six counties in the past three months. Naomi shook her head in disgust as she lifted a thirty-page fax from the Virginia Farm Bureau Federation, only to slap it back down a second later without reading a word. She was about to reach for another sheet when she realized that someone had slumped down in the chair next to her.

Her eyes opened wide when she saw the state he was in. "Oh my God, Ryan! Where have you been? Do you have any idea what time it is?"

He ignored her as he reached over to grab the coffee from her desk. "Anything come up yet?"

Her eyes drifted over his clothes—the same jeans and T-shirt he had been wearing the day before. His face was covered with at least a week's worth of stubble, and his eyes were red-rimmed and raw. He looked exhausted. "Nothing yet. Sixty-seven people are working on this, and that's just in this room. I'm starting to think it's impossible."

He snorted and said, "Of course it's impossible. The whole thing is a huge fucking waste of time." She watched as he drained the Styrofoam cup and tossed it onto the desk in front of him. "You don't know this bastard like I do, Naomi. He could be anywhere. He could be sitting in this room, for all we fucking know. He's just too damn good at what he does."

His voice had gotten louder with each passing syllable. When he stopped talking, Kharmai was aware of the silence around her. She looked up to see that the deputy director had crossed the room and was standing right behind them. Harper leaned down to whisper something in Ryan's ear, and she watched as both men walked out of the room a few moments later.

With a heavy sigh, she turned her attention back to the fax pages in her hand and tried to block out the cacophony around her that soon returned to its elevated pitch.

Jonathan Harper stood outside the glass doors of the CT watch center and jabbed a finger into the younger man's chest. "What the hell do you think you're doing, Ryan? I needed you here four hours ago. This was *your* idea, remember? What's the problem?"

"I was wrong, John," he snapped. "It's all bullshit. We're not *doing* anything. We're just sitting around waiting for the other shoe to drop—"

"That's all we *can* do at this point. We can't exactly go house to house and ask for William Vanderveen, can we?"

Kealey pushed a hand through his lank hair. "No, I . . ." He shook his head as he searched for the right words. "Jesus, I don't know. I just think we could be doing more."

Harper's voice dropped as he reached out to squeeze the younger man's shoulder. "Look, you made some good points yesterday, threw out some good suggestions, but I still need you. I listened to what you had to say because I trust your judgment. I know it's too passive for your taste, but I think this could work. In any case, it looks like our best option for the moment." He saw that his words hadn't changed anything. It was time to take a shot in the dark. "Something else is bothering you. Katie?"

When Kealey looked away, Harper knew he had it right. "What happened?"

There was a long pause. "She walked out on me at the hotel, went back to the Cape. She said she couldn't handle it . . ."

"She'll come around, Ryan." The dark gray eyes came up to meet his own. "She knows the deal. I went through the same thing with Julie a thousand times when I was in the field. The sooner we finish it, the sooner you can get back to her. That's how you have to look at it."

The younger man nodded his head. "I guess so." He let out a long breath and leaned back against the wall. "This shit is killing me, John."

"I've seen the way she looks at you. She'll be waiting when you get back to Maine, I guarantee it. Listen, go back to the hotel. Shower, shave, get some food and a change of clothes. Then do me a favor and get your ass back here. Naomi's lost without you."

The last part was said with a smile. Ryan managed to return it briefly before pushing off the wall and moving toward the elevators. He was almost there when Harper's voice rang out behind him.

"He's close, Ryan."

Turning to look into the other man's face, Kealey could do nothing more than hope to God he was right.

"Trust me, it's almost over."

When Jonathan Harper went looking for Kealey in the early afternoon at Tyson's Corner, he found him seated back at Naomi's side. Ryan had taken his earlier suggestions and now looked almost presentable, although his choice of clothing still left something to be desired. In a room filled with clean-cut FBI agents and representatives from the State Department, Kealey was wearing faded jeans and a threadbare dress shirt—over a T-shirt, untucked—with the first three buttons undone.

Harper shook his head at the younger man's pointed efforts to avoid conformity, but knew that he would let it slide. As far as results were concerned, the deputy director thought that Ryan was the most valuable person in the room, and at the moment, results were all that he cared about.

They looked up from the maps they were going over as he approached. "Got a minute?"

Naomi nodded and pulled out a chair. As Harper sat down, they immediately noticed that he was wearing a slight smile. He placed a pile of bank statements on the table in front of them.

"We finally got something on those Saudi passports the Feds picked up at National Airport. Theresa Barzan held accounts in three major banks in London, accounts into which several large deposits were recently made. Want to guess where the money came from?"

"Tehran?" Naomi ventured.

"Try Sudan. First Central Bank of Khartoum. Clever move on the woman's part . . . We have no diplomatic relations with the Sudanese, so we can't pressure them to release the depositor's name."

"But we can track the money from London, right?" Ryan asked. He frowned slightly. "It wasn't actually the Feds that came up with this, was it?"

"No, it got kicked up to the FATF. The Treasury Department figured that would result in more British cooperation."

Ryan nodded in approval. The Financial Action Task Force on money laundering had been set up in the late-1980s to combat organized crime, but since 9/11 had become increasingly involved in the process of tracking terrorist funds. Both the U.S. and the U.K. were charter members. "This is a definite lead, but the problem is time."

"I agree," Naomi said. She traced a finger down one of the long columns of numbers. "This is pretty typical, what she's done here. It's called smurfing. By breaking down the funds into tiny amounts, it usually ends up getting lost in the huge number of transactions that take place each day. And this is only the beginning. From London, she would have routed the original sum through at least another dozen banks. Even with the starting point, it's going to take a while to trace it to the recipient."

"All the more reason for us to follow up on Ryan's idea," Harper responded. He pushed a second sheet of paper toward them. It was the letterhead that immediately caught their attention. "This one is nothing helpful," Harper said. "So don't get your hopes up. The

French Foreign Office sent off a rocket to the State Department earlier today with an inquiry as to 'the current state of our terrorist threat.' Basically, they wanted to know if we have things under control, and they weren't too delicate about letting us know what they thought of our security measures."

Naomi looked surprised, and Ryan let out a low whistle. "I'll bet that didn't go over too well."

The deputy director smiled ruefully. "You don't know the half of it. If Chirac ever gets a look at the response we sent them, he'll probably have to break off diplomatic relations on principle alone. Same thing with the Italians. Nevertheless, they've decided to stick to the schedule. I just thought you should know that they're on their way. Whether we find him or not, this event is going to happen."

Standing before the open doors of the cargo area, Vanderveen stared with satisfaction at the simple elegance of his creation. It was almost a shame, he thought with a brief smile, that he would soon have to destroy it.

The Ford E-350 van had been purchased from a retired electrician, and the cluttered cargo area looked as if it might contain anything other than 3,000 pounds of high explosives. The previous owner had rigged up handmade wooden shelves that were bolted into the upper portion of the frame, running from back to front the length of the van. Beneath the shelves on either side were broad sheets of flat pegboard, from which hung tools of every type imaginable. All of it had been thrown in for a modest fee by the electrician, who had quickly discovered that retirement was much more expensive than he had anticipated.

Along with the tools had come four large steel trunks that were 32" x 18" x 14". It had not been enough, of course; after running some quick calculations, and allowing for space for the conduit on top, Will had purchased one additional trunk through a wholesale warehouse in Richmond. Then he had bolted the five steel boxes to the floor of the van. Even with the additional trunk, he still had nearly 25 pounds of the grayish-white material that would not fit in the compartments. He wasn't bothered by this development, though, as he was sure that the excess could be put to some good use.

His decision to use the trunks had necessitated a slight change in the circuit he had devised, but he still had plenty of number 6 caps at his disposal. At one cap per trunk, there was a little over 37 amperes running through the circuit, but the current moving over each detonator was the same as he had previously calculated: at just over 6.31 amps, it was enough to ensure the destruction of each cap, but not so much as to run the risk of an electrical arc, which would almost certainly result in a misfire.

He recognized that the use of the trunks was, at best, a weak effort at shielding the van's true cargo from prying eyes. At the same time, he didn't want to have to hang curtains in the rear windows if it could be avoided. Doing so would almost certainly arouse the suspicion of the police officers checking vehicles in the vicinity of the motorcade's route. The drive into the city, when detection was most likely, would be the most dangerous part of the operation. Once the van was parked, he would be able to detonate the bomb from the safety of his overwatch position if it appeared that the device was about to be discovered.

Even if the president managed to escape unscathed, a possibility that Will found highly unlikely, he knew with complete certainty that nothing would stop his creation from realizing its full potential.

Vanderveen turned away from the open rear doors of the van and sat back down at his worktable, gingerly stretching his hands out across the smooth wooden surface. His fingers were sore from the strain of packing the SEMTEX H into the steel compartments, but he ignored the pain and opened Shakib's document to page 117. As he scanned the compact lines of text and accompanying diagrams, Will thought that whoever had laid out the security plans for this event had made some serious errors in judgment, errors he was more than happy to take advantage of.

He settled back in his chair and took a long sip of coffee, enjoying the gentle draft of cool air that found its way through the ancient crevices of the timber walls. There were things still to be done, but he had time.

He had all the time in the world.

CHAPTER 30

TYSON'S CORNER • HANOVER COUNTY

Looking up from the exhaustive piles of paperwork covering his temporary desk, Kealey gazed over the limited space of the CT watch center. It was packed wall-to-wall by more than 80 people who, if being judged only by their frantic gesticulations and elevated voices, might have been traders on the floor of the New York Stock Exchange following a merger between Microsoft and IBM.

He wanted to smile at the mental image that arrived with that thought, but was too tired and worried to see any humor in the comparison. They had been going nonstop for three days straight, but their efforts had yielded almost nothing in the way of new information. Seeking to narrow the search parameters even further, Ryan had argued that they should cut out Washington, D.C., itself, on the basis that it was too confined an area for Vanderveen to safely complete his preparations. Emily Susskind, the deputy director of the FBI, had shot down the idea without a moment's hesitation.

Naomi had had a little more luck when she suggested that a general description of William Vanderveen should be released to the state police in Virginia and Maryland. The idea had been waved away at first: Director Landrieu argued that disclosure of another terrorist threat without definitive proof would only incite more panic, something that the president desperately wanted to avoid. Susskind had

agreed with him, but Joshua McCabe had sided with Harper in support of the idea. Since the National Special Security Event designation gave the Secret Service overall control for the upcoming event,
the decision was made to release the description, along with a carefully worded request for assistance in which the word *terrorist* did
not appear once.

Nevertheless, the telephones and fax machines in the watch center had been going nonstop ever since, leads pouring in from the
Area 17 office in Augusta, Division Four Headquarters in Wytheville,
and the Maryland Barracks in Forestville, College Park, Easton, and
Rockville. The tension in the overcrowded room increased in accordance with the workload, and as Kharmai watched yet another stack
of paperwork gather in the receiving tray, she began to seriously
question her own decision to involve the state troopers.

She felt a presence at her shoulder and looked up to see that Ryan
was standing next to her. "Anything worth looking at?"

She shook her head and showed him the crumpled sheets of fax
paper in her hands. "This stuff is worthless. If a Caucasian male between the ages of twenty and forty-five did anything to attract police
attention on the eastern seaboard in the last three months, I probably have a file on him," she said, gesturing at the pile of stacked reports. "You'd think they would know better than to waste our time
with this kind of garbage."

Kealey shrugged and said, "It's not every day that the state police
gets a request for assistance from the TTIC. We were careful with the
wording in the description we sent out, but they know where it's
coming from. They're going to assume there's a terrorist threat,
which makes their assistance valuable when the time comes to sub-
mit their budgets for the following year. They're looking to help
themselves first, Naomi."

"Yeah, well, it would be nice if they could help *us* out a little bit in
the process," she mumbled.

Ryan grinned and rested a hand lightly on her shoulder. "Come
on, I'll help you look at it. If this stuff is as useless as you say it is, we'll
be done by twelve, and I'll treat you to lunch. Sound good?"

A smile brightened her face for the first time that day. "It's a deal."

*   *   *

"What is *this* shit?"

Sergeant Richard Pittman looked up from the newest stack of paperwork on his desk and surveyed the room. "Where the hell did this come from? Jimmy?"

"Hell no, Sarge. That came straight from the lieutenant."

"Yeah, straight to *your* desk," Pittman grumbled. "Come on, man. Are you sure some of this isn't yours?"

The other officer shook his head and grinned as he lumbered toward the open door. "I don't see why you're complaining anyway, Pitts. We got a two-hour briefing this afternoon that you get to miss out on. Everyone else is already over there. Whoever dropped that shit on your desk probably did you a favor."

"Yeah, thanks a lot," Pittman mumbled. He was the only person left in the room, which he was grateful for, as it gave him the opportunity to issue a long string of profanities as he picked up the heavy stack of files and dumped them next to the fax machine. After eight years with the Virginia State Police, Rick Pittman had thought, on more than one occasion, that he was finally past these kinds of monotonous chores.

He flipped through the separate sheets of paper and saw that they all seemed to be going to the same place. *I guess that's something,* he thought. *There must be seventy-five different reports here. At least I won't have to enter a different phone number for each one.*

Pittman punched in the number listed at the top of the first page and began feeding the sheets of paper into the fax machine. Forty-five minutes and two cups of coffee later, he pushed through a Missing Person Report for NCIC Record Entry.

The report had been filed by Jack Milbery, whose wife, in roughly fifteen minutes, would have been missing for exactly three days.

As the fax machine whirred on the receiving end in Tyson's Corner, Will Vanderveen turned the Honda down his narrow driveway off Chamberlayne Road, leaving a spray of gravel in his wake. The day had been spent in Richmond, where he had picked up a few last-minute things. Small, inexpensive items, but items that were absolutely critical to his success. He had made the exact same purchases nearly three weeks earlier, but had exhausted his supply on two other occasions.

He had watched his speedometer carefully on the short trip south and back, but his brief sojourn into the city had passed without incident, and now most of the danger was behind him. When the time came for him to leave the farm again, regardless of what happened from that point forward, he would not be returning.

He parked the motorcycle behind the barn. There were several upturned flowerpots next to the exterior wall. Vanderveen lifted the third from the left, revealing a bulky object concealed in a carefully folded dish towel. After he collected the HK .40 caliber USP Compact, he took his time clearing the barn and the house before carrying his purchases up to the kitchen. He had learned from the unfortunate incident with the realtor. He would not be so careless again.

In the harsh light of the only bathroom, he propped his last remaining passport up against the cracked tile and stared deep into the face of Claude Bidault, and then up to his own reflection in the mirror.

His face, without cosmetic aids, was surprisingly youthful despite the fact that he was closing in on forty. He noticed for the first time that fine lines were beginning to appear around his eyes, but otherwise, he looked much the same as he had twenty years earlier. The subtle effects of aging did not bother him in the least. Like all people blessed with perfect aesthetics, Vanderveen had the luxury of indifference when it came to his own appearance.

Although his preference was to go clean-shaven, he had allowed his beard to grow untrimmed for the past two weeks, and it had filled in considerably. The blond hair on his jaw was a sharp contrast against his naturally tanned skin. His hair had been returned to its original gold with the aid of a chemical shampoo. Dyeing his hair brown had been the only cosmetic change he had made on his return to the States; in the first few weeks there was too much that had to be done, too much that required his undivided attention for him to deal with the added burden of a cumbersome disguise.

He had become Claude Bidault twice before: once to purchase the Econoline van, and the second time to pick up his registration at the DMV in Richmond. Now it was time for a third and final performance. First, he removed his purchases from the paper bag that rested at his feet, placing them one by one on the counter. He had stopped at four shops during his trip into the city, and had not purchased more than two items from any one store.

The hair coloring was of the semipermanent variety, easily washed out with warm water. He used a small brush with rigid bristles to pull the black tint through his facial hair, and then a larger brush for the rest. When the color had set, he scrutinized the photograph once more before lifting the scissors and beginning to cut. Claude Bidault was a laborer, an independent contractor who had come to America in search of work; it was not fitting that such a man would have an expensive haircut. A struggling immigrant would likely trim his own hair, with unflattering results.

When it was finished, his now black hair was still reasonably long, but the result was undeniably atrocious. The job was done, though, and done well; between himself and the man in the photograph, there was only one obvious discrepancy, easily rectified. When he put on the brown-tinted clear-vision contact lenses, he looked up into the mirror and saw that Will Vanderveen had disappeared without a trace.

The image would be completed by steel-toed boots and the careless dress of a man who spends much of his workday on a building site. According to the passport, Claude Bidault weighed in at just over 200 pounds. In actuality, Vanderveen weighed little more than 170, but was counting on several layers of clothing to effectively hide that fact from view. A jacket over several layers of long-sleeved shirts would not be an uncommon sight on the icy streets of Washington in late November.

He frowned and stared down into the sink, trying hard to think of anything he might have missed. He still had twenty-five pounds of SEMTEX H to dispose of; he would have to think of a good use for that. Shakib's document would accompany him into the city. It was a risk to travel with it; an unnecessary risk, perhaps, but it might still serve a purpose. He was loath to leave it behind. The leftover hair dye and other materials would be taken into the vast field behind the barn, where they would be burned. The house was leased in the name of Timothy Nichols, the same name he had used to acquire tags for the motorcycle. He would place that identification into the bag as well, to be destroyed behind the barn along with the other materials. The license plate would be removed from the motorcycle and hurled deep into the woods. Such precautions would buy him only a little time if the authorities tracked down the name of Timothy Nichols, but a little time was better than none at all.

It was all he could think of, but there was no hurry. He had plotted his timeline carefully, and it would pay to wait; the longer he was in the city, the greater the chance of discovery. Besides, he still had plenty of work with which to fill the empty hours, and it wouldn't hurt to catch a little sleep, either. The bed downstairs would suit his needs perfectly.

Heading back out to the barn, Vanderveen carefully surveyed the few remaining contents of his worktable. An idea was beginning to form in his mind. He selected several items and placed them in the worn duffel bag that rested at his feet. Then, swinging the pack over his shoulder, he climbed the gentle hill back up to the house.

He descended into the dark depths of his finished basement less than a minute later. The light, hesitant to follow, touched the back of his head for a fleeting instant before giving way to pitch black.

They had never gotten around to eating lunch, or even dinner, for that matter, settling instead for their share of an endless urn of luke-warm coffee. Ryan was on his fifth cup and feeling the effects. His stomach was churning acid, and his head was pounding from the dull roar that was inevitable when 87 people were crammed into a room designed for 60. The building was overheated and poorly ven-tilated, which didn't help matters at all, and the harsh fluorescent lights overhead neatly concealed the fact that midnight was rapidly approaching. The cold winds whipping over the rocky shore of Cape Elizabeth would have come as a welcome relief from the stifling heat of the watch center, but he pushed the thought from his mind when another image intruded on the picturesque scene.

He couldn't think about her now, no matter how badly he wanted to. There was just too much to be done, and they were running out of time. The president and his guests were scheduled to board the USS *Sequoia* in less than ten hours.

He rubbed his temples and tried to focus on the blurred text in front of him. After a few minutes, he realized that he hadn't read a single word. Shaking his head in frustration, he looked over to see if Kharmai was faring any better.

She was hovering over one of the many fax machines, a phone pressed between her cheek and shoulder as she fumbled with the buttons. Ryan watched with vague amusement as she swore and smacked the machine with the palm of her hand.

When he stood up and walked over, she held out a sheet of paper without pausing in her conversation: "Yes, as soon as possible . . . That's right, I need everything for the last three months, including photocopies of the driver's licenses if you have them . . . What do you mean, 'It's too late'? I don't care what time it is, call him at home if you have to . . ."

As she was talking, Ryan quickly scanned over the proffered document. When he got down to 'missing person's occupation,' his eyes opened a little bit wider.

Naomi hung up the phone a moment later. Ryan looked into her face and saw that her bright green eyes were sparkling.

"A realtor, huh?" he said. "That's interesting."

"It gets better," she said. "Nicole Milbery specializes in farm properties. Her office is in Ashland. That's Hanover County, right in between Richmond and Washington. It's the perfect place for him . . . Ryan, do you know how to fix this bloody stupid machine?"

He couldn't help but smile at the way she said it. He examined the unit and punched some buttons to clear out the backlog. "Who were you talking to?"

"The night duty officer at the VSP's Hanover office. He's going to call the investigating officer at home right now. As soon as he finds him, we'll get some more details."

"Don't get too excited," he warned. "It could be nothing."

Naomi wasn't going to be deterred that easily. "It could be everything."

The sergeant on desk duty in Hanover returned the call ten minutes later. Naomi snatched up the phone and listened intently while Ryan looked on, rooted in place by a strange mixture of anticipation and apprehension. For some reason, he knew they were finally on to something.

She pulled the receiver away from her mouth. "Milbery leased a property less than three weeks ago. Just under a hundred acres, three miles east of I-95." She turned her attention back to the telephone. "Did he leave a—okay, he did. That's great, I need you to fax that over to me. What was the name again?"

Ryan started to say something but she waved him away. "Okay, that's fine. Thanks for your help, Sergeant. Can you make your captain available? We're going to need to talk to him if this adds up to anything . . . Okay, thanks."

She hung up and turned to face him. "Timothy Nichols. Does that name mean anything to you?"

He thought for a minute, pushed the names out and together again, mixed up the letters, turned them around. When it came to him, the rest of the room seemed to fall away. "It's him."

"What?" She looked up, startled. "How do you know?"

"Timothy McVeigh and Terry Nichols, Naomi. He always was an arrogant bastard."

She went pale as she realized what he was saying. "Oh my God."

As if on cue, the fax machine started up and produced a single piece of paper. Although the driver's license was not blown up to magnify the features, and the face itself was blurred by copying distortion, Ryan knew exactly who he was staring at when he lifted the sheet to the light.

"That's Will Vanderveen," he said.

CHAPTER 31

TYSON'S CORNER, VIRGINIA

Patrick Landrieu stood at the head of the table and surveyed the people sitting on either side of the polished wooden surface. Despite the fact that he was the ranking person in the room, he knew better than to try to assert his authority over the group that he currently faced. The combination of their egos and ambition easily overruled his titular superiority, and he was well aware that they would crush him in an instant if they felt it to be in their best interest.

Landrieu was a round little man with a prominent nose, sparse gray hair, and cheeks flushed pink from the heart medication that he took twice a day, or at least whenever his secretary reminded him. The fact that he made a habit of working sixteen-hour days was reflected in his shabby appearance. His career, however, had never suffered from his slight physical stature. He had begun his government service as a terrorism analyst nearly twenty-three years earlier, and his rise through the ranks had been remarkable. He had served as chief of staff to the director of Central Intelligence, and then most recently as deputy executive director before being appointed by the DCI to his current position.

As he looked out over the sea of faces, he saw that they were appraising him in turn. Perhaps more than a few were wondering how much longer Landrieu's reign could possibly last. He was already coming under heavy fire for the intelligence failures that had led to the most recent disastrous events in Washington, as well as for the lack of success in capturing the man believed responsible for both terrorist attacks.

Aside from Landrieu, there were seven other people in the room. Seated immediately to his right was Deputy Director Emily Susskind of the FBI. Next to Susskind was Assistant Director Joshua McCabe of the Secret Service and its advance team leader, Jodie Rivers.

Also present was Colonel Stephen Plesse, the superintendent of the Virginia State Police. Plesse had arrived by helicopter from the VSP Administrative Headquarters in Richmond less than ten minutes earlier. He was in full uniform despite the early hour, and his face was still red from the harsh winter wind that had cropped up in the past few hours and was now singing around the building.

The three remaining people in the room were seated to the left of Plesse. They were Jonathan Harper, Ryan Kealey, and Naomi Kharmai.

"Well," Landrieu said, "you've all been made aware of the purpose of this meeting. I suggest we get right down to it. We have very little time to waste."

"Do we have any guess as to how much time, exactly, sir?" Rivers asked. She had no desire to be at this meeting, figuring that her rightful place was back on the waterfront finalizing the security arrangements. Even if she had wanted to, there was no way she could spare the resources for anything they might have had in mind.

The director looked around the room, his eyes settling on Jonathan Harper. "Does anyone have an answer for that?"

"The timetable depends on what kind of weapon he's planning to use, and that comes down to what kind of vehicle he's driving," Harper said. "Obviously, he'll need a bigger window if he's trying to bring a bomb into the city. I don't believe we've come up with anything solid on that yet. Emily?"

Susskind looked up from her coffee and debated for a second, her slender fingers dancing on the rim of her cup. "The only vehicle registered by Timothy Nichols in the state of Virginia is a four-year-old Honda motorcycle. Unfortunately, that doesn't really mean anything; he could have acquired another vehicle under a different name, or maybe he's stolen one—there's just no way of knowing.

"There's something else we need to consider, though. Once we had his alias, the link between Vanderveen and Theresa Barzan was quickly established. We still don't know her real identity, but we *do* know that, using that name on her Saudi passport, she wired him almost 35,000 dollars over the past several weeks. The funds were routed through the Caymans and the Cook Islands, which made it very difficult to trace. That's not enough money for a payoff, but it *is* enough to purchase a lot of expensive equipment." She paused and cleared her throat gently. "The kind of equipment he would need to construct and conceal a large explosive device."

A grim silence ensued as the people around the table considered this news. It was Jonathan Harper's measured words that finally shattered the calm.

"There's a chance he went back to the source, despite the increased security that was put in place after the Kennedy-Warren bombing. Has this information been checked against the records in Norfolk?"

"I have people working on that right now," Susskind responded. "We haven't been able to get in contact with the director of operations *or* the terminal manager. The highest we could get was an assistant supervisor of the container division, and that particular individual is not exactly the picture of cooperation."

It was the superintendent's sonorous voice that rang out in response. "I might be able to help you with that," he said. "Our department works pretty closely with the staff over there. I can save you a lot of time if you can get in touch with Gary Thompson and refer him my way. He's the general manager at NIT."

Susskind wrote the name down and nodded her appreciation to the heavyset colonel.

"Those records are going to be crucial," Harper said. "If Vanderveen did use the terminal a second time, he obviously managed to get past Customs, or we wouldn't be in this mess. At the same time, there will be a record of the type and weight of shipment he received. That could go a long way in telling us how he intends to deliver the package."

"Getting access to those records needs to be a top priority," Landrieu agreed from the head of the table. "We need to throw some weight around. It's going to take us long enough to get a search war-rant without wasting any additional time."

He turned his attention to the deputy director of the FBI. "Make sure they understand in Norfolk that there's going to be serious repercussions if they keep it up. We'll shut their whole operation down if we have to. What about the residence itself?"

"Surveillance is already in place," Susskind responded. "The SAC out of Richmond is running the show. Obviously, the Virginia State Police are on the scene as well. The state troopers have both ends of Chamberlayne Road blocked off, and a loose perimeter has already been formed around the house, extending a quarter mile out in every direction. The staging point is a half mile down the road—this part of the state is about as rural as it gets, which makes things a whole lot easier for us in some respects, harder in others. For instance, we can't bring any choppers in without making our presence known."

"Do we know if he's in there?" McCabe asked.

"No idea. The lights are off, but that doesn't mean much; at this time of the morning, he's probably asleep."

"What about infrared?"

"We tried that, but the windows are too small. We can't get a good scan of the entire house."

McCabe was nodding slowly. "Are there any vehicles on the property?"

"There's a fairly large barn," Susskind responded. "But the doors are closed and we can't get close enough to see inside without jeopardizing our cover. When we move, we have to be sure."

Plesse cleared his throat. "How about roadblocks? I would think, as a precautionary measure—"

"No way," McCabe said from across the table. "It's less than two hours into Washington from that part of Virginia. It would take us at least an hour just to get checkpoints set up on the main roads."

"Besides, what would we tell the people manning them?" Landrieu asked. "Let me remind you once again that the president is anxious to avoid drawing any unnecessary attention to this situation. Setting anything up that might approach an effective barrier around the city would mean bringing hundreds of people into the loop. That is completely unacceptable."

"Sir, with all due respect, I think we're past the point of worrying about publicity. By putting this much effort into keeping it quiet, we're giving Vanderveen a huge advantage."

Ryan flinched at Kharmai's unexpected outburst, and waited for the inevitable reprimand.

Patrick Landrieu straightened and fixed his gaze on the young woman at the other end of the table. "I'm sorry, miss, I didn't catch your name."

"Naomi Kharmai, sir. I'm with—"

"Central Intelligence, I know. I served that particular agency for more than twenty years. No offense, Ms. Kharmai, but I think the gravity of this situation is somewhat beyond the scope of your limited experience." He turned his attention away from her immediately. "Now, if anyone else has any reasonable suggestions . . ."

When Ryan tuned the man out and cast a quick glance in Naomi's direction, he saw that she had slumped down in her seat. Her eyes were downcast, and her cheeks were bright red.

"Excuse me, Director."

Landrieu looked up, surprised and annoyed. "Yes?"

"Do you know who *I* am, sir?"

Landrieu hesitated, a fact that was noticed by everyone present. "Yes, I do, Mr. Kealey."

"I would like to point out that Naomi's efforts at tracking this name down are the only reason we're even sitting here. If she has something to say, it would be well worth your time to listen to her."

Had he been a man of compromise, willing to endure a mild rebuke in the interest of maintaining a positive atmosphere, the director might have shrugged it off. Because he was not that kind of man, however, he chose to bluster. "While I'm sure that we're all grateful for Ms. Kharmai's efforts, I don't think we have time to—"

"Director."

With the single spoken word, Landrieu looked up into the coldest pair of eyes he had ever seen. He almost opened his mouth to speak again, and then decided against it. Landrieu briefly reflected that what he saw in Kealey's face might well have been the product, at least in part, of his own imagination. As a former deputy DCI, he still had connections at the highest levels of the Agency. He knew all about the man who was seated before him.

Patrick Landrieu swallowed his pride and cleared his throat. When he spoke, his words were barely audible, despite the stunned silence that had swept through the room. "By all means, Ms. Kharmai, if you have any suggestions, we would be happy to hear them."

Naomi was a little shocked herself at what had just transpired. She collected herself quickly enough, though, and unconsciously straightened in her seat. "Thank you, Director. I admit that the political implications of another bombing, especially during a state visit by two national leaders, are way over my head. At the same time, we can't afford to lose sight of the fact that the president is not the only person at risk here. There should be no doubt that a lot of people are going to die if Vanderveen manages to accomplish whatever it is he's set out to do. As you've all seen from the copies of the driver's license, Vanderveen made only minor cosmetic alterations while posing as Timothy Nichols. It's fair to say that he's probably already gotten rid of that identity, and has taken more dramatic steps to change his appearance for the final stage of his operation, if this *is* in fact the final stage."

This statement was greeted by the low rumble of unhappy voices.

"If Vanderveen is still there, then we clearly have nothing to lose by moving in right now. If, on the other hand, he's already gone, we need to know as soon as possible. Provided that the scene is treated with the utmost care and consideration, and any evidence remains intact, there's a good chance we might find something useful, something that could tell us what he looks like now. At this point, there is very little else we can do. I think that it's time to focus our efforts."

The unhappy sounds gradually changed to general murmurs of consent. All the same, Naomi was surprised when Landrieu hurried to agree. "That sounds reasonable enough to me. Let's hold off on the roadblocks. It would take a huge effort to mobilize that kind of force at this time in the morning anyway. Emily, I suggest that you start looking for a judge to wake up. When will you be ready to go?"

Deputy Director Susskind took a quick look at her watch. "Most of my people are already in place. Once we get the warrant, say . . . 5 AM."

"Excellent." Landrieu pulled back the cuff of his shirt and looked at his own watch. "That's three hours from now. Send me an update when you hit the ground in Virginia. There's no point in waking up the president at this hour. Let's wait and see if we have something useful to tell him. Whoever's not on the move will meet back here at 7:00 AM.

"President Chirac and Prime Minister Berlusconi arrived yesterday, ladies and gentlemen. The boating excursion is scheduled for 9:00 AM. That gives us six hours to catch a man who has eluded us for more than seven years. I suggest you get to work."

Five minutes later the room was almost empty. Ryan was one of the last to leave, and he looked around for a minute before he saw Naomi moving down a distant hallway. She was almost running, and he had to move fast to catch up.

"Hey, where are you—" He caught the look on her face. "What's wrong?"

"What do you mean, 'What's wrong?' You know exactly what's wrong."

"No, I don't." She was still moving fast, and he was genuinely confused. "Naomi, you give me way too much credit. For the record, I'm actually pretty dumb, and I have no idea what you're talking about."

She didn't smile. "You shouldn't have pulled that little stunt in there, Ryan. I didn't need you to do that, okay? It was embarrassing. I can fight my own battles."

"I know that . . . Naomi, stop for a second." When she unexpectedly complied, he had to backtrack a couple of steps to face her. "Where are you going, anyway?"

"I have a seat on the next helicopter to Richmond."

That came as a surprise. "With who?"

"Superintendent Plesse and the deputy director."

"Which deputy director?"

"Susskind."

Ryan lifted an eyebrow. "And Harper approved that?"

"It was his suggestion." Naomi crossed her arms and stared at him defiantly. Her cheeks were still flushed, and her glossy black hair spilled in riotous waves down around her face and over her shoulders.

Ryan thought she had never looked better.

"I'm going, too."

She shook her head slowly. "Harper specifically said you were to stay here."

"I don't give a shit what Harper said."

Her expression softened slightly, as did her tone of voice. "Ryan, we don't know for sure that he's still there, and we need to have both ends covered. You don't need me to tell you that."

He hesitated, knowing that she was right. When she started to walk away again, he caught her arm. "Listen, I'm sorry about what I said in there. I should have kept my mouth shut. It's just that Landrieu's such an asshole . . ."

"That's all right. I think so, too."

There was a brief moment of silence as they looked at each other. Impulsively, Ryan leaned down to kiss her cheek. "Be careful, Naomi."

"I'll be okay," she said. "After all, you won't be there to shoot me this time." She turned away before he could think of a clever response and resumed her rapid pace to the stairwell. When she stepped out into the icy wind and walked toward the waiting helicopter a few minutes later, she was wearing a wide smile, and despite the cold, she felt warm all over.

CHAPTER 32

RICHMOND, VIRGINIA • HANOVER COUNTY

As soon as the Bell 206 LongRanger touched down at VSP Administrative Headquarters, its three passengers disembarked and moved gratefully toward the stairwell and the warmth of the building. It was bitterly cold outside, and made worse by the frigid gusts of wind that whipped over the roof and penetrated their clothing. From a conversation she had overheard earlier in the day, Naomi knew the worsening weather to be the first gentle touches of a winter storm that had started off the coast of Florida three days earlier and had been working its way north ever since.

As she followed the two senior officials through the spotless halls, she reflected that they would all be saved a lot of trouble if the storm picked up enough to force a cancellation of the president's trip on the *Sequoia*. At the same time, she knew that they would never get off the hook that easily. President Brenneman seemed just as intent on fulfilling the demands of his schedule as Vanderveen was on cutting them short.

Deputy Director Susskind enjoyed the warmth of the building only for as long as it took her to ride the elevator down to the bottom floor. She had used the time in the helicopter to scream through several conversations over a static-filled line, and arrangements had been made for a car to take her directly to the U.S. Court of Appeals for the Fourth Circuit, where Judge Lucy Klein was already pouring her second cup of coffee and wondering what she could possibly have done to deserve such mistreatment at the hands of the government she had faithfully served for more than eighteen years.

While Susskind pleaded her case before the judge, Naomi would accompany Superintendent Plesse out to the staging area, where they were set to meet up with the SAC for the Bureau's Richmond Office. She followed Plesse through the big glass doors of the Administrative Center less than ten minutes after Susskind's departure, walking quickly toward the Lincoln Town Car that waited alongside the curb. Soon they were heading east on the Midlothian Turnpike, crossing darkened streets and following the gentle curves of the James River less than a mile to the north.

At 3:40 in the morning, the roads were virtually empty, and so it wasn't long before they reached I-95. The driver eased down on the accelerator when they took the entrance ramp, and soon they were pushing toward Hanover County as fast as the car could carry them.

They were in blackout condition at the staging area, which meant there were only a few light sticks, also known as chemical, or 'chem' lights, scattered around the perimeter. The staging area wasn't much more than a cluster of Bureau vehicles arranged in a vague circle, like a wagon train defending itself against marauding Indians. The side road was marked by a rusty gate that someone had thought to pull back and chain to a tree, thereby making it easier for vehicles to get in and out of the clearing in a hurry.

Naomi was hit by an icy gust of wind as soon as she stepped out of the Town Car. She blindly chased after Plesse in the dark, passing small groups of huddled agents as he hurried up to an idling Suburban and rapped on the window. When it came down he asked for the SAC, and was rewarded with a vague wave toward the largest vehicle in the clearing, a black Chevy conversion van. Ten seconds later he was pounding on the back door with a gloved fist.

There were two people already sitting in the overheated interior, which was lit up with communications gear. Naomi could clearly make out the two monitors displaying feeds from the infrared cameras on the perimeter.

Brett Harrison, the SAC, was a fair-haired, All-American type with big shoulders and clear blue eyes. Naomi was wary of him right off the bat, especially when she noticed that one of his front teeth was chipped. *Football injury*, she thought, and frowned. For some reason that she had never been able to figure out, she harbored a mild animosity toward jocks, especially middle-aged jocks who had never gotten over the fact that they weren't in college anymore.

Harrison grinned and stuck out his hand, which Naomi reluctantly shook, as did Superintendent Plesse. "Brett Harrison, good to meet you." He stuck his thumb over his shoulder. "This is Al Maginnes, the HRT commander."

"Maginnes?" Kharmai asked.

The commander smiled. "Ma, like mother, then Guinness, like the beer. Funny thing is, I can't stand the stuff."

Naomi smiled back at him. She didn't like the heavy Irish brew, either. Maginnes was a lightly muscled man in his early forties, she guessed, with a bald spot on top, a thick brown mustache going to gray, and careful brown eyes. He was wearing camouflage GORE-TEX pants and a black T-shirt. She saw that he had a heavy pistol riding in a leg holster, and there was an M4 carbine propped up next to him. He looked competent enough, and she briefly wondered if Susskind had worked him in to keep an eye on the younger SAC.

"Where are we at?" Plesse asked, shifting his weight impatiently on the uncomfortable little seat.

Harrison pulled his headset down around his neck. "Your boys have both ends of the road sealed off, so we're good there. There's still no movement inside the house, and we've been up and running since . . . what, Al? A little after one this morning?" The other man nodded. "So that's just over three hours without any movement. But there is something that I think you should see . . ."

Harrison placed the headset on top of his radio and swiveled to the center console. They all crowded around the low table, shoulders touching in the cramped space of the van. "These are the house plans. We got lucky and scooped them up from the owner, who built the place himself in '88 before he decided to rent it out. This is key, right here . . ."

The area he was pointing at showed two levels on what should have been a one-story ranch. "A basement?" Naomi asked. "In Virginia?"

"Not only that," Harrison said. "But the owner says it's a finished basement, complete with furnishings. Vanderveen is aware of our technology, which is something we need to keep in mind. He knows that the infrared can catch him through the windows, so he's safer underground. In other words, he might very well be down there, and—"

"The thermals wouldn't have picked it up," Naomi finished.

Another grin from Harrison. "That's right. So we're still up in arms over how to make the approach. We'll hold off on making a decision and see what trickles in from Norfolk. Until then, we're waiting on the deputy director and a search warrant."

Plesse asked, "Can you access the basement without going through the house?"

Harrison shook his head and the grin faded. "No, there's only one door leading down from the interior. No basement-level windows either."

"I couldn't see the house from the trees," Naomi pointed out. "I'd like to take a closer look."

The SAC opened his mouth, but Maginnes was the first to speak. "I'll run her out there, Brett. I need to talk to Larsen anyway."

The younger man nodded his consent, and Naomi followed the HRT commander as he snatched up his M4 and opened the rear doors to the van. Plesse didn't move from his seat.

Outside, she shivered and said, "God, it's freezing out here."

Maginnes, still wearing only the T-shirt on top, didn't seem fazed by the icy wind. "We can probably scrounge something up for you before we head out there. There aren't any vehicles on the perimeter, so we're gonna be outside for a while."

He pulled open the rear doors of one of the Suburbans and dug through a pile of equipment. After a few seconds, he stood up with a pack in his hand and a triumphant look on his face. "This belongs to the smallest guy on my team, which means his stuff is probably only eight sizes too large for you."

"Where can I change?"

He was already looking around. "Other side of that tree, I guess." He was pointing to a large oak about 20 feet away.

"There's nowhere warm?"

"Nowhere that isn't occupied. That's fine, if you don't mind twenty guys watching you strip."

"I think I'll pass," she said with a laugh.

Ten minutes later they were moving slowly down Chamberlayne after passing the two VSP squad cars positioned at the end of the road. Naomi had changed out of her pantsuit into a pair of dark blue Columbia utility pants and a black half-zip pullover, under which she was wearing several long-sleeved shirts. Her feet looked slightly ridiculous in black combat boots two sizes too large. She'd had to put on three pairs of socks to make them fit; her feet were sweating a little bit in the warmth of the vehicle, but it was better than getting out of the truck and freezing to death twenty minutes later.

"I don't want to take the truck any closer than we have to," Maginnes said. The Suburban's lights were doused, and he was navigating through a pair of night vision goggles clipped to a harness on his head. "We're going to have to hoof it the rest of the way."

They moved slowly through the darkened fields. Maginnes would stop every 15 feet or so, and then, without explanation, suddenly move off again. He called in his position periodically so they wouldn't get shot by his own men on their approach. It wasn't until nearly twenty minutes after leaving the comfort of the Suburban that they arrived on the edge of the perimeter.

Maginnes knelt in the dirt and adjusted his lip mike. Naomi slumped down next to him, already exhausted. "TOC, this is Magpie, radio check, over."

"Magpie, TOC," came Harrison's voice over the earpiece. "Read you Lima Charlie, out."

He called in several other radio checks. The last one was to his assault team leader, Chris Larsen. "Alpha One, Magpie. Give me a quick sit rep, over."

"Mags, this is Alpha. All weapons and personnel are accounted for. Sierra team is running through their own list. Still haven't spotted anything from our position, over."

"I'm . . ." Maginnes glanced around quickly, "about 300 yards south of the nest, in the dip next to the third stand out from the road. Do you have eyes on, over?"

"Negative, Magpie, over."

"Hold on a second, over." Maginnes peeled off the AN/PVS-7 goggles and handed them back to Naomi, who was basically operating blind. The moon and stars overhead were obscured by leaden clouds heavy with snow, but when she slipped on the harness and turned the knob, the world around her suddenly reappeared in strange, unnatural colors. The house, which she hadn't seen on the approach, now popped into view, pale against the darker green of the open air. From the stand of trees opposite the barn, she saw white lines streaking out of the woods toward the walls of the house.

"Oh my God," she breathed.

"You see them?"

She steadied the goggles against her face with her left hand and pointed with her right. "Over there."

Maginnes stopped fiddling with his radio. He turned on the Aimpoint sight attached to his M4 and pointed the weapon toward the woodline. "Got me, Alpha One?"

"That's a Roger."

"How soon can you get here?"

A brief pause, and then his earpiece crackled. "Ten minutes, fifteen to be on the safe side."

"Take your time, Chris. Magpie, out."

The SAC was sipping coffee and talking with Plesse when Schubert's *Symphony No. 8* suddenly filled the air. He picked up his cell phone and frowned at the number before flipping it open. "Harrison."

Plesse watched as the younger man's face turned pale, then red with anger. "You're shitting me! Does she know what's at stake here? Well, what do I do now? Okay . . . okay, fine."

He hung up a few seconds later and received an inquiring look. "The deputy director managed to wake up the most uncooperative judge in Virginia," the SAC explained. "We won't be getting a warrant, at least not fast enough to do us any good."

"Fuck."

"I couldn't have said it better myself."

There was a long, uncomfortable pause before Plesse unconsciously echoed the other man's words. "So what do we do now?"

Harrison didn't say anything in response. After thirty seconds of internal debate, he sighed heavily and reached for the headset.

When Larsen arrived thirteen minutes after the commander's call, he did it so quietly that Naomi almost jumped out of her skin. She was watching the house intently for any sign of life, with Maginnes lying prone at her side, when a low whistle sounded a few feet to her rear. She spun around, and then realized that Maginnes hadn't reacted at all.

"I heard you coming a mile away, Chris."

"Sorry, boss."

Naomi watched in amazement as a figure rose up from the ground before her.

"Still two minutes under time, though."

Maginnes smiled reluctantly. "Pop a few chem lights, will you? By the way, this is Naomi Kharmai. She's joining us from the Agency."

"Nice to meet you."

Naomi nodded in return and watched as Larsen reached into his pack and retrieved several small plastic tubes. He bent each one until the glass vials broke inside and the chemicals mixed. When he shook them and tossed them onto the ground, an area perhaps 5 feet in diameter was illuminated by a soft blue glow.

Larsen was maybe a few years older than she, with a narrow face and blond hair trimmed close to the scalp. His features were blurred by green-and-brown camo, but she noticed that his dark brown eyes were carefully appraising her. She watched as he called his team members to make sure the chem lights weren't visible from their position. Then he pulled a topographic map out of his pack.

The HRT commander grabbed a few rocks and placed them on each corner of the large sheet of paper. "Let's see what you got."

Larsen's finger hovered over the myriad of light brown contour lines. "I have one team here," he said, pointing to an area of heavy vegetation on the north side of the house. "I'm going in with them, if it comes to that. I gave the second team to Aguilar. He's across the road to the west. That was a problem . . . I wanted someone on the front door, but there's no cover and they have to cross about 200 feet of open space before entry."

"We'll work around it," Maginnes said. "What about the open-air option?"

Larsen pulled a grease pencil out of a loop on his flak vest and used it to mark several locations on the map. "Grierson stacked most of the snipers next to my second team of assaulters, because that's where most of the windows are facing. We've been sitting out here for hours, Al. I went over the sectors of fire and moved everyone accordingly. Then we checked it again and came up golden. My people know where they can and can't shoot. Oh, and one other thing: Jones is a couple hundred yards up the way with his .50. If, by some miracle, the subject manages to get to his vehicle, Jonesy can easily punch one through the block at that distance."

Maginnes gave an approving nod. "Good. Who's up on explosives?"

Larsen hesitated. "Canfield has the most practical experience, but Hudson spent a month training with Delta, so he's—"

"When was that?"

"Uh . . . January."

"Make it Canfield," Maginnes said. "Hudson's still a little green, but he can sit in on it. I want them to give your people a quick briefing on booby traps. Take these plans back with you, and have them look for trouble areas." A brief pause. "I want to take it slow, Chris. We know he's not on the ground floor, so that gives us time to maneuver. We'll use that time to get it right. I want everyone to walk away from this."

Larsen bobbed his head in acknowledgment and turned his attention toward Naomi. "We haven't gotten any specifics on this guy yet. What can you tell us?"

"He was a Special Forces engineer. He applied to EOD in 1993, then became an instructor in '94. They had to get a three-star general to sign the waiver; no one in the army has ever made that transition faster. He did the sniper school at Benning, and then the SERE course at Camp Mackall. You know about Senator Levy and the Kennedy-Warren . . ." Both men nodded. Larsen smirked a little as if to show that he wasn't impressed by Vanderveen's record, but she sensed it was mostly for show. After a brief hesitation, Naomi decided that they deserved to have all the facts. "One other thing . . . He killed five of his fellow soldiers in 1997 while on deployment in Syria. After that, he basically disappeared from the face of the earth, at least until now. I don't know what else to tell you."

Larsen's arrogant grin faded. He was about to respond when Maginnes held up his hand and cupped the other around his ear. He listened for a moment, then said, "Roger that, TOC. Give us a couple minutes, over."

He dropped his hand and looked up at them with pinched features. "Search warrant didn't come through."

Naomi dropped her head, and Larsen muttered an expletive. No one said anything for almost a full minute.

Finally: "How bad do you need to get in there?"

She looked up at Maginnes. "Pretty bad."

"How bad?"

"Bad enough."

He nodded his head slowly, then seemed to come to a decision. "Chris . . ."

"Yeah?"

"You got your throwaway?"

Larsen slapped the pack that rested at his feet. "Always."

The commander said, "Is it clean?"

Larsen looked offended. "Of course it's clean."

Al Maginnes nodded his head again, then turned his dark eyes onto Naomi's. When he spoke, his words were slow and precise. "What happened was, we decided to get a little bit closer, okay?"

"I can buy that," she said, and felt a little tingle between her shoulder blades.

"Chris, when you looked in the window, you saw a handgun lying on the floor."

"Right."

"Right." Maginnes scratched his head and considered. "Okay, so he's hardly going to have a registered pistol. An unlicensed firearm gives us cause to enter the premises." He looked up at her. "Are you okay with that?"

"Sounds kind of iffy, but . . . Yeah, I'm okay with it."

He looked at Larsen. "How about you?"

The younger man shrugged, tilted his head. "Sure."

"Then it's settled." Maginnes cupped his mike to block out the sound of the wind. "TOC, this is Magpie . . . Uh, there appears to be a handgun in the house. Does the subject own a registered firearm? Over."

Harrison caught his meaning and came back immediately: "HQ advises that the subject has not registered any firearms in the state of Virginia."

"We're going to check it out, over."

Coming back, with a little excitement over the static: "Roger that, Magpie."

Larsen was back with his men ten minutes later. Maginnes and Kharmai hunched together and watched the house through the trees.

"I could kill for some hot coffee right about now," he said.

She thought about that for a minute. "Figuratively or literally?"

"Literally."

"Wow, they weren't kidding when they said you guys were hard-asses." She yawned, leaned back and scratched her butt, then caught him smiling. "What?"

He shook his head. "I never saw a woman do that before."

"Then you haven't been paying attention," she said in a whisper. "We do it all the time." Then, a second later: "Besides, there's too much testosterone flowing around here. I was kind of feeling left out."

Another twenty minutes passed. A little snow started to fall, and although it was freezing cold and windy as hell, Naomi couldn't help but start to drift off a little. It was 5:05 in the morning when Maginnes furrowed his brow and cupped his ear.

"Roger that, Alpha One. Standby, over." He reached over to shake her, and she started, then looked up. "We're ready to go."

She was still shaking off the sleep. "Umm . . . okay. How? I mean, how are they going in?"

"If he's in there, I can't give him time to barricade himself," he said in a low murmur. "We're gonna go with Primacord on the door frame."

She said, unnecessarily, "They need to be careful."

"They will be." Maginnes had the individual teams call in, then got back on with Larsen. "Okay, Chris. Let's go."

"Roger that, Mags. Breachers are moving in, out."

Several minutes passed. Naomi couldn't see anything other than their own quiet breath condensing in the frigid air, and she said so.

The commander handed her the night vision goggles. "Try these. Don't watch the door when they shoot the charge."

Pulling on the goggles, she immediately saw dark figures advancing through the light snow. One stayed back with his weapon up, facing the front of the house, as the other moved up and started priming the door.

"Where are they?"

"Already at the door," she said.

Maginnes murmured into his mike. "Sierra One, what do you got? Over."

"No movement in the windows."

"Sierra Three, Magpie. Anything?"

"Negative. I'm drawing a blank, over."

Then, a moment later: "This is Alpha One. Door is primed."

"Take those off, Kharmai." When the goggles were up on her forehead, he cupped his hand and said, "Blow it."

There was a brief flash of light through the snow, followed immediately by a sharp crack. After a few tension-filled seconds, Larsen came on and said, "No secondary explosions, Magpie. Clear to advance, over."

"Head on in, Chris. Take it slow."

"Roger that."

Maginnes waited as long as he could bear it, then reached over to pull the goggles off her head. "Ouch."

He saw that he had caught a few strands of her hair. "Sorry." When he focused on the house, he didn't catch any movement in the windows.

Naomi was getting impatient. "What do you see?"

He shook his head in frustration. "Nothing."

Chris Larsen was the third man in the house after Canfield and Hudson. He was immediately followed by a team of five assaulters, who quickly followed his hand signals and moved to their predetermined positions.

"Magpie, Alpha One. Moving to secure ground floor, over."

"Roger, Alpha One." Larsen watched as his men cleared the first two rooms to the right, then followed them silently into the living room. The kitchen was past the open space, and he moved forward smoothly with the Heckler and Koch MP5 up tight against his shoulder, his eyes scouring the walls at knee- and ankle level, searching for anything that might indicate a trip wire. Then he was moving slowly against the textured wallpaper, taking a deep breath before poking his gun and his head around the corner . . . nothing.

He lowered the weapon and turned to see one of his men standing in front of a closed door. Larsen was the only one to spot the towel stuffed underneath. The operator said, "I think we got something here . . ."

Larsen had just enough time to say, "No—" before the door disintegrated. Kevin Hudson, who had been the one to pull it open, was thrown back and up by the blast. He passed through 8 inches of drywall before his head collided with the ceiling, snapping it forward and breaking his neck instantly.

Larsen turned to run, but then found, to his astonishment, that his feet were not touching the ground, and actually seemed to be going in *opposite* directions, as were the rest of his appendages . . .

Naomi saw a blinding flash, then heard a muffled *wumph* as the house was ripped apart. Maginnes was on top of her in an instant, shielding her body as fragments of brick, wood, and glass rained down around them.

Then there was silence and his crushing weight on her back. Nothing else, until he rolled off and she saw that there was part of a leg sitting two feet in front of her face.

That was when she began to scream.

CHAPTER 33

TYSON'S CORNER • HANOVER COUNTY • WASHINGTON, D.C.

Back at the TTIC, Ryan had finally stopped trying to fight the fatigue and decided to get some rest while he could. He tried to crash out in a secretary's office, but sleep didn't come. His mind was too occupied by everything that was going on, but most of all, it was Katie who held his thoughts.

Ryan recognized that he was largely responsible for their current situation, but he couldn't help but feel let down by the fact that she had just run out on him without even trying to talk about it first. He was thinking about this, and getting angrier, when he realized that he had done exactly the same thing to her when Harper first asked him to come to Washington.

He was not pleased by this recollection. It would have been a whole lot easier to blame the whole situation on her, but at the same time, he wanted nothing more than to see her again. If being the first to apologize made that a possibility, then it was a sacrifice he was more than willing to make.

And all it would take was a phone call. In the dim light of the office, Ryan looked up at the clock on the wall: 5:23 AM. He knew she wouldn't be awake, and Katie wasn't a morning person in any case. She would be much easier to apologize to in a couple of hours.

He shut his eyes and tried to let the exhaustion overtake him. He was curled up uncomfortably on the cot, thinking about how he would explain everything to her when the door swung open, the lights came on, and he heard a distant voice calling his name.

Suddenly, it didn't seem so distant. When he opened his eyes and saw the expression on the deputy director's face, he was instantly wide awake. "What? What is it?"

Harper's voice was strangled. "Vanderveen just got seven guys from HRT in Hanover."

Ryan was standing now, looking around for his shoes. "How? Was he there?"

"No, he rigged something up in the basement. They're still trying to figure it out."

Ryan stopped what he was doing and suddenly felt cold. He didn't want to ask it, but knew he had to. "Naomi?"

He breathed out a long sigh of relief when Harper shook his head. "She was 300 meters away when it blew. She's pretty shook up, though."

"Oh, fuck," Ryan said. He rubbed the stubble on his cheeks with open palms. "Oh, fuck."

The area around the house was swarming with police cars and ambulances by 6:45, their flashing lights less pronounced now that the sun was occasionally peeking through the heavy clouds. The fire-fighters had pretty much finished their work, slightly aided by the damp snow that was still drifting down over the wreckage and surrounding fields.

The barn, for the most part, was still intact. Naomi was sitting with her back against the timbers, wearing a thick blanket around her shoulders and staring at what was left of the house.

Looking around, she saw a group of Bureau investigators trying to determine the outer boundaries of their search area. Maginnes was aimlessly wandering around the charred remains with a strange mixture of pain and confusion on his face. He had lost Larsen, Canfield, and Hudson, as well as four other members of his unit. One assaulter had been blown back through the front door, and had managed to escape with second degree burns, a broken leg, and a concussion. He had already been airlifted to a hospital in Richmond.

Naomi's own injuries were minor; a few scratches was all she had suffered physically, but she couldn't get the sight of that blackened stump out of her mind, nor the sound of Maginnes's anguished moan when he had caught sight of it a few seconds after she did. She closed her eyes to block it all out, then opened them again when she heard someone calling her name.

It was Brett Harrison. He was standing next to a group of forensics people and holding a cell phone in his hand. As she stood up and walked over on shaky legs, she thought, if anything, the SAC looked worse than Maginnes. His face was as white as a sheet, and he couldn't seem to focus on anything for more than a few seconds at a time. When she reached him, he muttered, "TTIC," and handed her the phone.

"This is Kharmai."

It was Kealey. "Naomi! Are you okay?"

When she heard the concern in his voice, it finally caught up with her. She turned her back to the group and tried to stifle a sob. "No."

"Jesus," he said. She couldn't read his tone of voice. "Are you hurt?"

"No, I'm just . . ." Ryan heard some strange noises over the line and realized she was trying to hide the fact that she was crying. "It was pretty bad, you know? God, this was *my* idea, Ryan. I'm the one who—"

"Naomi, it's not your fault," he interrupted forcefully. "Those guys knew the risks going in. Vanderveen did this, not you. Okay?"

There was a long pause. "I'm sorry," he said in a softer tone. "I should have been there—"

"No," she said emphatically, unconsciously shaking her head in agreement with her own words. "You would have been in the house. I couldn't have . . . dealt with that."

On the other end, Ryan was lost for words. What he came up with, after about four seconds, was: "Come back to Washington, Naomi. I don't think you ca—I just think you should come back."

She could see that he was trying to make it easy for her. It would be so easy to give up being tough. She could go back to Washington, where he would show her some friendly concern and nothing more. She could sit behind a desk in the CT watch center and sip coffee, watch it play out on CNN, and remain perfectly safe.

But Vanderveen was still running free, and she wasn't ready to give up just yet. And Ryan had been about to say, before he caught himself, that there was nothing else she could do in Virginia. *Well, screw you, too.*

"I'm not coming back," she said. On the other end, Ryan was surprised by the sudden steel in her voice. "I'm going to grab one of Harrison's aides and go talk to some people. I want to know what he's driving, what he looks like. Otherwise, we're still running blind."

"Okay," he said, after a moment of indecision. "Hold on a second." He relayed the message to Harper, who broke off from another heated conversation with Patrick Landrieu to give his approval. "Harper says that's fine. And he's glad you're okay. I am too, you—"

"I know," she interrupted. "I'll let you know what I come up with."

Pressing the END button before he could respond, she looked once more at the surrounding devastation and wiped away her few remaining tears. *Okay, Naomi,* she told herself. *Time to get back to work.*

Washington, D.C., in the half light of morning. The clouds were rolling in from the south, but the sun still poked through occasionally, sending bright beams spilling down over random objects and people. Looking around the waterfront, Jodie Rivers sipped from her travel mug and stood in quiet appreciation of the sight. She had worked herself to the point of exhaustion over the past week, and although there was a lot going on, she'd be damned if she wasn't going to enjoy her morning coffee. Especially after getting called to the TTIC at one in the morning and the sleepless hours that had followed the meeting.

The colors of the city had that vivid look that is peculiar to a certain type of overcast weather. Across the sparkling surface of the channel, the grass of the East Potomac Golf Club seemed like an endless sea of emerald green. Although there was no precipitation, the air felt heavy and still, and she had received numerous reports of a storm moving in by early afternoon.

It would come too late to do her any good, though. For now, there was no trace of rain or snow on the ground, and no reason to cancel the boating excursion that was scheduled to begin in less than two hours. At least no reason that she could successfully argue to President Brenneman or his chief of staff, Ed Rigney.

She was painfully aware that they were presenting an irresistible target less than three weeks after two successive terrorist attacks. Unfortunately, the Secret Service served at the pleasure of the president, and once he had his mind made up, all they could really do was set up a good perimeter, surround him with as many agents as possible, and hope for the best.

The barriers leading into Maine Avenue were already doing their work. High above, using their high-powered binoculars the rooftop observers were scanning the assembled groups of demonstrators, now and then whispering a quiet description over the Service's dedicated radio link. In response to the description, someone would get bumped in the crowd by one of the interspersed agents. In each case, the target of the bump was completely oblivious to the fact that he or she had just been thoroughly checked for weapons. The Secret Service agents posing as demonstrators carried no signs and dressed neatly, if not conservatively, but they did shout out the occasional slogan to keep up appearances. So far the demonstration was peaceful enough, for which the uniformed Metro cops were grateful as they looked on with watchful eyes and neutral expressions.

Headed south toward the waterfront was the endless procession of embassy limousines bearing French and Italian diplomats. USSS personnel from the Uniformed Division checked each vehicle for explosives with CCTV wands, which projected the undercarriage onto a 4.5-inch screen positioned at waist level. Credentials and faces were scrupulously checked against existing documentation while other agents looked on with MP5s held low by their sides. Two junior aides from the French embassy who were missing their passes were pulled out of their vehicles and held for twenty minutes while their identities were confirmed, much to the consternation of the French ambassador and his head of security.

The preparations had been endless, and they seemed to be paying off, Rivers thought. Still, the integrity of the perimeter was largely dependent on the mind-set of a potential assassin. She knew that there was no way they could guarantee protection if an individual was willing to die himself in order to kill the president. An individual alone on a suicide mission was the greatest fear of any Secret Service agent, and Rivers was no exception. She found herself thinking about William Vanderveen: *God, I really hope he wants to live.*

"Daydreaming again, Jodie?"

She turned her head to smile at Joshua McCabe. "No, just enjoying the scenery. Pretty, isn't it?"

He followed her eyes to the golf course opposite the channel. "Yeah. Too bad for the golfers, huh?"

"I guess." The course had been shut down under PDD-62, on the grounds that it was too large a space to cover with their limited manpower. "What's going on?"

"Everything's moving right along. You did a good job getting the French and the Italians on file, by the way. We've been able to clear them pretty quick." She bobbed her head at the compliment. "Did you hear about Virginia?"

She looked up sharply. "No."

He grimaced and shook his head. "Someone should have told you . . . The raid went to shit. Vanderveen set a trap and took out a bunch of guys from HRT. They didn't find a vehicle in the barn."

"How did he do it?"

"Some kind of bomb. They're still looking into it. Anyway, they assume he's coming our way. So . . ."

She closed her eyes and thought about it. "I don't know what else to do," she finally said, giving a little shrug of her shoulders. "We don't have the manpower to extend the perimeter anymore. Did you pass this along to Storey?" Jeff Storey was the Agent in Charge of the president's detail, and scheduled to arrive in two hours with the main party.

"Of course. I took it to the president as well. Obviously, he wasn't happy about it. We're still on, though."

"Well, hell," she said in frustration. "What's with this guy? Doesn't he realize how serious the threat is?"

"He knows." There was a pause. "He's desperate, Rivers. If he pushes this through, he might pick up enough support to start thinking about another four years. Otherwise, he's done."

"It's kind of hard to run the country if you're dead," she mumbled.

McCabe winced. "Don't let anybody else hear you say that, for God's sake. Listen, I'm needed back at Tyson's Corner. You can reach me there if you need to, okay?"

"Okay, thanks." He nodded and walked back to his waiting car. Jodie Rivers stared into the gray waters of the channel as a series of awful scenarios raced through her mind, one after another. After letting her imagination run rampant for five minutes, she reluctantly moved off to double-check the perimeter and the list of foreign dignitaries who had been cleared for access.

Please, God. Not on my watch.

The TTIC was a nonsmoking facility, and Jonathan Harper had given up the habit years ago. With the pressure he was currently under, however, he needed some way to vent, and he wasn't a screamer.

He smoked outside as dawn broke, with Ryan standing next to him. The younger man was crossing his arms one minute, shoving his hands deep in his pockets the next, as if unsure of what to do with himself. They were alone on the broad expanse of concrete, and they had known each other for seven years. There was nothing awkward in the silence. The deputy director sensed that Kealey was coming to a decision, and waited for him to speak.

"I want to go to the marina."

Harper took another long drag and exhaled slowly. "Not much for you to do down there," he observed.

"I know that."

"What do you need?"

"Some kind of identification," Ryan said. "I want people to know who I am. I don't want somebody stopping me every five feet."

"I'll see what I can do. Not through us . . . through the TTIC, maybe. And I'll talk to McCabe."

"I need my gun. I have it with me . . . I just don't want it to be a problem."

"It won't be."

Harper finished his cigarette, and they stood in companionable silence as the sun topped the trees. "What do you think of Naomi?"

"I like her. She's . . . tough."

"Not bad-looking either."

Ryan smiled. "Not bad."

Harper tossed his butt toward the sandpit, missing badly. "I didn't really want her in on this at first. She's kind of rough around the edges, you know? Hasn't really learned to handle people yet. She's learning, though . . . Think she'll find anything?"

"I don't know. She's pretty quick. It depends on how lucky she is."

"Luck is part of it," Harper conceded. Then, after a few seconds: "Go to the marina. I'll call ahead for you. Would you know him if you saw him?"

"Maybe . . . Yeah, I'd know him," Ryan decided. He hesitated: "I think I'd know him."

"He'll know *you*," Harper said. "So watch yourself."

"I always do."

The room was just about what he'd expected: comfortable, but not lavish, with a few tastefully framed prints on the walls. There was the obligatory television in a tall wooden credenza, twin beds, and a nightstand, along with a small desk that sat adjacent to the door. Upon entering the room nearly twelve hours earlier, he had moved straight to the window to check his line of sight. It was perfect. The van was about 200 meters away, facing toward him, and approximately 75 meters away from the intersection of 13th and Pennsylvania Avenue.

The worst moment had come the night before; he had been forced to circle the block three times before finding a suitable location. Fortunately, he didn't think anyone had noticed. A considerable amount of pedestrian traffic had cropped up since daybreak, but not one of the passing people seemed too intently focused on the large commercial van that was parked at the curb. Since 12th Street had been closed to through traffic less than a half hour after his arrival, there were very few moving cars on this adjacent street, which made keeping an eye on the van easier than it otherwise might have been.

He had needed to rearrange a few things inside the room. The DO NOT DISTURB sign was hanging on the doorknob in the hall, a minor detail, but an important one. He had pulled the armchair out of the corner and maneuvered it in between the beds. Then he had grabbed the credenza from the narrow end and dragged it over to the space vacated by the armchair, turning it so it was at a right angle to the big picture window. The wooden chair had been taken out from underneath the desk, and placed next to the window in front of the credenza.

These minor efforts meant that he could watch the television and the vehicle at the same time. Vanderveen knew that MSNBC was scheduled to carry the president's address live from the waterfront. With any luck, he would be able to verify the president's approximate time of departure; he already knew from Shakib's document that Brenneman was scheduled to return to the White House at 11:40 AM, but it didn't hurt to double-check.

FOX News was already showing, on what appeared to be a continuous loop, coverage of the aftermath in Virginia. They had little footage and less information, settling instead on wild conjecture and a long shot of the smoking ruins provided by a low-flying helicopter with a shaky pilot at the stick.

Vanderveen did not know how the FBI had tracked him to that location, but he was not overly concerned. He was only hours away from achieving his goal, and there was no way they could stop him in time. Besides, he was pleased by the efficacy of his improvised device. If the anchor's estimates were correct, he had managed to kill eight members of the Bureau's vaunted Hostage Rescue Team. Hearing about it secondhand was somewhat less satisfying than watching the realtor bleed to death, but satisfying nonetheless.

He felt good, despite the fact that he was nearing the end of a long wait. The ringer on the cell phone was on, but the covered switch in the cab was in the OFF position, so there was no power going to the exposed circuitry. The phone he would use to trigger the device rested by his side, but if he was to call now, nothing would happen. He glanced at his watch, a cheap Timex, perfectly suited to his current persona. The digital display read 7:25 AM. At about eleven, he would go down to the van, ostensibly to pick up the notebook he'd deliberately placed on the passenger seat. With any luck, the president and a healthy number of his aides would be dead less than an hour from the time he flipped the switch.

He had done all he could. He leaned back in the chair and went back to watching the street below his window.

CHAPTER 34

WASHINGTON, D.C. • ASHLAND

Driving east on Interstate 66, it didn't take Kealey long to work his way into the city and toward the waterfront. In fact, the security check he endured on arrival took nearly half as long as the trip had, but it was still less than forty-five minutes after leaving Tyson's Corner that he was granted access to the Gangplank Marina. From there, it took him another five minutes to locate the person he was looking for.

Ryan felt more than a little foolish as he chased Jodie Rivers through the throngs of reporters positioned behind the metal crowd-control barriers. As they moved, they were jostled by the photographers and cameramen who were jockeying to get a good shot of the president's motorcade, which was due to arrive any minute. He needed to talk to her, but the woman seemed to be in perpetual motion.

He almost slammed into her when she stopped abruptly at the press gate. There were two men in dark suits and sunglasses checking IDs and the passes that had been specifically designed for the event and distributed the day before by the White House press office. Rivers turned her attention to the covering agent, leaving the other to continue his work.

"Did you get the photographs?" The man nodded. "Let me see them."

The man, who was at least 7 inches taller than Rivers and twice as heavy, immediately reached inside his suit jacket and pulled out a folded sheet of paper.

"You guys have been keeping an eye out?" she asked.

"Yes ma'am. Everybody's checked out on the list."

Ryan thought the deference showed by the burly agent to the diminutive Jodie Rivers was vaguely amusing, but kept the thought to himself.

The advance team leader turned to show him the sheet. It contained a blown-up shot of Vanderveen's driver's license in the name of Timothy Nichols, as well as several other images, showing him with glasses, long hair, dark hair, and a beard, among other things.

"These are enhanced photographs," she needlessly explained. "We took the original and made some minor alterations. It's not much, but it makes my people look a little bit harder, helps to keep them on their toes." Turning back to the agents: "Okay, good work, guys. Stay sharp."

She handed the sheet back to the man and moved off with surprising speed, Ryan close on her tail. She suddenly seemed to remember that he was there, and turned her head to address him as they pushed through the crowd. "I already talked to Deputy Director Harper, Mr. Kealey, as well as Director Landrieu. You're free to come and go in this area as you please . . . In fact, I'm happy to have you here. Every warm body helps. What do you need from me?"

He finally got an uninterrupted minute when they stopped to examine another checkpoint. "Actually, Agent Rivers, what I want to do is check the surrounding roads. You look like you have everything pretty much under control here, so I figure that the best place for me is where you're short on manpower."

"What are you looking for?"

"I don't know. Something that catches my eye, I guess . . . I would just feel better if I was on the move."

She was skeptical. "Sounds kind of pointless."

"I know, but there's not much else to do."

That seemed to satisfy her. "So, again, what exactly do you need from me?"

He shrugged. "I'm carrying . . . Harper told you that?" She nodded, her eyes instinctively passing over his body. He was wearing a
loose-fitting dress shirt with the sleeves rolled up, untucked, over a
pair of khakis. She didn't see the pistol, but realized it was probably
under the shirt at the small of his back. "I don't want any problems
from your people on the perimeter. Can you let them know that I'm
coming?"

She frowned, then said, "I can tell *my* people, but we're having a
hell of a time with communications. The boys from Metro are pulling
a lot of the vehicle checks, and they're using UHF radios. It's been
giving us problems all day, but I'll see what I can do. How are you
for ID?"

It was Ryan's turn to frown. "Harper couldn't get me anything.
You know, technically speaking, I'm retired from the Agency, and
Landrieu had some problems with that. He wasn't backing down."

Wincing, she said, "That could be a problem."

"I know." He hesitated. "If you can just get word to your top guy
out there, then I can probably start looking around without causing
any distractions."

She thought about that, began to nod when her earpiece sparked
to life. She listened intently as Ryan looked on.

Rivers glanced up at him. "The president is about to arrive."

Over her shoulder Ryan could already see the long procession of
vehicles sweeping around the corner onto Maine Avenue. The lights
on top of the Secret Service Suburbans were flashing, though the
sirens remained silent. The sight of the motorcade's approach caused
a storm of activity in the press pool, as cameramen and photographers
hustled for position in the overcrowded area. The distant roar of the
demonstrators started to pick up as well, despite the fact that their
view of the motorcade was all but obscured.

Ryan saw that Rivers looked nervous. She caught his attention and
tried a weak smile. "That press area is giving me fits. It's a lot bigger
than I wanted, but McCabe had to give in to the pressure . . . The
networks went crazy when he sent over our first set of requirements.
We got to a third draft before they stopped threatening to sue. The
first amendment is a terrible thing, at least from my point of view."

He nodded his sympathy. "The AIC for Brenneman's detail is here now," he pointed out. "That should take some of the weight off you."

"You'd think so." She sighed, then turned her attention back to what he had been saying. "Okay, as far as my people are concerned, everything north of Ben Banneker Park is pretty much relegated to the rooftop countersniper teams. That's a strange combination in and of itself; we've got Metro PD, Capitol Hill PD, and my own shooters up there, as well as a few Bureau people thrown in for good measure . . . All the same, comms are pretty good, with the exception of the Metro guys. I'll try to let them know you're coming, but I can't make any guarantees. I don't know what happened there; it was just one of the small things that we overlooked, and I'm pissed off about it."

She *looked* pissed off, Ryan thought, and she looked pretty good, too. He couldn't help but think it; her cheeks were flushed with anger, but it worked for her. If he didn't know better, he might have pegged her as a fresh-faced grad student, the enthusiasm making her seem a few years younger than her age. Because he *did* know better, he felt a little bit sorry for her; the Secret Service was an environment thoroughly dominated by alpha males, and someone who looked like Jodie Rivers would have had to work twice as hard to be taken seriously. He was sure that her current position had not come easily.

He let the thought go and tried to think of what else to ask her, but she was way ahead of him. "Do you need a vehicle?"

"No, I have one." Harper was going to be stuck at Tyson's Corner for the rest of the day, and had given Ryan the use of his forest green '98 Explorer. "They're still taking 12th back to the White House, right?"

She glanced at him, hesitated, then nodded. *If Landrieu said he was cleared* . . . "That's right, for the most part. Since 12th Street is closed for construction between Pennsylvania and H, we have to turn onto 13th. We're scheduled to head back around 11:40. Some of that depends on the weather. We're supposed to be getting hit pretty hard this afternoon."

"I heard it might pass us," Ryan said, looking up as if to confirm the rumor.

"Yeah, well . . ." she shrugged as the president emerged from the vehicle and flashed a broad grin at the press pool, which immediately responded with a number of clamorous questions. "We'll see."

Despite the fact that he had not slept in almost twenty-eight hours, Vanderveen could feel the energy coursing through his body. It was hard to remain seated in the chair, and the mind-numbing scenery offered by the hotel window did little to alleviate his boredom.

He had been surprised and gratified by the extent of MSNBC's coverage of the event. The cameras had transmitted a live broadcast of the president's motorcade nearly twenty minutes earlier. A quick count had yielded thirty-six vehicles, which was something of a relief, as it told him that Shakib's document had probably not been compromised. Of course, if it had, 12th Street would almost certainly not have been closed down, but it was reassuring to see that the Secret Service felt secure in its preparations.

It had never been his intention to attack the motorcade before the meeting took place. It was afterward, when they had already professed their profound commitment to one another, that the sudden death of the American president would do the most damage to the fragile coalition. And he was so very close . . .

He checked his watch: 9:31 AM. He smiled to himself. It was hard to believe it had all come down to these moments. Staring out the window, he marveled at the changes that would soon be taking place. The buildings at the intersection would suffer the most. Soon they would be faceless rooms, no longer marked by rough stone walls and sparkling windows, but by tangled steel and crumbling concrete, and the shattered bodies of those unfortunate people who resided within.

He was so lost in the images of fire and destruction that he didn't immediately notice the solitary figure moving up the street. His eyes opened a little bit wider, and he stood up and put his nose to the window to get a better look. When his suspicion was confirmed, his breath hissed out between his teeth and fogged the glass. *You should have been paying attention,* he thought, but it wasn't a problem; he still had time.

Vanderveen looked around quickly, thinking about what he would need. The decision came quickly; he pulled on his heavy jacket, and grabbed his key card and passport. Reaching for his temporary visa, but then thinking, *No, better not to try too hard*. Then he was moving fast toward the door.

Ryan had enough confidence in Jodie Rivers to believe that she would make the calls she had promised. He was tired of hanging around, so after a brief conversation with the same agents he had seen manning the press entrance, he passed through the metal detector with minimal fuss and headed back toward Harper's Explorer. It was parked on 7th Street facing north, but when he got in and looked through the windshield, he was suddenly struck by indecision.

The street in front of him was crowded with vehicles, and the same was true on the other side of the road. He could see police officers walking up and down the rows, calling in license plate numbers and performing quick visual checks. There would be just as many cars on the streets running into 12th, and it seemed like at least half the vehicles were some type of SUV, which was exactly what he was looking for.

He slapped his hands on the steering wheel in frustration and got out of the truck. The streets were crowded with commuters at this time of the morning, and there was little he could do from a slow-moving vehicle. It would be better to walk.

He started up 7th—the time-worn Beretta firmly secured in a drop holster at the small of his back—nodding a greeting to the Metro cops that he passed on the street. He was shivering in the cold air, then remembered that he had left his jacket back in Harper's vehicle. He debated for a second, then looked again at the long rows of vehicles. The sight gave him a sense of the enormity of his task, after which the decision came easily enough, and he walked quickly back to the Explorer.

After all, if he was going to be unproductive, he would at least be comfortable in the meantime. Soon he was coming back up the street, warmer in the leather jacket that still bore the tears and scuff marks from the Kennedy-Warren, and ready to begin what was sure to be a long and pointless search.

* * *

Jared Howson didn't have the benefit of a jacket over his uniform, and had been cold ever since his shift had started nearly two hours earlier. He would have welcomed the relative, and certainly heated, comfort of the 1st District Station on 4th, but knew it could have been worse. After all, he only had this one street to worry about, and it wasn't hard work. Simply look at the car, call in the license plate, do a quick visual scan, and move on to the next one. That was all the information he'd been given, but Howson had been on the force long enough to realize that the extra security had something to do with the presidential boating trip and the terrorist attacks that had rocked the city less than a month earlier. He had been as outraged as any American over what had taken place, and even more so than most because he was a guardian of law in this particular city, and those *bastards* thought they could come *here* and blow up *innocent people* . . .

Just thinking about it always got to him, and he had to shake off the rising anger as he finished with a blue Toyota and moved on to the next vehicle. It was a large commercial van, and exactly the kind of thing he had been told to look for. A Ford Econoline, he could see, with Virginia plates and a dented exterior that had seen more than its fair share of fender benders. He was about to call in the tag number when he realized that the passenger door was open, and a man was retrieving something from inside the van.

"Excuse me, sir. Sir . . . ?"

The man looked up, a notebook in his hand, wearing a big, friendly smile beneath the heavy beard. "Yes?"

Howson caught the accent right off the bat. "Is this your vehicle?"

"Yes, it is mine."

Howson studied him carefully. In his pocket he had the same sheet of paper that had been distributed to the Secret Service agents at the marina, and he had taken the time to look at it back in the station. This man didn't really resemble any of the superimposed photographs, although the general shape of the face *was* about right . . .

But that was true for at least 30 percent of the population, and the hair was all wrong. On top of that, the subject's eyes were reportedly a vivid shade of green, and Howson was staring into flat brown eyes the color of oak. Not to mention the fact that the man was clearly French.

Still, just to be safe: "Do you have some identification, sir?"

The man hurried to comply, pulling his passport out of his heavy coat. "Of course, of course. Right here, *monsieur*."

Howson accepted the burgundy booklet and peered at the cover: *Communauté Européenne*, and beneath that, *République Française*. Inside, all the requisite information for one Claude Bidault and what appeared to be a U.S. entry stamp, although he wasn't exactly sure what that was supposed to look like. Howson had never left the country, nor had he ever suffered from a burning desire to do so.

Satisfied, he handed the passport back to the man, who didn't seem at all bothered by the officer's inquiries.

"What is all this . . . activity? This is not usual, yes?"

"Actually, sir, your president is in town to meet with ours. I'm surprised you haven't heard about it."

"Ah . . ." The man beamed as though suddenly recalling that little fact, but the light of epiphany never reached his eyes. "That is correct. A big meeting, *n'est-ce pas?*"

The young police officer had to smile in response. "Yes, that's right." He moved closer to the van, taking the time to look through the back windows. Electrical equipment. A lot of it. "You're an electrician, sir?"

The man nodded enthusiastically. "*Oui.* I am with the big project on M Street. There is a new restaurant they are building there. Work is not so easy to find in Paris, you know. So I come here to work, and send the money back to my sister. She looks after my little ones."

"Your wife?"

Howson watched a look of pain cross the man's grizzled features. "She . . . How do you say? Passed away? When giving birth to my girl, my little Mirabelle. Four years ago next week."

"Oh." Howson could have kicked himself. *Better to shut your mouth now,* a little voice told him, *before you do any more damage.* "Well, sir, thanks for your time. You have a good afternoon, okay?"

The smile reappeared. "*Merci, monsieur. Et vous aussi.*"

The police officer watched as the man closed the passenger-side door, then walked back toward the stairs leading up to the hotel's main entrance. Howson hadn't seen him emerge in the first place, but now he looked up at the building's facade and frowned. The Marriott in this part of town was at least 180 dollars a night. Why would a construction company, even for a major project, pay that kind of money to put up an independent contractor? It didn't make any sense, and the thought lingered on the edge of his mind as he resumed his task.

The concern remained, though it was soon overshadowed by what seemed like a distant memory of a heated building and a full pot of hot coffee. The convergence of these two trains of thought left little room for anything else, and Howson failed to realize that he had not called in the plates on the Frenchman's Econoline van.

She had never bothered asking Harrison for one of his agents, instead settling for the use of one of the vehicles in the staging area. As a result, Naomi Kharmai, midlevel analyst in the CIA's Counterterrorism Center, had no more authority in northern Virginia than that of a private citizen.

She was in the restroom of a gas station directly opposite Milbery Realty. Looking in the mirror, she saw a woman who might have just emerged from a car wreck, except that she would have looked much better had that been the case. Her borrowed blue cargo pants were torn and dirty from lying in the field for hours on end, and the pullover was noticeably singed in several places. Her hair was matted and dirty, and the clothes she wore were thoroughly damp with melted snow. Her nose was totally stuffed up because she had a cold coming on, but she guessed that she probably didn't smell that great either.

Worst of all were her eyes. They reflected what she had recently seen, made her look scared when she needed to be confident and assertive, at least for the next few hours. Then she would be free to have her breakdown, which she was actually beginning to look forward to. After several minutes of scrubbing and adjusting, she emerged from the restroom looking just marginally better. She purchased two large cups of coffee from the attendant and tried to avoid his curious gaze.

She left the car where it was and crossed the street, simultaneously glancing at her watch. It was almost 11:30, much later than she would have liked for this conversation to occur, but tracking down Lindsay Hargrove had proven to be an incredibly time-consuming task. Naomi had finally managed to get hold of Hargrove's sister in Clarksburg, West Virginia, where Lindsay had apparently been staying for the week. She was now heading back to Virginia, and unfortunately didn't carry a cell phone. The sister *had* informed Naomi, however, that Lindsay fully intended to stop by the office on her way home.

And that was why she was here. The woman she wanted to talk to was a long shot for additional information, but better than nothing at all. Hargrove, whose name had been on the Missing Persons Report faxed to the TTIC, had seemed like a better bet than the realtor's husband, who wouldn't have had any reason to meet his wife's clients. Hargrove, on the other hand, had been working for Nicole Milbery for the past four years. Naomi was guessing that the woman might know more than she thought she did, despite the fact that she had already talked to the sheriff's office. At this point, all Naomi could do was hope that they might have been asking the wrong questions.

Once she was outside the office, she didn't have to wait long before a white Nissan Altima pulled into one of the empty spaces in front of the building, and an elderly woman hopped out with surprising agility. Hargrove's smile quickly faded to concern when she saw the state of the woman standing before her. "My God," she said, with genuine alarm. "What happened to *you*, hon?"

Kharmai studied her as she unlocked the door and they moved inside. Hargrove was a plump woman in her late sixties, with a pleasant demeanor and healthy skin that belied her age. Naomi liked her immediately, and saw no reason to lie. "My name is Naomi Kharmai, Mrs. Hargrove. I was on Chamberlayne Road this morning."

The older woman's eyes went wide as she took a seat and offered one to her visitor. Hargrove gratefully accepted a cup of coffee and didn't question who Naomi was, or how she knew her name. "That raid that was all over television? You were there?"

Naomi nodded. "Unfortunately."

"It was the only thing on the news . . . Are they any closer to find-ing Nicole?" she asked hopefully.

Naomi didn't have the heart to tell her that Milbery's body had al-ready been found in a shallow grave on the property, along with a red Ford Escape that had been driven deep into the undergrowth and strategically covered with mud and fallen tree limbs. That piece of in-formation had yet to make its way into the local news, and it wouldn't help matters to share it now. "They haven't found anything yet, Mrs. Hargrove, but they're still looking."

The older woman's faded blue eyes began to mist over. "She's such a good girl . . . I hope she's okay. I just don't understand it. Usually, I'm pretty good at reading people, but that man really fooled me, I don't mind telling you. He must be the devil himself."

"The one who leased the property?" Naomi asked. Hargrove nod-ded in agreement, but Naomi was confused. "Wait . . . How did you know that's why I'm here?"

"My son-in-law is a state trooper," Hargrove explained. There was a touch of pride in her eyes. "I asked him to keep me up-to-date, so he called me when your department asked for additional information."

Naomi frowned inwardly at the VSP's lack of discretion, but told herself to let it go for the moment. "Could you tell me exactly what happened, Mrs. Hargrove?"

The older woman shifted her weight in the seat and nodded en-thusiastically. "We were pretty slow on the day he came in. Nicole whisked him right into her office. She didn't say anything specific, but I saw that look in her eye . . . You know that woozy look a young woman gets when she sees a diamond necklace or a pair of shoes she really wants?"

Naomi couldn't help but smile at the analogy. "I've probably had it myself, more than once," she offered.

Hargrove shot her a knowing smile in turn. "I'm sure you have, hon. Anyway, that was the look that Nicole had. I knew what she was thinking, too, and her a married woman . . . Well, that's another story."

"And this man went directly into her office? He didn't say anything to you at all?"

"Oh, no," Hargrove said, taking a small sip of her coffee. "He was very nice and all, charming too, but he only said hello to me. I think he was just as interested in Nicole as she was in him."

"How long did he stay?"

"Not long at all. They were in there for . . . maybe ten minutes. Then they came out and drove off in Nicole's SUV."

"Together?"

"Yep." The older woman smiled at the scandal of it.

"How did he arrive in the first place?" Naomi asked. "You have some big windows in the front here. You didn't see him pull up?"

Hargrove was already shaking her head. "No, I didn't see anything at all. I already told that to the police."

"Are you sure, Mrs. Hargrove? This is really important."

"I'm completely sure. Besides, he told me he didn't have a vehicle."

Naomi looked up, suddenly interested. "I thought you said he didn't talk to you."

The older woman frowned. "Well, not coming in, he didn't . . ."

Naomi tried to be patient. "And?"

"Well, on the way out he mentioned that he didn't have a vehicle, but was in the market for one. So I asked him what he was looking for, and he said that he wanted a van."

"And what did you tell him?" Kharmai felt something stir in her chest, recognized it as excitement.

Hargrove looked embarrassed. "Well, you see, I have a brother who lives down by Rivers Bend. He quit workin' recently, so I knew he needed some extra money. And even though he's pretty worthless, he's still my brother, so I gave the man Walter's number."

"Walter's your brother?"

"Unfortunately."

"And he has a van?"

"Yep. It's a big one, too. He used it on all his jobs. He was an electrician for twenty years. Not a very good one, mind you."

Naomi was confused about something. "Why didn't you tell the police all of this?"

The older woman shrugged. She was a little nervous, trying to figure out if she was in trouble or not. "Well, I didn't see how it would help them find Nicole, for one thing."

Naomi had to admit that she had a point there. Up until about twelve hours ago, this had been a routine missing persons investigation, and there had been no reason to suspect one of Milbery's clients. "And the other reason?"

"He said that it wasn't what he was looking for. He didn't *want* a big, commercial van . . . too much on gas, he said. He just wanted something to run around to distributors in Richmond. I guess he was some type of salesman, but I'm not really sure."

She thought about that for a second. "How often do you talk to your brother?"

Lindsay Hargrove shrugged her shoulders once again. "Not all that often. Like I said, he's kind of no-good. I don't get nothin' outta talkin' to him. In fact, it usually ends up *costin'* me something."

"Did you ever find out if he sold the van?"

A third shrug. "I called him that day to tell him about it, but he didn't say 'Thanks for tryin' or anything like that, so I've been givin' him the cold shoulder ever since. Why?"

"No reason. What kind of van does your brother have, Mrs. Hargrove? Specifically, I mean."

"I can't be sure, hon, but I think it's a Ford. A white Ford, and really big."

"What about the outside? Anything unusual about it . . . ?"

"No, not really. It might have a ladder rack. Apart from that, it's just a plain-old white panel van, maybe a little dinged up. Walter isn't a very good driver."

Naomi got to her feet, sweeping a lock of dirty black hair behind her ear and trying hard not to show her excitement. "That's great, Mrs. Hargrove. You've been very helpful. Do you think I could use your phone?"

"Sure, hon. Anything you need." She hesitated. "Um, Walter's not in trouble, is he?"

Naomi looked up and said, with complete sincerity, "Trouble? No, not at all. In fact, his information could be vital to national security."

"National security? Walter?" Lindsay Hargrove thought about that, appraising the disheveled state of her visitor once again. She lifted an eyebrow. "Huh."

When the call came in to the TTIC, Jonathan Harper had to stop her twice before she slowed down enough to give him a coherent account of the conversation.

When Kharmai was finished, he said, "But you don't know if the van was actually sold or not?"

"No, but the story he told her doesn't sound right to me, sir. Maybe he was just trying to keep her out of the loop, you know? One less witness he'd have to worry about."

Harper heard the excitement in her voice, and had to admit that it sounded promising. He looked at his watch. "Jesus, Naomi, they're wrapping up the speeches right now."

She was almost frantic. "Sir, you *have* to stall them, or at least have them take a different route. He kept coming the whole time, despite every effort on our part to stop him. He knows something, or he would have backed off. He *has* to know something."

"You might be right about that." He was thinking back to Kealey's warning about the missing laptops at the State and Justice departments, a warning that they had both quickly dismissed at the time. If Vanderveen had managed to get his hands on something like that, he would have certainly known how to put it to good use. And the Secret Service still hadn't released their report on the matter. "I'm sending this all the way up, Naomi. I hope to God this isn't a false alarm."

She had never been more sure of anything in her life, but knew that he wasn't questioning her judgment. It was just that he had to ask it. "He's there," she said emphatically. "He's pushed it too far to stop now. He's there and he's waiting."

A brief hesitation. "Okay. I gotta run. See if you can pin down Hargrove's brother, find out for sure what he did with the van. And listen . . . good work."

"Thank you, sir."

* * *

"... And so, I am pleased to join President Chirac and Prime Minister Berlusconi in announcing a gradual downsizing of European oil interests in the Republic of Iran over the next three years, beginning with an immediate decrease in production by 200,000 barrels per day in the South Pars gas fields, and culminating with the complete withdrawal of survey and exploration teams in the region by 2008. Production will also be reduced in the Dorood, Salman, and Abuzar oil fields which, combined, account for more than 70 percent of Iran's offshore output.

"The United States has made no secret of the fact that it has maintained sanctions against Iran since 1979. These measures have been strengthened over the years, most notably with the Iran-Libya Sanctions Act of 1996. While it is our wholehearted desire to see these sanctions lifted and the full restoration of diplomatic relations between the U.S. and the Republic of Iran, there should be no doubt that we are willing to stay the course if the Iranian government persists in its attempts to acquire tools of mass destruction."

President Brenneman paused, then held up his hand to quell the sudden surge of voices from the crowd of reporters standing before him. "I'd like to take this opportunity to personally thank President Chirac and Prime Minister Berlusconi for accepting my invitation, and for working as hard as they have to make this goal a reality. The agreement that has been brokered here today is the direct result of their commitment to the Nuclear Non-Proliferation Treaty and its intended purpose: to render the threat of nuclear war a thing of the past, and to make the world a safer place for future generations. Now I'd like to step aside and let them tell you more about the specific implementations that are scheduled to occur . . ."

As she surveyed the scene, Jodie Rivers shook her head and thought, *This is insane*. Despite the fact that the guest list had been kept to a minimum and carefully screened, the area bordering the waterfront was packed by more than 200 people, each and every one of whom, in her eyes, was a potential threat.

The three heads of state were standing on an elevated podium perhaps 50 feet wide and 20 feet deep. President Brenneman was moving aside to give the French ambassador room as he stepped up to introduce President Chirac. Although there were large numbers of Diplomatic Security and Secret Service agents both on and around the podium, Rivers was well aware that this was a huge security risk. As a result, her eyes never left the stage, even when she flipped open her ringing cell phone and lifted it to her ear. She definitely didn't appreciate the interruption.

"Agent Rivers? This is Director Landrieu."

She recognized the urgency in his voice immediately, and felt suddenly cold. "Yes, sir."

"Let me start by saying this is a four-way line. You're talking to Deputy Directors McCabe and Susskind as well. Listen carefully. We have some information that puts Vanderveen in the city with an Improvised Explosive Device. I can't give you better than 90 percent on that, but it was enough to put the wheels in motion, and I don't need to tell you who the target is."

Dear God, she thought. Her worst nightmare was coming true, and she had to force herself to pay attention.

". . . Rivers? Are you still with me?"

"Yes, sir. Go ahead."

"You're looking for a white Ford van, commercial type, probably an Econoline. We don't have a plate number or a name for you yet, but we're only a couple of minutes away, so keep your line open."

"What about the—"

"Jodie." It was a new voice, and one she recognized immediately. "AIC Storey has already been alerted. We're gonna keep the question-and-answer session with the press pool going as long as we can without arousing any suspicion, okay? We finally got through to the people in Norfolk . . . Under the name of Timothy Nichols, Vanderveen took possession of forty crates at a total weight of just over 3,000 pounds less than two weeks ago."

Her eyes went wide at the numbers. "Jesus, the city is packed—"

When he cut back in, McCabe's voice had the clear ring of authority. "Listen to me, Jodie: Your only concern is for the president, okay? You have that waterfront locked down, I've seen it myself. There's nothing Vanderveen can do to you there unless he's suicidal, and the general consensus, the *hope*, is that he isn't. Normally we'd move the president as fast and far as possible, but that's not going to work in this case. So we'll keep him at the marina for now; Storey knows what to do, just follow his lead. As soon as I get off here, I'm headed to your location."

Yet another voice, coming fast before she could respond: "Agent Rivers, this is Emily Susskind. HRT is already up and running. They're fanning out around the area, and some are in plainclothes, okay? You need to get that to your observers as soon as possible. I don't want my people getting shot by mistake."

She was nodding to herself as the instructions came fast over the phone. "Got it."

Then, from Deputy Director Susskind: "Hold on." Over the sounds of the crowd around her, Rivers heard static and voices raised in excitement. It seemed like minutes later when McCabe came on and said, "Got a name, Jodie. Claude Bidault, French national. The vehicle was registered in Virginia less than a month ago. Plate number is . . . RND-1911. Ready for a description?"

"Go."

"Black hair and brown eyes. He might have a beard, but that's not 100 percent. A little heavier than Vanderveen, at about 200 pounds. We're not sure how he's doing that; padding, maybe. Same height, of course. There's nothing he could do there."

"I'll get it out to my observers." Rivers was a little bit frantic now. "Sir, I have to move."

"I know." McCabe's voice was tense over the line. "Get to it, Jodie."

Ryan had been on the street for two-and-a-half hours. Nothing so far had grabbed his attention, although he had to remind himself that Vanderveen wasn't exactly going out of his way to appear conspicuous.

There had been nothing planned out or expedient in his route; he had headed north from 7th and Maine, scanning faces and checking vehicles along the way. There wasn't much he could do other than to look through the windows and drop down to visually inspect the undercarriages, and his strange behavior had earned him some curious glances, as well as a few fearful ones.

He recognized the futility of his search, but there was one overriding fact that bothered him more than anything else: there was no feasible way to detonate a bomb by command wire on a crowded city street, and a timer wasn't practical, either, even if Vanderveen had somehow managed to get hold of the Secret Service's list of scheduled movements.

In other words, the only realistic way for Vanderveen to succeed was by remote detonation, which meant that he would be close by in an overwatch position. Kealey knew the man well enough to know that he would detonate the device regardless of whether the president was in target range; the public would believe it because of what they had seen him do to the Kennedy-Warren on national television, but proof enough for Ryan was the raised scar that resided an inch to the right of his own sternum.

He stayed on 7th until the National Air and Space Museum appeared on his right, then crossed the street onto the wide open space of the Mall. Heading northwest over the grass, with the dome of the Capitol Building framed high at his back, he smiled at the excited noises coming from a group of schoolchildren who were lined up at the glass doors to the Smithsonian. The smile soon faded, though, as he was too tightly wound to share in their enthusiasm. For all he knew, their bus might be passing Vanderveen's position on its way back to their school . . .

He pushed the thought from his mind as he came up on 12th Street. It was better not to think about it. When he heard his cell phone ringing, he was grateful for the distraction, but not for long. "Ryan, it's Harper."

"John, listen—"

"No time, Ryan."

He caught the urgency just as Rivers had done less than a minute earlier, and fell silent immediately.

Harper continued: "Naomi turned out to be lucky, after all. Our man has a driver's license and a French passport in the name of Claude Bidault. The passport is real, but the actual owner reported it lost six months earlier while on vacation in Crete. Got that?"

"Yeah. Keep going."

"Susskind finally hooked up with this guy Thompson in Norfolk. Using the Nichols ID, Vanderveen picked up 3,000 pounds' worth of material at NIT exactly eight days ago. The arrogant bastard walked right under our noses *twice* at the same port . . . Anyway, he has a vehicle that we can't account for. It's a Ford Econoline van, white, maybe with a ladder rack on top."

Ryan was already running. Standing on 12th when the phone rang, he had taken two long looks either way down the street, then decided to go north, for no particular reason he could think of. Harper's voice seemed to bounce at his ear as he dodged the heavy crowds of pedestrians, most of whom were people leaving work for a quick lunch. Some of them shot him angry looks or curses as he pushed through the throngs, and the whole time the deputy director's words were hitting him with the force of a sledgehammer: ". . . and Virginia tags, Ryan, RND-1911. HRT is moving out in plainclothes, but they—"

"Tell them to stay north of the Mall." His mind was moving in a blur, trying to recall a white Ford van, but . . . No, he hadn't seen one. He was sure of it. He said again, "North of the Mall, John. That's where he's gotta be. What's happening at the marina?"

"That whole area is locked down tight. They doubled up on the barriers, and the CAT team is moving into place," Harper said, referring to the Secret Service's Counter Assault Team, a highly secretive group that managed to keep a low profile, despite the fact that they accompanied the president wherever he went. "They've been able to keep it pretty quiet so far."

"That won't last," Ryan said, already breathing hard from the exertion of a full-blown sprint. He was passing cars in a flash, and there was a white van *right there* . . . But no, it was a Chevy. He didn't break stride, racing past the parked vehicle as a number of pedestrians turned to gawk in his wake. He was scanning faces, too, looking for anyone who might resemble the description that Harper had just given him.

He made a quick decision. "Can't walk and talk, John. Gotta go."

"No, Ryan, WAIT—"

He cut the connection and jammed the phone into his pocket, slowing down for a second to feel for the Beretta and get a long look both left and right down Constitution Avenue.

Nothing. He stayed straight on 12th, running hard.

*   *   *

Jeff Storey, the agent in charge of the president's detail, was floored by the message that he had just received. A terrorist, in the city with a van full of fucking explosives, and they wanted him to *sit tight*? It was beyond belief . . .

Storey had been a special agent in the Secret Service for nearly sixteen years, with the last four spent on the president's detail, and the last two of those four in charge of that detail. He looked around nervously. Jesus Christ, the assistant director had said 3,000 *pounds*. The concrete bollards would stop the van itself, but the kill radius for that kind of weight was at least . . . what? He tried to remember. It had to be at least 1,500 feet, and from his position on the podium, Storey could easily make out the medium-sized print on the barriers where 6th turned into Maine. *Sit tight, my ass,* he thought. *We're sitting ducks.*

Standing there on the podium, listening to the French ambassador lead up to the introduction of President Chirac, thinking about how easy it would be for a van to come barrelling down that street, Jeff Storey came to a decision. *He* was the one in charge of the president's detail, not Joshua fucking McCabe, and there was no way that he was going to see the president dead on his watch. In sixteen years with the Secret Service he had never found the need to draw his weapon on the job, but he did so now. He was standing on the podium with a group of diplomats and aides, blending into the background with the others behind the three heads of state when he convinced himself it was time to act. As the Sig 228 came up and out of his holster, the eyes of the two agents standing next to him went wide, and there was no turning back.

The AIC lifted his sleeve to his mouth and said, in a calm but forceful tone, the words that caused the world to come crashing down around him: "Storey to detail! *Hurricane!* I repeat, *Hurricane!*"

Moving behind the press pool with two junior agents in tow, Jodie Rivers looked up in surprise at the sudden movement on the podium. Her surprise quickly turned to horror, however, when she saw that Storey had grabbed the president roughly, and was pulling him back as the other agents surrounded the pair with their weapons out. The French president and his aides were looking on with confusion clear in their faces, as was the Italian prime minister, when the DSS agents assigned to each man came crashing onto the stage, following the lead of Storey and his detail.

The reporters and photographers on the gangplank were in a frenzy at the scene, cameras flashing everywhere as the people in the press pool tried to make sense of the situation. Their screamed questions went unanswered as a line of agents formed to block the president's predetermined escape route, but the metal barriers came crashing down as the media let go of the last shreds of decorum. The thin line of agents was quickly overrun by the huge crowd of reporters and cameramen.

Rivers couldn't believe what she was seeing. This was *exactly* why McCabe had ordered Storey not to do anything rash. *"What the hell is he DOING!"* she screamed, before realizing that the two junior agents standing next to her had even less of a clue than she did.

Back in the CT watch center, McCabe, Susskind, Landrieu, and Harper were also staring in horrified disbelief at the scene that was playing out live on MSNBC.

McCabe was the first to lose it, his face flushing a very deep red. "This is *exactly* why I told him to sit tight!" he shouted, unconsciously giving voice to the thoughts of Jodie Rivers. "We need to cut that feed *right now*!"

Harper's face was pale, and he was shaking his head. "It's too late. If Vanderveen saw that, he has nothing to lose by blowing it."

"Fuck!" McCabe slammed a closed fist down onto the table in front of him. A moment of clarity cut through the reactionary anger, and he suddenly realized that his career with the Service was almost certainly over, not to mention the fact that a lot of people were probably about to lose their lives. *"FUCK!"*

Ryan crossed the street when he reached the Pavilion at the Old Post Office, cutting under the arches of the Ariel Rios Federal Building and breaking into a wide open space less than 100 meters away from the Ronald Reagan International Trade Center. He ran north as 13th Street loomed ahead, and then found himself facing the pink-gray granite expanse of Freedom Plaza. He was breathing hard and there was a painful stitch in his side, but he kept his head up as his eyes scoured the line of cars in front of the National Theatre.

There. He knew immediately that it was the right one, even though the vehicle didn't have a ladder rack and he couldn't tell for sure if it was a Ford from the side. He knew because the van was sitting low to the ground, much lower than it should have been. Whatever that vehicle was carrying, it definitely wasn't light.

Then he was running again, despite the fact that Vanderveen was probably just waiting for him to get closer to the van before blowing it. Something inside Ryan's head told him that he should be feeling fear, that there was definite cause for it, but he couldn't lock on to any single emotion. He only knew that he had to get to that van as soon as possible.

Although he didn't make a conscious effort to do so, his right hand went back to the holster and came up with the pistol. It turned out to be a bad move; Vanderveen wasn't anywhere in sight, but there *were* a lot of people walking around, and a lot of people eating lunch on the benches around the fountain. One woman saw the gun in his hand and began to scream, and then there were a lot of screams . . .

Trooper 1st Class Jared Howson couldn't believe what he was seeing. He was about 50 meters east of the Ford on Pennsylvania when he saw a distant figure with what looked like a gun in his hand, racing through a crowd of cowering pedestrians.

Howson just stared for about ten seconds before he remembered that he was a police officer, and had a gun of his own. He pulled the standard-issue Glock 17 out of its holster and sprinted back down the street toward the van, not once taking his eyes off the other man or the weapon he was holding.

Although Jeff Storey had undeniably broken standing orders, he was still a Secret Service agent with sixteen years of experience, and knew that, given the current situation, he would be a lot better off on the water than he would on the streets. Still surrounded by the members of his detail, he dragged President Brenneman, who was still too shocked to be angry, down the dock as a number of agents peeled off to cover their movements.

The AIC grabbed a UHF radio from one of his men. It was already set to Channel 4, their dedicated maritime link. "Storey to Coast Guard cutter Alder, Storey to Alder. I need immediate escort for Boater at LZ number 3. Do you copy?"

Coming back a split second later: "Storey, this is Alder. Roger that, we're two minutes out, over."

"Two fuckin' minutes," Storey mumbled. "Unbelievable." He put in a second hurried call for transport at the designated landing zone, which was on the southern tip of the East Potomac Golf Club, as well as asking for additional helicopter support, never breaking stride as he pulled the president toward a turbocharged motorboat manned by USSS personnel less than 50 feet away. Behind them, the chaos continued to build as some of the reporters, finally realizing that they might actually be in danger themselves, began to trample each other in their rush to get away from the waterfront.

The DS agents for the French and Italian delegations, unaware of the specific threat, bundled their respective principals into armor-plated limousines and screamed at the drivers to move. The heavy vehicles pulled away from the curb at a surprising rate of speed, minus motorcycle outriders, following Maine onto 12th Street, and then heading north toward Pennsylvania Avenue and the safety of the White House.

Ryan was amazed when he reached the van and it was still intact. He didn't know where Vanderveen was, but knew the man was definitely somewhere in the area, and had to be watching him at that very moment. He arrived at a dead sprint, pulling up short and slamming his left elbow into the glass on the passenger side.

A wave of pain shot up his arm, but the safety glass gave way immediately. Another three judicious blows pushed the crumpled sheet of glass onto the passenger seat. He was reaching to unlock the door from the inside when a voice yelled, "HOLD IT!"

He whipped his head around to see a young police officer pointing a heavy black pistol at his chest. The adrenaline coursing through his body, Ryan's mind took in the scene at the speed of light: Metro PD uniform, two chevrons on the sleeve, young kid, scared eyes, and shaky hands on the gun. It all combined to give him a very bad feeling.

"DROP THE GUN!" the officer screamed.

"I'm a Federal officer," Ryan snarled. "I have to get into this vehicle right—"

"SHUT UP! DROP IT!"

"Ah, fuck. *Fuck*!" Ryan could see he wasn't going to win, and he was out of time. "Okay, I'm dropping it. Don't shoot me, for Christ's sake." His right hand left the gun on top of the shattered pane of glass, and slowly, ever so slowly, he pulled his hands out of the interior and held them out by his sides. "Listen to me—"

The policeman was coming down a little bit now. "Keep your hands where I can see them! Turn around and—"

"Shut up! *You* listen to *me*. I'm a Federal officer. The person who owns this van is the same man who killed Senator Levy and blew up the Kennedy-Warren." Ryan watched a look of disbelief spread over the young man's face. "There is a bomb in this vehicle. I'm stepping back . . . Take the gun off the passenger seat and let me get in there, okay? I *need* to get in there."

"I saw him . . ."

Ryan latched on to it, talking fast: "Black hair, brown eyes? About my height, heavy?" The officer nodded, the confusion spreading to his eyes. "He's a terrorist, and there is a bomb in this van. Take the gun, man. *Take the fucking gun*."

More wavering. Without taking his gaze or his weapon off the man standing before him, Jared Howson reached in through the door frame and lifted the Beretta off the seat.

Will Vanderveen was absorbed by the live footage on MSNBC. He had known, or felt, rather, that something was wrong when the conference was still going on ten minutes after it was scheduled to end.

Although it didn't seem like much to get excited about, Vanderveen knew that every second of the president's schedule was accounted for by the agents comprising his protective detail, and the unusual length of the Q&A session following the return of the *Sequoia* was definitely out of the ordinary. Then, in that shocking moment when the president had been grabbed from behind by one of his agents and dragged away from the podium, his single violent expletive could have been clearly heard by the guests in the next room. His anger had been made worse by the fact that the agents were taking the president farther down the dock, which meant he was moving *away* from 12th Street.

Still, he hadn't given up hope. He was still watching intently, trying to see if the DS agents who arrived on the podium a split second later were pulling their principals back toward the motorcade. It was hard to see, because the cameraman had removed the camera from its stable platform, and judging from the jerky image, was having a hard time holding it steady in the crowd. Vanderveen knew that with all the people currently spread out over the marina, the Service would never be able to land a helicopter. So it was either the cars or a boat, and he felt a little bit better when it appeared that the agents *were* moving the French and Italian leaders back toward the cars. His earlier reconnaissance of the waterfront had served him well, and he might still be able to salvage some of his plan.

It was only then that he realized, with a sudden feeling of dread, that he had missed the whole point. *Why* had they pulled the president off the podium in the first place? He felt a tingle of fear as he stood up and turned to look out the window. What he saw turned the fear to shock in an instant.

It couldn't be, he thought, but try as he might, there was no denying it: the person standing on Pennsylvania north of the plaza, held at gunpoint by the same police officer Vanderveen had talked to earlier, was none other than Ryan Kealey.

He nearly smiled at the scene. There was something almost comforting about the sight of his former commanding officer—it was like seeing a living link to the past. There was something vaguely amusing about it, too; after all, it wasn't every day that a former Delta operator was caught out by a rookie cop, and that kid in particular didn't look as if he belonged anywhere near a loaded firearm. *Ryan must be getting sloppy.*

Then the smile faded as he realized that they probably weren't

alone. The Bureau's Hostage Rescue Team might already be surrounding the hotel, and they wouldn't be interested in merely arresting a man who had killed eight of their own.

The decision came in a heartbeat: it was time to cut his losses. He
had flipped the switch in the cab two hours earlier, right before his
conversation with the police officer. Everything was ready. Vanderveen
picked up his .40 caliber USP and jammed it into the waistband of his
jeans, then pulled on his long, heavy coat to conceal the bulge. In his
pocket was the cell phone, which he withdrew as soon as he stepped
into the hall.

He briefly wondered how much of the blast he would feel in the
shelter of the hotel, then decided that he didn't care. He couldn't
wait for the motorcade, but for all the failure of the day, there was
one small feeling of triumph: Ryan Kealey would not live to see the
end of it.

Walking down the hall toward the elevators, Vanderveen flipped
open the cell phone and pushed and held the number 1.

They were making some progress, but the young officer still had
his 9mm trained on Kealey's chest. "You come running down here
with no ID, waving a gun, and now you say there's a bomb in this
van? I . . . look, I can't let you in there."

Ryan couldn't understand why they weren't already dead. Was this
the wrong vehicle? Had he made a mistake? "I'm getting into this
van," he said. It wasn't a request, and he began to move cautiously
back to the passenger-side door. "Shoot me if you have to, but I'm
getting in."

The gun wavered, then finally dropped. "Shit! I'm not gonna
shoot you." Howson slipped Ryan's weapon into his holster, lower-
ing his own to his side. Then, a second later: "What do I do?"

Ryan opened the door from the inside, flinching when he realized
that he hadn't checked for a trip wire. "You talked to the guy?"

The officer nodded and pointed to his right. "Yeah, I think he
went in there."

Ryan glanced toward the dark gray facade of the JW Marriott
hotel. He pulled his cell phone out of his pocket and handed it over
while simultaneously turning his attention back to the van. "Speed

dial 3, then ask for Rivers." He was glad he had stored her number. "Tell her where to come . . . *Don't* go into that building."

Ryan was in the cab a few seconds later, head down and busy as the police officer raced toward the hotel. In his right hand Howson carried the standard-issue 9mm Glock. In his left hand he held nothing, as he had already slipped the cell phone into his pocket and promptly forgotten about it.

Vanderveen stopped dead in the hall, staring in disbelief at the message on the cell phone's display: *Network Unavailable*. What the fuck did that mean? He cursed low, under his breath, and didn't notice when a passing woman shot him a disapproving glare.

He hoped it wasn't the hotel. For all of his planning, he had not anticipated this possibility. If it was something to do with the building materials, he'd have to get outside before he could get a signal. That was thirty seconds in the elevator, forty seconds through the makeshift hall leading to The Shops at National Place, and another twenty seconds through the stores themselves to F Street. He knew because he had already timed it. Ninety seconds total—more than enough time for any number of unpleasant things to occur. Plenty of time for Ryan to get into the hotel, and more than enough time for the HRT to set up a hasty perimeter.

Maybe it wouldn't come to that. He pushed and held the button a second time, willing his creation to do its work.

Ryan was in the van for less than five seconds when he found what didn't fit. His hand was sweeping between the seats when it banged into a boxy metal object. Shifting his weight over the seat to stare down at it, he couldn't see what practical purpose it might have served. It looked like a cover of some kind, but when he tried to lift it, it didn't budge. Then he pulled on the other end and it came right up. He flinched, waiting for the inevitable blast. When nothing happened, he looked down and saw a single switch.

He flipped it without hesitation. Leaning back in the seat, breathing hard from fear and the long sprint, his mind raced to figure out what had just transpired.

Two seconds later, sounding distant through the thin steel partition, Ryan heard the unmistakable high-pitched tone as a cell phone began to ring somewhere in the cargo area.

After another few seconds had passed, he looked in the rearview mirror to see a procession of black limousines turn from 12th onto Pennsylvania at breakneck speed, only to make another sharp turn onto 13th a split second later.

Jared Howson burst into the lobby with his gun up, oblivious to the wide-eyed stares and screams that accompanied his entrance.

A security guard was standing just inside the door, but didn't move to interfere with the policeman or the gun in his hand. Howson turned right toward the concierge, scrambling to recall the name he had seen on the passport.

"Bidault! Claude Bidault! What's his room number?" No one responded. They just stared at him with their hands held high. *"WHAT'S THE ROOM NUMBER?"*

One of the men finally grabbed a keyboard, his hands shaking. "Bidault?" Howson nodded impatiently. "Room 545," the concierge said. "Elevators are that way."

But Howson was already gone, the Glock 9mm down low in a two-handed grip. He moved fast toward the elevators, then caught a flash of a dark green oilskin jacket and stopped instinctively, trying hard to remember. He had seen that jacket somewhere before . . . He sprinted past the atrium toward the escalators.

Kealey moved into the hotel with less fanfare, but everyone knew why he was there. A few fingers pointed him past guest registration on the main lobby level.

Indecision for a moment. He didn't have a weapon, but Vanderveen was running and would soon be gone. Hold or follow? A glimpse of a Metro PD uniform at the top of the escalator made the decision for him.

He moved in that direction, only to find his path was blocked by a large security guard. The man had a radio up and was speaking into it urgently. He turned his attention to Kealey: "Stop right there, sir! I said stop!"

Ryan slowed to a fast walk, his hands up in front of his chest, palms out in a conciliatory gesture. "I have a reservation here. I'm sorry for the trouble, I'm just late meeting someone . . ."

He hit the security guard hard in the solar plexus, then lifted his knee into the man's face. The guard fell back, tumbling into a coffee cart and sending several steaming urns crashing to the floor.

Ryan was aware of swarming blue uniforms in his peripheral vision as he sprinted up the escalator. He was passing covered glass doors when he heard a popping noise up ahead, and then what sounded like two more shots carrying over the cries of terrified onlookers.

He picked up the pace as the screams intensified in volume.

Howson knew he was moving too fast, but he was young and his adrenaline was through the roof. More importantly, there was an open area up ahead, and he'd definitely caught another flash of the oilskin jacket.

The whole way, from the van to the lobby, the lobby to the escalator, the escalator to here—all forty-five seconds of it—all he could think about was the story it would make. He couldn't wait to tell it on the old man's porch . . . There was no little voice, nothing inside telling him to slow it down, otherwise there wouldn't *be* any story, and he was running hard. He saw light spilling from left to right at the end of the hall, heard the sound of a bustling crowd, and kept pushing forward. Past a steel-shuttered elevator pit, past a plastic Dumpster filled with trash, and then into the basement level before realizing his mistake, because the lure of the light had prevented him from turning right.

It came without warning. There was no explosion of sound, no tunnel of light, and no pain. All he felt was a grazing sensation at the back of his head, and then darkness.

Ryan was about twenty steps and seven seconds behind. He saw the prone figure of the police officer as soon as he entered the construction area, and tried not to look at the gaping exit wound in the young man's face, or the spray of blood and tissue on the tile in front of him as he reached down and snatched up Howson's Glock.

Ryan sensed that Vanderveen was not waiting to get the drop on him, and he needed to move fast now if he wanted to catch up. He turned into the open area recklessly, the 9mm down low in the same two-handed grip that Howson had adopted less than two minutes earlier. Twenty feet in front of him, Ryan saw people running in his direction out of Filene's Basement, the only store on the lowest level. He bounded up the stairs, passing black bins of cashmere and racks of discounted Prada, forcing his way through the frantic crowd, knowing full well that this might be his last chance at getting close enough to put the man down for good.

Vanderveen was about fifteen seconds ahead of Kealey when he passed through the glass doors leading out onto F Street, moving quickly but casually. His posture was relaxed, and calm enough so that none of the passersby immediately noticed what was dangling from his right hand.

The few extra seconds gave him the time he needed to scan the street for police cars or the unmarked Suburbans that were favored by so many of the government's more notorious agencies. He wasn't thinking about what had gone wrong; there would be plenty of time for that later. At the moment, his only goal was to get out of the city as fast as possible.

He stepped into the road, crossing the first lane before a west-bound Camry with a dented hood screeched to a halt a few feet to his right. As the shocked and relieved driver furiously leaned on his horn, Vanderveen walked around the side of the vehicle.

The man had been smoking while he drove, and the window was rolled halfway down, despite the cold. He started to say something smart as the person he had nearly hit approached his door, but never got it out. Vanderveen smoothly lifted the .40 with his right hand and jammed it into the driver's ear, pulling the trigger once.

Ignoring the screams of nearby pedestrians, Vanderveen pulled open the door and yanked hard on the driver's body, which tumbled lifelessly out into the road.

Then he was in the car and moving away, not bothering to fully close the door until he had already upshifted twice. Looking up to the rearview mirror, he saw the glass doors of the National Place building swing open as a figure emerged at a dead sprint.

* * *

Kealey burst out onto F Street in time to see the red Camry pulling away in a squeal of tires. He had the Glock up in a heartbeat, banging away two shots at the retreating vehicle, going for the tires but catching the bumper instead.

Then it howled around the corner onto 14th, disappearing from view. Kealey swore under his breath, saw the body on the street and moved to pull someone out of their vehicle. Seconds later, a pair of black Suburbans with light racks flashing on top came flying up behind him on 13th Street, slamming forward to a halt at the intersection. Then there were men streaming out of the vehicles with their MP5s locked onto his head, screaming, "FBI! Drop the gun! *Drop the gun right now!"*

Kealey turned and shouted back, for what seemed like the tenth time in as many minutes, "I'm a Federal officer! Susskind knows me, for Christ's sake! The guy you're looking for just turned that corner—" He almost pointed before he realized he still had the gun in his hand. "In a red Camry. I got the plate—"

"Put the gun on the ground! *Do it!"*

The people approaching him didn't look all that accommodating. He had his left hand on the door handle of a silver Mercedes, the middle-aged woman behind the wheel staring up at him in fear and shock. Ryan took his hand away and lifted his arms at the elbows, the grip of the gun pinched between the thumb and forefinger of his right hand. Swearing again, he set the weapon on the pavement and stepped back as the agents swarmed in around him.

It was over, and Vanderveen was gone.

CHAPTER 35

LANGLEY • CAPE ELIZABETH

The debriefing was held at Langley more than eight hours later, with very few people in attendance. The director's office was spacious enough to accommodate the small crowd, which included Naomi Kharmai, who had been flown back from Ashland courtesy of the Virginia State Police, Jonathan Harper, DCI Andrews, and Ryan Kealey.

It had been relatively easy for Harper to get Kealey out of FBI custody. Susskind spoke to the D.C. field office's HRT commander just minutes after the second shooting on F Street, and orders had been relayed from there to the team that was holding him. The handcuffs came off almost immediately, and his Beretta was retrieved from Howson's body and returned to him. The agents that he rode with expressed regret at the incident, but only reluctantly; the muted apologies he received were next to inaudible. The Suburban in which Kealey was seated departed immediately for Tyson's Corner, but most of the agents remained behind to secure the scene and wait for reinforcements.

He couldn't really blame them for arresting him. He had been out on the street in civilian clothes with a gun and no identification, standing less than 5 feet from a man with a gunshot wound to the head. In retrospect, Ryan realized that being confronted by the highly trained HRT operators was a lot better than most of the alternatives. At least they hadn't shot him out of panic.

When he arrived at the TTIC less than twenty minutes after leaving the scene, the helicopter blades were already turning. Despite angry protests from Director Landrieu and Joshua McCabe, Harper had arranged for transport for Ryan and himself so they could be immediately flown back to Langley. Unfortunately, that was where the rapid movement ended. They had been forced to wait for hours, as the DCI had been caught up in a lengthy inquisition by a shaken President Brenneman at the White House. Now, seated in the director's capacious office, the events of the morning seemed like nothing more than a horrible dream.

It wasn't a dream, though, and Ryan had proven it by recounting his story to Director Andrews no less than three times, all the way from the time he received Harper's telephone call up until his detainment by the FBI. Kharmai had also been asked to thoroughly describe the events that had transpired in Hanover County. The two junior officers did most of the talking, but they got some of the answers they were looking for as well.

Naomi was seated next to Ryan, while the two senior officials sat in comfortable armchairs on the other side of a low coffee table. She had enjoyed a long hot shower in the women's locker room upon returning to Langley, and someone had been dispatched to her house to pick up some clothes. Her unknown benefactor had chosen well. As a result, she looked a thousand times better than she had that morning, and was anxious to learn more about the disastrous raid in Virginia.

Harper was the one to explain it to her. "The Bureau's Explosives Unit concentrated their efforts on the basement. They found damage consistent with a gas-leak explosion, but leaks almost always originate from the output valve, which is located on the ground floor. So they think that Vanderveen disconnected the fittings to the stove, drilled a hole into the tile and rigged up a hose leading down to the basement. Then he used duct tape to seal off the hole and all the air vents leading out, so that the gas was just trapped down there."

Harper took a sip of coffee and continued: "They found other evidence that corroborates that account as well. There were pieces of a gasoline can—one of the old-fashioned metal ones—jammed into the walls, and what appeared to be two contact plates and traces of SEMTEX H. He didn't have time for anything fancy, so he simply taped a block of explosives to a gasoline can, then wired up a battery to an electric cap. The device was set to go off when the buffer was removed from between the steel plates."

Ryan was shaking his head. "What about the bomb in the van?"

"That one was a little more complicated, though not overly so," Harper said. "They only got around to moving it a few hours ago; there were some concerns about booby traps, especially after what happened in Hanover. The ATF guys that are taking it apart all say the same thing: simple, but efficient. He wired up a cell phone to the SEMTEX H, which was concealed in five steel trunks. By the way, you would have been screwed if you'd gone in through the back, Ryan. He had antihandling devices on the phone and two of the trunks."

"But not the switch."

"Not the switch," Harper agreed. "He didn't want to risk a premature explosion, so a wrong number to the phone wouldn't have made a difference as long as there was no power going from the battery to the circuit. You said you heard the phone ring?"

"Yeah, it rang about two seconds after I flipped it."

"That was Vanderveen trying to set it off. Those few seconds made all the difference, Ryan."

Ryan felt a little bit sick over how close he had come to being wiped out, along with about eight city blocks. "Jesus Christ," he said, "all I did was flip a switch."

Harper was nodding slowly. "He needed to be able to activate it quickly, but he couldn't exactly get in the cargo area and start rooting around in the middle of a busy city street. It was the best way for him to do it, and if it wasn't for you showing up when you did, it would have worked."

Ryan fell silent. He didn't want to think about what had almost happened. There would be plenty of time for that later, but Naomi didn't notice his hesitation, and she wasn't finished: "What kind of damage are we talking about?"

The deputy director cleared his throat. "Well, there's no definitive answer. I talked to Bateman—that's the guy heading up the ATF task force, by the way—and he gave me some round numbers. We would have been looking at serious damage to every building in a four-block radius, plus some varying damage out to twelve blocks from ground zero. That would have included Freedom Plaza and Pershing Park. Estimates, and there is some dispute on this, are between 400 and 500 dead, plus anywhere up to 2,000 injured. The time of day was factored in to that as well; if it had been a few hours earlier, for example, the casualties would have been much lower."

Ryan looked at his hands.

Director Andrews turned to stare out the window, ashen-faced. "My God."

"What about the angle?" Ryan asked. "He was going after the motorcade, right?"

Harper nodded and said, "That's right. There's even more dispute over *that* question. He was definitely going after the motorcade, but it's not clear if he would have been successful. Bateman thinks it would have worked, but the Bureau's people are saying otherwise."

The DCI broke in and added, "He stacked the odds in his favor by placing concrete blocks against the partition. That close to the actual device, it would have pushed most of the force of the blast directly out into 13th Street. I think he came closer than anyone wants to admit."

Kharmai and Kealey fell silent at the candor of the remark, but Director Andrews was only getting started. He turned back from the window to appraise them carefully. "Needless to say, there's going to be some serious fallout in the next few weeks. The first choice, of course, would have been to keep the whole thing quiet. After Senator Levy's assassination and the Kennedy-Warren, the last thing we need are reports of a 3,000-pound bomb nearly taking out the president's motorcade. If it had just been the evacuation on the waterfront, we could have explained it away. A few heads would have rolled, but we might have swept it under the mat.

"Unfortunately, it didn't stop there. Vanderveen killed two people in his escape, including a Metro police officer. Both of them died in crowded areas, so there's no way we can play it down. This is going to be headline news for the foreseeable future, so the president's advisors, in all their wisdom, are trying to spin it into a positive thing, a major success for U.S. law enforcement. No one wants to call it what it really was."

"A near disaster," Ryan said.

Andrews nodded in agreement. "Exactly. But it's out of our hands now, so if they want to play politics, we have no choice but to play along. Anyway, the president is looking to publicly slap some backs. That means you two. Especially you, Ryan."

Kealey's response was immediate and heartfelt. "There's no way that's going to happen." He saw the DCI's reaction, checked himself, then said, "Excuse me, sir. I just don't want to have anything to do with it. Besides, we've never operated that way, and the president knows it. I don't want my face on television, and I don't want to give any interviews. I just want to know what we're doing to catch the bastard."

Harper looked up and sighed heavily. "He didn't get far in the Camry. It was found in an underground parking garage in Anacostia, and in the trunk, the body of a twenty-nine-year-old secretary." Ryan swore and looked away, thinking about how close he had come to stopping Vanderveen. "He chose carefully; there were no cameras in the garage, no way to immediately determine what kind of car he switched to. The woman was missing her purse, so it took a while to track her down. They started with the neighboring buildings . . . When they found her employer, they got her name and a vehicle registration from the DMV. Then, of course, they found out that her car was missing. So there's a nationwide APB out on her Camaro, but no one is especially hopeful. Just taking the woman's ID gave Vanderveen a two-hour jump on Susskind's people." The deputy director paused to take a sip of coffee. Studying Harper's weary expression, Ryan thought that the man looked exhausted, then realized that he probably didn't look much different himself.

Harper was still talking. "Since this is all going public anyway, the president has given us free rein to track Vanderveen down. His name is already on the list of Most Wanted Terrorists, and we've gotten his face to passport control at every major airport in Western Europe, as well as Africa and Australia. He inadvertently helped us out with that . . . The picture on the Nichols's driver's license is probably less than two years old, which makes it much more recent than the army shots we were working with before. We've sent those updates to Interpol as well."

"Vanderveen's been tied to Iran and Al-Qaeda," Ryan reminded them. "He has access to money, so he's not exactly obliged to fly commercially. They might have arranged for a charter months ago, probably to some dinky little airfield out in the middle of nowhere."

"You think he's gone, Kealey?" asked the DCI.

"It would make sense, sir. If he stays here, he's opening himself up to the biggest manhunt in the history of U.S. law enforcement. Besides, you know as well as I do that if he gets to Iran, we're pretty much screwed. We have no assets there to speak of, unless something's changed in the last twelve months."

Harper sighed heavily. "Nothing's changed." He thought about it, then said, "He failed, though. If he's on his way back to Tehran, he probably won't be getting a very warm reception."

"I hope you're right," Ryan said. "But I wouldn't count on it."

The meeting adjourned five minutes later. Kealey and Harper walked side by side down the hall, neither finding much to say, each lost in his own private thoughts.

Harper, just to break the silence, said, "You'll be getting a medal, you know. Naomi, too. Probably something pretty."

Ryan shrugged halfheartedly but didn't smile. "I don't really care about that." He glanced over at the other man quickly. "It's not that I don't appreciate it. It's just that I really don't care. Besides, it's not like I can show it to anyone anyway."

Harper laughed a little at the way he had phrased it as they approached the elevators. "Not this time, Ryan. This is one of our few public accomplishments, our day in the sun. Might as well enjoy it while it lasts."

Kealey didn't respond right away, once again lost in his own little world. Finally, he said, "You can mail it to me, John. I'm going home. Tonight."

Harper found himself nodding in agreement. "Landrieu won't be happy," he observed. "He's already pissed that you came here instead of getting debriefed back at Tyson's Corner."

"Fuck him," Ryan said. "*Fuck him.* He fought you on that ID thing, and I really needed it. I was ten seconds behind Vanderveen when those guys from HRT drew down on me. I don't have anything against them . . . They were just doing their job. If I could have shown them something, though, we might have been able to catch up to him. Hell, I *know* we would have been able to."

"He's probably done, anyway," Harper observed, steering the conversation back to the TTIC director. "Brenneman threw a lot of the blame for the senator's death and the Kennedy-Warren at Landrieu, and a lot of it's sticking." He hesitated, then said, "I really did fight him on that, you know. He was going to shut you down the whole way, Ryan. I had to compromise."

"I'm not blaming you, John. I didn't mean it like that. I'm just sick of people like Landrieu. There's a thousand like him in Washington, and they all seem to hold the most dangerous jobs."

"I couldn't agree more," Harper said, and realized that he meant it. As the elevator doors opened on the first floor, they stepped out onto the clean white marble, and he turned to give the younger man some last-minute advice. "Get back to Katie, Ryan. I'll handle the fallout over your speedy departure. You did a hell of a thing today, so think about taking some of the credit for it, okay? And don't worry about Vanderveen. He'll turn up sooner or later."

"I still want that bastard, John." Ryan hated to break his promise to Katie, would dread trying to explain it to her, but the words had come out unexpectedly, and he knew that he meant them. "I want back in. Officially, I mean."

Harper smiled. It was what he had wanted to hear. "We'll talk about it in a few days. Until then, get some rest and go see your girl."

"If I can even catch a flight," Ryan said, with more than a little frustration. "That storm passed us, but I heard it's headed north pretty fast. By the time I get to Dulles, they might have the airports—"

He stopped when he saw that the other man's smile had turned into a big grin. Harper shook his head, handing Ryan a card with a number on the back. "Got your cell phone?" he asked. Ryan nodded. "Call that number when you're ready to go. I'm the DDO, Ryan. Sometimes you forget that."

Kealey was about to ask what he meant by that cryptic remark, but instead just reached out to shake the other man's hand. "Thanks, John. I'll see you Monday."

"Have a safe trip. I'll meet you at the main gate when you get back. Call it 9:00 AM." Harper was looking over Ryan's shoulder. "I think someone else wants to have a word with you."

Ryan turned to see Naomi Kharmai standing a few feet away, wearing a nice smile and looking good in a white pantsuit that contrasted well with her caramel-colored skin. She tilted her head and said, "Where are *you* off to in such a hurry?"

They sat across from each other in the dismal cafeteria, which was mostly empty at this late hour. Awkward silence at first, as Ryan left his coffee untouched, and Kharmai rolled a mug of tea between her shapely hands.

"Just gonna run out on a girl, huh?"

He looked up. She was smiling, maybe a little bit sadly. "I'll be back next week, Naomi. You'll get tired of me in no time."

"I thought you wanted out. I thought you *were* out."

"I can't leave. Not while he's still out there."

She thought about that, was about to say something, then decided against it. "Are you going into the CTC?"

"That's where you work, right?" She nodded. "Then no."

She scowled as the grin spread over his face. "Seriously."

He shrugged. "Probably. That's where I'll have the most access to resources, so, yeah, I think so."

She smiled, and they both fell silent. Finally, just to make conversation, Ryan said, "They're giving us medals, you know. Pretty ones."

She shrugged, and what followed kind of surprised him. "That's not so important to me. I don't know why . . . I always thought it would be."

He read in her eyes that it wasn't an act. She meant the words, and that surprised him even more. "Harper likes you, Naomi. You got noticed on this, so take what they give you and smile for the cameras, okay?" She looked up to see if he was making fun, but his face was completely sober. "I'm not trying to be arrogant, but I don't need this job, and I don't really want it all that much either. It's more time away from Katie, because she's back at school in the spring and won't be able to come down here with me."

He paused to take his first and only sip of coffee, then said, "You, on the other hand, have the goods, Naomi. You could go high here . . . You couldn't be DCI, because of the nationality thing, but just about everything below that is open to you. I mean, you could definitely head up the CTC. To get there, though, you're going to have to fake it once in a while. You don't care about the medal . . . This is one of those times. It's in your best interest to play it up a little bit, believe me."

She took the advice for what it was worth, flattered by the compliment, wishing that he hadn't brought up the other woman. *I want you to come home with me!* she wanted to scream, and it must have been all over her face, because his words were followed by a long, awkward silence.

Eventually, though, she decided to spare him. It was clear that he wanted to go, and making him suffer wouldn't change his mind. "Well, I guess I'll see you Monday," she said.

They both stood up. "I guess so." Then they were looking at each other for a long moment, Naomi waiting, hoping that maybe he'd lean in and . . .

It didn't happen. Instead, he just reached out to lightly touch her arm. Then he turned and walked out of the cafeteria.

She looked after him for a long moment, a number of expressions mixing on her face. When he passed through the doors and disappeared from view, she sat down to finish her tea, and tried not to think about it.

When Ryan called the number that Harper had given him, he was reminded for the first time in a long time just how much sway the man really had. It was easy to forget, because there was nothing flashy about the deputy director's personal lifestyle; although he lived in a nice house and dressed well, he took his wife to the same resort in Colorado every year, and drove a six-year-old Explorer with 100,000 miles on the odometer.

When it came to his position at Langley, though, Harper had the power to move mountains. Five minutes after placing the call, Ryan was met at the main gate by a dark-suited man who, after introducing himself as George, showed him to a glistening black Mercedes with tinted windows. Judging from the way it hunkered down over its wheels, the aggressive-looking sedan was also fitted with armor plating in the door panels and engine compartment.

George opened the rear door, but Ryan shook his head and climbed into the front. He didn't want to get too used to this kind of treatment, and wondered for a moment if Harper had gone through the trouble as a favor, or to intentionally remind him of some of the perks to be found at Langley. Ryan smiled when he decided that the occasional chauffeured ride in an armored Mercedes didn't really compensate for the government salary because, after all, it was the salary that determined your actual living conditions. Maybe not for him, but certainly for most government employees.

He was forced to reevaluate that assessment, however, when they squealed onto the runway at Dulles International. He couldn't believe they had been cleared onto the tarmac, and was even more surprised when he realized that he would be returning to Maine on one of the Company's Gulfstream executive jets.

He turned to his driver and said, with a hint of a smile, "You must get a kick out of driving this car, George. You have a hell of a job."

The other man, burly and stoic throughout the whole trip, couldn't help but crack a smile of his own. "That I do, sir," he said. "That I do."

It wasn't long before the G-V had reached its cruising altitude of 41,000 feet, and they were streaking north at a little over 561 miles per hour. Ryan knew he should kick back and enjoy the ride, and he did, at first, but being all alone almost 8 miles up soon became a little unnerving.

When he noticed that the cockpit was shielded by only a privacy curtain, he drifted up there to reassure himself that someone was actually flying the aircraft. Both men seemed to welcome the company, and it turned out that Steve Kearns, the pilot, had been flying jets for the Agency for almost seventeen years.

"Where was the last place you flew to?" Ryan asked, knowing full well what the answer would be.

Kearns grinned imperceptibly. "Can't tell you that."

"Where are we going now?" He honestly didn't know.

"Can't tell you that either."

The grin spread, but Reynolds, the navigator, laughed and said, "Portland International Jetport, sir."

That was good news to Ryan. Portland was much closer to Cape Elizabeth than Bangor was, which was where he usually flew in and out of.

"I'm surprised they didn't shut down the runway," he observed. "That place isn't really built to handle traffic in this kind of weather."

Reynolds nodded in agreement. "That's true. Of course, we're more than 10,000 feet over the worst of it right now. Things are getting pretty messy on the ground, though. Half the state is out of power, and they had to kick in the generators at PWM. The storm is pushing out a little bit due to the Canadian jet stream, but it's still pounding the east side of the state. We'll be okay, though the landing might be a handful. Hey, Kearns, you *do* know how to land, right?"

The pilot shrugged. "I tried it on *Microsoft Simulator '98* once," he said, smiling broadly. Ryan noticed that Kearns was one of those people incapable of keeping a straight face when telling a joke. "It didn't work out too well."

Reynolds, surveying something on his myriad screens, looked up and said, "Well, I hope you learn fast. We're about ten minutes out."

"Jesus Christ," Ryan said, a little shocked. "We just took off."

The pilot smiled. "Welcome to the wonderful world of corporate travel."

The landing, as Reynolds had predicted, wasn't fun at all, even though Ryan had tightly strapped himself into one of the soft leather seats just aft of the cockpit. He got up on shaky legs after they rolled to a stop, poking his head up front to thank his couriers. Kearns looked a little pale, but both men acknowledged his words, which were difficult to hear over the pounding rain on the fuselage.

"Did you guys hear anything about my transportation on the ground?" Ryan yelled over the roar.

Kearns said, "You're going to Cape Elizabeth, right?"

"That's right."

"It's only about twenty miles," the pilot said. He was grinning again, and the color had returned to his face with the landing out of the way. "That isn't much of a walk. I have an umbrella if you need it."

Reynolds shook his head with a rueful smile and turned from his console to face Ryan. "You need to find Andreno in the security office, on the second level. He has a key for you. I guess you have the car for the weekend, but it's due back at Langley on Monday."

"Andreno?"

"That's all I know." The navigator shrugged. "How many can there be?"

Ryan realized he was right. "Yeah, it's not that big of an airport. Or jetport. Whatever." Reaching in to shake their hands: "Thanks, guys."

"Not a problem. Drive safe."

The jetway had already been extended to the outer door with a resounding metal-on-metal clank. Reynolds came back to open the door from the inside, and then Ryan was in the elevated tunnel, nodding his appreciation to the jetway operators before moving forward to the bustling terminal.

The open space was filled with stranded passengers, and Ryan reminded himself once again to thank Harper for cutting what would have been a severe headache out of his trip. Navigating his way through the occupied seats in the terminal, he quickly found the cramped office and asked for Andreno, who turned out to be the chief of airport security.

"Yeah, I got your key right here," the heavy man said with a grunt. "Mercedes . . . nice."

Accepting the key and some verbal directions, Ryan left the office and headed for the underground parking garage. The car that was waiting for him was very similar to the one in which he had ridden to Dulles. Sliding onto the cool black leather, he grinned like a little boy when he turned the key and the engine purred to life.

Soon he was leaving the parking garage, the sound of the powerful engine ripping off the concrete walls like thunder, mixing with the hollow boom of the rain outside. With the wipers going full blast, he accelerated down International Parkway, the bright lights of the Mercedes cutting a swath through the dark swirls of rain, then

turned left on Johnson Avenue before reaching I-95 South a few minutes later.

As he drove, he couldn't help but think about the upcoming argument with Katie. She would probably be furious that he was going back
on his word, but he knew that he had to track down Vanderveen
once and for all. It was an argument that she couldn't win; he was
going back to the Agency either way, but there were a couple of
things that might make it easier for her. He *had* gotten her the ring,
after all, and maybe he could dangle the use of his BMW in front of
her to keep the argument as short as possible. He knew she loved
that car almost as much as she hated her Corolla.

Ryan had been thinking about that, too. At the risk of spoiling her,
he knew that she had her eyes on a new Volkswagen SUV . . . Shit, he
couldn't remember the name. Tureg, or Tourag, maybe . . . something like that. It was pretty big, though, and solidly built, which was
all he cared about. Katie was not very skilled behind the wheel, and
while he teased her constantly about it, he secretly agonized over her
frequent trips to and from Orono. He remembered how excited
she'd been after seeing the latest model in the parking lot at the grocery store . . .

Why not? he thought. It would be worth it just for the look on her
face. Tomorrow, a Saturday, would be a good day for that. He'd slip
away in the afternoon and go see the dealer in Augusta. He wondered if she would notice if he had a roll cage installed . . .

The random thoughts began to fade as he left the highway in
favor of the narrow side roads running along the coast. Harder going
here, as the towering trees carried over the road and blocked out
some of the rain, but also some of the light, which wasn't all that
much to begin with. The road was covered in fallen branches, too;
some were almost as big as small trees, so that he had to brake a few
times and swerve sharply once, which rattled him almost as much as
the bumpy landing had back in Portland.

The house came up fast on the left, the steep roof showing up
now and then through the evergreens from a distance. He was
pleased to see lights in the windows, which meant that Katie was
there and they still had power.

Ryan was glad she was home, and it took him a few seconds to realize how relieved he actually was. She had nearly broken his heart by walking out on him at the hotel, and they hadn't spoken in the few days since that incident. He'd had a good idea how she felt, though, and had decided that the best thing was to give her some space. Surely it would have blown over by now. All he cared about was seeing her. He had wanted to call to let her know he was on the way, but she liked surprises, and he liked surprising her. The Volkswagen would top them all, he thought with a grin. Again he was reminded of his idea for a sunset ceremony on the Mediterranean. Lots of plans . . .

The argument first, though. There would be no getting around that, but maybe it wouldn't last too long. It was only fair to be upfront with her about it.

Then he found himself thinking about what his profuse and heartfelt apology would most likely result in, and decided that the argument could definitely wait for one more day.

The one disadvantage to the house on Cape Elizabeth, he thought, stepping out of the Mercedes and into the storm, was the fact that it didn't have a garage, not to mention the fact that the distance from their improvised parking area to the front door seemed much farther on a moonless night during a torrential thunderstorm. Ryan finally made it under the awning, the raindrops beading and rolling from his thin leather jacket. Although his jeans were soaked around the ankles, his feet were still dry in his waterproof Columbia boots.

Sliding the key into the door and turning the handle, he immediately realized when he stepped inside that the house did not seem as brightly lit from the interior. In fact, apart from a dim glow at the top of the stairs, the only light he could see was coming from the kitchen directly in front of him. Then he heard her moving around, and an involuntary grin crept up on his face as he silently moved down the hall to sneak up and scare her.

Stepping through the doorway, though, he was surprised to find that she wasn't moving anywhere. Instead, she was sitting at the dining room table and staring up at him with a terrified look on her face. Her bottom lip was trembling, and her dark blue eyes were filled with tears.

And standing directly behind her, wielding a razor-sharp knife and a terrible smile, was William Vanderveen.

He tried to tell himself that it wasn't real.

It *couldn't* be real. It couldn't be real because it wasn't rational; Vanderveen had the contacts to get out of the country almost immediately, but had decided instead to drive more than 450 miles, with every police officer in the country out looking for him, to come *here*? It just didn't make any sense . . .

And he didn't look anything like Claude Bidault. That meant it must be a dream, because there was no way that he would have had time to drive all the way from Washington to Maine *and* remove the heavy beard and the tint from his hair. It just wasn't possible . . . was it?

He instinctively reached for his Beretta, then went cold when he realized that it was sitting on the passenger seat of the Mercedes.

All the tools in the world, but nothing at hand when he needed them most. And no one to blame but himself.

"Hello, Ryan."

Said conversationally, in the tone of voice that Ryan remembered from so long ago, and the same voice that chased away the last of his desperate hopes. This was not a dream.

"Will." He tried to keep his voice steady, but it was almost impossible.

The smile grew wider. Vanderveen tilted his head and said, "It's hard for you to call me that, isn't it? You want to say March, don't you?" The flat side of the knife moved slowly across Katie's throat, but Vanderveen's vivid green eyes never strayed from Kealey's face. "I'll let you in on a little secret, Ryan. You can call me what you like. It doesn't make a difference. Not here. Not anymore."

The man's gaze was almost hypnotic. Kealey broke it with a huge effort, forcing his eyes down to Katie's. She was pleading with him, the tears finally breaking free and streaming down her cheeks. "Ryan . . ."

Vanderveen looked down when she spoke, but his head came up

very fast before Kealey could move. "She's stunning, you know. I couldn't have chosen better for you myself. Her eyes are so . . ." He put on a show of searching for the words, the knife doing little circles in his hand. "Expressive. So full of life. It can make an otherwise plain woman seem very beautiful indeed. And Katie here was never plain, was she?"

Ryan noticed, with some strange clarity of vision, that the weapon Vanderveen was holding had come out of his own kitchen drawer, a 4½-inch Kyocera paring knife, much like the one he had brought into the detention center. It was dancing in rhythm with the killer's words, but never strayed more than 6 inches from Katie's throat.

He dragged his eyes away from them, searching for something, anything he could use as a weapon.

It was useless. Three feet to his right, a slate-topped counter that had nothing to offer. He could charge, but it would never work, he would never get there in time. Vanderveen would start cutting her the instant he moved.

And outside, pounding through the exterior walls of the house with its own incomparable rhythm, was the sound of the building storm.

He had to say something. "Listen, she . . . You don't need to . . ."

The other man was watching him intently, but Ryan stopped, and something clicked in his mind. When he opened his mouth again, the pleading note was gone. Instead, he spoke the truest words he knew. "If you do it, you won't be able to run far enough."

"There it is," Vanderveen said, genuinely pleased. "That's what I wanted to hear. It's good to see you can still get your back up."

Ryan took a quick step forward. Before he could take a second, Vanderveen had pulled Katie out of the chair in a blur. He held her tight against his chest, his left arm wrapped like a steel bar around her slender waist. The tip of the knife was digging hard enough into her skin to draw blood.

"*No, Goddamnit! Don't*—" Ryan stepped hard on his rising panic. He snapped his hands up and tried to keep his voice level. "Just let her go, Will. She has nothing to do with this."

"Wrong!" Vanderveen snarled. "She has everything to do with this. You *made* her part of this when you decided to play hero today."

Ryan couldn't find the words to respond. Katie was crying hard now, stricken by the helpless look she saw in his eyes, struggling to find words between her heaving sobs: "Ryan, don't let him . . . hurt me . . . *please*."

"It's okay, Katie," he managed to choke out. "I'm here. I'm here."

"That's very touching," Vanderveen remarked. "But I'm getting bored now, so let me ask you something, Ryan: Was it worth it? Was it worth the fleeting gratitude of a few hundred people you'll never even meet? If you could go back and let them die so she could live, wouldn't you do it? Wouldn't you do it *in a heartbeat*?" He waited for some kind of response, but Kealey couldn't focus on anything but the look of sheer terror and desperation on Katie's face.

Vanderveen was visibly disappointed. "Let's try it this way," he said. "Do you remember the first time you ever saw her?"

Ryan knew what the man was doing, but he couldn't help what happened next. The image appeared in his mind before he could stop it: Katie, legs curled up beneath her, hair shimmering golden brown in the sun, a pretty smile and inviting blue eyes, sitting on the grass in Orono.

Vanderveen's gaze had become even more focused. When he saw Kealey's eyes cloud over, remembering, he smiled again and said, "That's it. Hold that thought . . ."

Ryan snapped back in time to catch the last part of the sentence. ". . . and watch this."

Then, with a single, powerful thrust of his arm, Vanderveen pushed all 4 ½ inches of the blade into the right side of Katie's neck.

Before he could fully grasp what had just happened, Ryan heard an anguished scream and, not recognizing it as his own, broke forward across the wooden floor, completely focused on taking the other man's life. He was oblivious to Katie's reaction.

Her eyes opened wide and her lips parted, but no sound emerged. She tried to pull away from her captor as her legs went out from under her. Then she crashed forward against the side of the table, her right hand coming up to feel for the source of so much searing pain.

Suddenly she found herself on the floor, kicking out frantically, trying to find some air through the choking sensation of blood in her throat. She had sudden sparks of insight, brief bouts of lucidity that brought her the terrible truth. She tried to push it away, but the facts were fighting through . . . She had been hurt, seriously hurt, and the nearest hospital was 20 miles away, and she couldn't breathe, and Ryan wasn't looking, didn't see how bad it was, and she *couldn't breathe* . . .

Kealey and Vanderveen were struggling for control of the gun that had materialized out of nowhere. Wrestling for control of life and death, one driven by rage and despair, the other by a hatred born of many years—a visceral evil that was the sum of many parts, traceable back to no single point in time.

The .40 roared once, then came sliding across the polished wooden floor, pulling through a thin trickle of blood before coming to rest beneath the refrigerator. Vanderveen made a quick decision as Ryan went for the gun, getting to his feet and throwing his full weight at the back door once, then twice before the lock broke and he burst out into the storm, just as two rounds splintered the door frame where his head had been a second earlier.

Passing the door, Ryan glanced quickly to make sure that the other man wasn't lying prone in the mud, ready to spring back up and into the kitchen. He saw a distant figure merge with the dark, then disappear through the sheets of rain.

With the door open, the sound of the storm was deafening as he went to Katie and kneeled, pulling her close. Her shoulders were over his thighs, the back of her head resting in the crook of his right arm. As he held her, he felt her left hand reaching out to find his, the long fingers gripping tight to squeeze out the pain.

Ryan didn't try to remove the knife; it only would have hurt her more and made the bleeding worse. Her lips parted as she tried to speak, and when she turned her head toward him, a thin trickle of blood ran down the side of her mouth. Although she couldn't make any words, he knew that she was in agony because she was still kicking weakly and the tears had not stopped building.

Worse yet, her luminous blue eyes were losing some of their animation, and when he put his face close to hers, he couldn't feel her warm breath on his skin.

"Katie." He wasn't sure if she could still hear him, and it was hard to tell because her face was blurred by his own tears. "Don't go, Katie. Stay here. God, just . . . stay with me. Please . . ."

It was all he could say. He wanted to tell her he loved her, that he was sorry, but the words wouldn't come.

Instead, he held her close and rocked her back and forth, refusing to believe that he would not hear her laughter, her voice, or see her beautiful smile ever again. And still rocking, as gently as he could, until the light finally left her eyes altogether, and she died in his arms a few moments later.

Vanderveen was tearing along the path through the woods, disoriented and full of adrenaline. Despite the fact that he had not slept in almost three days, he had never felt more alive. For the first time in seven years, he was actually glad that Kealey had survived the bullet in Syria. It was so much more fitting for it to end here, and now, perhaps, Kealey might understand something of his own pain . . .

The pine and oak trees were all around him, the pines still full and green, the oaks nothing more than towering, writhing arms of tremulous wood. He was already soaked to the skin, freezing cold, and the roar of the ocean was like a living thing. He had his bearings now, heading forward to the great dark expanse of the Atlantic, feet pounding in the mud as he raced, unknowingly, toward the edge of the towering cliffs.

Kealey emerged from the back of the house at a dead sprint with Vanderveen's gun in his hand, moving fast toward the water. He was numbed by what had just happened. It couldn't last, though, and cutting through the emptiness was the inescapable truth: that he was responsible for all of it. By putting the hunt for William Vanderveen ahead of Katie, he had killed her just as surely as if he had stabbed her himself, and he couldn't get the image out of his mind: Katie, kicking and writhing on the floor, trying to cry out through the blood that was filling her throat, the hideous gurgle that had emerged instead. God, no. *No!*

Vanderveen spun around when he heard what might have been, carrying high over the howling wind, a scream of agony and bottomless pain. The sound brought a smile to his face. Kealey was coming.

The path had ended in a wide clearing, several solitary fence posts standing guard on the perimeter. The mud was churning around his feet as though attempting to swallow him whole, but far more terrifying was the precipitous drop that ended the world just 10 feet in front of him. The sky above was in constant motion, twisting black clouds lit bright by sheets of lightning, the thunder pounding hard just seconds later with enough force to make the ground shake. The wind was icy cold and constant, bringing silver streaks of rain in from over the tortuous swells of the ocean.

He tried to think. Kealey had his gun, and he was without a weapon. He had to get out of the clearing immediately.

Directly behind him, where the path turned into the underbrush, Vanderveen heard the unmistakable sound of splashing feet.

Kealey turned the corner and stepped into the empty clearing. He was buffeted hard by the wind, which didn't seem to be going in any one direction, but the USP Compact was up and steady in front of him. He had dropped the magazine on the self-loading pistol on the way out of the house to see that it contained four bullets. That meant that Vanderveen had not reloaded after his bloody escape from F Street, as only three rounds had been fired inside the house. There was one in the chamber, though, so he actually had five Federal 155 grain Hydra-Shok rounds with which to kill the man, and he planned to use every last one of them.

He wasn't sure if that would be enough. In the recessed lighting of the kitchen, Vanderveen had seemed almost inhuman. Part of it was his appearance. It had been Ryan's first close look at the man in almost eight years, and he clearly hadn't lost a step in that period of time. If anything, he looked even stronger and leaner than he had during his time as one of the most capable soldiers in the U.S. Special Forces community.

More than that, though, was the fact that Vanderveen appeared to be driven by something far more powerful than his natural physical strength. It was the way his eyes burned with that strange light that others, not knowing better, might have mistaken for ambition, religious fervor, greed, or any other kind of overpowering emotion.

Kealey was under no such illusions. He knew that Will Vanderveen was driven by hate, and hate alone.

For Ryan, these were not specific thoughts, but vague considerations that drifted on the edge of his tortured mind. In the confusion of fact and fiction, however, he was able to grab hold of one thing that may or may not have helped him: *When it comes to that man's eyes, it all looks the same.*

Listening to this strange epiphany in his head, everything else went quiet for a minute. The shrieking wind seemed to drop to a murmur, the storm fell blessedly silent, and he heard footsteps coming fast behind him.

He turned without looking, the gun coming up. As he fired, he felt a stinging in his face. Then he was falling, but still on solid ground. The muzzle flashes were lost in a sheet of lightning that briefly turned night into day.

Did I hit him? Ryan didn't know, couldn't see as he stood and wiped what might have been water out of his eyes. He hadn't counted the number of rounds he had fired, wasn't sure if it was two or three. He didn't know how far he might be from the edge, and he was still trying to get his bearings when something slammed into his left side. He felt his ribs give way with a sickening crack.

The breath left his lungs in a rush as he crashed to the ground. Ryan tried to face the other man, but still couldn't see much more than a vague outline through the blood streaming down over his forehead and into his eyes.

He became aware then that Vanderveen was towering over him, but when he blinked, the man was gone. Ryan wondered why until he realized that the gun was no longer in his hand. Staggering to his feet, his vision cleared momentarily and he saw a dark figure scrambling across the clearing, the outstretched hand reaching for an object in the mud.

Ryan took two steps forward when the pain hit him like a hammer in the side. His ankle felt like it had been crushed in a vise, but somehow he was still running as Vanderveen turned with the gun, getting off one shot before Ryan hit him low and sent him tumbling out into space.

Vanderveen reached back for the ground, shocked to find that it wasn't there. He was caught by a sudden downdraft and carried away from the cliff wall, pelted the whole way by stinging beads of rain. Looking up, the clouds were getting very far away, and when he began to turn in midair, his eyes finally locked onto the churning waters below.

The impact came, crushing the breath out of his lungs as the ocean sucked him down. He was instantly paralyzed by the cold, but it couldn't last; the pain followed a split second later, rippling through his body in an agonizing wave, pulling him back from the brink of conciousness. He struggled for the surface as the darkness closed in around him.

Ryan was still in the clearing, less than 2 feet from the edge. He lay motionless in the freezing mud, trying to take account of his injuries. He knew without looking that most of the ribs on his left side were broken. His ankle didn't feel right at all; he remembered that it had almost collapsed when he tried to run on it. Gingerly, he reached up to touch the jagged cut on his forehead when he was stopped by another sudden pain.

It didn't take long to locate the source. Vanderveen's last round had caught him in the right side. Pulling back his jacket and lifting his shirt to expose the neat hole, he saw that it was bleeding slowly but steadily. Carefully reaching back with his right hand, he felt for, but didn't find what would have been a much larger exit wound.

He wasn't sure how much damage the bullet had done, and after thinking about it for a while, decided that he really didn't care. Vanderveen was finally dead, but at what cost?

Katie.

He had been numb to this point, but the sense of loss he suddenly felt was far more painful than the injuries he had sustained.

Lying there in the damp, he idly wondered how long it would take for him to join her. His eyelids were already getting heavy, and the cold didn't seem as pronounced as it had been a few minutes earlier. The pain wasn't as bad either. Not nearly as bad.

His right hand moved up and away from the hole in his side, drifting over a lump in his jacket. He felt delirium coming on, so he double-checked to make sure he had not imagined it. No, there was definitely something there. He pulled it out to see: his cell phone.

Ryan put his head back in the mud and thought about it. If he called now, they might make it in time. They might not. He didn't know.

Was it important?

Why should he care?

A few minutes later, he returned the phone to his pocket and settled back to wait.

CHAPTER 36

CAPE ELIZABETH • WASHINGTON, D.C.

Callie Palmer hunched over her steering wheel and tried to see through the rain streaking down her windshield. The storm had gotten progressively worse since her departure from Orono more than two hours earlier, but she was now down to the last few miles of the trip, much to her relief.

She was tired after a full day of classes, but she was also worried about her best friend. That was why she had decided to drive down for the weekend, bringing with her the few things that would be needed to lift Katie's spirits: two six-packs of Rolling Rock and a few good movies on DVD.

Usually that did the trick, but Callie wasn't so sure this time. Her closest friend was really upset over her latest spat with Ryan, and didn't seem inclined to stop brooding about it anytime soon.

She sighed as she turned onto Village Creek Road, the house coming up fast in front of her. As she drove up the muddy drive-way—*Ryan really needs to pave that*—she saw something that made her frown. A black Mercedes, sitting on the grass in what had become their unofficial parking area. When she saw that it had government tags, she swore under her breath. Ryan must have returned from Washington early, and Callie knew they were probably way too wrapped up in each other at the moment to even think about answering the door.

She got out of the car anyway and ran through the rain to the shelter of the porch. She had come too far to just turn around and go right back, and she got more and more annoyed as she thought about her wasted trip.

She knocked on the front door. No answer. *Hmmm.* After a brief moment of hesitation, she turned the knob and stepped inside, shivering again, but with pleasure this time when the warm air hit her face.

Not that warm, though, and she could see why: directly in front of her, down the long hall, the back door to the kitchen was hanging open, swinging back and forth in the wind.

She saw shattered panes of glass.

She felt a cold ball of fear in her stomach, a wave of apprehension that turned into outright terror when her eyes moved down, and she saw what looked like thin crimson streams working their way across the wooden floor.

God, no. She was carried forward against her will. Turning the corner, she found Katie carefully arranged on the kitchen floor, eyes closed, lips slightly parted. Her friend wasn't moving.

Then she saw why, and she started to scream uncontrollably.

Jonathan Harper was fast asleep when something roused him from the dark.

He sat up and reached out, fumbling for the nightstand without turning on the light, swearing under his breath when he heard a glass of water hit the carpet below. Then he had the receiver up and next to his ear. "Hello?"

He would have answered the telephone differently had it been the second set residing by his bedside, but this was his house phone, and not the secure unit that was checked every two weeks by DST personnel from Langley. Thus, he was surprised when he heard a young female voice: "Director Harper? Sir?"

He swore again and fumbled again for the lamp. "Yes, this is Jonathan Harper."

"Sir, this is Sarah Bernstein, the night-duty officer at Langley. I tried to reach you on the secure line, but it didn't go through . . ."

Harper glanced over and spun the unit around with his left hand. The cord had been pulled out from the back. He scowled and looked over at Julie's stirring form.

He'd give her an earful in the morning. "What do you have for me, Bernstein?"

She hesitated. "Sir, perhaps you'd like to call me back through the switchboard."

Rubbing the sleep out of his eyes, he silently reprimanded himself for thinking so slowly. "You're right. Give me a minute."

He slammed down the phone hard enough to wake his wife. She sat up and copied his sleepy gestures, running her palms over her face and back through her sleep-tossed hair. "Who is it?"

"I've told you a thousand times, Julie. I need to be able to take calls here immediately."

"Sorry. I just thought you deserved a break . . ."

There was no use in arguing with her. He plugged the STU-III back in and dialed a number from memory. "This is Deputy Director Harper." He recited his authorization code. "Give me the duty officer, please."

A series of clicks and whirs, then: "Bernstein."

"Yeah, this is Harper . . . What's going on?"

Her voice was clipped and efficient. "Sir, I have a call here you probably want to take. Benjamin Tynes from the Cumberland County Sheriff's Office. He says it's important."

"Cumberland County . . . ?"

"It's in Maine, sir."

He sat straight up in bed. At the look on his face, Julie's eyes grew wide. "What is it?"

"You have him on hold?"

"Of course, sir."

"Patch him through."

More clicks, then a grizzled old voice cutting over the line: "Mr. Harper?"

"You've got him."

"My name is Ben Tynes, sir," the man said unnecessarily. "I'm the sheriff for Cumberland County, and I got something here you might want to know about."

Harper was already losing patience; he wanted to know how the man had gotten his name and number, but he wanted answers first. There was only one person he knew in Maine. *Jesus, Ryan* . . . "What do you have, Sheriff?"

"I'm at 1334 Village Creek Road. We got here twenty minutes ago in response to an emergency call. What we found was a young woman, DOA, and a man in critical condition. The woman has been identified as Katherine Leah Donovan, twenty-four years of age. She was a student at Orono. The injured man's wallet has him as Ryan Thomas Kealey . . . Is this making sense to you?"

Harper squeezed his eyes shut. After a long pause, he let out a strangled, "Yes."

The sheriff seemed confused, expecting the other man to elaborate. Finally, he said, "We're still trying to figure out what happened here. From what it looks like, we're missing a third person—"

Jonathan had a pretty good idea who the third person was. "What about Kealey, Sheriff? What's his condition?"

"Not good, sir." Another long hesitation. "Not good at all. He was outside for a long time. He's got a badly broken ankle and a gunshot wound to the right side, in addition to a few broken ribs on the left. The bullet's still in him, but there doesn't appear to be any major damage. That's the good news. On the other hand, his core temperature was 91 degrees Fahrenheit when they brought him in. That's severe hypothermia . . . They think he'll pull through, but it'll be close."

"What about the girl? Are you sure that she's . . . ?"

"She was pronounced twenty minutes ago, Mr. Harper. She's gone."

"Give me a second, okay?" Harper lowered the receiver and, ignoring Julie's panicked inquiries, took a moment to collect himself. Finally holding up a hand to quiet her, he got back on with Tynes. "What's it look like to you, Sheriff? Any ideas?"

"Me and my deputies haven't been here all that long, sir, but . . . I think that your third person got the drop on one or both of them. He did the woman in the kitchen, and we found your man in a clearing 200 feet behind the house. There were signs of a struggle."

"How did you know he's my man?" Harper asked.

"One of Donovan's friends found the body and called 911. They had to take the friend to the hospital with Kealey—she's in shock—but she was still reasonably coherent when we got here. Somehow, she knew your name, and there's a car outside with government plates, so I thought it made sense to at least try and get hold of you."

"You did the right thing, Sheriff. Uh . . . any sign of the third person?"

"Nothing. They warmed Kealey up with heat packs and blankets, trying to get some information out of him. What he gave us wasn't much, but from what I gathered, the other guy went over the side—"

"What do you mean, over the side?"

"Into the ocean, sir."

Harper pushed his left palm hard against his temple, thinking about it. Ryan had moved to the house only a year earlier, and Jonathan had never been there. He had no picture in his mind to refer to. "What does that mean, Sheriff?"

"It means that he's gone." The deputy director heard Tynes clear his throat over the line. "Dead."

"How can you be sure?"

"It's about 180 feet to the water, sir. From that height, it's like hitting cement."

A long pause. "I hope you're right about that," Harper finally said. "I *really* hope you're right about that."

Ben Tynes could tell that he wasn't convinced. "Sir, unless you hit at just the right angle, whatever's left of your rib cage will tear your insides to shreds. And even if you *do* make it through the initial impact, you'll either go so far down that you drown before you can get back up, or you'll be too badly bruised to get out of the water. They usually get dragged out by the current, but I've seen what was left of the few jumpers we recovered. Trust me, it's not a pretty sight."

He took a deep breath and let it out slow. "Okay, Sheriff. That's good enough for me. I have to make a lot of calls, but I'll get back to you as soon as I get transportation lined up. Call in forty-five minutes."

"There's one other thing, Mr. Harper . . ."

Jonathan detected a new note in the man's voice, a reluctance that instantly caught his attention. "Go ahead."

"This man, Kealey . . . How well do you know him?"

"Pretty well. He's been a good friend of mine for a long time. Why?"

"What was it between him and this Donovan woman?"

It was the last thing Harper wanted to think about. He was about to snap at the man, but Tynes seemed to be going somewhere with this. "They were engaged. Just a few weeks ago." He wasn't sure what the sheriff was looking for. "Apart from the usual couple stuff, things were good between them. Really good."

Tynes carried on, more sure now of what he was about to say: "The reason I ask, sir . . . I think he saw what happened to her. When we found him, he was turned over on his stomach. The bullet went in about four-and-a-half inches right of his navel, and the wound was . . ."

"Was what?" Jonathan didn't feel good about this particular line of inquiry.

". . . leaking a lot faster than it would have been if he'd been lying on his back." Another long pause. "And he had a cell phone, sir, but he didn't call anyone. Do you see what I'm saying?"

Harper felt cold, despite the relative warmth of his bedroom. "Oh, no . . . Jesus."

The longest pause yet, what seemed like minutes on end. Tynes maintained a respectful silence, waiting for the deputy director to continue.

"I'll be there in three hours," he finally said.

Harper put the phone down and looked at his wife.

"*What?*" she asked.

The storm lingered over Cape Elizabeth for a very long time, raging from Portsmouth to Bangor, although those two cities did not define the outer limits of its wrath. The perimeter of this particular hell was not marked by geographic features or the opinions of overpaid meteorologists.

When it was done, many hours later, there were estimates of more than 130 million dollars in total damages, although some of those figures were padded in anticipation of the forthcoming inquiries from the insurance companies.

As always, it was the oceanfront properties that sustained the worst damage.

There were exceptions, of course. Some structures managed to remain largely unscathed due to the quality of their building materials, or to their particular placement on the erratic coastal landscape. One such home belonged to Richard and Brenda Cregan, a retired couple who had moved north after selling their modestly successful landscaping company in the Boston area four years earlier.

The house was everything they had been looking for: quiet, secluded, comfortable but not lavish at four bedrooms and two-and-a-half baths. It was smaller than most of the other homes in the area, but the vast quantity of land that came with the property more than made up for the lack of square footage. The Cregans were avid outdoorsmen, and the trails leading back through the heavily wooded lot behind their home had factored heavily into their decision to purchase the property.

An argument could be made that the trees were more important than the trails, as they served as a natural buffer between the house and the destructive power of the ocean.

The Cregans loved the trails, though, as they made for an easy quarter-mile walk through the heavy woods that came to an abrupt halt just 15 feet over the lapping surface of the Atlantic. In a mild squall, the waves sometimes made it more than two-thirds of the way up the rocky precipice. The cliffs were considerably closer to sea level than those of Cape Elizabeth, which could be found less than a half mile to the north.

In this particular storm, however, the ocean merged seamlessly with the land, as though the 15-foot barrier had never existed to begin with.

The Cregans were not disturbed by the wind and rain that pummeled their home, or by the sudden drop in temperature that had accompanied the elements; after more than four years on the coast, they had already seen more nor'easters than they could remember. They knew, with the same hard hearts of the natives, that there was little they could do, other than to wait it out and assess the damage in the morning. They also reminded themselves that they were not in any danger from the trees surrounding the house, as most of the towering pines within several hundred feet had been cleared the previous year.

Reassured that the sturdy walls of their home represented safe refuge, they were not concerned when the phone lines went dead and they lost power. It was a commonplace occurrence in such weather, and though they had access to a powerful generator, they chose instead to make an early night of it, and headed off for bed.

They slept lightly, but they did sleep. Their house was surprisingly well insulated from the crashing sound of the storm by heavy brick and mortar, and expensive windows whose stout wooden frames had been well installed by local contractors.

As midnight approached, the trees farthest from their home seemed to grow out of the ocean. The writhing limbs bowed and swayed with the force of the wind and the water pounding against and swirling about their trunks.

The trails also emerged from the gray depths. As they moved farther inland, they began to take on more distinct shapes. Some of them were lined by fence posts, but all were marked to some extent by their previous travelers.

Smaller prints, such as those left by deer and some of the forest's smaller occupants, were soon washed away by the pounding rain.

Others lasted longer, such as the deep tracks left by the considerable weight of Richard Cregan, and the lighter, distinctive tread of Brenda Cregan's Timberland hiking boots.

There was a third trail that would have confused them had they seen it. It was a trail marked by uneven footprints of varying depths. Strange dragging marks followed each solid mark in the mud.

They were spaced in unusual increments, and each varied widely in depth and integrity. The differences were obvious, but the combined marks in the earth left no doubt as to the injured man's destination.

The footprints cut a straight path, leading directly from the tortured swells of the Atlantic to the calm, darkened exterior of the house that Richard and Brenda Cregan shared.

They were unaware as the storm raged on.

They slept lightly, and they did not dream.